WHEN SHIFT DOESN'T HAPPEN

A novel

Christo Louis Nel

Website - ChristoLouisNel.com

First Kindle Edition - March 2019
First Print Edition - March 2019

ISBN 978-1-7337326-0-4 (paper back)

Cover design by Marna Pritchett

Dedication

To Mart - my best friend for life, for better or worse.

And to those who helped me on the way to make this book happen
THANK YOU!

Thank you Mart, Marna, Esmé, Christa and Elma
for being the first readers and your comments.

Thank you Alet for editing the draft version and your advice.
Thank you Aimeé for the final editing. You are awesome!
Thank you Marna for the design of the cover. I love it!

SECTION I

Discovering the Truth

CHAPTER 1

Hotel Room

The two camouflaged motorcycles approached the crossing from the east. Leading the squad was Sergeant Keith James of the 8th Infantry Battalion. He kept a watchful eye on the road ahead, searching for any disturbance that could indicate the presence of a landmine. Following Keith was Lieutenant Charlie O'Neal, a communications specialist. The road between the military bases had to be cleared daily before the troops were allowed on the road.

Dust swirled up from the dry gravel road behind the bikes before it slowly drifted back to earth - another hot windless summer day. The rider in front suddenly slowed down and with his fist signaled a stop. Charlie skidded to a halt next to Keith. Fifty yards in front of them was one of many crossing. A narrow road, only wide enough for one vehicle, ran north to south and crossed the main road Charlie and Keith were sweeping.

Tonight, he was back in the Caprivi Strip. The "strip" is the stretch of land in Namibia between Angola and Botswana. The border war between the South African Defense Force (SADF) and the South West African Peoples Organization (SWAPO) was still in full swing. It was Christmas Day, 1973.

They carefully observed the surrounding shrubs, small trees, and the gravel area around the lonely baobab tree on the southeast corner of the crossing. They sat motionless and listened for a few moments. It was still early morning and the silence sent a chill down Charlie's spine.

Keith pointed to the intersection and looked at Charlie. "Four mines!" he said with a soft voice.

"Where?" Charlie whispered as he strained his eyes. "I see nothing. Only dirt."

"Use you far-eyes," Keith said as he took his binoculars from the bag strapped to his chest. He scanned the surrounding area before zooming in on the spots where the mines were strategically planted in the middle of the crossing.

"Wow. You know what to look for," Charlie said as he turned to Keith who was still studying the landmines.

"It was a rushed job," Keith said. "Something spooked them. They didn't even cover the mines completely. Look there," he said and pointed to the right side of the crossing. "You can see their tracks leading north. If we startled them, they may still be close-by. Be ready!" Keith said with an alarmed voice and a worried look on his face.

"This is not good," Charlie mumbled as he turned around to study the road behind them. He felt the vibration in his legs straddling the bike before he heard the rumbling of a vehicle approaching quickly. Keith lowered his binoculars and turned to Charlie.

"You hear that?" Keith said as he got off his bike. "What're they doing on the road? We haven't cleared it yet!" Aggravated, he reached for his rifle and took a few paces forward. Charlie turned his head from side to side trying to identify the direction the sound was coming from. He looked to the south and saw dust rising above the trees. It was clear the vehicle was traveling at a high speed and had no intentions of stopping. Local residents believed speed could outrun the explosion of a landmine - a myth proven wrong so many times in this area.

"Hit the deck!" Charlie shouted at Keith. "They're not going to stop!"

He grabbed his rifle and scrambled in the opposite direction from Keith. Charlie slid underneath a bush and turned around. He saw Keith disappear behind a tree and cover his head with his arms. He did the same. He knew instinctively what was about to happen.

The black Mercedes Benz entered the crossing going at least 60 miles an hour on the gravel road.

It all happened in super slow motion. Charlie saw the left front wheel roll over the first landmine. It exploded under the mid-section of the car and flipped it over. Gravel and rocks flew in all directions as the car skidded on its side to the other end of the crossing. The second landmine on the north side exploded under the engine of the car. It was propelled high into the air, and landed with a thump a few yards down the road. The car and its occupants were ripped to pieces. Charlie stared at the wreck as it came to a stop. The windows were shattered and the interior of the car was tinted red by the blood.

"They're all gone!" he thought to himself. His arms still covered his head and ears. The wreck held his gaze like a magnetic force that just would not let go. He saw the waves of gravel approach him from the impact area. But he couldn't move. The shockwave lifted his body a few inches from the ground and dropped him back into the same position. Everything went silent and the only sound he could hear was the high-pitched ringing in his ears. Nothing more.

From underneath the bush Charlie looked in the direction of Keith. He had his hands covering his ears. For a few moments they stared at each other realizing the graveness of what they had just witnessed. Slowly Charlie got up and walked towards the wreck. He stopped next to his bike that was toppled over from the impact. It was lying in the middle of the road and he picked it up and set it on its stand again.

Keith stopped in the middle of the road, bent forward and picked something up. A smile appeared on his face as he looked at Charlie.

"It worked!" he shouted at Charlie and pointed into the air. Charlie saw his lips move, but the ringing in his ears blocked most of the sound. He looked up and saw the mushroom cloud of dust floating back to the earth. As the dust drifted down, it turned into money. Millions of dollar bills floated in the air and slowly drifted down. He looked at his feet and saw the dollar bills under his boots. He bent over and picked up a few bills.

"Is this real money?" he shouted back at Keith still busy picking up money.

"Yes!"

Suddenly Charlie stopped and turned his head sideways to listen.

"You hear that?" he shouted again as the high-pitched monotone ringing in his ears faded. From a distance far away, he heard a phone ring. He looked at Keith oblivious of the sound. He was too busy stuffing the pockets of his uniform with the money. Satisfaction was written all over his face.

"What?" Keith asked. "We are rich man! Look at all the money! Sir Archibald didn't get away with it."

The ringing got louder and got more persistent. Charlie turned around and looked curiously down the road.

Charlie was plucked out of his deep restless sleep, and the dream quickly faded away. Reality set back in. He was only vaguely aware of a dream and an explosion. He reached for the phone and glanced at the alarm clock.

"Hello?" he said as he put the phone to his ear.

"Good morning, Mr. O'Neal," a perky and friendly voice said on the other end. "This is your five-thirty wake up call. Can we send up your regular morning coffee?"

With a dry mouth and scratchy voice, he confirmed the wakeup call, and accepted the offer for coffee.

"What happened?" he mumbled to himself. *"Feels like I just fell asleep!"* He

4

looked around the room just to make sure he knew where he was.

On the table he saw his laptop and the documents he worked on the night before. Everything was spread out on the table and on the floor. When he arrived on Sunday evening from Nashville, TN, he moved the table so he could watch TV while working. He mostly listened to the local news and weather while editing documents or responding to e-mails. As a systems integration consultant for Professional Information Technology Staffers, PITS in short, he was required to travel to the client's location. He worked ridiculous long hours, and sleep seemed to be his enemy. He was on assignment with a client in Springfield, MO. The initial three months had turned into two years. The night before he had worked on the final details of a specification for a new interface. The project's deadline was approaching fast and he had stayed up late to complete one more item before he could call it a day. The developers were quick to shift blame for late deliverables and he didn't want to give them any reason to throw him under the bus.

Charlie was used to long hours and late nights. This morning it was different though. He woke up with an uneasy feeling in his gut. He could normally survive many days with little sleep and weird working hours. When he was back home in Nashville for the weekend, he'd crash and sleep until he woke up mid-morning the next day. One night's good, deep sleep would take him through the next week or two. A hard knock on the door startled Charlie. He instinctively knew who it was.

"Room service!" a voice at the door announced. Charlie got out of bed and felt the stiffness in his knee from an old injury. With a slight limp he walked to the door.

"Good morning, Josh," he said as he opened the door and let the night shift manager in.

"Good morning, Mr. O'Neal," Josh said as he squeezed by Charlie. He put the tray on the small fridge next to the dresser. There was no space on the table, but he was used to it. After all, Charlie was one of his favorite hotel guests. As night shift manager, he personally delivered Charlie's coffee on Thursday mornings. He knew it was the day Mr. O'Neal was very generous with his tips. He turned around with a big smile on his face. He knew what was coming and he slowly made his way to the door.

"Enjoy the coffee Mr. O'Neal. Breakfast will be ready at 6 a.m. Will you be joining us this morning?"

"Thank you Josh. Yes, I'll be down shortly. It's Thursday. Two poached eggs, bacon and toast, please?"

"It'll be ready when you arrive Sir," Josh said. "With the usual orange juice, a banana and an apple to go."

Charlie put a ten-dollar bill in Josh's hand. The smile got even bigger as he walked out and closed the door behind him. Charlie was generous with tips the day he left the hotel to travel back home. As a traveling consultant, hotels and airports were an extension of his home. Sometimes, as with his current project, he stayed at the same place for long periods of time. Over the years he learned the benefits of small rewards in the form of a good tip. He treated hotel staff with respect and kindness. His generosity would often come back to him in the form of special treatment when he needed it most. The first time he requested a favor from Josh, he was reluctant to help. Charlie asked if he could leave one of his bags at the hotel and retrieve it Sunday evening when he returned. Josh hesitated with the excuse that he first had to consult with the day shift manager. Only after he agreed to keep the bag in the closet in the office, did Charlie give him a generous tip. It was settled. One of Charlie's bags stayed at the hotel over weekends. He used his carry-on bag to take dirty laundry home. His toiletries, an extra charger for his PC, a second pair of shoes, and other smaller items he would not need at home, stayed at the hotel. Charlie requested a specific room with every reservation. It had to be away from the elevator, far from the noisy ice machine, and on the second floor. Eventually the staff realized Mr. O'Neal would be an easy guest. They reserved the same room for him most of the time. His breakfast was ready at the same table when he arrived in the dining room every morning. The shuttle driver dropped him off first in the mornings. It was the small things like this that made hotel life easier for a frequent traveler.

Charlie walked to the tray and poured his morning coffee, added creamer, stirred, smelled the aroma and took his first sip.

"Just what I need," he thought to himself as he started to get ready for another long day. A day destined to disturb the stable and routine life of Charlie O'Neal.

* * *

CHAPTER 2

Project Meeting

T he project meeting started on time. It always started on time on Thursdays.

"Settle down please!" Tessa had to raise her voice to get the group to order. "I know you want to get out of here, but you know the rules."

Tessa Morris, experienced project manager from Bird, Immelman and Graham Systems Auditors, or BIGS as she referred to her employer, managed the team she assembled with calculated finesse and a razor sharp tongue. Her attitude matched the red color of her hair. She scheduled the weekly status meeting for Thursday afternoons at two o'clock. An hour long meeting everybody understood would impact travel schedules for out of town consultants. If the meeting dragged on for longer than the scheduled time, flights could be missed. The project offices were in the data center of the client located on the east side of Springfield, MO between highway I-44 and Route 66. The airport was located on the west side of the city. In normal traffic, the airport could be reached under thirty minutes.

Charlie, deep in thought about a new problem he discovered right before the meeting, missed Tessa's first request for an update.

"Sorry, I missed that. What was the question?" Charlie asked.

"I wanted to know if your team will be ready for a test run of the payment interface next week?" Tessa repeated her question with a hint of frustration. Everybody knew it was a micro trigger point for the project manager. She didn't like to repeat herself. Charlie knew she could be very bitchy when someone didn't pay attention during a meeting.

"No. It will not be ready," he replied. "The file layout for the middleware was different than the specs and we need to make another change. It should be ready the week after next. It will be better to reschedule." Charlie saw on her face she was not happy with his response and the delay in testing.

"Let's discuss it after the meeting. Before you leave," she said forcefully before moving on to the next team for an update.

After the meeting Charlie followed Tessa to her office. He had worked with many project managers in his career. Only a few had the ability to control a bunch of stubborn, know-it-all, traveling consultants effectively. A diverse group from multiple staffing agencies assembled as a project team, each one was hand picked for a specific reason and skillset. Unfortunately, some of the chosen ones came with big egos, and even bigger attitudes. A conflict of personalities was common and the client company had to find the correct project manager. Tessa Morris was just the person for the task.

Staffing for the project was not a simple process. Tessa insisted on participating in the interview process. Consultants from various companies were carefully screened, background checked, and interviewed. By the time of the kickoff meeting, she knew each person on the team very well. Locked in her desk drawer, was a confidential folder for each person. The folder contained a resumé, notes from the interviews she personally conducted, and a comprehensive background check. She progressively added her own notes.

The client was First Midwest Financial Services, a new financial institution established by the merger of First Bank of Missouri and Midwest Financial Services. The new company obtained the professional services of dependent auditors to oversee the merger. BIGS staffed the project management office with a strong team and was contractually not allowed to provide any consultants for the project. The terms of the service agreement specifically stated that BIGS was hired exclusively to manage the project budget and the project timeline.

"You make sure the project is completed on time and on budget," was Tessa's final instruction from Matthew Jenkins, the newly appointed Chief Information Officer of First Midwest. He had interviewed the final three candidates put forward by BIGS for the project management position. Tessa Morris stood out from amongst the rest due to her proven success with a recent project similar to the one the client had in mind. She was assigned the job, and was responsible for the successful integration of the two financial systems.

"I will give you a choice," Tessa said during one of the early status meetings. She already had to reschedule the meeting a couple of times. Some key members declined and had the excuse of an early flight on Thursday afternoon.

"Those who travel from out of town, will ALL, and with all I mean all, be here Monday mornings at eight or you will ALL be here on Friday mornings at eight. We cannot have some come in late on a Monday and some leave early on a Thursday. I know it is difficult to get direct flights, and most of you have a connection somewhere. But, the project is on a tight schedule and we cannot keep on rescheduling meetings because somebody missed a flight or had to leave early. You can all fly in on Monday morning, and then leave on Friday morning after the status meeting. Or you can ALL fly in on Sunday evening and leave Thursday afternoon after the status meeting."

The debate that followed lasted for almost an hour and she listened patiently to both sides of the arguments. Some heated discussions and valid arguments for and against both sides were made. After an hour she called for a vote. All but two voted for the Sunday and Thursday travel days. Most preferred to work from home on Friday mornings and have the afternoon off.

"That settles it," she concluded. "The status meeting will be on Thursday afternoons. Sub-teams will schedule a conference call for Friday mornings to recap the status meeting, discuss open issues, and plan for the following week. All issues need to be updated on the shared drive before noon. The Project Lead Team will review the issues list at noon on Fridays. I will call the team leads on Friday afternoon if the updates are not timely. Any questions?"

It was not the first project Tessa managed for her company. BIGS specialized in mergers and acquisitions - M&A - in the financial industry. Early in her career, she chose the project management track and not the technical track as a career path. At some point she had managed each one of the sub-teams now involved in an M&A project. The implementation for First Midwest would be the largest project she had ever overseen. The budget was not an issue and resources were available in abundance. They wanted the best, but the timeline was the critical aspect. A successful project would mean success for her career and a step closer to partnership.

Charlie's name was submitted by Professional Information Technology Staffers, PITS. Tessa was intrigued by his impressive resumé. He had the technical skills and financial services experience she was looking for. She interviewed him for one of the team lead positions and the final decision was a no brainer for her, but she had to convince him to take on the position. Charlie was not interested in people management, and preferred to stay close to cutting edge technology. The integration of systems didn't require him to deal with personal issues. He agreed to be the team lead on the condition Tessa would handle personal issues and resource admin. He also wanted to personally review the credentials of candidates for his team before she appointed them.

Charlie's role expanded as the project continued. It required him to coordinate activities for all the interface specialists of the sub-teams. The project required each team to have an interface specialist, or somebody who was supposed to be a specialist. Charlie had to ensure specifications were completed on time and met the internal audit controls. He had enough experience to write most of the required programs but preferred to complete the specifications and have a developer deal with the mundane task of coding and debugging. He would become more hands-on during the test cycle.

One of the tasks Charlie dreaded most was the constant bickering with representatives from external service providers. They had no appreciation for the project timeline and caused frequent delays in deliverables Charlie was responsible for.

"I can deal with the technical issues," Charlie one day complained towards Tessa. "If you can just get them to commit to the timeline."

"I will handle it," Tessa responded. "Give me the details of incidents where they missed the timeline. Nothing will get them to respond faster than a financial penalty."

Charlie deferred negotiations about the scope of work and the fees to Tessa, and made it her problem. She frequently had to pull Charlie in for conference calls to cover the technical jargon they threw at her. In the process, Tessa and Charlie spent many hours working together. They had a good professional working relationship. Personal discussions were limited and Charlie avoided talking about himself. He was single, a loner, never talked about his past, and had almost no social life.

Tessa preferred relationships with other women. She was not aware that Charlie knew her secret, and Charlie preferred it that way. It made the relationship so much easier for both of them.

"What's going on Charlie?" Tessa asked Charlie as she settled behind her desk. "You are normally ready with answers when I need them. I had to repeat myself, and you know I don't like to do that. Why is the interface not ready for the test cycle? You know how critical the interface is. Where did the new requirements come from?" Tessa blasted Charlie with a string of questions. She didn't really expect an answer, but it was her way to voice her frustration.

"Sorry about that," Charlie said calmly. "It was not mentioned in the discovery phase. Another gap, but we will be able to catch up," he said and downplayed the severity of the problem he still didn't have a solution for.

"About the interface," Tessa was still upset. "We have to be ready as soon as possible. We cannot afford any more delays."

"I know. The problem was not on our end," Charlie defended himself. "The company responsible for the middleware mapped half of the fields wrong. They will have to make some changes. And yes, it was in the original specifications we provided to them. They just messed up. Again! You know this is not the first time. Sometimes I wonder if they really know what they are doing." Charlie worked hard to control his own frustration. He normally had everything under control and was not frequently caught off-guard. He just could not tolerate the inability and inefficiency of others.

"Ok, just make sure you get it under control," Tessa replied. She opened a folder on her desk and Charlie recognized his resumé. Some sentences were highlighted, and he noticed comments were scribbled in the sideline next to the highlights.

"My resumé?" Charlie asked and looked at Tessa. "Something going on that I should know about?"

"Yes. I do have something else I want to talk to you about." The angry tone in her voice was gone.

"This must be serious," Charlie commented and leaned against the doorframe.

"Close the door and sit down please." She said while flipping through his resumé. Charlie closed the door and sat down facing her.

"What are your plans once this project is completed?" she asked. The question and sudden change of subject caught Charlie by surprise.

"Well," Charlie paused for moment. Not sure how to respond, he tried to stall first. "I have not really thought about it yet. There are still a few months left on my contract and I'm not planning to jump ship."

"BIGS has a few projects in the pipeline. I'm gathering resumés for a future assignment I may get pulled into." Tessa sat back and looked at Charlie. "You are one of our star resources on this project. I enjoy working with you, and appreciate all the long hours you put in. Your technical skills and specifically your knowledge about the financial sector are extraordinary. It's not easy to find somebody with your skills."

Charlie's instinct and gut feeling threw up some red flags while he listened to Tessa.

"That's a first," Charlie said with a smile on his face nodding his head. "You don't normally give complements, you must want something."

"Of course I want something," she said. "I first need to let you know how good you are and then ask if I can trust you. What I'm about to tell you is confidential."

"You know me. Of course I will run out and tell everybody about what we discussed the moment I leave this office," Charlie said with sarcasm.

"Very funny, Charlie," Tessa said. "I'm serious. I know I can trust you, but I need to ask."

"Yes. I will keep it confidential," Charlie responded seriously.

"Ok then," Tessa continued. "I reviewed your resumé last night again. Seems you have worked with REAL-TIME in your past. Did you do a lot of development?"

"REAL-TIME? Wow, that goes back a long way," Charlie said. "It was just one of many programming languages I used earlier in my career. The programming environment grew up, and I don't really like the development aspect anymore." Memories about the past flashed through his brain and something deep inside stirred. His stomach twitched, but he continued. "I used it extensively in the eighties while working for a bank in South Africa. I was a DBA at the time. The banking industry was very excited about the new application. For me, it was something new to learn. The bank paid for my training and the rest is history. So, yes, you can say I have some development experience with REAL-TIME." Charlie completely downplayed his experience and tried to sound nonchalant about it. "But, why are you interested in my past experience?" Charlie asked and looked straight at Tessa. It was his time to study her reaction.

"We are looking at a big M&A," Tessa said and shared more details with Charlie. "One of the institutions involved in the acquisition still uses REAL-TIME. The other party prefers their own homegrown system. They plan to switch over to the homegrown system and save on licensing fees to REAL-TIME in the process. The problem is finding somebody with enough experience to help us understand what we are looking at. We need somebody who we can put forward as a resource to secure our bid. That is where you come into the picture. If we can get you on our team, it will give us the advantage we are looking for. BIGS will again staff the Project Management Office, like we did on this project for First Midwest. We plan to select some of the key resources from this project for team lead positions. The technical teams and developers will mostly be subcontractors. We will hire extra bodies as and when they are needed. It will be a nice long-term project. And, the money will be good. Really good."

"What about this project? Are you quitting on us?" Charlie asked, not sure exactly how to respond. It all sounded exciting, but in his gut he still had this strange feeling of uneasiness.

"No, I will not" Tessa said quickly. "This project is under control and will be done in a few months. I plan to take some time off afterwards. The new project will start early next year. That is, if the M&A process gets past the regulatory approval. We have nothing on paper yet." She looked at Charlie for a few moments and then continued. "I would like to add you to my short-list. What do you say? Can I put your name down?"

Charlie looked at Tessa for a long time. He thought about the reaction from Heinz, the PITS HR manager. If he took the opportunity, he would have to leave the company that helped him become a US citizen. This was not an easy decision.

"This will not be an easy decision." Charlie said. "But, put me down and give me some time to think it over. You will have to give me some more details. You know I like to make decisions based on facts and not just some idea."

"Of course," Tessa replied. "That is exactly what I expected from you. I just wanted to see if you would be interested. We can talk again next week."

Charlie left Tessa's office with mixed feelings. For a moment he felt excited, but he didn't like change. There was no pressing need for him to change the routine he'd gotten used to for so long. On his way to the airport he thought about the conversation with Tessa. A feeling of intense sadness, and a longing for something he didn't know, came over him. It was going to be another long lonely weekend for Charlie O'Neal.

* * *

CHAPTER 3

The Lie

"Good morning," Charlie said as he knocked and the open door to Tessa's office. "Do you have a minute?"

"Good morning, Charlie. Yes, sure. Come in." Tessa briefly looked up, smiled at him and continued typing. He stepped into her office and leaned against the wall. After a moment the typing stopped and she sat back and looked at him.

"Sorry, just had to get that e-mail out," she apologized. "What can I do for you?"

"About our discussion last week," Charlie started and looked in the hallway to make sure nobody could hear him. "I did some research over the weekend, and I couldn't find anything about a big merger and acquisition looming. How sure are you about the project?"

"We are an audit company. We know stuff," Tessa said with a smile. "There is a very tight lid on this one and it's still very confidential. When the news media catches on, it will definitely stir the market. I'm sure you will hear about it on all the news channels."

"Umm, that doesn't really help me. How do I make a decision based on that?" Charlie wanted more info, but he also needed to know how much Tessa trusted him. Working in the finance sector for so long, he knew how fast rumors spread. Some ideas became reality, while others faded away the moment the sun went down. He had to make sure this was not just another dead end.

Tessa looked at Charlie for a few seconds. In her eyes he saw she was considering her reply very carefully.

"Charlie," she started and her big blue eyes widened as she looked directly at him. "I have known you long enough to know I can trust you. Trust me on this one. I know what I'm talking about."

An awkward silence hung in the air for a moment. Charlie trusted very few people. Since he immigrated to the US, he had kept to himself. He worked long hours, became good at what he did, and lived a comfortable life. He earned a decent income, but didn't have an abundance of money.

"How long have you been a consultant Charlie?" Tessa asked. Charlie frowned about the strange personal question.

"Long enough, to not answer a question if I don't know the motive for the question," Charlie responded with a smile on his face.

"Typical consultant," she said and smiled back at Charlie. "Let's talk about the one thing consultants always wants to know first. The rate. What did you have in mind?"

"We can discuss the rate later," Charlie responded and he could see she was surprised by his response. "I'm more interested in the project details and who is involved. What systems are we talking about, what type of financial institutions; traditional banks or investment firms? You know there are only a handful of companies still running REAL-TIME? It will not take long for me to get a list of those who still use it."

"Wow, lots of questions. Seems like you did give our conversation some thought over the weekend."

"Yes, I did" Charlie said with a somber look on his face. "You know I'm a loyal person and I don't like change. There has to be a very good reason for me to leave PITS. They have treated me well up to now and I'm sure they will treat me the same in the future."

Tessa listened to Charlie and shook her head. Again Charlie noticed how she weighed her response before starting.

"Sorry Charlie. I cannot give you any more specifics if you are not on board. I cannot share anything more if you have not signed a non-disclosure agreement."

"That's an insult, you know?" Charlie said teasingly. He also realized that this might not be just some normal project. "I sign one for every project I have worked on. You either trust me or you don't trust me. I'm willing to sign one any time, and you know that."

"Ok then. What do I need to do to get you on board? Let's talk rates and get it out of the way. Maybe I can get you interested. We can do the paperwork later."

"Before we get to the rate. I have one more question. If you are willing to answer it, I will know you are serious and we can talk more."

"Ok. What's the question?" Tessa asked with a curious look on her face.

"Why do you want me on the project? Why me specifically? Is one of the parties involved in the merger the bank I used to work for?"

"That's more than one question?" Tessa responded with a smile.

"Ok, ok. Semantics. Answer any one you wish and we can go from there."

Tessa looked at Charlie and for a moment their eyes locked. They both knew the seriousness of the situation. Deep inside, Charlie remembered a few times in his life that he felt he could see into the soul of the person sitting across from him. He recalled the incident with Mr. Burns, his high school math teacher. And who could forget Mr. Kramer? His dad got him the job at a bank when he graduated high school. Mr. Kramer was his first manager and a good man, but he did have his little secret. There were some others, but when he looked at Tessa, he had the same feeling he had before. In his gut he knew he could trust her.

"I looked at your contract. We are willing to increase your rate twenty-five percent. All travel expenses will be paid on top of that. We are willing to give you two-fifty an hour." She sat back and waited for Charlie to respond. Charlie just stared at her in total disbelief. The blood slowly drained from his face.

"What?" he said with a frown on his face. "Did you just say two-fifty an hour?"

"Yes." Tessa answered hesitantly. "Is something wrong? Did you expect more?"

"Wait" Charlie said, looked down and shook his head. When he looked up he had an angry look on his face. "How do you add twenty-five percent and get two-fifty?" Charlie asked with a soft, but deliberate voice.

"We took your current rate paid to PITS, and added twenty-five percent. Basic math. As an independent consultant, you will get the full rate and there will be no middleman. No staffing company will be involved to take a cut."

"I have a non-compete. I cannot do that," Charlie responded. His mind still stuck on what he just heard.

"It will not violate the non-compete agreement. You are not negotiating directly with the primary client, who is First Midwest. The new agreement will be between you and BIGS. The offer is directly to you, as an independent consultant. I just wanted to make sure we got your attention. That's why we added twenty five percent."

"You sure got my attention." Charlie sounded very angry. Tessa shifted uncomfortably in her chair.

"Charlie! What's going on?" she asked with a sharp voice.

"How do you know my rate?"

"I'm the project manager, Charlie. I approve every time sheet, and every payment. I have to account for every minute the client is billed for. Expenses are capped at fifteen percent, and I want details if it goes one penny over the allowed rate. I need to know since I have to explain it. You really thought I didn't know what the rates are?"

Charlie stayed silent for a long time. He battled to control the anger inside of him. He was furious and tried to hide it.

"I was told my rate is a hundred dollars an hour. My company takes twenty percent of the rate. That leaves me with eighty dollars per hour. So, the rate is not two hundred as you said. Either you are lying to me, or what you are telling me is that PITS charges double what I was told. Who do I believe?"

Tessa unlocked her drawer and pulled a file from the desk drawer. It was the same file she had before. She dropped it on the table and looked at Charlie.

"I have the proof Charlie. Right here," she said and tapped with her finger on the file. "The signed contract between First Midwest and PITS. I'm not the one lying!"

Charlie looked at Tessa more confused than before.

"I do my best to deliver good results. Then the company I work for lies to me? This project has been going on for almost two years now, and only now do I find out the truth? How long has this been going on? Have they been stealing from me the whole time?"

Charlie looked at Tessa and saw how the truth slowly dawned on her. His words sank in and he knew she was making the same calculations he was busy with in his head. At $120 per hour, working 2000 hours a year would give PITS $480,000 just for the past two years. Double what Charlie made, and he did all the work.

"The agreement with all staffing companies allows them to take a maximum of a twenty percent cut of the rate paid for a consultant's service." Tessa tried to explain. "It is fair to all the parties involved. If what you say is true, then they are in breach of the contract with the client."

Charlie dropped his head and stared at the floor. Perplexed and not knowing what to do or say, he just stood there in silence. It became very quiet in the office. After a while he looked up and with a calm and soft voice said: "I need fresh air and time to think. Nothing wrong with your offer, I just need to figure out what I'm going to do right now."

"I understand," was the only thing Tessa could say.

Charlie walked out of her office, and out of the building. He just wanted to get out and think. He didn't feel the cold air outside as he walked a few blocks to the coffee shop he stopped by every morning. At the counter he ordered his favorite caramel macchiato, paid for it and sat down in one of the chairs in the corner. Customers were coming and going, but he didn't notice anything.

"Two hundred dollars an hour! They don't even pay me half of that!" He didn't know what to do with the information Tessa accidentally provided to him. He was sure she had her facts straight. She had the contract. He knew all staffing companies took a cut from the rate negotiated with the client. PITS did exactly the same. But for them to make more than double what he got out of the deal was too much for Charlie to digest. He felt sick just thinking about it. He calculated what they had made and compared it to what he had made. He thought back over the more than ten years he had been working for them. Their deception fueled his anger exponentially.

"After all the years I worked for them! Now I find out they have been cheating me the whole time. If you can lie, you can steal, and they stole from me."

Charlie sat alone with his thoughts. Every minute that passed, he got more upset with Heinz Conrad. Heinz was the one who recruited him and convinced him to make the move from his home country South Africa. The way he explained the American dream and the advances in the tech industry, made it all sound so futuristic and achievable. It was a time in his life when he needed to make a change, a drastic change. But now, after all these years, he discovered that he had been cheated for so long. It stirred the pain of what had happened many years ago from deep inside of him.

He thought about Heinz and what he was going to do when they met again. He wanted to just leave immediately, drive all the way from Springfield to Atlanta and smash his face to pulp. But he knew it was a bad idea and he would never do anything like that. He had to plan it carefully. The same way he had planned his revenge for the bullies in high school. His time would come. He just needed to be patient.

She found Charlie an hour later in the coffee shop, slumped forward, staring at the table with a mug in his hand. The coffee was cold.

"Charlie?" Tessa said as she stood next to him. He didn't respond. "Charlie!" she reached over and touched his shoulder. He looked up at her with a blank stare in his eyes.

"Are you ok?" She took the cup from him and walked to the counter. She asked the barista to heat it up, and make her a cappuccino.

"I will just make him a fresh cup. Is he ok? He was just sitting there. I didn't know what to do."

"He will be ok. I'll take care of him. How much for the coffee?"

"Oh, it's is free. He is a regular and is always generous to us. Please take good care of him," the barista said with concern in her voice.

"Thanks. I will."

Charlie was back to his normal self again. Tessa sat down across from him.

"What's going on, Charlie?" Tessa asked. "And don't you dare say nothing! I know you and I can see something is wrong, really wrong. Talk to me." Charlie just stared at her.

"How much do you really know about me? How do you know something is 'wrong'?" he said and used his fingers to make air-quotes. He tried the defensive act first.

"Charlie. I have your resumé on file. I will not make an offer to just any person off the street. Of course not! We do our homework very well. I know you have worked for PITS for more than ten years, and they sponsored your green card application. You became a citizen early in 2002. Do you need more?"

"So? Do you also know how much they pay me? How long has this been going on?"

"I know the rate structure the client pays each staffing company. The contract with First Midwest allows them to take a twenty percent cut of the consultant's rate. I assumed PITS would honor the agreement. And no, I didn't verify each individual consultant's rate. Maybe I should have done my homework better."

"Obviously," Charlie said sarcastically.

The barista delivered the drinks and Charlie looked at her and said: "Thanks, Wendy. I will make it up to you."

"I know," she said with a smile and walked away.

They tasted their coffee in silence, not sure what to say or do next. Tessa broke the silence.

"They are in breach of the agreement with First Midwest. If I mention it to the Matthew Jenkins, he will have them off site in a flash." Tessa expressed her thoughts out loud.

"Maybe that's not too bad of an idea," Charlie said angrily. "That will cut their profit also. If all the consultants PITS has on this project leave, it will be a major blow for them."

"That may be true, but I cannot lose you now. You know that very well. If you leave, we will miss the deadline. If we lose all the consultants from PITS ... I don't even want to go there." Her voice faded and when Charlie looked at her he realized she was sincere. She was also caught off guard by the discovery of the truth.

"I won't put your project at risk" Charlie said. "I'm not sure what I'm going to do, but I'm not just going to let this one pass unnoticed." Charlie thought how he had felt many years ago when Project Maroela was shelved. He was the lucky one that stayed on when the contractors were let go -

a different time, a different reason, but he still remembered it clearly. He didn't want to deal with the same situation again. His initial knee-jerk reaction was to just walk off the project and quit. *"That would teach them to mess with the wrong person,"* he had thought to himself. He also knew he would not follow through with his threat.

"Please Charlie," Tessa begged. "Think about the other consultants. What will happen to them if the project gets cancelled or delayed? You may be ok, but it will hurt them too, maybe more. I know for sure I will lose my job for giving you the info."

"And if I do nothing, it's business as usual! No repercussions, and no penalties for PITS? Now I know why this has been the 'most profitable' project for them. They cheated all the time."

"I'm afraid there's not much we can do right now." She shook her head and clenched her teeth. They both realized that there was nothing they could do without causing a major upset for everybody involved.

"You know" Charlie said as he put his cup down and looked at Tessa. "I think I've had enough. This may just be the straw that breaks the camel's back."

"What are you going to do?" Tessa asked concerned.

As quick as the anger flared up inside of Charlie, he suppressed it again.

"I don't know exactly," Charlie said, shaking his head. "But I'm going to have a serious conversation with Mr. Heinz Conrad."

"Who is Heinz Conrad?" Tessa asked.

"He is the HR manager from PITS - just a regular HR person with a fancy title. Many years ago, I responded to an ad in a newspaper in South Africa. He recruited me to come and work in the US. That's a long story for another day. He frequently travels all over the world to hire more consultants. There are a whole bunch of them working for PITS. Not only on this project, but on multiple other projects also. He thinks he is one of the big shots at the company."

"But he didn't sign the agreement with the client. It was Vince Milner." Tessa said with a puzzled look on her face.

"Oh, no! Not Heinz. He would never sign a contract with a client. That would be Vince Milner, the CEO. He is responsible for marketing and customer relations. He does the negotiations with clients and signs the contracts. Heinz only focuses on building a pool of resource. He only signs the contracts with consultants."

"So, Heinz negotiates the contracts with the consultants, and Vince negotiates the contracts with the clients. And the CFO - what's his role? What's his name again?" Tessa asked.

"Dan Oliver" Charlie said.

"So, is he the one who is cheating?" Tessa said while nodding her head. "Sure sounds shady to me."

"I don't know yet. But it's payback time." Charlie still sounded bitter and determined. "I have been working my butt off to survive, and they are the ones laughing all the way to the bank."

"Charlie. Please don't risk the project. Maybe there is an explanation." Tessa begged again. "You know how hard you and everybody else have worked to get this far. If we lose a group of consultants now, it will be disastrous for all of us. Think about the others. What will happen to Ben, Gracey and Jackson? They also work for PITS. You have spent so much time helping them get settled. You want them to lose their jobs also?" In her voice Charlie heard the emotions welling up. Tessa continued and a tear formed in her eye. "I'm so sorry Charlie. I should not have disclosed confidential information to you. They will blame me for the failure of this project."

"Sorry? Why would you feel sorry? For telling me the truth?" Charlie was angry and upset. "I will never blame you for telling me the truth. You just opened my eyes."

"I know. But I still feel bad. I didn't know. Honestly!" Tessa took a deep breath and exhaled slowly. She wiped a tear from her eye with a napkin from the table. "I can kiss the next project goodbye for sure," she said with disappointment.

"I thought you said you had the project in the bag? Does it depend on the outcome of this project?"

"No, we don't have it completely in the bag yet. We are on the shortlist - one out of three companies. There is still a lot of work to be done before we can say we have a deal. Failure of this project will set us back a few steps and we might just lose it altogether." Tessa hesitated before she continued. "Why don't you give it some time? Think about your reaction and the consequences before you do anything."

"Yeah. I need to think this through. My Dad always said 'Never make a decision when you are angry or upset.' I learned my lesson on that one."

"Please!" Tessa pleaded with Charlie again. "Wait a couple of weeks. Help me get this project done, and I'll return the favor to you someday."

Charlie thought for a moment and then looked at her directly.

"Maybe there is something you can do for me. Can you get me a copy of the original agreement signed between PITS and First Midwest? I may just need it for my discussion with Heinz. I need the hard facts to show him."

"It's confidential." Tessa objected, but didn't sound convincing. She looked at Charlie and he could see something brewing in her mind. "Maybe I can do something for you. I told you we do our homework. Let me see what I can get." Tessa sounded like the project manager again. "But, I will need you to sign the non-disclosure first."

Charlie was deep in thought. He was not sure what she would be able to give him, but his plan was starting to take shape. He had a good working relationship with Tessa, and he didn't want to make life difficult for her. This just made their relationship stronger. Maybe she held the key to the door for the next phase of his life away from PITS.

"Ok. You think about the contract while I think about what I should do next." He said and smiled at her.

"Thank you Charlie." Tessa sounded relieved that the immediate crisis was averted. "Until this project is over, I have to consider what is best for the project. Once it is over, you can quit and become an independent consultant. You can negotiate your own rates and nobody will get a cut from it. You can earn a lot more without the middleman."

"Until then, I still have to take the financial knock for what they have been doing? Is that fair? How many other consultants have they screwed over?" Charlie said with bitterness.

"Let's get out of here," Tessa said as she got up. They walked out and Tessa motioned toward her car. "I'll give you a ride back to the office."

"Thanks," Charlie said and got into the passenger seat. They didn't speak much on their way to the office. Charlie stared outside and noticed the traffic. A cold shiver rand down his spine as a black Mercedes Benz passed in the lane next to him.

* * *

CHAPTER 4

Dog and Pony Show

The receptionist at the front desk looked at the displayed on the switchboard before pressing the blinking light to answer the phone.

"Professional IT Staffers, good morning! This is Emma speaking. How can I help you?"

"Good morning, Emma. Can I speak to Heinz Conrad, please?"

"May I ask who is calling?"

"This is Charlie O'Neal. I'm a consultant with PITS."

"Please hold, Mr. O'Neal. Let me see if he is available to take your call." Soft music played in the background as she put Charlie on hold. A few seconds later the music stopped and Heinz greeted Charlie in his loud, boisterous voice.

"Good morning, Charlie! What a surprise?" Heinz had the gift of the gab, was a smooth talker, a promise maker, but unfortunately for Charlie not a promise keeper. "You never call me, I'm the one who normally has to make the call. How are you doing today?"

Heinz had sold the American Dream to Charlie. The Utopia world for any IT consultant who wanted to travel and see the world; an opportunity to work with the best of breed, wine and dine in the finest restaurants in the world, and find a place to eventually settle. Charlie had believed the pitch from Heinz when they first met, taking the bait Heinz threw out to him. Charlie's intentions were to stay in the consulting service for a short while, gain exposure in the international arena, stuff his resumé with enough global experiences to find a full time position with a major financial institution and then settle down. His plans were to build a new career in the technology environment of the financial services industry.

"Good morning, Heinz. I'm fine. We need to talk."

"Wow, Charlie! What's wrong? You sound upset. Did something happen?" Heinz sounded concerned.

"Yes, I'm upset. I need to meet with you in person. I have to be at the dog and pony show on Friday..." Charlie said with sarcasm and Heinz interrupted him before he could complete his sentence.

"It's not a dog and pony show, Charlie. You know that. It is in the interest of the company and all consultants. It's an opportunity for knowledge transfer, and to learn something new." It was a sensitive nerve Charlie touched on purpose. Many of the senior consultants had heard the same stories over and over. New consultants drank in the words and presentations from the executives, the "Three Musketeers", and from other consultants. One of the most dreaded tasks for a benched consultant was to participate in the presentation during the quarterly meeting. Charlie had given his share of presentations early on in his career with PITS. As he gained more experience, he skipped the obligation since his billable hours were more important to the company than spending time preparing for a presentation. There was always somebody new willing to use the opportunity PITS provided. Charlie got used to the diverse group of people at the quarterly meetings. He recognized those he had worked with at some point during a project, but only a handful had stayed with the company. It was a constant revolving door of consultants.

"That's your story, Heinz. Will you be available, or should I just skip the meeting?"

"What do you want to talk about?" Heinz sounded a bit more irritated than when he answered the phone. "Can we discuss it over the phone?"

"No. I want to have a man-to-man conversation with you. I don't want to discuss it over the phone."

"Ok then. What's it about? Give me some details so I can at least be prepared for the meeting."

"No, Heinz. I'm not going to explain it over the phone. Can we meet Friday morning? Early, before the other consultants arrive for the show?"

"I can be here early. What time?"

"At seven will be fine."

"Ok. I will be here. Are you sure you don't want to tell me what this is about?" Heinz tried again.

"I'm sure, Heinz. See you on Friday." Charlie hung up before Heinz could respond.

Charlie knew it was rude, but he didn't want to talk too much on the phone. He was worried that he would lose his cool and verbally attack Heinz. That would be disastrous and he would miss the opportunity to see Heinz's first reaction when confronted with the facts. He wanted to see the surprise and fear in Heinz's eyes when he put the evidence in front of him.

Charlie had never liked people that lied to him. He vowed to always tell the truth no matter the consequences. He trusted his own gut feeling, and from the day he met Heinz, he had uneasiness deep inside of him. He managed to put his feelings about Heinz aside and blamed it on his personal circumstances at the time. But every time they met, there was something in Heinz that made him cringe.

Charlie met Heinz for the first time in South Africa after he responded to an ad in the Sunday Times newspaper. The initial communication happened via e-mail, and a few days after Charlie submitted his resumé, Heinz called him. They arranged for a meeting during one of Heinz's recruiting trips. He had already lined up a few interviews with new recruits from the local University in Pretoria, but Charlie had some experience they were looking for. Heinz wanted to meet in person.

The interview was scheduled at a restaurant in a shopping center close to where Charlie lived. Charlie arrived early and waited for an hour past the scheduled time before he finally left. Heinz had been a no-show. Charlie left very worried and he battled with his own thoughts. *"Is this a sign? Is this the right thing to do?"*

When he got home, there was a message from Heinz apologizing for not making it to the meeting. He had some lame excuse about traffic and getting lost when he tried to take a short cut. He asked Charlie to give him a call so they could reschedule. Charlie returned the call and they arranged for a meeting at Charlie's apartment. When Charlie met Heinz, they shook hands and it made him squirm. His hand was cold and sweaty, not the normal firm grip Charlie was used to when men shook hands. It could just as well have been the hand of a corpse he shook. He could hear his dad's words echo in his mind: *"A man without a firm handshake cannot be trusted. He will eventually stab you in the back. Be careful, be very careful."* Every time they met, Charlie feared the moment of the customary handshake.

"Why did I not listen to my Dad?" Charlie thought as he turned his attention back to work. The project was in the final phase before going live in the productive environment. There was the normal frenzy of activities to get everything ready before the last switch was flipped to activate the new system. The required quarterly meeting on Friday interfered with the project, and the PITS consultants had to work extra hours to make up for the lost time while attending the meeting in Atlanta.

Charlie arrived early on Friday morning. Based on the number of cars in the parking lot, he was not the only early riser. He swiped his badge at the front door and stepped into the reception area. Caterers were setting out trays of breakfast foods and snacks. He skipped the food, walked straight to the elevator and pressed the button for the fifth floor where the PITS offices were located. As he waited he thought about the many quarterly events he had attended. *"The same routine, the same food, and the same speeches."* The meeting would start at 8:00 AM. Lunch would be served at 12 PM. The afternoon session would adjourn at 3 PM. The evening event would be sponsored by the company, and would be held at the home of the PITS CEO. It would be the same tired food, endless drinks, boring desserts, hyped presentations and predictable discussions.

On the fifth floor he stepped out of the elevator and smelled coffee brewing in the break room. He helped himself to a cup and walked to Heinz's office. The door was locked so he settled into the conference room down the hall. Charlie heard him before he saw him as he greeted some of the early risers. He asked a few questions and gave instructions to somebody about the meeting. He walked passed the conference room, and when he saw Charlie, he walked in with his hand stretched out. The moment Charlie dreaded most. Charlie rose from his chair and took hold of the dead fish. He shivered as he shook it once and let it go as fast as he could.

"Good morning, Charlie."

"Good morning, Heinz." Charlie acknowledged the greeting without any trace of friendliness. He expected the discussion would not go well.

"Had a good trip?"

"It was fine."

"Let's go into my office" Heinz said as he began walking to his office. He unlocked the door and settled in behind his desk with his coffee in hand. Charlie stepped in and closed the door behind him. He sat down facing Heinz. They each took a sip of their coffee, and stared in silence at each other for a moment.

"Nothing like a good cup of coffee," Charlie broke the uncomfortable silence. He tried to be calm, and not sound too aggressive.

"Yes. The fuel that runs IT," Heinz commented and attempted a smile.

"Thanks for coming in early."

"Not a problem. I planned to be early anyway, so no effort for me. What's on your mind, Charlie? You sounded upset when we talked earlier in the week."

Charlie looked at Heinz and took a deep breath.

"Heinz. We have known each other for a while now. I have been working for PITS since the early days when the company just started up. You recruited me, and helped me settle in. You even helped me go through the immigration process. Remember it?"

"Yes, I remember. Those were the good old days. We were trying to get traction in the financial services sector. We just could not get the breakthrough we needed. We had a promising opportunity, and needed an expert to get our foot in the door. Then out of the blue you contacted us, and the rest is history."

"The good old days." Charlie echoed back and Heinz continued his monologue.

"I still think you are one of the best hires I have ever made. Yes, immigration was not easy, as you know, but we eventually got through the process. I'm glad that is over." Heinz paused for a moment. "But, that's not why we are here. What can I do for you?"

Charlie knew Heinz had a full day ahead and had a show to run. He also didn't want to dwell too long on the small talk and wanted to do what he came for.

"That's right, Heinz. I have something to discuss with you. Something personal." Charlie reached for his laptop bag. Took out a copy of the agreement between PITS with First Midwest Financial Services. He dropped it on the desk in front of Heinz and said: "This is what I want to discuss!"

Heinz looked down and picked up the document. He started to read it and Charlie saw on his face the moment he recognized what he was holding in his hands. It contained the full statement of work to be performed, the normal legal disclosures, the non-compete agreement, confidentiality agreement and payment terms. This was it. He flipped through the pages and stopped on the page with the signatures for PITS as the service provider and First Midwest as the client. Then he turned to the addendum that listed the names of the consultants engaged in the project. The list had changed over time and Charlie was the only one from the original group who was still on the project. The page also contained the rate for each consultant.

Heinz's face turned gray before it became as white as the paper he was holding. His eyes grew wider, and for a moment Charlie thought they were going to pop out of their sockets. Charlie enjoyed every detail of the moment intensely. This was exactly why he wanted to meet in person. He wanted to see and experience the shock and awe on Heinz's face the moment he realized what the meeting was about.

"Perfect! It was worth the wait. Got you!" he thought and took another sip of his coffee.

"Where... How... Who..." Heinz stuttered. He was at a loss for words. Charlie had not seen him so stunned and the look in his eyes told him that Heinz knew exactly where the discussion would go. This was his worst nightmare coming to life.

"I have my resources." Charlie responded calmly. For the first time since they met, Charlie felt fully in control of Heinz. The tables had turned.

"This is confidential information." Heinz tried to shift the blame. "If the client disclosed it to you, they are in breach of contract. We will sue the guts out of them!" He sounded angry, but in his eyes Charlie saw fear. His face began to turn red as the blood started to flow back to his cheeks and embarrassment took over.

"Oh. Now, *they* are in breach of contract?" Charlie said with sarcasm.

"Page eighteen. Section four, second bullet point; and I will quote just in case you cannot read! 'The service provider agrees to a maximum margin of twenty percent of the consulting fees paid in compensation to the consultant. Actual expenses will also be capped at twenty percent of the base rate. Violation of this section will void all terms and conditions as stipulated in this agreement and statement of work.' Who is in breach of contract?" Charlie had memorized the sentence, since he anticipated Heinz would threaten suing somebody immediately.

"We haven't violated the terms of that section," Heinz tried again.

"No?" Charlie sat up. Anger engulfed him, and he was ready for the fight. "What is my rate? What rate are you using to bill First Midwest for my services? You have the contract I had to sign when the project started. Get it out so we can compare notes."

"I can explain," Heinz switched to defense when he realized Charlie had his facts and knew what was going on.

"You'd better explain! How long have you been screwing me, Heinz? How long have you been skimming from the top? You took sixty two and a half percent of the rate! I only get eighty dollars. How many other consultants are you screwing this way?" Charlie was on a roll and had many more things to throw at Heinz.

"Charlie. Wait. Wait!" Heinz interrupted and held up his hands. "It is not what you think."

"How do you know what I'm thinking?" Charlie exploded again. "What do you think is going to happen if I stand up at the meeting today, and tell all the consultants how PITS has been screwing us the whole time?" Charlie's face was red in anger. He was ready to jump up and hit Heinz. Heinz's face turned back to gray and he sat on the edge of his chair.

"You wouldn't dare."

"Don't underestimate me, Heinz!" Charlie was still furious, but he slowly regained control of himself. He still had some fight in him and he wanted to get it out.

"What is it you want, Charlie?" Heinz surrendered but still wanted to take a stab at Charlie. "Money? Now I see it. It's just greed? You want more money!" Heinz said with a smirk and a sarcastic look on his face. Charlie could not believe what he had just heard! He was indignant.

"Greed! YOU... you want to accuse me of being greedy!?!" Charlie said while shaking his head from side to side in astonishment. "Wow! Come on, Heinz. You can do better than that."

"What do you want?"

"The truth Heinz. Just tell me the truth. I want to know it all. And, yes, I do want the money you owe me. We will start with what I can prove with the contract in your hand. The rest will be for you to prove as we review all previous contracts I have signed."

Heinz sat back in his chair, stared at Charlie for a while. He was deep in thought about his next response. Charlie knew he would stall and have an excuse to avoid a direct answer.

"I will have to discuss it with Vince and Dan."

"As expected. The Three Musketeers! So, are they in on this scheme also?" Charlie got up and stepped towards the door. "Oh, just so you know. I left a full statement and a notarized affidavit with somebody in Springfield to hand to First Midwest if I don't show up at work on Monday. I still mean to honor my part of the agreement to the client. I'm not sure what you are going to do, Heinz. I want an answer before I get on the plane on Sunday evening. My flight leaves at 7 PM." Charlie opened the door and turned back to Heinz. He was a defeated man, staring at nothing. "The client doesn't know that I have a copy of the agreement. The ball is in your court."

Charlie took the elevator down to the first floor where breakfast was ready and where the meeting would take place. He suddenly had an appetite and loaded a plate full of food and got a fresh cup of coffee. He had not finished his previous cup and had left it on Heinz's desk. Other consultants began to arrive and the crowd grew. He greeted a few familiar faces and introduced himself to new ones.

Charlie had expected Heinz to stall with the excuse that he had to discuss the matter with Vince and Dan. He wasn't sure when Heinz would have time do it. The day already had a full program and Heinz had a show to run.

The dog and pony show continued. Charlie made sure he sat far to the back and so he could observe the Three Musketeers going through their paces. Heinz was the only one a bit off of his normal self, but Vince and Dan made up for it. All throughout the day Charlie avoided contact with Vince and Dan. He knew Heinz would not come close to him unless he had discussed the issue with the other two.

Vince was the last one to address the group and thanked them for another successful quarter.

"To celebrate the success of this quarter, and this will be our best year yet, you are all invited to dinner at my house tonight. There will be lots of food, and drinks will be on the house. If you need directions, the address and a map of how to get there is on the invite at the front desk. Grab one as you leave. See you there!" Vince ended the session and started clapping his hands for himself. The group applauded and the exodus started.

One of the consultants Charlie worked with stopped to talk to him. They made their way to the door and Charlie could see Heinz and Dan in a discussion in the front of the room. At the door, Vince was greeting everyone. Charlie had no choice but to talk to him.

"Glad you are here, Charlie," Vince said after the customary handshake and pat on the back. "I have something to talk to you about. Will you be at the party tonight?"

"Yes." Charlie said uncomfortably. His first thought was that Heinz had already talked to him. "What is it about?"

"I'm working on a new prospect. Something big. We are going to need you for this one. I want to talk to you about it."

"Sounds interesting. Yes, I will be there."

"See you tonight!" Vince said as he greeted the next person in line.

Charlie left the building and walked to his rental car. He had a smile on his face and he thought about what Vince had just said. Before he left Springfield on Thursday, Tessa had called him into her office.

"I have some information for you."

"About?" Charlie asked. He had too many things on his mind and thought it was something about the new project.

"I have the names of the other companies on the short list for the project. PITS is one of them."

"What?" Charlie was surprised but not really shocked.

"Yes. I owe you one, and I wanted to give you the info before your quarterly meeting. Just remember, my offer still stand. You owe me an answer."

"I know. But thanks for the heads-up."

He knew exactly what Vince wanted to talk about. *"This is going to be interesting,"* he thought as the headed to the hotel to get ready for the party.

* * *

CHAPTER 5

The Party

Charlie turned into the neighborhood where Vince and Alice Milner lived. Cars were everywhere and he had to park a few houses away from the Milner's. The neighborhood was classified as a "Residential Estate" with a minimum 3000 square feet per house and a minimum lot size of one acre. Vince and Alice lived on a two-and-a-half acre lot and the house was well over 5000 square feet. It was Charlie's second visit to the estate. His first visit was also after a quarterly event when PITS sponsored a house warming party for their beloved CEO. The house was custom built under the watchful eye of Alice while Vince tended to business. The interior decorations were still a work in process according to Alice, and Charlie wondered what had changed since his previous visit.

The front door was open and Charlie walked in. Alice Milner was in the foyer talking with another guest and welcomed him in.

"Hi. Welcome to our home. I'm Alice, Vince's wife."

"Hi. Alice. I'm Charlie," he said as he shook her hand.

"Charlie! Of course! How could I not have recognized you? You were here for the house warming party!" She felt embarrassed for not recognizing Charlie immediately. They shared pleasantries, and she walked him through an elegantly decorated living room. Above the fireplace was a majestic painting of Table Mountain.

"This is beautiful!" he commented.

"Ah, thank you," Alice said with a face full of appreciation. "Vince inherited it from his parents when they passed. His father bought it as an investment many years ago. I used it as inspiration for the interior decor."

"It wasn't here when we had the house warming party."

"No. The frame got damaged during our move from South Africa many years ago. I had it reframed when we built this house."

The wall next to the fireplace was decorated with family pictures. In the center was a large canvas print of a young Vince and Alice looking through the back window of a car with the words "Just Married" written on it.

"That you and Vince?"

"Yes." Alice said with a smile and stared at the picture."

"Beautiful car," Charlie commented. "Oh, and beautiful bride too." He said embarrassed about not first complementing her.

"Oh, I know," she said as she touched his arm. "All the men have the same reaction. They first notice the car. That was in one of his dad's vintage cars."

"Well. It's a great picture of you and Vince. Good photography. The wedding survived, obviously. You haven't changed a lot, or you got married when you were very young."

"Oh, thank you Charlie," she acknowledged his attempt to complement her. "This is our memory wall to remind us of the family and friends we left behind when we emigrated."

"And those are his parents?" Charlie said as he pointed at a picture of Vince and his parents. The three of them were standing on a beach with Table Mountain in the background.

"Yes." Alice said with a soft voice that made Charlie look at her. "It's one of the last pictures taken of them together." He noticed a sudden look of sadness in her eyes.

"I'm sorry," Charlie apologized. "I didn't mean to stir any sad memories."

"No. It's OK. That's just me. They were such good people. Always willing to help. The accident was such a shock for us. On Sunday afternoons, they would drive around Cape Point and over the Chapman's Peak mountain pass. In Houtbay they usually stopped to buy ice cream from a street vendor. If it were a nice day, they would take a walk on the beach. It's a very scenic drive, as you may know."

Charlie just stood next to Alice and listened. He thought about his own family he had not seen in many years. She took a deep breath and then continued.

"It was such a tragedy. Apparently he lost control in the mountain pass and went over a cliff. The car tumbled down the mountain and plunged into the ocean. They didn't survive. It was a very sad time for Vince. His Dad meant so much to him." With her finger she carefully wiped a tear from her eye, making sure not to spoil her makeup. "They had worked together for a long time. When his Dad got the promotions they moved to Cape Town. We followed not long after they moved."

"Oh. I'm so sorry to hear. I didn't know."

"Of course you didn't know. You never come visit so we can share stories of South Africa. But that is not why you are here." Alice said with a cheerful voice. She took him by the arm and showed him the counter loaded with all kinds of drinks and mixes.

"Help yourself. The rest of the group is outside." She smiled at Charlie, and returned to the foyer to welcome more guests arriving.

Charlie looked at her. The emotional moment stirred something deep inside of him. He swallowed hard as memories about Hanna formed in his mind. As he had done so many times before, he immediately suppressed it. He turned to the counter with all the drinks and scanned the open bottles. He studied some of the labels, and selected a bottle of cabernet sauvignon from the Napa Valley. He poured a small amount into a crystal glass, juggled it around and smelled the aroma. The taste was smooth, not dry, a hint of spiciness, but not sweet. He liked it and filled his glass before walking towards the open sliding doors leading to the back patio where the party was just starting.

He saw a group of other senior consultants he had worked with at some point. He joined the group and they chitchatted about work and life in general. It was not long before the group was once again called to order and faced one of the executives. Vince Milner, as the host and CEO, addressed the crowd from the stairs leading up to the gazebos next to the pool area. He welcomed them and congratulated all the hard workers for another successful quarter. He gave some accolades and special recognitions to select individuals. Charlie was glad there was nothing for him this time. Vince completed his spiel and handed the platform over to the CFO.

Dan stepped forward to announce the quarterly bonuses - the main reason for the party. The bonus structure was complicated, and for most it seemed Dan was the only one who understood it. The employees were not really interested in the bottom-line of the company, and wanted to know what the percentage was. Dan once again congratulated the group on the successes of the quarter.

"And now for the moment you have all come to this gathering for." He tried to stall and the group cheered him on to make the announcement. "The bonus percentage is.... eight point four percent!" The crowd cheered and Charlie's smile on his face didn't reflect in his eyes. In his head he quickly calculated what his loss over the past two years was. If they had not cheated him on his rate, his bonus would have been much more. He made a mental note of the number. He may need it when he meets with Heinz again.

Dan handed the platform to Heinz who attempted to bolster some excitement with recruitment of new consultants. He had some envelopes in his hand. Before reading the names on the envelopes, he reminded the group again of the incentive PITS offered for referrals that lead to employment. It was not only Charlie who noticed the sub-standard performance by Heinz. He looked in the direction of Vince and Dan and saw them looking at each other with a question mark on their faces. They seemed concerned about Heinz's low energy. With every envelope he handed out, he would normally have some one-liner comment about the person that would excite the crowd. This time, he had a somber look and the commentary was flat. When he was done, Vince stepped forward and took over the motivation session. He used his marketing flamboyance to inspire the crowd. He emphasized the importance of new talent for the long-term growth of the company. He thanked those who had completed their assignment in the US and would be returning back to their home countries. He adjourned the formalities with a loud, "Let's party!"

From a distance Charlie watched as Vince and Dan gathered around Heinz. They seemed to be asking questions, and Heinz in return just shook his head. He didn't seem to have a lot to say to them. For Charlie it was clear that Heinz had not talked to Dan or Vince about the meeting they had earlier in the day. Charlie was puzzled since Heinz's excuse this morning was that he had to discuss the situation with them. It seemed obvious to Charlie that Vince and Dan had no idea what was going on. He turned and walked towards the food table to get dessert.

"Hello, Charlie," Vince suddenly appeared next to Charlie and with a slap on the shoulder stretched out his other hand to greet Charlie. "We didn't get time to talk today. How are you doing? Project still going well?"

"Hello, Vince. Yes, everything is fine." Charlie quickly had to change his line of thought, and pushed his concerns about Heinz aside. "We are in the final stretch before go-live. The system will be in production by the end of the month. Then the critical care phase of four weeks, and we will be done with First Midwest." Charlie responded.

"That's great. Any new assignments planned for you?"

"Not yet. I'm planning a few weeks off. It has been a long stretch and I have not had any vacation in over six months," Charlie replied.

"Well deserved. Where are you going? Visiting your mom?" Charlie was surprised that Vince remembered his mother, and was even more surprised that he didn't mention anything about Heinz. It was even clearer to Charlie that Heinz had not talked to Vince, and he decided to test the waters.

"Nothing is finalized yet, but I thought about visiting her. I talk to her at least once a month. She is still in good health and has a busy schedule for an old lady. Can I ask you something?"

"Yeah. Anytime."

"Is Heinz ok? He seemed off the mark tonight."

"Yes, I noticed, but I have no idea what's going on." Vince looked at Charlie and Charlie saw in his eyes that he knew nothing about his meeting with Heinz. "Maybe just the work load. We have something big in the pipeline. If we can land this one, we will need a lot more resources than what we currently have."

"Is that what you wanted to talk about?" Charlie asked.

"Yes. Walk with me." Vince said and made his way to the fire pit. When they were out of earshot of the others, he stopped and turned to Charlie.

"Charlie, I'm going to need you on our next project. Your skills are going to be a key factor for us."

"Why me? There are many others who can do what I do? I trained many consultants and there are some really good ones." Charlie objected, but in the back of his mind, he remembered the conversation he had with Tessa. He knew where this was going.

"Well, you see..." Vince paused for a moment. Charlie saw he was choosing his words carefully. "This is very confidential, but I know I can trust you. We are going to need somebody who knows REAL-TIME. I know you have some experience with it."

"That was a long time ago. I thought I was done with it."

"Yes, me too. We are looking at a potential merger, and one of the parties involved still uses REAL-TIME. We are on the shortlist of companies to manage the project and provide resources. I have included your name on our list. I just wanted to make sure you are not already committed to another project. Can I count on you?"

"It sounds interesting," Charlie said. "Didn't know you were a REAL-TIME person too."

"Yes." Vince said with touch of nostalgia. "Did some good stuff back in the days with it. But I'm glad that is behind me now. Never want to go back. I will leave it to the experts."

"I assume it will be in the financial sector then?" Charlie asked.

"Yes. We are pitching our combined REAL-TIME experience as a key factor. Between you, Dan and myself, we may have enough to clinch the deal. But keep it quiet please. It's still confidential. Seems money will not be an issue, and when it's announced, there may be some ripple effects in the whole sector. This is big, and we have to be ready for it."

"And my rate? Will it be reviewed?" Charlie asked. He had to bite his tongue not to sound bitter and too aggressive. Vince looked at Charlie puzzled.

"Talk to Heinz or Dan about it. I stay out of individual rate negotiations. I just deal with the clients."

"Oh, I see."

"So. Are you ok with me putting your name on the list?"

Charlie looked at Vince. He wanted to say no, but he knew he couldn't. For the time being, he had to play along.

"Why not? I have not committed to any other project yet. What is the timeline? Will there be some time to take vacation?"

"Oh yes. This will be early next year when it kicks off. Once the announcement is made, we will need to move fast. I'm sure there will be enough time for vacation."

"Sounds good to me."

"Enjoy your vacation," Vince said, and patted Charlie on the shoulder before walking away to start a conversation with the next person.

Charlie greeted a few people, had some casual conversations as he slowly made his way towards Dan. Charlie waited for the right moment, and when he saw Dan ending a conversation with one of the other employees, he stepped closer.

"Hello, Dan. How are you doing?" Charlie said and stretched out his hand to greet him.

"Hi, Charlie. Good to see you. I wanted to talk to you this morning, but ran out of time. I'm glad you could make it to the celebration."

"Seems there are a lot of things going on right now." Charlie tried to sound relaxed, but inside his mind was running at full speed. He took another sip from the glass of the wine in his hand.

"Yes. Heinz mentioned to me that you wanted to take some vacation after the project. He said you did a great job on the First Midwest project, and were a cornerstone for us to get new consultants assigned to the project. Thank you for that." The conversation was not headed in the direction Charlie thought it would go, but he had the answer he was looking for. Heinz had not talked to Dan either.

"Well, that is just what we do, is it not? Always mentoring newbies. Some a pure waste of time, but there are some really good ones also."

"Did you find any good talent we could consider for the long term?"

"There were a couple of good ones. I liked working with Benjamin and he seems to be a quick learner. He has a great attitude. Gracey is very smart, does more than is required, and never misses a deadline. If you keep them around, they will not disappoint you."

"Good to know. I will keep them in mind and see what we can do."

"I'm just sorry we cannot keep some of them for longer periods of time." Charlie said as he thought about the number of junior consultants he had to train while working at First Midwest. "Why do they have to leave so soon? We recently lost a good developer right in the middle of a complex development. It set us back a few days to find a replacement.

"Well, his I-94 expired and he had to go back to sort out his visa. We cannot let them overstay the expiration date." Charlie noticed Dan's uneasiness. Having been through the process himself, he knew something about dealing with immigration.

"Oh, I didn't know. I thought the L1 visa allowed them to stay longer." Charlie knew he had Dan in a tight spot. Dan looked around to see who was within earshot.

"In some cases yes, but with Jake there was an issue with the dates. He had to go back and get it corrected. If he can sort it out, we will take him back again. Can I get you a refill?" Dan asked in an attempt to change the subject. He held his hand out to take Charlie's empty glass.

"I'll walk with you," Charlie said and walked with Dan towards the sliding doors.

"Oh, Charlie. About my conversation with Heinz." Charlie almost stopped in his tracks when Dan went back to the conversation with Heinz. For a brief moment, he thought he had it all wrong. "He asked if we could award you a special bonus this year. He said you went over and above with the training of new consultants. You also took on more responsibility with the First Midwest project."

"Heinz said that?" Charlie asked with disbelief in his voice. He really wanted to add, "Don't lie to me," but managed to keep his mouth shut.

"Yes. I just wanted to let you know, it's approved. I agree one hundred percent with Heinz. We appreciate what you have done over the years for the company. I saw you and Vince talk so you know we have something special planned for you in the future. I will leave it to Heinz to discuss the details with you."

"Wow, that's very generous of you. Thanks, Dan," Charlie responded with unnoticed sarcasm. He knew Heinz was hiding something from his partners. Neither Vince nor Dan knew anything about the meeting he had with Heinz.

Dan excused himself and walked away to fulfill more of his task as one of the executives of the company. Charlie filled his glass, greeted a few more people and made his way slowly to where Heinz was involved in a group discussion. Charlie observed from a short distance and when Heinz made eye contact with him, he left the group and approached Charlie. The usual pleasantries were not exchanged. Charlie kept his hand in his pocket so he didn't have to shake the dead fish again.

"Charlie."

"Heinz," they said with an uncomfortable presence between them.

"I saw you talked to Vince and Dan. Anything I need to know?" Heinz asked with arrogance.

"Maybe I'm the one who should ask that question," Charlie responded.

"Why?"

"It doesn't seem they know anything about our conversation this morning."

"No, they don't."

"Uh, are you lying to me again? You said you needed to discuss it with them."

"I needed time to think."

"So, you are doing things without their knowledge and approval? That would be a first. You can never make a decision without first consulting with Dan." Charlie responded with surprise.

"That's not true." Heinz sounded irritated by the suggestion from Charlie. "I do have the authority to make decisions. We don't always have time to discuss the finer details of what goes on in the business. Some things are best if not shared."

"I wonder how Vince would respond if I confronted him with the contract. Since he was the one who signed it, he should also be responsible for the execution of it. How many others are you ripping off?" Charlie asked, and the sound of his voice increased in intensity enough to make Heinz look around nervously.

"I think we need to discuss this in private. Not here in public." Heinz tried to lower the tone of his voice. "Why don't we meet again tomorrow? Can you stop by my house before you leave? Then we can discuss the situation and finalize the details."

"What details?" Charlie tried to prolong the discussion. He didn't feel like letting Heinz off the hook so easy.

"The demands you made. I'm trying to get you a *special* bonus," he said using his fingers to make air quotes.

"Oh, so that is what you and Dan were discussing this morning."

"Yes. I think you deserve it, and the company owes you one."

"It better be *special*," Charlie said and mimicked Heinz with the same gesture of air quotes. "I will be at your house around 2 PM. My flight leaves at 7 PM, so we will have enough time to talk." Charlie turned around and walked away without waiting for Heinz to respond.

* * *

CHAPTER 6

Sir Archibald

C harlie sat in his rental car a few houses down from Heinz's home. Compared to the neighborhood where the party was held the night before, this was the total opposite. Houses were close together. Driveways had multiple cars parked in front of the single garage. Some also had cars parked in the street. Yards were not taken care of and a few of the lawns had not been mowed in a while.

The dark clouds drifting in from the west made the uneasy feeling Charlie had, feel even heavier. He was not sure what to expect from Heinz or how to approach the meeting. He had lost some of his bravado from their meeting in the office, but was concerned that his anger would flare up as soon as he caught Heinz in a lie again. He planned to arrive early to determine if Heinz had invited anybody else. There were no cars in his driveway and the garage doors were closed. Either his car was parked inside or he was not home. He looked at his watch and saw it was five minutes till two. He started the car, pulled into the driveway and walked to the door. He rang the doorbell and Heinz opened the door almost immediately.

"Hello, Charlie. Please, come in." He stood aside and Charlie walked in. The house was scarcely decorated and it was obvious Heinz lived alone. The house inside was clean, at least as far as he could see. He looked down the

51

hall and saw all the doors were closed.

"Hello, Heinz. Still living alone?"

"Yes," Heinz said and they stood facing each other in the middle of the living room. The awkward silence lasted only a few seconds but felt like an eternity for Charlie. No one wanted to make the first move. Heinz finally broke the silence.

"Please, sit down." He tried a much more friendly approach than what Charlie expected. "Let's have a calm discussion about this."

Charlie sat down in a chair and faced the door. Heinz took a seat on the couch on the other side of the room. Charlie didn't say a word, but only stared at Heinz, waiting for him to be the first one to talk.

"Charlie. What exactly do you want from me? I'm not sure where you got your information, but I can explain." Heinz tried, but it was obvious he was not sure how to do it.

"As I said before, Heinz. How about the truth?" Charlie intended to be calm, but could not keep the aggressive tone completely out of his voice. "Just be honest with me and don't lie to me anymore." Charlie hesitated, and before Heinz could start with his excuse, he asked his first question. "To start with," he said staring at Heinz, "how long this has been going on?"

"What do you mean 'how long this has been going on'? What is 'this'?" and he used his air quotes again.

"How long has PITS been cheating consultants on their rates? I know the rate I'm being paid, and I never questioned it. I trusted you and PITS to be honest and fair to your consultants. It seems I'm the stupid one. PITS made more from the hours I billed than I did. How many other consultant's rates have you cut and skimmed from the top?" Charlie stayed calm and tried not to raise his voice.

"It's different contracts." Heinz seemed to have thought about his response and presented his excuse to Charlie. "The contracts PITS has with its clients are different from the contracts with consultants. There are overhead and administration costs to be covered and we negotiate the best possible rates with clients to ensure we can sustain a good organization. How else are we supposed to find new clients, manage an office, run the payroll and provide the usual admin stuff taken for granted by consultants? It costs a lot of money to run a back office."

"That may be true Heinz, but we also had an understanding from the beginning. When you recruited me, you sat across from me and explained to me how generous the company was towards consultants. Our initial agreement was that PITS would not take more than fifteen percent of my billable rate. Thinking back, I can remember the first contract where you disclosed the rate to me. There may have been a couple more where it was mentioned, but then you never mentioned it again and, because I trusted you, I never bothered to verify the rates."

"We changed our policy a long time ago. Our contracts with consultants don't specify a percentage anymore."

"Changed the policy?" Charlie could not believe the lame excuse Heinz used. "When? I was never informed about it. Maybe I should ask some of the other senior consultants if they were informed. I wonder how many of them know about this change in policy?"

"Don't get upset, Charlie. Please." Heinz tried to calm Charlie down and for a while the insults and argument about the contract and the fairness of it continued. After a while Charlie sat back in his chair and stared at the ceiling. He could not believe all the excuses Heinz brought up. He thought for a moment and then sat back up.

"What you are saying, is that the contract between you and First Midwest, or any other client, cannot dictate to PITS what they should pay the consultants."

"Correct. They have nothing to do with our internal business."

"But the contract with First Midwest has a stipulation about it. How do you get away with it?"

"It may be stipulated, but we don't have to disclose anything to them. As long as the expenses are within the allowed range, there are no questions or queries."

"So." Charlie hesitated for a moment before he continued. "You will not have a problem if I go back to Springfield on Monday and show my contract to the CFO at First Midwest? Maybe I should ask him what the purpose of the clause in the contract is."

"You cannot do that! You signed a non-disclosure agreement." Heinz sounded a bit too cocky for Charlie to stay calm.

"I cannot?" Charlie said and it was clear he was trying hard to stay calm. He took a deep breath before he continued. "Do you think I care? I'm ready to quit and just walk away! I don't need you anymore. Let's see where Vince will find somebody for his next big project!"

"What?" Heinz suddenly sat up straight and had a surprised look on his face. "He talked to you about it?"

"Yes. You didn't know?"

"No! I was supposed to discuss it with you. We wanted to make sure we have you on board."

"Well! Good luck with that." Charlie snarled as he realized he had hit a soft spot. "Seems I'm not the only one caught by surprise. You lied to me! You cheated me! Why would I want to continue working for PITS? Maybe I will get a better offer somewhere else."

"Charlie, wait! You cannot quit now?"

"Why not? Let's call Vince and tell him I'm not available for the next project. Let's hear how he feels about it."

"No! He doesn't know about this!"

"What do you mean he doesn't know?"

The silence in the room lingered for a while and Charlie waited for Heinz to respond. When he started, it was a different Heinz. Defeated, he explained to Charlie what was going on.

"Charlie, I needed the money. Vince and Dan don't know about your contract. Vince negotiated the overall terms with First Midwest, but I did the paper work. I took a chance and put in a very high rate for your services as one of our senior consultants. I contacted the client and I promised to give them a discount on the rates for less experienced consultants. I couldn't believe it when they fell for it."

"And Vince knew about this when he signed the documents." It didn't make sense to Charlie.

"Vince doesn't know. I changed the rates after he signed the document. He is only concerned about the bottom line. He doesn't care about individual rates."

"How did you get away with this? Is Dan also involved?"

"No. He doesn't know. I opened a separate account where clients transfer the money too. I then transfer the amount according to the original rates on file to PITS. Nobody else knows about it. You are the only one."

"How many times have you done this before?"

"Only this one time. I swear, Charlie, it was only this one time."

"How can I believe you? How can I ever trust you again? You lied to me! How do I know you are not lying to me right now? Why did you do this to me?"

"I told you, I needed the money."

"For what?"

"I was being blackmailed." Heinz closed his eyes and dropped his chin on his chest. His secret was out. For a moment Charlie almost felt sorry for the pathetic figure on the other side of the room.

"What? Who blackmailed you?"

"It's a long story." Heinz looked at Charlie with embarrassment written all over his face. Slowly he explained to Charlie. "When I came to the US initially, it was on a visitor's visa. I found somebody who was willing to marry me for money and in return would sponsor my green card application. We got married and I started the process. Two years after my green card was approved, I qualified for citizenship since I was married to a US citizen. We never lived together and were married on paper only. I basically bought my citizenship. I paid her a fixed amount every month until I became a naturalized citizen. The payments were supposed to stop then, but she had other plans. She threatened to expose me to the USCIS. I was too scared to think straight and gave her a final lump sum. I had no choice. I gave her almost all of my life savings on the condition we get divorced immediately. After the divorce she tried to blackmail me again, but I had enough of her. I told her I didn't care anymore and to go ahead. I also told her that we would be in the same boat since I had the proof of how she had blackmailed me and of the payment I made to her. I never heard from her again."

"So, you stole from me to cover your fraud?" Charlie said with bitterness.

"No, that was a long time ago. I had to make a loan to pay her. I needed money to recover and with your contract I saw an opportunity. I was tired of living from paycheck to paycheck."

"Heinz. It is very difficult for me to believe one word of what you are telling me. If you said you had a drinking problem I would have believed you. Or, if you had gambling debt, but this story just doesn't make sense. It sounds like BS to me."

"You have to believe me. It's true. I will pay you back every penny that is due to you."

"How are you going to do that?"

"The contract allows PITS to take twenty percent of any consultant's rate. I will make sure you get every penny due to you. Dan has already approved a special bonus for you."

"I know that. He mentioned it to me. Will it cover everything you stole from me?"

"I will pay any difference out of my own pocket."

"And where will you get the money to pay me? Steal from somebody else?"

"No, I've tried to save as much as I could. I will find the money."

"When?" Charlie asked.

"Give me seven days to make the arrangements."

"How much?"

"I'm not sure. I will have to calculate it."

"I will make it easy for you," Charlie said. He had already done a rough calculation of what PITS owed him. "I worked for almost two years on this last contract. I booked a lot more than the normal forty-hours per week. Roughly two thousand hours a year. I was paid eighty dollars an hour and you charged two hundred. Less the allowed twenty percent gives a rate of one hundred and sixty I should have received. I was paid half of that. The calculation is easy. You owe me exactly what you already paid me. Three hundred and twenty thousand for the last two years."

Heinz didn't blink an eye. He made his own calculations and had a counter offer.

"Charlie, this will raise a lot of questions. I have an offer for you." It was Charlie's turn to be stumped.

"I'm listening."

"If we pay you through the payroll, there will be taxes involved. To avoid any questions and tax issues for PITS, for you, and for me, I'm willing to pay you two hundred thousand in cash."

"What portion will come from the bonus?"

"I may be able to get fifty thousand approved. I asked Dan for more, but he objected. I think I will be able to convince him to approve it."

Charlie stared at the floor for a while thinking about the proposition. An idea flashed through his mind. *"Maybe I can use an offshore account again!"* he thought to himself. After a while he looked at Heinz and said: "Two fifty. A hundred thousand through payroll with the appropriate tax deductions." He hesitated and felt a shiver run down his spine as he continued. "The rest will come from you. In the mean time I will honor my part of the contract with First Midwest and complete the project. At the correct rate of course." He looked at Heinz to make sure he was understood. "

The shock on Heinz's face gave Charlie a feeling he hadn't experienced in many years. As kid he was bullied at school many times. He planned his revenged carefully and when it came to fruition, he had the same feeling of satisfaction.

"That will be very difficult to explain to Dan. He will have to get Vince's approval."

"That is your problem," Charlie said with a smirk. He was ready to be done with the conversation and leave.

"I will need more time." Heinz tried again to stall.

"I want the first payment from PITS as part of the quarterly bonus." Charlie said as he laid out his demands. "If it doesn't happen, I will give the contract to the CFO. You have until the end of the project in Springfield to get your side organized. I will provide you with the account details where the money should be wired. You will have twenty-four hours to complete the transfer." Heinz listened to Charlie's demands without a word. "Just remember - I have the evidence in a safe place. If it doesn't happen as agreed, I will send the details to Vince, Dan and First Midwest. It's up to you." Charlie stood up to leave. Heinz got up and looked at Charlie.

"I'm sorry this happened, Charlie. I never intended to do you any harm."

"We all have to live with the consequences of our decisions. This is one you will have to live with."

"I know." Heinz said and opened the door. When he opened it, a cat meowed and came running to Heinz. He bent over and picked the cat up in his arms.

"Charlie, meet Sir Archibald, or Archie in short. He's a very friendly cat." Heinz said as he stroked the cat's fur. Immediately Charlie felt the blood drain from his head. His eyes bulged out of his head as he stared at the cat. It turned it's head and stared at Charlie with big dark eyes. Charlie opened his mouth to say something, but he couldn't breathe.

"Charlie?" Heinz said as he looked from the cat to Charlie. "Are you OK? It seems like you have seen a ghost! Are you allergic to cats?"

Charlie put his hand against the wall to stabilize himself. His legs felt like jelly.

"What... What did you say?" He whispered with a soft voice.

"Are you ok? Do you need some water?"

"No. The cat. What did you call him?"

"Sir Archibald. What's wrong? Are you sure you are ok?" Heinz sounded concerned.

"The name? Where did you get the name?" The blood returned slowly to Charlie's face but he could not take his eyes off the cat.

"Oh, just a name that I overheard somewhere. He was a stray cat that showed up one day. I started feeding him and he stayed. Just never left. He will disappear sometimes for a day or so, but always comes back. I just had to call him Sir Archibald. Sounded like a cool name to me. Why are you asking?"

"It doesn't matter. I have to go," Charlie said and hurriedly squeezed past Heinz. He walked to his car, got in, backed out of the driveway and drove off. He looked back and saw Heinz standing at the door with Sir Archibald in his arms.

"Who is this guy? Where does he come from? What does he know about Sir Archibald?"

It had been many years since he last heard that name. Suddenly he was scared, very scared. The uneasiness he felt before he entered Heinz's house returned and a cold chill covered his body. Many unanswered questions flashed through Charlie's mind as he drove to the airport.

For the first time in many years, he thought about Hanna again. An intense sadness came over him, and tears started running down his cheeks. He didn't bother to wipe them away and let them flow down his face. He blinked his eyes a few times to focus on the road in front of him. With a loud voice wrought with emotion, he groaned. "Why, why, why!" he yelled as he hit the steering wheel.

CHAPTER 7

The CD

The after effects of the quarterly event took its toll in the following week. The intense emotional experience made Charlie struggle to stay focused as the demands for his attention increased as the project came to a conclusion. The emotional roller coaster after his meeting with Heinz caused more distractions than he expected. He couldn't get the image of the cat out of his mind. He worked longer hours to catch up with overdue tasks. Something was about to give.

On Thursday morning Tessa called Charlie to her office. With a feeling of guilt he entered. He was not sure if he missed another deadline or what the reason for the meeting was, but subconsciously he expected a scolding. He got the opposite.

"How did the meeting with Heinz go?" she asked and caught him by surprise. That was all he could think about the last few days. "Did you knock the daylights out of him like you wanted to?"

"No, to the second question." Charlie responded. "The meeting went OK. He had some lame excuse that a client cannot dictate the terms of a contract with employees. He also mentioned the age-old excuse of overheads. The usual stuff."

"As expected." Tessa said with sarcasm. "What are you going to do? Quit?"

"Not yet. They promised me a special bonus."

"Did you think about my offer?"

Charlie looked at Tessa for a moment before responding. This was one of the reasons he was so distracted. He was not sure if he should mention to Tessa about his discussion with Vince. He trusted Tessa, but he also had a sense of loyalty towards Vince. In the early days after his move, it was Vince who spent time with him to explain the process of immigration. They were only a small group of consultants then. As the company grew, Vince had more responsibilities and Charlie was not interested in managing people. He just wanted to focus on the technical side.

"I did. But I need time to think about it. When will you know if BIGS got the project?"

"It's to early to tell. We will just have to wait."

The conversation turned back to the project and pending deadlines. Charlie assured Tessa his tasks were on schedule.

Charlie arrived home late Thursday evening. The alarm clock woke him at 7 AM, and he felt tired and grumpy. He completed some work related tasks, the required Friday morning status call and then started his chores in and around the house.

At some point during the day he ended up in the attic of his house. He was on a mission to find a timer he could use with his new crockpot. His previous attempt to cook chicken thighs and vegetables was a disaster, and the crockpot was ruined. "*How do you burn food in a crockpot?*" Charlie had thought after the incident. He had set the pot on high with the intent to turn it off after 4 hours. As usual, he got lost in his own world of coding and debugging. He lost track of time and forgot about the food still cooking. He worked late into the night and went to bed in the early morning hours. He woke up the next morning to the smell of burnt chicken. It was not only the food that was a loss, but the crockpot was ruined and he just threw it all in the trash. The odors of burnt chicken stayed in the house for a few days as a reminder. He bought a new crockpot and prepped his food for the weekend. When he switched on the crockpot, he remembered the terrible smell and decided not to make the same mistake again.

He knew he had an electric timer switch stored in his attic with the small fake Christmas tree he bought one Christmas. While searching and rearranging the bins in the attic, he saw the box in the corner. He had seen it many times before and never really paid attention to it or looked at it twice. This time however, he had the urge to pick up the box and take it downstairs with him. The meeting with Sir Archibald awoke things he had managed to suppress for many years. He knew exactly what items were in the box marked *"computer stuff"*. As he picked up the box a string of memories flashed through his mind. He found the timer he was looking for, and carried the box with him down the stairs. He placed the box on the sideboard in the hallway and went to the kitchen to set the timer. He set it for four hours so he would have a warm dinner, and maybe some leftovers for the weekend. When it came to food, Charlie preferred food with basic ingredients. He loved crockpot chicken and enjoyed it on top of a bed of cheese-grits. Over the weekend he didn't want to leave the house and subject himself to the temptations of fast food. He had enough of that during the week while traveling.

The box remained on the sideboard for the weekend. On Sunday evening while packing his bag to leave for Springfield, he walked past it and finally opened it. Inside were old floppy discs CDs he brought with him when he left his home in South Africa. He scanned through the pile and smiled when he saw some of the junk he had kept. He remembered what was saved on each one - some old programs he developed for clients, dumps of old e-mails, DOS and Windows installation disks, and so many other things now totally obsolete. The CDs were stored in a plastic container with a round peg in the middle. The peg fit inside the hole of a CD and held about forty per container. He liked the storage format since the discs were protected from dust and accidental damage. There were four containers in the box, and one was marked with the word, "WORMS". He opened it and started to unload the discs from the top of the stack. This was his treasure - his memories captured on CD discs. They contained information more precious to him than any amount of money. He couldn't do much with them, but it was still his treasure. It was his handwriting on the labels, his creation from many years ago. When he'd packed his bags for the move to the US, he had to carefully decide which CDs would make it into the box and become part of his personal archive. The rest he destroyed by breaking it into small pieces. As he scanned the content, he read the labels on some discs. *"E-mails and docs before Y2K."* *"Backup-clipper-db4 before Y2K."* One by one he read the labels to himself. He remembered a life he had chosen to forget. A life he had to leave behind. One that it would be better if he could just forget about. It was the second to last CD he looked at that made him stop and read it again and again. The labeled read, *"Keep forever - 1977 mods!!"* That was a very long time ago.

Many things had happened since he transferred the files from his old backup tapes to floppy discs and eventually to CDs. When compact discs became the newest tech "thing", he went through the laborious task of restoring his backups from floppy drives. He burned the files he wanted to keep onto CDs.

After the accident, he yearned for something more meaningful than work. He was alone and missed Hanna. He struggled to identify what he was looking for, but he kept on searching with a hope to one day find it. His decision to emigrate was an impulsive one. He had an argument with his boss and decided it was time for a change. Maybe he would find happiness in a place far away from the memories. That was when he saw the ad in the paper and responded.

As he browsed through the CDs he took one out of the pile and put it aside. He stared at it for a long time, not sure if he wanted to go down this path again. It was marked as *"Project Delta"*. He closed the box and left it on the counter with the intent to return it to the attic after he had copied the CD to the next new tech thing - a flash drive.

"So, Sir Archibald. You are back again. I wonder if the account is still active?" he mumbled to himself and slipped the CD into his laptop bag. He carried the leather messenger bag with him wherever he went. In the bag was his laptop, chargers, flash drives, an emergency fund of cash, documents he had to review and other random stuff he might need while waiting in the airport for a connection.

Charlie's flight back to Springfield on Sunday evening got delayed in Atlanta - again. He settled in at a desk in the frequent flyers lounge. With all the traveling he had done over the years, he had complimentary access. He used the comfortable environment to get some work done and prep for the week ahead. He made use of the free snacks and drinks from time to time, but never indulged in more than one glass of wine.

As a boy, Charlie witnessed how alcohol would affect his dad after the third or fourth beer. He saw the hurt in his mom's eyes and, although his dad never got violent, he became overly happy and loud. Charlie saw how embarrassed his Mom was when it happened. One night on their way back home, they had a close call with a tree. His Dad fell asleep behind the wheel of the VW beetle they were riding in. His brother Stephen had fallen asleep next to him on the back seat, but Charlie couldn't sleep and observed the entire scene unfold in front of him. He could see his mom's face. She tried to keep his Dad awake and focused, but he would not listen to her. The argument following the investigation of the damage to the car and his mom insisting on driving the rest of the way home, had such an impact on Charlie, that he vowed to never get into that state of mind. Through his whole life, Charlie had never gotten drunk from alcohol. As a student he became the de facto designated driver and had to put many of his friends to bed, a task he performed very reluctantly.

Charlie settled down in his regular spot and pulled his laptop from his travel bag with the intent to complete the document due by the end of the week. *"What else do you do when the flight is delayed?"* was his normal excuse. As his computer booted up, Charlie reached for the folder with the documentation he needed to review. When he opened the folder, the CD he had placed in his bag earlier slipped out. He picked it up and read the label again.

"Why not now?" he thought to himself. *"I'm not on the clock and it is my time. Let's see what is in here."*

He placed the CD in the drive of his laptop, opened Explorer, and browsed through the list of files. The folders in the root directory indicated the content. Documents, e-mails, programs and then there was one zip file named, *"shift_for_delta_1977.zip"*.

When he saw the file name, that deeply unsettled feeling returned and once again he felt shivers move down his spine. He looked around, but nobody was near him or staring at him. The anxiety stayed with him for a while and he didn't know what to make of it. From time to time he would get that same feeling when he realized something important was about to happen, or when the outcome of something he was about to do could be either very good or bad, very bad.

He hesitated for a moment before he copied the file to his flash drive. He clicked on the filename to unzip it and a popup window for a password appeared. *"Of course!"* Charlie thought to himself. He stared at the screen, and his brain went into overdrive as he tried to remember the correct password. He knew that it would not be simple since he always used passwords that weren't easy to guess. His passwords were normally a pattern of three or four different, but related items. The date of an event, some characters to describe the event and a few characters from the tag of the car he drove at that time. The three factors made it easy for Charlie to figure out the password if the event was more current, but he also had the habit of throwing in a kink by substituting letters with numbers and vice versa. An "E" became "3", an "O" became "0" and a "L" became "1".

"Why do I always have to make it so complicated?" he thought. *"Could I not just have used a simple password? Now I have to figure out all the old stuff again!"* He was annoyed with himself as he worked his way through the puzzle to remember when he made the backup and the car he was driving at the time.

The date of the file was the date it was zipped and not the date associated with the password. It became a guessing game as he started working backwards on old passwords he remembered. Eventually he had to give it up when his flight was called. He scrambled to make it to the gate and board.

It took Charlie a few days before he finally got the password file correct. While he worked through all the versions he'd used in his life, the content of the CD became more real. Each password attempt stirred up a memory about an event or a time in his past that he had tried to forget. He knew exactly what was in the zipped file. It contained the information he needed, but he also knew there were files that would lead him to things he wanted to forget. The world he tried to run away from, the time when he was young and stupid. A time of pain and hurt he didn't want to remember. But there was also that one unsolved mystery that lingered, the one thing that he had not dealt with and never wanted to deal with again. It was the time when he first encountered a mysterious Sir Archibald.

During his meeting with Heinz, Charlie thought about the bank account he had used before. He was not sure if it still existed, but if it did, he could use it again. He just needed the account number and login details to confirm and the information was in the file he was trying to access.

Eventually Charlie reverted to his archives of passwords he maintained in spreadsheets. The most current version he kept on a flash drive on his key-chain. He had to go back a few versions before he found one old enough that contained the passwords of forgotten sites, places he work at before, computers he had and systems he had worked on.

"This is mind boggling," Charlie thought as he scanned all the hundreds of references and places where he had to use a password. *"The brain must have one massive CPU just to be able to remember all the passwords and pin numbers we have to use every day."*

Lucky for Charlie he kept the master password for the spreadsheet the same. The master password was the first secret code he'd used before passwords were even required. He created the secret code when one of his clients, Sam Griffin, didn't pay him as promised and he used the code to get Sam to pay his dues.

* * *

CHAPTER 8

First Ransom - 1982

C harlie was in his late twenties, single and depressed. A friend of his brother approached him with a request for a simple accounting program he could use for his business. He ran a gas station with a small convenience store and bakery in the back. They used a manual cash register to record the daily sales, but he needed a program that would allow him to manage the system from the back office. He needed the front unit to operate independently of the back office, but it should be able to reconcile the daily sales in the back office. At the time, there were not many point-of-sales programs available for small businesses. Computers still used floppy drives and hard drives were small and expensive. This was just a side job and a favor for his brother.

At the time Charlie worked as a programmer for a bank and used mostly mainframe systems. In his spare time, he played around with PCs and studied new programming languages. He used the opportunity to learn Clipper as a database system. He wanted to keep a door open to maybe in the future get more involved in the small business sector.

The program for Samuel Griffin, would net him around three thousand Rand in South African currency, the equivalent of about $2,700 based on the exchange rate in 1982, which would be just enough for the upgraded

IBM compatible PC he had in mind. Sam became a friend, and promised to pay him in cash when the system was fully functional. Charlie delivered the system as promised. Sam, the sneaky businessman he was, only paid Charlie a third of the money he owed him. His excuse was that he first wanted to make sure the program worked as he requested and that there were no bugs in it.

The system worked fine. Of course it did.

When Charlie asked for the final payment, Sam came with a counter offer to Charlie. He wanted one more "small" change to the system. The change eventually took Charlie more than forty hours to complete. For Charlie it meant long hours after his normal workday and over weekends.

The change Sam requested was the real reason he initially wanted the program developed according to his own business specifications. The cash, check and credit card transactions were kept separate from transactions for customers with an account that was settled monthly. The kink in the process was to allow a user, being Sam or his wife Linda, to backdoor into the system and modify the cash transactions. Sam pocketed the cash and transferred the amount to a fake customer account. The fake customer would never pay his bills, and Sam would write off the amount as uncollected debt. It reduced his monthly tax liability and the annual income tax payable. He kept a separate ledger in a small black book in his bottom drawer. The cash takings were all pure profit. On paper the business seemed to barely break even every month, but the black book had the correct numbers and showed the actual profitability of the business.

The only people who knew about the backdoor were Charlie, Sam and Linda. *"That will not be a secret"*, Charlie thought when he explained to Linda how to use it. She talked way too much to keep it a secret.

Charlie spent long nights and a few weekends with Sam and Linda to get the program completed and operational. It was during one of his late night sessions that he thought about the secret code to imbed in the program. Everyday when the system booted up, the code checked the system date against a date hidden in a file somewhere on the hard drive. If the date on the computer were six months past the hidden date, the program would activate the secret code. It was a simple routine. The program would display a message on the screen, and would not continue until a special key combination was pressed. Charlie wanted to hold the system hostage until Sam paid him.

As Charlie expected, six months passed without Sam paying him. Early on a Saturday morning, he got a call from a very upset and angry Mrs. Linda Griffin.

"Charlie!" she yelled on the other end. "The computer is going to blow up!"

"What?" Charlie replied not immediately knowing what was going on and still asleep at 5 AM on a Saturday morning.

"It says right here… 'Press any key and this computer will blow up'. What should I do, I don't want to lose everything I have on here?"

Charlie burst out laughing when he realized what was going on.

"Did you pay all your bills last month?" Charlie asked.

"Of course I did. You know me. I always pay my bills."

"Did Sam pay all his bills?" Charlie replied.

"I pay the bills. He will forget half of it, so I pay all our bills."

"Well, go ask him if he paid for the program you are using."

There was dead silence on the other side.

"You still there?" Charlie asked after a while.

"Charlie! Explain!" Linda demanded. She sounded upset and Charlie wished he could be there to experience the conversation she would have with Sam.

"Linda. You know how long and hard I worked to get the system up and running. Sam has promised many times to pay me, and I got paid once. He only paid one third of what we agreed on for the first version of the program.

He still owes me the balance for the first version, and the full amount for the changes I made six months ago. I built a check into the system to hold it hostage until the ransom money is paid. I made sure you cannot use the program if he didn't pay for it."

"Charlie. I didn't know." Linda said and started to apologize. She explained all the bad things she was going to do to Sam. In his mind Charlie could see her face and how embarrassed she was. He could also see how mad she was at Sam for not paying Charlie.

"Doris!" She suddenly yelled in Charlie's ear. "Go call Mr. Griffin. Tell him I want to see him right now. You don't come back here if you don't bring him with you. You understand?" she instructed one of the workers.

The gas station was in a busy part of town and on Saturdays it was all hands on deck. Charlie had spent many weekend mornings with them while installing the system. He trained Linda, and she trained the other users with Charlie on standby.

Charlie smiled when he heard Linda go off on Sam. Sam had all the excuses in the world, but could not escape the fact that he didn't pay Charlie.

"Charlie," Linda said in the phone. "Come and get your damn money and fix this thing."

"Linda, listen to me. I know I can trust you. If you promise me you will make sure I get paid, I will tell you how to bypass the screen. It will only work until I install the new version of the program. I will stop by a bit later after I've had my coffee and then I will fix it for you."

"We have lots of coffee here. You know that. You come here right now! How do I bypass this message? Are you sure my computer will not blow up? It says right here if I press any key it is going to blow up."

"Trust me. It will not. Hit Alt and F4 at the same time." He waited a few seconds and then asked:

"What happened?"

"It's asking for a secret code."

"Ok, enter 'Sam-owes-me-6k' and hit enter."

"What do you mean? He owes you six thousand?" She asked in disbelief and Charlie enjoyed every moment of it. He could only imagine the loaded atmosphere between her and Sam. They loved each other dearly, but she had a fast tongue and a short fuse – a 'get things done now' type of person. Sam was the more relaxed and easygoing type. For him there was always another time to do anything and everything. As it goes in many relationships and law of the magnets, opposites attract. As soon as she hung up, Sam would get an earful from her.

"Yup." Charlie said.

"I will have it when you get here," she said and hung up the phone.

"This is going to be a good day," he said to himself as he got out of bed, smiling with satisfaction after feeling vindicated.

* * *

CHAPTER 9

The Discovery

I t was travel day again. The wakeup call woke Charlie the usual time on Thursday morning, but today something was different. He had another one of his dreams, but could not remember what it was about. It was not the dream that made it different, something else had happened. It took a few moments to settle into his mind. When he saw the hotel writing pad on the table, the discovery of the night before hit him between the eyes. In an instant the confusion, disorientation and vagueness from only a few hours' sleep were gone.

"No, it cannot be real!" He said and leaped from his bed. He jumped over the second queen size bed and grabbed the pad from the table. He stared at the number he had circled multiple times. He flipped through the pages and pages of numbers. He went back to the first page and stared in disbelief at the circled number.

"No, no, no!" he yelled with his inside voice and fell back into the chair. He stared at the pad he held with both hands and hit it against his head.

"*How could it have happened? It was not supposed to be working anymore! Project Delta never worked!*" he thought out loud as the eight-digit number was engraved in his memory. He could not get his brain to believe that what he had discovered the night before was true.

He read the number out loud, "Thirteen million, four hundred sixty six thousand, nine hundred and seventeen Euros!" *"Holy crap! I'm in big trouble. How did this happen? How did it get so out of control?"* Memories from the previous night returned. His anxiety increased and turned into a full-blown panic attack. His heart rate rose to a point where he got so dizzy he almost fainted. Only then did he realize he wasn't breathing normally. He exhaled and took a few deep breaths to calm down.

He picked up the writing pad and studied the numbers on the paper again. "I still cannot believe it!" he said.

At the top of the page was the number for his account at the Bank of Zurich. He had opened the account more than twenty years ago. The rest of the numbers and scribbles were his attempts to figure out the password for the account. He knew he had a limited number of tries to get access. He had not accessed the account for many years and didn't want to waste an attempt with his regular passwords that he knew would not work. He knew the password for the bank account would have been based on the car he drove at the time he opened the account. He remembered the make and model, but the tag number was a bit more of a challenge to recall.

Frustrated, he had to search through his archives to find the correct account number, username and password. In an older version of the spreadsheet containing all his passwords, he found the login details. With his last attempt, he decided to use the "forgot password" option and immediately regretted it. He realized the account was linked to an e-mail account he seldom used. He continued his search now focused on finding the password to his e-mail account so he could retrieve the "forgotten password" e-mail. At least he had used it more recently than twenty years ago.

Eventually he managed to access the bank account. His relief quickly turned into fear and anxiety as he wrote down the account balance. Each time he circled the number, his panic level increased. Faster and faster he circled the amount. An abundance of consequences flashed through his mind. He closed the browser window and shut down his computer. With his arms lifted above his head, he paced the room for a while, taking deep breaths as he tried to regain control of his rushing heart beat.

For many years he had managed to control his anxiety, but this was just too much for the calm and controlled Charlie O'Neal. When project deadlines approached, he was the steady and relaxed one while others seemed to panic. When plans went awry during the final stages of a project, everybody turned to Charlie for help and guidance. He calmed everybody down, not by saying much, but just by getting things done. Project managers loved Charlie.

Exhausted from the excitement and panic, he fell on his bed praying for rest to come. Eventually he fell asleep, but it was a restless night with dreams he could not remember all the details of. Suddenly the money Heinz owned him seemed like a drop in the bucket compared to what he had in his account at the Bank of Zurich.

During the day, the project demand his attention and kept Charlie occupied. He had to rush to get to the airport on time. His flight home was delayed as usual in Atlanta, and Charlie arrived in Nashville close to midnight on Thursday evening. During the flight, Charlie replayed the events of the last few weeks in his mind. It all started with the offer from Tessa that stirred the pot. Then it was his discussion with Heinz that fueled the fire inside of him. On top of that, his casual conversation with Vince about the next project that indicated it may be the same one Tessa mentioned. Finally the moment he met Sir Archibald and was thrown back into a time he would rather forget.

He thought about the discovery of the money the night before, and wondered if he had accidently logged into a wrong account? It was the only explanation he could come up with, but in the back of his mind he knew that the account number was correct. It was his name on the account and

When Shift Doesn't Happen

his old address. He decided to analyze the transactions the next day to determine where and when the money went into the account. *"Where did all the money come from?"* was his last thought as the plane touched down and taxied to the gate.

Charlie drove from the airport to his home as if he was on autopilot. It was late and he was tired. There was not a lot of traffic on the road. At home he dropped his bag with dirty clothes in the laundry room, and went straight to bed. He was physically exhausted and emotionally drained, but still sleep didn't come easily.

The house was quiet when Charlie woke up late the next morning. He lived alone in the three-bedroom house he bought from a co-worker that had to return to South Africa. They bought the house in Nashville after Michael DeWet managed to secure a two-year contract with a client. Michael and his wife Karen, planned to settle down there, but it didn't work out for them. Michael and Charlie were some of the early employees at PITS, and when the demand for Michael's skills as COBOL programmer declined, he and Karen decided to return home. It was a good deal for Charlie and he was able to get Michael out of a pickle.

Charlie and Michael had stayed in touch with a couple of calls over the years. Every call ended with an invitation from Michael for Charlie to stay with them whenever he decided to visit his family in South Africa again. They had settled in a beach house north of Cape Town and Charlie had them on his list of people to visit during his planned vacation. Charlie didn't know all the details, but he knew PITS had paid for Michael and Karen to have first class tickets for their return to South Africa. When he asked Michael how he had managed to get them to agree to the deal, the only response he got was a cryptic indicator that there was a lot more to the story than he was willing to share. He still remembered his last discussion with Michael.

"I used some leverage with Dan," Michael said. "I know about something he did in his past, but got only a portion of what those cheating bastards

77

owe me." On his face Charlie saw the bitterness and resentment of a deep wound. He decided not to pursue the subject. His wife Karen had gone through a deep depression and was in seventh heaven about returning to her roots and to her family. Charlie made a mental note to give Michael a call again.

Charlie was not very much interested in his normal weekend routine. The first thing on his mind when he woke up was the bank account. He got his coffee ready while his computer went through startup. He logged in and accessed the account using the new password. He reviewed the details to make sure it was really his account and saw the address listed. It was the same one he had used at the time he opened the account. He stared at it for a few minutes as the memories flooded his mind. His eyes filled with tears.

"It is more than twenty years ago," he thought. He remembered the trip when he and Keith opened their individual accounts in Zurich, Switzerland. He looked at the balance and got an uneasy feeling. From experience he knew that he could brush the feeling aside forever. He continued to study the transaction history.

"How did it get there?" he asked himself every time he saw the balance. *"What should I do with it? Is this really my money? I sure can use it."* One question after another popped in his mind and he had no answers for any of them. He had nobody to discuss his problem with. He didn't know what to do next. He thought the time in his life that was linked to the account was over forever, but on the screen he saw the proof that it was very much still alive.

"Did it come back to haunt me? Why now?"

When Charlie left South Africa many years ago, he destroyed all evidence of the account. Over time he tried to erase it from his memory, but it took a long time. He left his home country, his family, the life he had and he just wanted to get away from it all. From time to time when he saw a stranger in the airport or at a store, they would remind him of people he knew. Sometimes he had the urge to go and ask the person if he or she was related to people he remembered, but he never had the guts to do it. He just walked on struggling with his own memories. He forced himself to forget and as time passed, he managed to push those memories to the distant background. It worked until he met Sir Archibald.

He continued to analyze the transactions from the account. The initial deposit was a 1000 Euros. Six months later small deposits were made daily, some only for pennies, and then the amount deposited daily jumped to ten times the previous amount deposited.

"That was when Bravo paid out. Shift happened and it paid off," he thought to himself.

There was a withdrawal that almost cleared the account and then no further transactions for a few months. He looked at the date of the withdrawal and remembered the time and the reason for the withdrawal. He needed the cash to pay for a ring. The deposits then started again with small amounts and slowly increased for almost a year. A year after the withdrawal, a large deposit of a few thousand Euros was made, and then no further transactions for a few months. The account earned interest and for months only the interest was added to the balance.

"That must be when we ran the first test for Project Delta."

A few months later the deposits started again when they launched Project Delta. He smiled when he thought about the time when he and Keith thought they had struck gold! The smile disappeared again. Or, did they not?

Six months later the deposits stopped and Charlie's life changed forever. He stared at the screen and saw the date of the deposit. It was the day before the accident. Chills ran down his spine and memories flashed through his brain as he continued to analyze the details. Every line brought back more memories.

Charlie paged down and he could almost not believe his eyes. The deposits had started again and, when he looked at the date, he noticed it was shortly after he left his home country. The activity on the account had increased dramatically.

"But I wasn't even there. Who did this?"

At first glance the deposit amounts seemed to be random. Some amounts were only pennies, and then it would jump to thousands of Euros. It took him a while before he saw the pattern and realized what had happened. The random pennies were not random at all. Somebody played with the decimal and shifted it around. Exactly what he and Keith did.

The number of zeros added changed. Sometimes it increased ten times, and then the next day a hundred times. Who ever did this was experimenting with the decimals. A few times the amount was increased a thousand times.

"That was right after I left. What happened? Did somebody activate the code by accident or on purpose? They shifted the decimal place exactly like we did. They played around with it!"

The deposits continued for almost eight years and then stopped. He looked at the date and realized it stopped a week before Y2K. After that no further deposits were made. The interest rate had increased to eight percent when the account reached a million Euros. That was one of the reasons they decided to use the Bank of Zurich. The interest rates were good. He continued the analysis and did some calculations of the interest added to the account. Although the interest rate fluctuated over the years, each month interest was added. There were no withdrawals from the account and the balance steadily increased.

"What!" Charlie said out loud when he saw the amount added monthly in the past year.

"Twenty five thousand a month interest alone. That's crazy. I can retire with that income."

His initial excitement about the money slowly disappeared and turned the opposite way. The more he thought about the money, the higher his anxiety became. Fear started growing inside of him as he realized the magnitude of what had happened and the implications it could have if somebody found out about it. Thousands of questions ran through his mind.

"Whose money is this?"

"Did I steal it?"

"Who knows about it?"

"What should I do with it?"

"It's not mine. Or, is it?"

"How can I get some of it?"

He thought about the code they had put in place. He and Keith only took half of the money and split it between them. When he thought back about the time and what happened, something clicked in his mind.

"Sir Archibald! He must have done it." In that moment he thought about what they had done many years ago and an image flashed through his mind. He saw Heinz with his cat in his arms. Charlie struggled to control himself when he suddenly realized that Sir Archibald might be closer than he thought. It felt like it was yesterday when it had all happened.

"It cannot be a coincidence. Does he know who I am?"

Charlie got up and paced the floor. The walls came in closer and closer, and the room became smaller with every step he took. His breathing was shallow and short and it felt overwhelmingly claustrophobic. He opened a window but the hot air from outside didn't bring any relief. His mind was spinning in all directions, and he didn't know what to do.

After a while Charlie dropped back into the chair and stared at the screen. The amount was already burned into his memory - 13,466,917 Euros. Exhausted, he took a few deep breaths to calm down and control his anxiety. He counted backwards from twenty, and when he got to one, his nerves were calmed to a point where he could think rationally again. He got up, closed his computer and walked down the stairs to the garage. On the way he grabbed a bottle of water, loaded his bicycle onto the bike-rack and drove to the park. He started riding on the paved greenway bike route. Riding was like therapy for him. He used the exercise to stay in shape and get relief from work related stress, but mostly to forget. But today, every turn of the wheel brought back a memory.

* * *

SECTION II

Project Alpha

CHAPTER 10

The Math Teacher

igh school wasn't easy for Charlie. When his older brother went to first grade, he begged and whined nonstop for days to also go to school. To keep him quiet, his mother promised that he could go to school the following year. Charlie remembered her promise. In the afternoons when Stephen, two years older than Charlie, had to do homework, they did it together. When the school started the next year, he reminded his mother about her promise and she had him tested for school readiness. He was only five years and six months old when he set his foot in first grade. He was not only the youngest in his class throughout the rest of his school career, but also the smallest. What he lacked in age and size, he made up for in smartness.

Charlie grew up in the northwest part of South Africa. His father was in the navy when Charlie was born, and when his dad retired from the military, the family of four moved frequently. Finances were tight, and his Dad struggled to find a job and keep it. The frequent moves put Charlie in a new school at least once a year while in elementary school. He became the target of bullies at every school. Academically he was the smart kid in the class, and the teachers liked him. He learned the hard way that his popularity with the teachers made the target on his back so much bigger.

Charlie loved math and it was easy for him. Spelling was a different story, but Charlie loved to read and his comprehension was phenomenal for his age. Being the new kid in the class so many times, Charlie struggled to make friends and instead books became his friends. He was not the fastest, but had a great memory and could very easily recall what he had read. His teachers and parents didn't recognize that Charlie had a photographic memory and he could visualize the words and pages he had read. It was easy to recall facts and, unlike the majority of students, he loved taking tests.

The school system split the required twelve years of school attendance into two phases: Elementary school till 7th grade and high school from 8th grade through 12th grade. When Charlie entered high school, it was already his eighth school. His parents rented a farmhouse from a relative and they lived so far out of town that there was no school bus route. Charlie, like so many other kids his age from the area, was put into boarding school. There was only one kid in the whole school smaller than Charlie on his first day of high school. Charlie however, was the youngest in his class for the rest of his high school career. Boarding school would provide the opportunity for Charlie to complete high school in the same place. His parents moved a few more times, but Charlie and Stephen begged their parents to let them stay in the same school.

Charlie remained popular amongst the teachers and eventually his classmates accepted him as one of them. He was still the smartest kid in his class, enjoyed sports, and was very competitive for his age and size. The other kids stole his books from his room to copy his homework. Initially it bothered Charlie when his friends did this. He could not understand why they would cheat. At least he didn't have to actually do their homework for them anymore. In his freshman year of high school, the bullies threatened to hurt him if he did not do their homework. Being in a boarding school, supervision by an adult was missing most of the time. Bullies ruled and the seniors made the rules. He learned very quickly to just do as he was told and avoid being knocked around or ridiculed. Charlie secretly planned his revenge. It took some time to find the right opportunity, but he was patient. He waited for just the right moment to put his petty plan into action. He made some obvious mistakes in the finer details of the math problems, but still made sure the answers were correct. He transposed numbers in complex equations, swapped lines of the solutions and, especially in geometry, he would change some of the symbols. He overcame his fear of being caught and it became a secret game for him. Sometimes the math teacher discovered the mistakes, and whoever it was got a severe scolding. Sometimes, and this was the part Charlie secretly enjoyed, it led to the bully having to bend over and take the traditional two strikes from the teacher with his cane. Charlie still suffered the consequences of the mistake at the hands of the bullies, but somehow he felt vindicated. His answer was always, "Sorry man, I'm just human. Next time you can just do it yourself."

Charlie's first severe panic attack was due to his own wrongdoing though, and not one of the bullies. Every Friday was pop quiz day in math. Charlie never failed a test. The test covered new work from the past week. You either had it right or you had it wrong. There was no middle ground. No gray area. It was black or white. Girls had to write the correct solution ten times as punishment. The boys had it easy. Two strikes with the cane in the back of the classroom. Those who failed would line up and Mr. Burns stood in the ready position. The first student would step up to the spot, bend over and touch his toes. Mr. Burns would place two quick strikes on the buttocks. If you dared jump up between strikes, you would just have to go down again and take an extra one. The boys were used to the strikes and made fun of the one in the ready position. The girls were not supposed to be spectators, but they watched over their shoulders and giggled at the reactions from the boys.

Mr. Burns and Charlie had their own inner battle going on. Charlie didn't want to endure the punishment. Not because of the fear of it, but he hated making a mistake. Mr. Burns on the other hand, wanted to get Charlie to bend over for the two strikes at least once. Over the years, from eighth-grade to his senior year, Charlie sat in Mr. Burn's math class. Mr. Burns never had the opportunity to have Charlie bend over and take the two strikes. At the beginning of Charlie's senior year, Mr. Burns in his opening monolog, called Charlie out.

"Charlie, you have been the best student last year. No strikes. Maybe this is the year you will get them." Charlie just smiled at him and responded sarcastically in front of the whole class.

"And if I don't make a mistake? Will you take the strikes?" The class burst out in laughter, but Mr. Burns was not impressed with Charlie's cocky response. He ignored Charlie for a few weeks and everybody knew the battle was on.

Then it happened.

It was a Friday and the geometry quiz was handed out. Charlie didn't pay attention to what he was doing. It was an easy quiz. His thoughts were around the early release and the upcoming tennis match. The school's tennis league played their matches on Friday afternoons and they frequently had to travel to different cities for them. In his eagerness to leave early, Charlie made a mistake. He forgot to put the correct symbol in one of the statements to indicate the measurement of the triangle was in degrees. Something he frequently did when doing homework for the bullies. Mr. Burns used it as excuse to fail him. There was no gray area.

The punishment didn't fit the crime. Mr. Burns enjoyed the lineup and dished out the strikes with enthusiasm. He made Charlie wait till the end.

"Charlie!" He said. "So, I got you. Who is giving and who is receiving today? I told you this was the year."

Charlie was steaming with rage about the unfairness, but didn't say a word. He stepped up to the spot, and assumed the position. The strikes were hard and fast. Slowly Charlie stood up and walked to his desk. The class was very quiet. There were no giggles or comments. Everybody thought it was unfair and that Charlie didn't deserve it. When the bell rang at the end of the period, Charlie was first out of the room. He didn't bother to greet Mr. Burns. It was Friday and he was on his way to play tennis.

That was the only time Mr. Burns had the *pleasure* of giving Charlie two strikes. It upset and confused Charlie. Mr. Burns was his favorite teacher, his rugby coach and one of the track and field coaches. Occasionally he invited students to have lunch on his farm on Saturday mornings when there were no organized school activities. Many residents in the dorm had to stay in the dorm over weekends. Mr. Burns and his wife knew the hardship some of the students were living under at home and that life in the boarding school was far more luxurious than the conditions at home. Food was the most important reason for the visits. Mr. Burns raised cattle on his farm, and meat was in abundance during the occasion. In return for the food, the boys would help Mr. Burns with the cattle. Mrs. Burns used the opportunity to give the girls extra cooking lessons as they prepared the lunch. Charlie went on many of these trips to Mr. Burn's farm. He was a good man and by far Charlie's favorite teacher. He could not come to grips with the unfair treatment he had received. It was a common mistake he always overlooked. This was the first time he used it to fail Charlie in a test.

For weeks Charlie refused to answer any questions in math class. He made sure his work was impeccable and there were no more errors. Never would Mr. Burns find another reason to fail him again, or have the *pleasure* to have him bend over for two strikes. The atmosphere in the classroom remained tense. All the students waited for the confrontation to happen.

One day Mr. Burns asked Charlie a direct question. Again Charlie ignored him. He asked Charlie to stay behind when he dismissed the other students so they could discuss whatever was bothering Charlie. When the bell rang, the class emptied in a flash and the hallways became filled with speculations of the outcome.

Charlie waited in silence as Mr. Burns patiently walked to the door and closed it. He returned to his desk and picked up a piece of paper. Charlie made his way to the front of the class. With his book bag in his hand, he stood in front of Mr. Burns' desk.

Mr. Burns was the first to speak and he completely surprised Charlie.

"Charlie, I'm sorry about the strikes," he said in the same tone he used when students visited his farm. This was not the voice of the match teacher or the coach. "You are one of the best students I have ever had. Don't think about the strikes as punishment, but remember it as a lesson about life. Life is not always fair." The same words Charlie heard so many times from his dad.

"But it was not fair," Charlie protested with uncertainty in his voice.

"I know. But remember, the simplest mistake can sometimes cause a disaster. It can even lead to death. Remember that. Yes, it was only a stupid symbol you forgot, but it was the only way I could teach you something more about life."

Charlie just stood in front of Mr. Burns staring at his feet. He didn't say a word. Mr. Burns handed him the piece of paper he had in his hand.

"Look at this example. I can prove to you that 1 = 2. You have one minute to study it and tell me where the mistake is." Charlie looked at Mr. Burns for a moment and then took the piece of paper from him. He glanced over it and got confused. He started from the top again and looked carefully at the equation Mr. Burns had written down.

$a=b$	*Assume as a known fact.*
$a^2=ab$	*Multiply both sides by a.*
$a^2-b^2=ab-b^2$	*Subtract the same from both sides.*
$(a+b)(a-b)=b(a-b)$	*Factor both sides.*
$(a+b)=b$	*Divide both sides by (a-b).*
$a+a=a$	*Substitute a with b (known fact).*

$2a=a$	*Add together.*
$2 = 1$	*Divide both sides by a.*

Charlie didn't immediately notice the error and was totally amazed by what he saw. His anger at Mr. Burns overshadowed his attention to detail. The more he tried to find the error, the more confused he became. He started to panic. Slowly his heartbeat increased. It beat faster and faster. It started to feel like he couldn't breathe, and the panic inside of him grew stronger by the second.

"This is wrong," he said with certainty. A smiled appeared on Mr. Burns' face as he watched and listened. "It is impossible! This is so wrong. How can one equal two? What is wrong...?"

Deep inside Charlie just knew there was a mistake somewhere. The harder he tried to find the obvious mistake, the more confused he became. The anxiety continued to rise.

Mr. Burns looked at his watch. "Time is up. One minute is over."

He reached for the paper in Charlie's hand. Charlie didn't want to let go of the paper until he knew where the error was.

"No, no, no!" Charlie softly whispered. "This is wrong. This is really wrong."

And then he saw the mistake. He sighed deeply and let go of the paper. He realized that his gut feeling was right. Math was still great and this was just a rookie mistake.

"You cannot divide by zero," he said triumphantly and looked at Mr. Burns. Their eyes met and for a few moments they stared at each other. For Charlie it felt like he was seeing all the way into the soul of Mr. Burns. He saw admiration from a teacher for the best student he could ask for. Charlie almost never made a mistake; he paid close attention to details and was an exceptional student.

They talked for the rest of the recess time. Mr. Burns told Charlie he expected great results from him in the final exams. Charlie apologized to Mr. Burns for ignoring him in class. He told him that he respected him very much as a teacher, a coach and a person. He thanked him for all the input he gave into his life.

When the bell rang to end the recess, they shook hands like men. They both knew they would be friends for life. It would not be the last lesson he learned from Mr. Burns.

A month before the final math exam started, they called a meeting with the students who took the advanced math class, a required subject for submission to university. The exam consisted of two papers, each a three-hour session - one for Algebra, and the other for Geometry and Trigonometry. Failing the exam was not an option for Charlie. He had his mind set on qualifying for university and would be the first in his family to attend.

Charlie knew something was wrong when he saw the look on Mr. Burns' face. He stared at his feet and could not look at the students. Charlie thought he saw tears in his eyes, but wasn't sure.

"There has been a terrible mistake," the principal said. "The advanced math curriculum sent out by the Education Department at the beginning of the year was not complete. Some sections were left out. We received the study guides for the final exam last week, and when Mr. Burns reviewed it, he discovered the mistake. We contacted the Education Department, and they have confirmed the final exam for advanced math will include the missing sections from the curriculum." The students moaned and grumbled and the principal had to ask for silence a few times before he could continue. Charlie remained silent and stared at Mr. Burns the whole time. As he realized the implications he felt disturbed and became upset at somebody he didn't know. He wanted to blame Mr. Burns, but deep inside he knew it was not his fault.

The principal continued and tried to downplay the severity of the problem and the impact it would have on the students.

"There are only a few new topics that were not covered during the year. New textbooks are available at the Education Department in Pretoria and Mr. Burns volunteered to leave immediately to pick up the books tomorrow. The new books will be available on Friday morning. I will answer any questions now."

The question and answer session continued for a while. The principal and Mr. Burns tried their best to remain positive and keep the students calm. The students had two options. Those who didn't plan to attend university could take the exam based on the standard curriculum. Students who needed the advanced math course to be eligible for admission to university had no choice but to attend additional classes Mr. Burns offered after hours and over weekends.

The last few months of Charlie's high school career was brutal. When the new textbooks arrived, he became a loner. He lived, breathed and studied math every minute available. Students taking the advanced math course and who lived on campus were given special privileges. They were allowed to study at large and at will. The normal house rules and restrictions were relaxed on their behalf. The study hall became their new math class. Junior students, who were required to study under supervision in the hall, were ecstatic. During the afternoon and evening study hours, they were allowed to study in their bedrooms. Supervision was increased to prevent any disturbances for the math students. Mr. Burns was as committed as his students. He made himself available after hours and in the evenings. He spent many late nights with the students and when he left to perform his duties on the farm, Charlie became the substitute teacher. He helped the strugglers and those who had not yet mastered the basics of the new topics. The more difficult questions were noted and presented to Mr. Burns during his next visit. During the day, school continued and the math students still had to complete all the other required subjects.

When the students sat down for the first math paper, algebra, they were all tired and exhausted, but their spirit and motivation were high. Over the course of a few weeks, the senior class completed the national exam administered by the Education Department. When it was all over, they celebrated with a party at a nearby lake. The results of the exam were published three weeks after the final paper was written. As was the tradition at many schools all over the country, the whole senior class attended the unveiling of the final results ceremony. The principal opened the package containing the results in front of the students. There was complete silence as they waited in anticipation for the final verdict. The principal announced the names of those who had an A for all their subjects. Everybody cheered as the names were read. Charlie was not one of them. The homeroom teacher received the copies for each student and handed them out. A list of all the results was pinned on the bulletin board outside the hall. Local and national newspapers printed a special section with the results the following day. It was an event with mixed feelings and emotions. Some laughed with tears of relief when they saw their own score. Some were surprised when a student passed the exam they were not expected to pass. Unfortunately for some, the reality and shock of not passing lead to disappointment and more tears.

Charlie aced four out of his six required subjects. He was very excited and relieved to see the A for math on his report card. Like many of the other boys in the same situation as Charlie, he was already drafted for military service. His plans to attend university were put on hold for a couple of years.

Students and teachers said their goodbyes. Promises to stay in touch were exchanged. Some would and some would not remain in contact. Charlie greeted his friends and teachers. He left Mr. Burns for last on purpose. They looked each other in the eye and shook hands. It was a strong handshake, and Charlie would remember the moment for a very long time. Both of them had tears in their eyes and it was Mr. Burns who let go of Charlie's hand, stepped forward and gave him a fatherly hug. When they let go, they smiled at each other and shook hands for a final time. Mr. Burns gave his last words of advice to one of his most memorable students.

"Take care of yourself Charlie, and remember the most important lesson I taught you," he said.

"Pay attention to the details," Charlie started. "If not, a simple mistake can prove one-equals-two, and then shit will happen." Charlie repeated Mr. Burns' words. He used the "s" word that a student would normally never use in front of a teacher, but Charlie was done with high school and he said it with respect. Mr. Burns laughed and gave Charlie a friendly slap on the shoulder before turning around and walking away. When he got to his car, he looked back and saluted Charlie. With tears in his eyes, Charlie returned the salute and walked to where his mom was waiting. Unlike all the other students in his class, Charlie was not yet old enough to qualify for a driver's license when he graduated high school. His Mom had to drive him. They lived a couple hours away, and there was nobody else from the area he could get a ride with. When he gave her the results, tears ran down her face as she proudly hugged and kissed him.

"I knew it!" She said with a proud voice. "You are a very smart kid Charles Guillaume O'Neal. You will be the first one in our family to go to university. I'm so very proud of you, my son." She started the car and they left the parking lot. Charlie took one last look at the buildings where he had spent so much time and effort over the past 5 years. It was time to start the next chapter in his life. He had no idea where it would take him, he was just glad this one was over.

* * *

CHAPTER 11

First Job

C harlie got his math genes from his dad. Being an accountant at the mining company, he oversaw the procurement and inventory management departments. During summer school vacations, Charlie helped with the annual stock counts. His dad was a genius with calculations. They competed against each other by adding long lists of numbers and then checking each other for accuracy. It was only in his senior year, that he realized his Dad had been letting him win. This was before computers entered the business environment and inventory was managed on index cards with details of the item and the supplier on the front. On the back of the card the transactions were listed with the current balance and value noted. Every withdrawal and receipt was recorded on the card. One day Charlie observed his Dad from a distance. He saw how he picked up a stack of cards, held it tight in one hand, and flipped through it as you would through the pages of a book. When he was done, he would write down a number on the ledger. Charlie walked up to him to find out what he was doing.

"Oh, I'm just updating the stock ledger."

"How?" Charlie asked. He wasn't sure if what he saw was true.

"I just add the value from all the cards. You know. You helped me many times to update the cards."

"Yes. But how did you get the total? You were just flipping through the cards."

"Practice makes perfect" he replied with a smile.

"So," Charlie sounded suspicious. "The challenge for adding numbers. The game we always played, you let me win sometimes?" His Dad laughed and looked at Charlie.

"Of course. But, you got better and it will be hard to beat you now."

"No" Charlie said and shook his head. "I will never be able to do what I just saw. You're a genius Dad. Nobody can add numbers as quickly as you just did."

Charlie realized the time he spent counting stock and updating the index cards was not only a game but also the way his Dad had instilled a love for math in him.

After graduation, Charlie worked with his Dad as usual. He got paid in the form of free lunches at the cafeteria, and an unlimited supply of sodas. He roamed the property of the mining company on foot and on a bicycle. His job was to locate and count specific equipment and critical spares parts. Life was good for young Charlie O'Neal, but it was time he got a real job.

Charlie started his first job at Anglo Bank of South Africa in the early seventies a few weeks after he graduated high school. He got the job due to his dad's relationship with the bank manager. The platinum mining company where his dad worked was a client of the bank. When Charlie graduated from high school, his dad somehow got him an interview with the bank manager.

The military draft in South Africa required all boys 18 years and older to perform one-year military service to their country. Charlie was drafted six months after graduation when he turned 18. His plan was to go to university before military service, but he didn't have a scholarship. His parents didn't have enough savings to pay for his tuition and his dad saw the military as a way to kick the can down the road. The dreaded conversation about funding Charlie's university dreams was delayed for a while. During his interview Charlie discussed a student loan with the manager, Mr. Kramer. When Charlie presented his grades from high school, the bank manager proposed an alternative to Charlie.

The bank was always in search of new talent, especially those with good grades in math and accounting. Being a small rural town, most young people ventured out to the big city lights and seldom stayed local. The proposition was attractive to Charlie. The bank was willing to offer him a full scholarship and a salary while performing his military service. The only condition was that Charlie would complete his studies and return to the bank upon completion of his studies. The salary and scholarship would be a loan repayable in the form of years of service. If he didn't complete his studies, or didn't return to the bank, the full amount would become a loan. The 'golden handcuffs' Mr. Kramer called them.

Charlie discussed the options with his Dad.

"Charlie," his Dad sounded serious and had a look of guilt on his face. "You know there is no way for your mother and I to pay for you to go to university. We just cannot afford it. It's also a big risk for you. It's a lot of money if you don't complete your studies and return to the bank."

"I know Dad. But this is a good offer. Where can I get a scholarship that will beat this one?"

They talked for a while and discussed the implication for Charlie. It was not only the discussion about their financial position that Charlie would remember for a very long time, but also the real reason he got the interview.

"The bank needs people who can do math. Somebody who understand basic calculations" his dad started his tirade. "You know how many times I have to go and fight with them to correct errors? There is always a mistake with the interest calculations. They are terrible with rounding. And those random fees - it drives me crazy!" he said and hit the desk with the palm of his hand.

"Who does the calculations?" Charlie asked.

"I don't know. Mr. Kramer blamed the dumb clerk he had. I used the opportunity to get you the interview. I bragged about your skills and how good you are with math. I told him you were looking for a job. He owed me one for not reporting him to his head office, so he agreed to the interview. Seems you made an impression on him."

It was many years later that Charlie would think back to the conversation with his Dad and realize how he had hit the nail on the head. If he only knew how close to the truth he was.

The mining company had a huge overdraft agreement in place, and interest charges were a sensitive subject for the mine manager. Maybe the frequent bottle of Scotch whisky Mr. Kramer received had something to do with Charlie getting the interview and the job. The decision was easy for Charlie.

Anglo Bank was one of the big national banks in South Africa and Mr. Kramer the typical autocratic manager. The staff was scared of him, and tasks were mostly performed to avoid being summoned to the *"principal's"* office. Although rules were very strictly enforced, the staff knew he was always fair in his decisions. He had very little tolerance for errors, but when it came to personal matters, he cared for his employees and they knew they could trust him.

One morning Charlie arrived at work and instinctively knew there was a change in the atmosphere. Mr. Kramer cared for this staff, but he cared a lot more about the opinion of *"head office"* and the branch's performance in their eyes. He was scared stiff every year when it was time for the annual audit review. When the time drew closer for the arrival of the auditors, the environment was so charged with emotion that an eruption or explosion could happen anytime. The annual audit was an especially stressful time for Mr. Kramer. The longer the audit lasted, the more his stress level increased, and the more intensely he micro managed his staff. Everyone hated the time when the auditors were there and wished they would just leave.

During one audit, Mr. Kramer, as branch manager, got *"dinged"* because of an incorrect interest calculation. It didn't pass the cross check of balances perfectly. The auditors used a weird method to calculate a check sum of the interested paid daily. The sum of the daily interest charges was used to calculate the base amount according to the interest rate. The total charges for the month was verified and had to balance with their calculations. If it didn't balance, the manager got *"dinged"*. Branch managers knew they had to perform a cross check daily, but it was an exercise in futility due to the interest rate used. There was always a minuscule decimal difference and the auditors knew it. They used this simple method of calculation to generate fear and anxiety amongst the branch managers. The explanation was always that incorrect interest calculations could negatively impact the financial performance of the bank as a whole. If a manager could not balance the fractions of calculations, they were not competent enough to be a branch manager. The bank made its profit from the interest and the fees charged to its clients. A branch should be profitable or run the risk of closure. The complex calculation caused many headaches for Mr. Kramer. He just could not come to grips with it and eventually employed a person with the sole responsibility of calculating the interests and fees.

This was Charlie's first experience with the auditors. On the top of the list of audit items were the interest calculations. It was a basic formula to be verified. They randomly selected a few days of the previous year to validate the calculations. The task was normally assigned to one of the rookies on the audit team. Even the auditors hated the execution part, but they were ecstatic when an error was discovered.

Charlie stood on the sideline and observed as one of the rookie auditors followed a carefully choreographed script. He memorized the script and just smiled as he noticed how even the auditors battled to follow their own calculations. The rookies followed the script provided by the senior audit manager. They were authorized to ask any staff member any question at any time, and boy, did they ask a lot of questions. As auditors they were only allowed to ask questions and never, as in never, answer a question from a staff member. The audit manager was the only one who answered questions. A mistake that was smaller than a fraction of a penny would turn into a big issue.

The length of the audit was undetermined and kept secret by the auditors. This time the audit manager walked into Mr. Kramer's office on Thursday morning and announced their departure by the end of the day. The afternoon was spent behind closed doors, and based on the length of the review, not many issues were found. The rating of the branch, and the number of *"dings"* the manager received, was used to prorate the annual bonus paid to branch managers. Staff members were guaranteed a thirteenth check and it was paid every year on the Monday before Christmas. The branch managers received their bonus at the end of the year.

The scrutiny by head office the following year depended on the results of the annual audit. Mr. Kramer was no different from all the other branch managers. He cared about the result of the audit. And like most other branch managers, the one thing they all dreaded the most was losing out on their annual bonus. They would do almost anything to make sure their bonuses were not impacted. Yes, they even cheated the system, and spend a lot of time making sure they got away with it.

One of the tasks Mr. Kramer assigned to Charlie was the daily settlement for the interbank transfer account. Each bank tallied the checks from competing banks in the area. Joint meetings with other clerks were held daily. Checks were exchanged and each clerk signed an IOU for the difference. Differences were never paid immediately and the balance from the previous day was used as the opening balance for the following day. A running total was kept, and the manager checked the balance of the IOU. If the balance exceeded a specific threshold, it was forwarded to head office for clearance and settlement. A final clearance was done monthly, and confirmed during the next joint meeting between clerks.

The interbank transfer account also had an interest component. The daily balance and agreed rate was used to calculate the interest on the spot during the joint settlement meeting. The clerks were required to verify the calculations and sign off on the interest component.

It was during one of these settlement sessions that Charlie questioned the calculations by the competing bank. He had a problem with how the rounding was settled. The opposing clerk always rounded down when they had to pay interest, and rounded up when interest was due to them. Charlie questioned the practice, and was not happy about the answer.

"Oh, this is how we have done it forever," the clerk from the competing bank explained with a grin and a tone of superiority in his voice. "As the leading bank in the country, we can dictate the terms and methods of calculation."

As the rookie in the business, Charlie didn't want to argue his case of simple mathematical principals. He reluctantly accepted the answer as a bank rule, but it continued to bother him. He decided to discuss it with Mr. Kramer. Mr. Kramer listened in silence and didn't comment when Charlie suggested they just truncate every time and then over time it would balance out more evenly for both sides. The way it was done only benefited the other bank.

"Close the door, Charlie," Mr. Kramer eventually said. From the bottom drawer of his desk he pulled out a black and red journal. It was one of the cheap ones from the stationary store down the street. It had a black cover with a red spine and graph pages. He recognized it. He had seen a similar one in the bottom drawer of his dad's desk. When he asked his dad about it, he explained its purpose to Charlie.

"Son, this is my 'good boy-bad boy' journal. I update it every time people do something special for me. When somebody does something I don't like, I write it down. Do you remember all the gifts we receive at the end of the year from the mining supply reps?" his dad asked.

"Yes. You always give them to other people. We get the candy and chocolates."

"Exactly!" his dad said. "The 'good boy-bad boy' journal decides who gets what. Lots of people know about it, and they always want to be on the 'good boy' list at the end of the year." He stopped for a moment, and then looked at Charlie. "You know, people will never cease to amaze me. Before they knew about the book, they treated me like crap, but as soon as they heard about the book, they suddenly changed and everybody wanted to be my friend. Isn't it funny how people change when they know they can get something from you?"

Charlie had heard the same lesson from his dad many times over the years. It became part of his being and he grew weary when somebody unexpectedly became friendly towards him.

"Do you know what this is Charlie?" Mr. Kramer asked.

"It's a journal, Sir. My dad uses one at the mine also."

"This is the bank manager's 'auditor repellant' book. What I'm about to show you, only a few people know. Most branch managers have one in their drawers and when I say we live and die by this book, I mean we live and die by this little book." He shook the book in front of his face and sounded very serious. Charlie thought it must be a very important book. He would like to know what was in it.

"You've heard the rumors that I once got dinged by the auditors for a simple calculation error?" Mr. Kramer asked.

"Yes. Somebody told me."

"Well, it is true. I hated it then and I still hate it. I have to hear about it every time I attend a branch managers' meeting at head office. I don't want it to happen to me again. This little book helps me to balance every day and it keeps the auditors happy. All branch managers have this little book. It is our way to get around the auditors."

Charlie had this weird feeling that this was something he was not supposed to know. Mr. Kramer spoke in a soft voice and leaned forward as he showed Charlie the entries for the last few months.

"Each branch has a discretionary expense account for the branch manager. We call it our marketing and sales expenses. We have a budget amount every year, and what is left at the end of the year is used for the annual function."

Charlie had not been with the bank long enough to have experienced it, but he had heard the stories of the excessive amount of food and drinks the previous year. The staff could not believe the bank was so generous, but they enjoyed the party.

"You see, Charlie," Mr. Kramer continued. "I use my discretionary expense account to balance the interest calculations daily. The difference from the settlement meeting is added in this book. We do the normal interest calculations, and then we use the auditors' crosscheck to calculate the difference. Any difference is then added to the spending account to balance the books daily with a journal entry to the account. I got the idea from another branch manager with a lot more experience than me. He also got dinged once, and was never dinged again. When I asked him how he did it, he told me that you always round up when the client owes interest on an overdraft, and round down when you pay interest to the client. It's the same process we use with the interbank settlement account. This will cause an overcharge to the client that is offset with an entry to the manager's account. A small amount is added every day. The auditors are happy and by the end of the year it adds up to a nice little sum. The more accounts you have, the more entries you get. The bigger the balance, the bigger the party at the end of the year."

Charlie listened intently to the explanation and at the bottom of one of the pages he saw the entry 'Balance carried forward'. He could not believe the amount and realized why the party the previous year was so good. It was more than his dad had paid for his new car a couple of years ago and it was still early in the year. Charlie did a quick calculation. He could not believe that such a small value could add up to something so significant. *"If you have one account, calculate the interest and then round it up, it is less than a penny on average per account. That's not much."* Charlie thought to himself. *"You need a thousand accounts just to get five pennies a day. Over a year, it would add up to eighteen bucks and twenty-five cents. The bank must have a lot of accounts to get to that balance?"*

Mr. Kramer continued with his explanation. "The auditors are happy, the managers are happy and we all have a great party at the end of the year!" He leaned back with a big grin of satisfaction on his face.

Charlie had his doubts about the accuracy as a million questions formed in his brain. *"But hey, who am I to question the bank manager? I just graduated high school and have very little experience. I know nothing about banking and how to balance the books. If this is the way it is done and the auditors are happy, why bother to change it?"* he thought to himself.

"How many accounts do we have?" Charlie asked.

"Not as many as I would like. With all the mines in the area, we are close to twenty thousand. Nationally we have millions."

"That's a lot," Charlie responded. *"Twenty times twenty-five cents will give you five bucks a day,"* Charlie thought.

"So," Mr. Kramer continued. "I want you to help me with the calculations every month. It seems like you understand the math side of it." He went on to explain to Charlie the steps he performed daily and how to record it. Charlie would do the calculations and Mr. Kramer would make the entries in the book. He would then prepare the journal voucher to capture the entry in the ledgers.

Interest calculations were added only once a month to a client's account. It was calculated based on the daily outstanding amount. The daily balance was recorded on a journal voucher, or JV as referred to by the staff, the size of an index card. The piles of vouchers were stacked everywhere, and nothing happened without a JV. It was preprinted with spaces for the details of each entry to be made on an account - red sheets for credits and blue sheets for debits.

The first week after he started at the bank, he had watched in amazement how the daily routine unfolded. Nothing happened in the bank until the vault door was opened. Two senior staff members with the keys were needed to open the door. Nobody could get into the vault before the ledger carts were rolled out. The same process over and over, day in and day out. Charlie sat behind his desk and watched how the ledger entry staff would go through the piles of JV sheets every day. Like robots they would repeat the same actions day after day.

The carts were pulled up next to the desk with the account ledger charts stored in large bins. First, the JV sheets were sorted by the account number and then split between the carts. The ledger charts were stored in the bins based on the account number. Then the typing started. The same action; pull the ledger chart - roll to the line where the entry should be made - type the entry based on the JV - remove the ledger chart - put the chart back in the bin - flip to the next JV - find the ledger chart - repeat. Over, and over and over. The whole day the same thing was repeated with the rhythm of the rolling and sorting and typing filling the air. Talking was restricted until the JVs were done. The last day of the month, the interest and the fees were recorded on the account ledger charts. One JV sheet for the interest, and one JV sheet for the fees. The charges for the fees were fixed and were prepared daily. It was piled up till the end of the month. The interest sheets became Charlie's responsibility.

Once a week, Charlie would get full access to the ledger charts. He pulled every ledger chart for accounts with an overdraft and placed the pile on his desk. He would then go through the charts, calculate the daily interest based on the rate noted on the chart, and record it on a JV sheet. A JV sheet was prepared for each ledger chart. There was one entry per week with the sum of daily interest charges as Charlie calculated it based on the directions he received from Mr. Kramer. At the end of the month, the weekly totals were added and the monthly interest charge noted at the bottom of the JV. The JVs were kept in a pile on his desk and he performed the computations on a calculator that printed the calculations onto a paper tape. The tally roll was wrapped around all the JVs, and then held together with a rubber band. Charlie kept the completed sheets in his drawer until the end of the week when it was all handed over to Mr. Kramer for verification. After he signed off on it, it was handed to the ledger staff to capture on the ledger charts. Mr. Kramer would make the entries in his book, and add the JV for the *'discretionary'* expense account.

All savings accounts were kept in a separate ledger and in a separate bin. The bin was pushed to Charlie's desk and he would repeat the same process to calculate the interest the bank had to pay on savings accounts. This time, instead of rounding up, he would round down.

At the end of the first week, Charlie gathered a pile of JVs he had worked on. He walked to Mr. Kramer's office and left the pile of JVs for him for review. He noticed on a separate JV sheet on his desk. It was for an amount that should be posted to the manager's discretionary expense account. The JV entry was to offset the interest over-charges for the overdraft accounts. It was for sixty-two bucks. The entry for under-payments to savings accounts was just forty-seven bucks.

"At this rate, there will not be much for a big party come year-end," Charlie thought. *"Where did the rest of it come from if the party was a good as I heard? Something just doesn't add up,"*

The time came for Charlie to leave for his military service. There were only a few weeks left before he had to say goodbye. He met with Mr. Kramer about his future and asked if the bank would honor their commitment to pay his monthly salary. He promised to get back to Charlie.

Two weeks before his last day, Mr. Kramer called Charlie into his office. He handed Charlie a folder with all the paperwork to be completed and contracts to be signed. It was a lot of forms and some long-term commitments for a boy not yet 18 years old. Charlie asked permission to discuss it with his parents first.

"This is a big decision, Charlie" Mr. Kramer explained. "Read the fine print carefully and discuss it with your parents. Remember, once you have signed on the dotted line and you receive your first salary while in the military, it becomes a loan. The agreement is for you to repay through the work-for-pay program. If you don't return to the bank, you have to pay back every penny plus interest. The bank sees it as desertion and the interest rates are brutal."

"I plan to honor my commitment, Sir." Charlie saw the concern on Mr. Kramer's face. Mr. Kramer continued with his explanation.

"If you want to return, I will be very happy to employ you again. I already asked if you could come back to this branch, and head office said it would be fine, but I doubt it will happen. If you want to continue with the application for a scholarship, you have to start the process immediately. It will not become binding until you actually receive the scholarship. It will pay for tuition, books, room and board, and there will be a monthly allowance for incidentals. The same terms will apply as with the military service agreement. If you don't return to the bank, it will become a loan with interest added from the day you received the first payment. The terms will not be in your favor."

Charlie understood most of the details Mr. Kramer mentioned. He also noticed the serious undertone. The offer from the bank was very lucrative and for Charlie it was the only opportunity he had to further his education. There was no alternative.

If he said no, he would go to the military and live on the ninety-four cents a day military pay. There may be some danger pay if he was sent to the combat zone on the border, but not much would be left for saving. When done with the military service, Charlie would have to return home and apply for a job at the mining company where his dad worked. Charlie preferred life away from the platinum mines. He knew what his decision would be.

"When do I need to return the forms?" he asked.

"The military form a week before you leave. The scholarship any time before your last day." Mr. Kramer replied.

"Mr. Kramer," Charlie started and looked him in the eye. "If I were your son, what advice would you give me?"

There were a few moments of intense silence. In the background Charlie could here the sound from the typing machines in the ledger section. Mr. Kramer looked down and stared at nothing particular on his desk for a while. When he looked up at Charlie, there was a tear in his eye. It reminded Charlie of the incident in high school when his eyes met those of Mr. Burns. It was not too long ago.

"Charlie," Mr. Kramer started. "I don't have a son anymore. He died in the same war you are going to fight in. If he had asked me the same question, given your circumstances, my answer would be the same." With a quick brush of his hand, he wiped the tear away and then he continued. "I have known your parents for a while now. I know their personal financial situation. Charlie, there is no way they can afford to pay for your education. You have a very special gift and a lot of talent. I have never seen anybody in my life that understands math the way you do. Use the opportunity and change your future forever. It will be a waste of talent if you don't go to university.

Get out of this rat hole. Get out of the mining community. You cannot come back and just work at the mine. You need to break out of this rut and find the destiny God created for you."

Charlie listened intently to the advice Mr. Kramer gave him. Every word burned into his memory forever. Mr. Kramer took a deep breath, exhaled slowly and then continued.

"Charlie, I already recommended to head office that your application be approved for military service pay and for the scholarship. What the heck! If you go to the big city to work at head office, so be it. You deserve the best opportunity to get out of this place and go make a difference somewhere else. Talk to your parents and let them know if they have questions, to contact me. You are still a minor and they have to co-sign the contract for the military service. Complete the scholarship application and when you sign it, date it for the day after you turn 18. I will keep it in the drawer and will not submit it until after your birthday. That would make it a binding contract between you and the bank and would not become a burden on them if you decide not to return to the bank."

Charlie was overcome with relief as he realized that his dream could become true. He opened his mouth to speak, but no words came out. He was afraid he was going to cry, and he just stared at Mr. Kramer. He stood up and offered his hand to Mr. Kramer. They shook hands to confirm the agreement and acknowledge each other. It gave Charlie time to recover and he managed to get a word out again.

"Thank you, Sir. That is exactly the advice I was looking for. Not from the bank manager, but from the person who cares for his people. I will never forget it."

That evening, Charlie left work early and drove to his parents' house where they lived in the small mining community. There were only seventy-five residential houses for mining officials. The mine captain lived in number 1. A store assistant lived in number seventy-five. His parents lived in number seventeen. The house numbers were assigned according to an employee's position at the mine. As child, your social status was determined by the house number your parents lived in.

Charlie and his parents sat around the dinner table and had a long conversation about his future and the direction he wanted to go. Charlie explained the advice Mr. Kramer gave him. He saw tears in his mom's eyes when he told them about it. His dad promised to make sure Mr. Kramer got the best bottle of whiskey at the end of the year. His dad co-signed the contract for Charlie to receive a salary from the bank while performing his military service. Then he explained to Charlie what had happened to Mr. Kramer's son. He was killed on the northern border a few years ago in a land-mine explosion. It was their only child and was a big loss for them.

A week before he had to leave for his military service, Charlie made his final rounds and said goodbye to the group of people he had worked with for the past six months. Some of the older ladies cried. Most of them had a son or a family member serving in the military and knew what awaited Charlie. Mr. Kramer was the last one on his list and Charlie still had one more question for him.

Charlie knocked on the door and walked into the bank manager's office to say goodbye. Mr. Kramer looked up at Charlie. He was busy making entries in his journal. It was the same red and black journal from the bottom drawer. Charlie used it as the opportunity to ask his question.

"Mr. Kramer. I have one last question before I leave."

"Yes. What is it?" He closed the ledger and looked at Charlie.

"Sir, I heard about the annual party last year. I have never experienced it and you said it was paid from the manager's discretionary expense account. How did you really pay for it? I know, and I think you also know, the pennies from rounding the interest was not enough to pay for the lavish party from last year. I have my suspicion, but I'm not sure about it."

The blood slowly drained from Mr. Kramer's face. Charlie realized he had touched on something sensitive. *"Maybe I should just have kept my big mouth shut,"* he thought as he waited for a response. His scholarship application was still in the drawer. Mr. Kramer could very easily just conveniently forget to sign it and never submit it.

"How do you think it's paid for?" Mr. Kramer asked Charlie after a few minutes with a grin on his face.

"The additional transaction fees?" Charlie started. "I noticed the fees when I did the interest calculations for the overdraft accounts. I didn't realize it immediately, and thought it was a special arrangement. I think it was called the 'overdraft-processing fee'. I saw the pile of JVs and the contra account entry was made to the branch manger's discretionary expense account."

Mr. Kramer exhaled slowly. Charlie knew he was close, but not hundred percent.

"Charlie, you are smart, really smart. Please never become an auditor. All bank managers would be in serious trouble if you were one of them." He tried to make a joke and relieve the tension hanging in the air.

"I don't plan to become one," Charlie said.

Mr. Kramer then explained what was going on. "Branch managers are allowed to use creative measures to provide funds for additional expenses not covered in the budget. It is all above board and every penny is recorded. Yes, the fees you noticed are just one of many methods branch managers implement to ensure profitability and strengthen the discretionary expense account." He hesitated for a moment before he continued.

"Remember, everything that happens inside the bank is confidential. You signed the non-disclosure agreement when you started on your first day. You signed another one when you applied for the military service payment, and there is a signed one in my drawer." He smiled at Charlie, who knew there was something more, but didn't know exactly what. Charlie would eventually find out many years later.

Charlie left the bank and went home to see his parents before he had to report for his service to his country.

It was fourteen days before Charlie's eighteenth birthday.

* * *

CHAPTER 12

Basic Training

C harlie reported for basic training at the 8th Infantry Battalion, located in the outskirts of Upington, in the Northern Cape province of South Africa. He boarded the troop train at the small railway station closest to the home of his parents. They were the only ones at the station to see him off. Like the handful of other moms there, his mom cried. She held him for a long time before she eventually let him go. Charlie swallowed hard on the lump in his throat and tried to look brave. The train stopped frequently and those who boarded were about the same age or older than Charlie. Charlie stared through the open window at those boarding, but didn't recognize anyone. The same scene repeated at many stations. Parents and siblings said goodbye to a son or brother. A few recruits managed to smuggle alcohol onto the train, and their singing and bravado continued all hours of the day and night. From a central rendezvous point, the boys were regrouped and under military police supervision departed to their different units for three months of basic training.

In Upington, there were no permanent buildings for the troops. They took residence in tents. The green canvas tents were aligned military style. Sandbags were placed at the bottom of the tent walls to keep it anchored when the wind started howling across the barren fields of the Northern

Cape. Small rocks were aligned between tents to demarcate the walkways. New recruits attempting to take a short cut through the tents eventually tripped over a tent wire and discovered the reason for the walkways. In return for his blunder, the recruit would be ridiculed and laughed at. Oh, and beware your soul if the drill sergeant saw you. The army's goal was to break down new recruits physically, emotionally and spiritually in the first few weeks, and then build them up gradually as soldiers. It had to be done in a three months timeframe. Every opportunity to punish a recruit was seized by the drill sergeants. Running was always part of the punishment.

Inside the tents everything was setup, organized and aligned in exactly the same way. Beds were made the same way, clothes were hung in the metal lockers in the same order, rifles were disassembled and the parts laid out on the bed in the exact same way. Outside the tents the two fire buckets were aligned from the first tent in the row to the last one. One bucket filled with sand, and the other filled with water. The buckets had to be filled to the same level, and God forbid if one tent didn't have enough sand or water in it. Somehow the drill sergeant could *"smell"* when one bucket missed a single drop of water. He would randomly kick over buckets not filled to the correct level. If even one bucket didn't meet his expectations, all buckets had to be emptied and refilled for inspection before sunrise the next morning.

At night tent flaps were closed to keep out the bitter cold. First thing in the morning, tents flaps were opened again. It was winter, and some mornings the water in the buckets were frozen. The drill sergeant even used the cold and freezing water as an excuse to send the whole platoon to the north gate to ensure it was closed.

"Somebody must have left the gate open! That is where the cold is coming in. On the double! Go check if the gate is closed." Words Charlie heard so many times, he would never forget them.

"How do you think you will kill a fire with frozen water?" the short drill sergeant yelled in the face of the closest recruit. He kicked the bucket over and then ordered every bucket to be kicked over.

Every day the short and obnoxious drill sergeant of Charlie's platoon would pick on a different recruit to demonstrate his superiority in yelling and intimidation techniques. The sole purpose was to drive more fear into the recruits. He specifically liked to pick on the bigger guys. His verbal attacks would irritate them to the point where they would eventually explode and respond in like manner. It was just what the drill sergeant wanted. He used their reaction as an excuse to punish the whole squad with all kinds of exercises and extra drills. All the show and tirades from the drill sergeant had one goal - build a sense of comradery and unity amongst the troops and direct the anger against a faceless enemy. Luckily for Charlie, he was one of the smaller recruits and was spared the verbal attacks.

"To the north gate you go! Everybody! On the double!" was the drill sergeant's most famous words. The whole squad would move in unison to the gate, bodies were still frozen from the frigid night. The young kids, soon to be turned into soldiers, were not used to the brutal cold and sleeping in tents. The drill sergeant knew it was freezing, and that there was no other way to get body temperatures rising. He had to get the blood circulating. The recruits scrambled, quickly assembled their weapons and made their way to the north gate of the base. The sergeant used the opportunity to go through the tents like a tornado and give the recruits more reasons to hate him. He randomly selected a bed in each tent and tipped it over. If he found an open locker, the contents were emptied on the groundsheet. He was obnoxious, mean, loud, cruel, and the recruits hated his guts. He had to be that way. He was everything the army wanted him to be to transform boys into men, and men into soldiers - and he only had three months to complete the task.

Basic training concluded with a final day of testing. A big deal was made about the written test. Recruits were left alone for one whole day to study.

The drill sergeant turned into a human being overnight. He helped those who needed help with the study materials and even wished them luck. He told Charlie that he had better ace the test or he would make sure Charlie stayed at the base. The test covered every possible subject and military topic mentioned during the past three months of basic training. Nothing was off limits. Those who failed the test were by default volunteered to remain on base and become part of the infantry unit. The army needed as many foot soldiers as possible and ninety percent would fail the written test.

The physical trials and endurance tests were used to further separate recruits. The more physically abled bodies were capable of surviving the harsh environment where the infantry combat battalion would be deployed. The fitness trials started immediately after the written test. It started with the legendary 1 and 1/2 mile run. Contrary to the first three months where it was done every Saturday morning with full gear before breakfast, the test was performed with only combat clothing, boots, steel helmets and rifles. The run was timed and the results recorded. Then followed the regular obstacle course done at least once every day during the fourteen days before the test.

The secondary motive with the written and the physical tests was to divide the troop into different categories for the specialist phase. The national draft, decreed by the government in 1966, required all men 18 years and older to endure the basic training phase. They came from all walks of life and were thrown into the same situation. Not everyone was willing or able to participate. The pool of talent was thinned in the first three months by the drill sergeants. Some were assigned admin duties, some became medical ordinances and others were sent to the kitchen to become chefs. The vast fleet of military vehicles required as many resources to maintain and operate the fleet. Many of those who didn't meet the physical requirements for combat were sent to the vehicle yard. There were more than enough tasks to keep a military base running. Those mentally and physically unfit for combat against the enemy, were identified as early as possible in the process, and then re-assigned.

Charlie, although young of age and one of the smaller in size, was savvier than most in his platoon. Navigation, map reading, communications and all the military jargon required to pass the written test, were easy for Charlie. It was no surprise to the drill sergeant to see Charlie in the top one percent. His hunting skills on the farm with his BB gun and his dad's .22-caliber long rifle put him in the top five during the shooting competition. The physical fitness test was a different story. The scaling of the wall slowed him down when his size forced him to make a second attempt to get ahold of the 10-foot high wall. He nevertheless made it into the top ten in the battalion. The time came for Charlie to make an important decision, one that would impact his life forever.

During a short one-hour session, the top one hundred recruits in the battalion were introduced to the different military divisions. The ultimate goal was to get them to enlist as career soldiers and join the permanent force of the military branch of the government. Charlie listened and considered all information thrown at him by overly enthusiastic pen pushing lieutenants. They were all smooth talkers. The presentations focused on the glamour and adrenalin of combat. Every group mentioned how they were destined to make a difference in the outcome of the war. Internally Charlie still struggled to fathom the purpose of the war.

After the presentation, he had to make a quick decision. He considered two divisions. The reconnaissance brigade would put him right in the center and forefront of the action. The only problem was that as a part of the Special Forces it required a two-year commitment. The other option was officer training at the infantry school. Although they encouraged a two-year commitment, it was not yet enforced. The only thing Charlie was sure about when considering his options was that he didn't want to stay at the base in Upington. Anywhere else would be a thousand times better.

The biggest selling point for Charlie was when they showed the new barracks and facilities at the officer's training school. The presenting officer boasted about the kitchen and the mess hall. He compared it to the open tent they were sitting in which was also used as the mess hall. Food would taste so much better without sand in it.

Charlie had to constantly remind himself of the contract he signed with the bank. He could not go back on his word and sign up to become a professional soldier. The bank still held the key to university for him. He needed a college education to be able to move away from the mining community.

His decision proved to be the wrong one. The officer's training school was located at the foot of the Black mountain range and they spend most of their training in the rugged terrain. A week before the final test and graduation to become an officer, Charlie got injured during a maneuver in the mountain areas of Oudtshoorn. He'd spend a month in the hospital and after knee surgery returned to the base in Upington to complete his basic training. The officer's class he was part of, would move on and graduated without him. Charlie was devastated.

Two other soldiers were with Charlie when he arrived back at the base in Upington. They all stood nervously outside the tent of Major Martin Kruger, the new Company Commanding Officer. Oscar Company provided support to the troops from the battalion on the frontline. The CO had a brief interview with each soldier returning from officer's training school. He flipped through the folders containing the full details of the past four months of their short military career. His split decision determined where they would spend the rest of their year of service.

When he read Charlie's file, he commented on Charlie's achievements during basic training and at officers' school.

"You did well on the signal and communications test. Are you any good?" he asked Charlie.

"I got the highest score on the test and was the fastest in the cipher translation test, Major, Sir!" Charlie responded, still standing at attention and staring directly in front of him. He knew not to make eye contact with a ranking officer.

"You, stay behind." He said and pointed at Charlie. "Corporal!" He shouted at the soldier waiting outside the CO's tent. The corporal appeared on the double, saluted the major and stood at attention.

"Take these two to logistics and give this to Captain Jacobs." The major signed the internal memo and handed it to the corporal. The instruction assigned the other soldiers to the equipment maintenance group.

The major asked Charlie a few more questions about Infantry school and his injury. He asked specific questions about signal training and after ten minutes, made his decision. Charlie was assigned to the CO's communications team. The unit operated the central communications for the battalion, and when deployed to the battlefront remained on base instead of going on patrol.

The initial excitement about being in the central command tent soon wore off. It was a boring and tedious job. Long hours spent in a small tent. The daily sit-raps (situation reports) submitted up in the chain of command stayed the same. Troop strength, supplies status, transportation status, and random statistics needed by somebody on the receiving end.

There was one area that Charlie enjoyed the most during training and in preparation for deployment to the war zone. All messages sent over the air had to be in a coded format.

"Remember!" Charlie could still hear the officer's voice when he drilled it into them. "The enemy is always listening!" The class repeated in unison after him. "The enemy is always listening! Code the message!"

The coding and decoding of military messages used basic ciphers and Charlie stood out from amongst the rest of his class as a genius. The training officer made a side note in Charlie's file, and it caught the attention of Major Kruger. The intelligence officer in charge of the communications squad, Lt.

Lambert, soon discovered this skill and Charlie received longer messages to code. For Charlie it was something more interesting to do than the daily sit-raps.

The messages to and from HQ were for the eyes of the commanding officer and the intelligence officer only. Gradually these messages made it to Charlie. Like everything else in the military, it always had to be done on the double and nobody did it faster than Charlie. Every message to and from a higher-ranking officer was always regarded as an "urgent" message. Even a routine base visit from the Battalion Brigadier, Bravo-Bravo as the troops called him, was treated with the highest priority.

The most important item for the day was the tee-time at the local golf course. Charlie discovered this when Lt. Lambert asked him to decode a message and give it to the CO. He walked to the CO's tent and handed him the message he had deciphered. Major Kruger looked at it and without a word dismissed Charlie and destroyed the message. Charlie could never understand why they couldn't just discuss it over the phone. The golf game was unofficial business being conducted as top secret. Eventually Charlie learned that one of the privates acting as a caddie for the major was not just any private. He had won the national junior golf title before reporting for his year of military service. The brigadier and the major were getting "private" golf lessons from him.

"The games men play" Charlie thought when he figured out what was really going on.

A few weeks into Charlie's new assignment, he received another message to decode. As soon as he started working, he immediately realized this was important. It was time for action. All games were at an end, and it was time to deploy.

* * *

CHAPTER 13

When Shift Doesn't Happen

T he 8th Infantry Battalion unit arrived in the Caprivi area on the northern border of South West Africa (now known as Namibia) with Angola. Cross border patrols and raids were common and the purpose of the *"war"* was to keep the insurgents from the north out of the home country.

"Stop them at the border, and they will not get to your family and your home," the politicians and advocates of the *"Bush war"* proclaimed over the radio and at public gatherings.

The operations control room - the *"ops"* - was the center of action at every base camp. It had a sign on the door barring any unauthorized person from entering. It hosted the squads tasked with radio communications and gathering of intelligence. The tent flaps were always closed and area maps indicated the positions of their own troops and targeted enemy locations. Coffee was available 24/7 and officers knew it. Charlie, one of three unranked soldiers authorized to enter the tent, was tasked with coding and decoding messages. New cipher sheets were issued daily. Charlie was not officially cleared to handle confidential reports, but his reputation for the speed with which he could code and decoded messages outweighed the risk of information being leaked to the enemy. His rank didn't fit the role he was in. He read messages of activities and operations no private should read. Sometimes he felt sick about things he came across, but there was no time for anxiety attacks. He quickly learned the value of taking a deep breath and holding it for as long as possible to get his emotions under control. The frantic behavior in the tent when contact was made with the enemy very quickly healed him from his anxiety. He realized that a simple mistake could very well cost someone their life. *"This is not a game, O'Neal. Stay focused! One does not equal two."* The incident with his math teacher, now in the distant past, played in his mind every time a life was lost and he had to code the message. When Russia and Cuba got involved in the war to support Angola, casualties increased and occurred frequent.

Charlie was the only person without a rank in the ops room when the Bravo-Bravo paid a visit to the base camp on the front line. The brigadier immediately wanted to know who he was and what he was doing in the tent. Lt. Lambert explained that the CO had cleared Charlie to be in the tent. The brigadier, obviously not satisfied with the answer, continued on with the discussion about ongoing operations. From that point on, Charlie's presence became a hot button during every visit. Finally the brigadier called the CO out about it. The battalion commander insisted that no private should be reading and handling classified information. It was not according to the book. He scolded the CO again and ordered Charlie to leave the tent. Charlie stood outside the tent and overheard the argument between the CO and his commanding officer.

"If you want to keep him, then do something about it," the brigadier said. "And do it quick! Military style quick," he hollered as he stormed out of the tent.

Major Kruger depended on Charlie. There was no way he would get rid of him. He made an executive decision and promoted Charlie to the rank of "candidate" officer. He instructed Lt. Lambert to complete the paperwork and obtain formal approval from the battalion headquarters to make Charlie an officer. This put Charlie in an awkward position since he was the only candidate officer on the base. He felt isolated from all of the other groups. He couldn't associate with officers or non-commanding officers or privates. He was on an island surrounded by people.

Fourteen days after Lt. Lambert submitted the paperwork, the authorization was received in a coded message. Charlie was cleared to handle classified military intelligence and immediately promoted to second lieutenant. Lt. Lambert had mixed feelings about it. Charlie was by far more effective and equipped to do his job. He felt threatened by Charlie's presence and made sure their schedule for duty didn't overlap. The time Charlie spent at the officer's training school, and the justification from Major Kruger, was enough to get Charlie the required level of clearance to remain in the ops-room. The new status and special treatment he received as an officer, suited him a lot better than floating between ranks. He met a few new officers and made some new friends. On Christmas day in 1973 he became friends with Keith James.

It was Christmas day and special meals were prepared for all soldiers on the frontline. Charlie sat inside the mess tent across from Sergeant Keith James, the NCO of the biker squad. The biker squad, followed by a support squad in an anti-landmine vehicle, roared out of the base every morning before sunrise. The V-shaped hull was supposed to increase the survivability of the occupants during an explosion from a landmine. The bikers had to "*sweep*" all roads between bases and declare the road safe for travel. They left early each morning from their home base, completed the patrol, and spent the night at the destination base. The next morning they would execute the same task but in the opposite direction. The two bikers in front scanned the road for any disturbance that could indicate a newly planted landmine. If anything out of the ordinary were noticed, the supporting squad would provide protection while the bikers would investigate up close.

They were trained sappers and responsible for neutralizing landmines, booby traps, or any of the improvised explosive devices the enemy used. If a disturbance in the road were a landmine, they would carefully remove it and detonate it on the side of the road. If it were booby trapped, they would detonate it from a safe distance. No military vehicles were allowed on the main roads until the bikers cleared them for travel. The local population knew they should stay off the roads until they saw military vehicles using the roads. That was their sign it was safe.

Something that should have been a routine task led to a tragedy that day. The daily foot patrol left the front gate to scout the perimeter of the camp. They came across the tracks of a group of twenty or more insurgents and radioed it in. Trackers were dispatched and they followed the trail that led south. They determined the general direction of the group and multiple squads were ordered to set up an ambush. The goal was to capture as many insurgents as possible. The CO wanted them alive. They needed a break-through and this was an opportunity to gather more intelligence.

The bikers already cleared the routes troops would use to advance to the ambush point. Sergeant Keith James had just returned after the daily trip and was having lunch with Charlie. They met recently after Charlie became an officer and was allowed into the officer's mess tent. They were from the same region back home, about the same age and size, and a natural friend-ship developed. They were discussing the ambush and what it would mean if they could capture some of the insurgents.

The table rattled and they felt the tremor caused by an explosion before they heard the sound. They both stopped eating, looked at each other, and then looked in the direction of the sound. A cloud of dust rose slowly into the air about four or five miles from the base camp. Everybody froze in place for a moment while silence engulfed the whole area. The dust floated away and dropped back to earth.

Life returned to the spectators in the base camp when somebody shouted with a load voice:

"Scramble! To your positions!"

The responses came immediately and everybody ran in different directions with a specific goal. Some ran for the trenches on the perimeter of the base camp. A siren started wailing and commands were issued in every direction. Order returned in an instant as soldiers reacted instinctively. The continuous drills performed everyday became second nature. Keith had turned as white as a ghost.

"Did we miss one?" he asked to nobody in particular.

Charlie got up and made his way to the ops room. A private came running towards him.

"Lt. O'Neal. The CO wants to see you on the double!" Fear was written all over his face.

"What's going on?" Charlie asked as they ran towards the ops room.

"I don't know. I was on guard duty outside the ops room. I think one of the vehicles on its way to the ambush hit a landmine. Somebody said the road wasn't cleared."

"What road were they on?" Sergeant James asked. He was now running with them.

"I don't know. But it was not on one of the main roads." The private replied.

"Did they have clearance for the road? Who gave it?"

"Lt. Lambert gave the clearance. Alpha asked for directions when they left base this morning." The guard was talking as fast as he could, trying to explain the situation before they got to the ops room. "They were dropping squad 'alpha-two-two'. They must have been on the wrong road. The CO is mad as hell. The 'ters' must have heard it also. The trackers radioed in and said they scattered in all directions and were running wild. They left all their weapons and got rid of their uniforms. They are in civilian clothes now. We will never get them."

Charlie stepped into the ops tent and observed the chaos inside. The radio operators were all talking at the same time. The CO was barking orders left and right. Lt. Lambert sat at a table with the cipher sheet and the coded reports in front of him. All protocol was abandoned as operators used native codes to confirm troop locations.

Something was wrong. Lt. Lambert didn't move and sat frozen on the bench at the table. He seemed to be in shock. Charlie made his way to the table. When he saw Charlie, he tried to speak, but no sound came from his mouth.

"What happened, Lambert?" Charlie asked.

"I don't know." Life slowly returned to Lt. Lambert. "There is the report from the bikers with the list of roads that were cleared this morning. Sergeant James dropped it off himself." He looked at Keith standing on the doorway of the tent. "This is the route they were supposed to take. We looked at the map together and confirmed the route. I coded it and gave it to the operator to transmit. They must have sent the wrong message. They went down route-74 and not route-82. They went east and not west. How did that happen?"

"Where's the message?" Charlie asked.

"Here," he said as he handed Charlie the message. Charlie looked at the cipher sheet and the messages. His heart rate spiked and his anxiety level peaked. He immediately knew what was wrong. He saw the face of Mr. Burns and heard his voice.

"An obvious mistake can be the difference between life and death," The words echoed through his mind.

"Did you calculate the shift this morning?"

"The shift?" Lt. Lambert asked with a withering voice. His eyes wide open staring at Charlie. Tears formed in his eyes when he realized what had happened and the mistake he had made.

They were young men captured in the bodies of soldiers, pawns in the war game between nations for a cause they barely understood. Charlie and Lt. Lambert were just a few months past their 18th birthdays. The rest of the people in the tent were about the same age. Only a handful of officers, career soldiers, were in their early twenties. Some of the higher-ranking officers, like the CO, were older. *"This is how messed up it is,"* he thought to himself.

"Yes. The shift. We calculate it every morning. Where is the shift?" Charlie asked.

"I...I forgot to change it." Lt. Lambert said with a shocked look on his face. He knew what the implications were.

"What!" Charlie shouted with a raised voice he seldom used. "You know what happens if you don't use the shift." The tent turned silent. The CO stopped mid-sentence, turned around and looked at Charlie.

"What's going on O'Neal?" he demanded with the authority of the officer responsible for the wellbeing of his soldiers.

"He coded the message without the shift factor. He sent Alpha Platoon on route-74. It should have been route-82. The shift factor for today is eight." Charlie explained it in simple terms to the CO.

"You mean, he screwed up?" the CO asked with a threatening voice while pointing to Lambert.

"Here is the message. The direction from the green road was to take route-82 and go west. Without the shift, it became route-74 and going east."

The CO took the message and cipher sheet from Charlie and looked at it. The rage he immediately felt inside was hard to control. His knuckles turned white as he crumpled the message and threw it at Lt. Lambert.

"Get out!" he shouted at Lambert, who scrambled for the door and left as quickly as he could.

The CO fell silent and nobody dared to breathe or move. He leaned on the table with his hands supporting. After a minute he looked at Charlie.

"How long was he in here today?"

"Since 06h00 this morning, Sir. I worked last night and he had the morning shift."

The major stood up and took command of the situation again.

"Get me a list of all the messages he sent and where he sent them," he instructed Charlie. He turned to an operator and gave the next order. "Cancel all pursuits. Tell everyone to hold their positions until further orders are given." He turned back to Charlie and looked at him.

"O'Neal! Fix this! Confirm the messages and make sure you use the correct shift before any more shit happens. Tell Lambert I want to see him in my tent in five." He turned around and exited the ops tent barking orders at officers to ready his Casspir vehicle and assemble a support squad to escort him to the site of the explosion.

Charlie sat down and got to work. Sergeant Keith James stood at the door watching. He saw how Charlie managed to shut out the world around him and focus on the task at hand. He sat down across from Charlie and followed his movements as he ciphered and deciphered messages. When he was done he gathered the messages, looked at Keith and with a nod, left the ops tent to report to the tent of the CO.

The driver of the vehicle and three soldiers lost their lives that Christmas Day. The insurgents headed south from Angola and crossed the border into Botswana. They knew the SADF would follow them, and planted landmines at multiple locations around the base. The landmine detonated by the buffalo vehicle, was double stacked to cause maximum damage. Multiple others were booby-trapped and throughout the day controlled detonations could be heard. No more lives were lost, but the insurgents managed to escape.

Lt. Lambert was sentenced to a fourteen-day detention and got stripped of his rank as officer. He was demoted to a NCO and never returned to the ops room again. After his detention period at the battalion headquarters in Rundu, he was transferred to a base far away from the combat zone. Charlie was promoted to Lieutenant first class and put in charge of the communications squads. He reported directly to the CO, Major Martin Kruger.

The experience they shared that day brought Charlie O'Neal and Keith James closer and they became best friends for life. They ended up at the same university and chose the same dormitory for three years. They had the same majors and chose the same subjects. They were inseparable and spent many hours together writing computer code. In their final year at university, they worked together on Project Alpha in remembrance of the soldiers of Platoon Alpha who lost their lives in the explosion. The phrase "Shit happens, when shift doesn't" had a new meaning for Charlie and Keith.

* * *

CHAPTER 14

Project Alpha

I t was their final year at the University of Pretoria, one of the most prestigious Universities in South Africa. As seniors in their dorm, they had first choice of single rooms and selected adjoining rooms. They shared the ups and downs of life with each other. They were both computer science majors, worked hard and made good grades. An unspoken competition developed between the two of them. Charlie won most of the time when it involved academics, but with social life, it was a different story. Keith was the initiator and nagged Charlie constantly to go out with him and have a life beyond school. It became a lot easier when Hanna got involved.

"How did the date go last night?" Keith asked Charlie on their way to the Science and Technology building for the early morning math lecture.

"Went ok," Charlie replied without looking at Keith. He kicked at an invisible rock in front of him. He felt embarrassed and didn't want to discuss the subject.

"Just ok?" Keith questioned Charlie's halfhearted response. "You and Hanna seem to be a perfect match. Why just ok? Did something happen?" He wanted more details about Charlie's first official *"date"* with Hanna. It was their first evening out where nobody else tagged along. Keith had to work hard on Charlie and plotted with his girlfriend, Marlene Adams, to set up the date with Hanna Shultz.

Charlie and Hanna met during their first year math course. Charlie majored in math and computer science and Hanna in math and physics. Charlie had admired the most beautiful girl in the class from a distance. Destiny intervened in their second semester. The class was divided into work groups for the practicums and they were placed in the same group. The workshops required them to be friendly towards each other and they worked together solving problems. They were both brilliant students, but had the same introverted personality types. Socialization outside class was awkward and difficult.

The friendship got elevated to more than a platonic relationship when Keith and Marlene became more serious in theirs. Keith dragged Charlie along on nights out with Marlene. Marlene invited some of her friends to tag along hoping to find a match for Charlie. It didn't work and Charlie was not interested. One day Keith suggested Marlene should invite Hanna. The whole atmosphere changed and Charlie became a different person. Needless to say, the four became best friends. They double dated and shared life on campus together. During school breaks when everyone went home to visit their family, Charlie could not wait for the next semester to start.

Although the friendship grew between Charlie and Hanna, he could never muster enough courage to ask her on a date where it would be only the two of them. The group outings continued for a while.

"I don't want to ruin a friendship," Charlie explained to Keith one evening after another group outing. They had dropped the girls off at their dormitory and were making their way back to their rooms. Keith had nagged Charlie constantly to take the friendship to the next level by asking her for a date.

"Nothing really happened. We just had a good time together. We ate dinner at the Spur and I dropped her off at her dormitory. Done it many times, so why should this be any different?"

"It was supposed to be a date Charlie! She is not your sister!" Keith said with frustration. "Did you hold hands?"

"Sort of," Charlie said with a red face, blushing with embarrassment when he recalled the events of the previous night. Since he had been a little boy, Charlie did not like to discuss his feelings and girls always made him feel inferior because of his age and size. He kept to himself and focused on his academic achievements.

"What do you mean, 'sort of'?" Keith stopped and caught Charlie by the arm. He wanted the full details. He would not let go of Charlie until he spilled it all out.

"Well, I did as you told me to do. I was playing with the car keys as we were walking from the car to the entrance. I then switched the keys to the other hand. I made sure I was walking close to her. When I dropped my hand that had the keys, it touched her hand and I just took it. It was weird man. But I did it." Charlie sounded excited when he eventually got to the point where he explained the event to Keith.

"What! What did she do? What was her reaction?"

"Nothing. She just looked at me, and smiled. But, she didn't let go of my hand. We walked like that to the door, and said goodnight."

"Come on Charlie! What happened at the door? Did you kiss her?"

"No! Are you crazy? It was the first time we held hands. You expect me to kiss her just because she didn't let go of my hand? I was not sure if I should do anything more so I just hugged her like we usually do and said good night."

"Man, you are ignorant." Keith was totally frustrated with Charlie's lack of action. "Do you not realize she likes you? Everybody knows it except you!"

"What do you mean everybody knows it?" Charlie gave Keith a puzzled look.

"Charlie!" Keith said. The tone in his voice made Charlie stop and look at

Keith as he continued with frustration in his voice. "Hanna is the best thing that will ever happen to you. She is beautiful, she is smart, she can pick and choose from a lot of guys on campus who would love to take her on a date. Man-oh-man, if we were not friends, I would have asked her out on a date myself. She only has eyes for you."

"How do you know that?"

"Marlene told me."

"Marlene? When?"

"Some time ago. Remember the rugby match? The four of us, and the dinner we had that night? Well, afterwards Hanna and Marlene had a long chat. You know they are best friends for a reason." Keith put his finger on his own chest and then pointed at Charlie. "Because of us."

"Oh." Charlie said sheepishly.

"Hanna opened up to Marlene. There were some tears involved. Hanna wasn't sure if you liked her or not. She wanted to know if she was wasting her time hoping that you would just say or do something."

"Why didn't she say something?"

"She doesn't want to make the first move. She believes that it's the man's responsibility. Why do you think I gave you all those tips? I know Hanna likes you. You just need to get over yourself and do something about it. Talk to her!" Keith said as he turned and started walking. "Let's go. Class is starting in a few."

The lecture dragged on. Charlie's thoughts were still with Hanna and the conversation with Keith. He was not paying attention to what the assistant had to say. The professor had assigned the boring tasks of explaining the guidelines for the final practical exam, to his assistant. It was their final year and the practicum had to be submitted by the end of the semester. It would count as one third of their grade. The rest of it would be from tests, attendance and the final exam. Charlie already knew all the facts and continued with his thoughts about Hanna.

"Am I really that blind?" he thought to himself. He liked Hanna. They spent a lot of time together as a group, but were seldom alone. Since their first year when they had a few classes together their friendship had evolved from inside the classroom to the outside world. It started when she held a seat for him next to her in a lecture hall. From then on they always held a seat for each other. Keith and Marlene seldom had classes together, and spent time together between classes. Charlie depended on Keith to help keep his friendship with Hanna going. Conversations were lighthearted and friendly and seldom veered to the serious part of life or feelings from the heart. Charlie found it easier to talk to Marlene than to Hanna. When he was alone with Hanna he was at a loss for words and felt dumb. He was concerned that he would say something that offended her. He didn't want to ruin their friendship. He was just not sure how to talk to her or how to express his feelings towards her.

Marlene, planning on a career as an elementary school teacher, was the most talkative one. The four spent a lot of time together. They frequently had lunch together on campus and attended social events in a group.

"It suddenly makes sense. Why did she not leave and find a better friend? Maybe she feels the same way as I do? I think I should ask her about it?" Charlie's thoughts stayed with Hanna, while the assistant continued his monolog.

On their way out of the lecture hall, Charlie turned to Keith and continued the conversation they had before class.

"I'm going to ask her if it's true." Charlie said to Keith.

"What?"

"What she told Marlene."

"No man, you can't do that! You can't let her know Marlene told me. You will ruin their friendship! And do you want Marlene to kill me? I wasn't supposed to tell you."

"So, how do I ask her then? What do I say?" Charlie had very little experience with dating and this was his first real girlfriend. High school went by without him ever dating a girl. His focus had been on making good grades and playing sports. There were some that he secretly liked, but he never got to the point of dating anyone.

"Wait for the right moment. When we are together again, I will disappear. Take her for coffee in the cafeteria and then you can talk to her. Just talk to her like we are talking now. Don't make it awkward. When the right moment is there, ask her what she thinks about last night and about holding her hand."

"Wow! Talk about not being awkward," Charlie replied. He was very unsure of himself and how to start the discussion.

"Different topic." Keith said. "Have you decided on a subject for the final practical project for the year?"

"Yes. I have an idea. You ok if we team up again this year? I kind of like the idea of a team project. Makes it easier to discuss details and get things done. As long as I don't have to do all the work."

"Yes, we can. If it wasn't for me, you would never have solved the problem last year."

"Yeah, right." Charlie said and laughed at Keith. "Whose fault is it that all the punch cards were dropped when I had to stack it into the card reader? And, who moved the memory position of the answer?"

It was the late seventies and computer science was still in its infancy at universities in South Africa. Programs were typed on punch cards and fed into a card reader. Job control cards were added at the beginning of the program and the mainframe computer would process the logic. The results were then printed on reams of continuous feed paper. Boxes and boxes of computer printouts were stacked all over. If you weren't available to retrieve your results when they were printed, you had to search through the piles of printouts. Many times it was a lost cause and it was better to just run the job again. The curriculum required students to learn multiple languages. Some was of no use in real life and others eventually became mainstream in the business world. The languages Charlie and Keith had to master included SAMOS, ASSEMBLER, FORTRAN and COBOL. They spent many hours in the basement of the science and technology building where the keypunch machines were located. Each card represented one line of computer code. The programs they wrote had thousands of lines of code and therefore thousands of cards. Boxes full of cards were stacked in the room until the code was completed. To execute the program, they had to carry the boxes up the stairs to the card reader in the computer room. Somebody came up with the smart idea of using a colored pen to mark the cards on the top, as they were stacked in a box. Charlie and Keith discovered the importance of the markings early on. Charlie dropped a box full of punch cards and it took them hours to put the cards in the correct order again. From then on they drew all kinds of patterns on the cards. During the final exam their junior year, Keith dropped a box and the pattern help him to arrange the cards within a few minutes. They still managed to get the assignment completed in the allotted time.

The project for the final exam the previous year was to write an ASSMEBLER program, retrieve a specific phrase and decode it. The professor wrote a program and hid the phrase somewhere in the mainframe memory. He provided some clues to where the phrase was located. Memory space was limited at the time and the critical component in the logic was to write an algorithm that would utilize memory space efficiently before running out. In the process, Charlie and Keith made an error. Although they found the location of the phrase, it would not print. Unknown to everybody, including the professor, most of the programs were correct, but the phrase was not in the specific memory position anymore. When the professor eventually discovered the error, the reserved mainframe time was running out fast. He had to reset the system and rerun his initialization process. When it happened the second time Charlie and Keith ran their program, they ran out of time and the exam could not be completed. The professor gave everybody a passing grade for effort, and took the program Charlie and Keith used to analyze the problem. A few days later he explained to the class what had happened.

The program Charlie and Keith submitted had an infinite loop and a logical error. Instead of reading the memory positions, the program wrote the character to memory instead of printing. In the process, they filled all available system memory and when the logic reached the position of the hidden phrase, there was not enough memory available to continue. A lesson learned by everyone on how not to fill system memory. Charlie and Keith were happy to take credit for the innovative way to make sure everyone passed the exam.

"So, what is your idea?" Keith asked Charlie. "What futuristic ideas do you have for this semester?"

"I have a calculation procedure I want to research. What is the impact of rounding on interest calculations?"

"What?" Keith said with shocked and disbelief. "You want to do what?"

"Let me explain," Charlie started.

"You know I worked at a bank before I went into the military. That same bank gave me the scholarship, and when I graduate, I'm going back to work for them."

"Yes. At least you have a job lined up. I still need to find one."

"You will get one. There are lots of jobs for programmers out there."

"Yeah, right." Keith said sarcastically.

"Anyway," Charlie continued with the story he started. "Mr. Kramer, the bank manager, had a way to balance the books. When he did the interest calculations, he would truncate the result at two decimals. He never rounded up or down. To balance the books, he calculated the interest on the sum of all the accounts. He then used a creative method to post the difference between the total of the individual interest and the check total, to a discretionary expense account. The only problem is, there was more money in the account than I thought there should be. I did my own calculations and I'm sure he either made a mistake or he had something else going on to have so much money in that account."

"And why should I care about this?" Keith interrupted Charlie's explanation of the calculations.

"We have to find a subject for our project. I want to create a function routine that will show what the difference is between rounding up, rounding down and truncating when doing interest calculations. My theory is, that if you round every time to the nearest penny, it would even out over time. Only a small difference will remain if you compare the sum of the interest of individual accounts to the interest calculate on the sum of all accounts."

"That's just math. That will not meet the criteria for the project." Keith didn't really understand yet what Charlie's intentions were.

"I know, but we can spruce it up with some additional functionality to meet the criteria. This can be the foundation for something to develop in the future. Maybe we can sell the logic to a Tech Company to embed it in their operating system. It will look good on our resumés one day if we can get somebody to buy into the idea."

"And what is in it for me?"

"It's our project. We are in this together, and we share whatever we get from it."

"You believe we can make something out of it?" Keith was not yet convinced with Charlie's idea.

"We could, but I don't exactly know how yet."

"How?"

"Let say we develop a rounding function that can be called on demand. We feed it a list of accounts and it calculates the interest for each account. It keeps a running total of the fractions lost and calculates a check sum.

An auditor would love to have something like this. The sum of the interest for each account needs to match the interest calculated on the sum of all the balances added up. In theory it should be a small difference. From experience I know it will never balance one hundred percent. The only way to balance the calculations is to use a contra account. At the bank I worked at, we posted the difference from the interest calculations to a contra account and the books seemed to be in balance."

"So if you don't round, but truncate, your theory is the difference will be bigger?" Keith tried to keep up with Charlie's argument.

"Yes! Exactly. Mr. Kramer used the discretionary expense account for this. If you truncate, it will not even be a penny difference. The clients will not notice a small rounding error. I have never heard anybody query the method Mr. Kramer used, except my dad. He checked the calculations every month. I tell you, there was a lot of money in that account."

"Is that not stealing from the client?" Keith asked skeptical.

"Well, I thought about it a lot, and I'm not sure. What is really being stolen? Can you show me one tenth of a penny? It's basic fifth grade arithmetic, and it's only a fraction of a penny. Do you ever verify the interest calculation on your bank statements?"

"But if you add it up, it is more than a penny?"

The conversation continued for a while. The arguments and theory about the calculations became deeper and more complex. Eventually they both decided to take on the idea as the subject for the project to prove who was right and who was wrong.

"Let's name our project." Keith said. They both thought for a few moments, threw around different names, and couldn't find one that sounded just right.

"How about Project Alpha?" Charlie said.

"Alpha? Why Alpha?"

"Remember the Caprivi? The guys from Alpha Company who died in the landmine explosion? This project will be a reminder that a simple mistake can kill somebody. When shift doesn't happen..." Charlie didn't complete his sentence, but they both knew what the results were.

"Yes. Bad things will happen. I don't know, man, it's creepy, and it's a bad memory."

"Let's just say this is the first of many projects we will do together. We start with Alpha, and then Bravo and we go through to Zulu. We can call it - Project Alpha: The Theory of Rounding and the Impact in the Banking Sector. By OJ - O'Neal & James."

"Ha-ha...Very funny." Keith didn't seem impressed, but didn't have any alternative suggestions.

Project Alpha proved to be more difficult than anticipated. Charlie and Keith spent many hours to get the idea working and meet the criteria as specified by the professor. They started with a small number of accounts in their list. They had to manually check all calculations, and it took time. Over and over they did the math to confirm the results. Keith was the first one to get bored and would find an excuse to go do something else. Charlie spent many hours checking the results on his own.

Keith was the one who came up with the wild idea that changed the direction of the project. Charlie and Keith were on the squash court. They were very competitive and evenly matched. A game frequently stretched over the allowed time they could be on a court. Charlie played tennis for the varsity team. Keith grew up playing badminton, and was also on the varsity team. They both learned to play squash at university. It was an unfair match whenever they played badminton or tennis, so squash became the equalizer. They both had to adjust their style when playing. The casual games became a serious competition over time. Charlie had a slight advantage over Keith since he was the taller one. The height disadvantage he had experienced during his teenage years disappeared when he hit a growth spurt in the military. The extreme and strenuous exercises he was exposed to, combined with the genes from his dad who was over six foot tall, contributed to his growth. Charlie was close to six foot, and Keith was a good three inches shorter. Keith was the faster and more agile one on the court, but Charlie had the longer reach. The competition stayed healthy, and on court arguments and squabbling over points were left on the court.

"I got it!" Keith said in the middle of a game.

"No. You missed it. It was out of bounds. My point." Charlie said as he reached to pick up the ball and serve for the next point.

"No. Not the game. Project Alpha!"

"What?" Charlie was totally surprised by this sudden change in focus as it was very unlike Keith to think about an academic subject while on the court. They were too competitive to think about anything else during a game.

"We need to shift."

"Shift?" Charlie asked totally confused.

"Yes. How many clients did your bank have?"

"Maybe a few thousand at the branch, but millions nationally. It is one of the big three."

"Exactly. We have been using small numbers. The calculations are too small. Let's shift to bigger numbers. If you combine the total number of clients for the big three, how many clients will there be?

"Well, I'm not sure. Anglo is not as big as Barclays, and Barclays has ties to the UK. If you consider only the local branches, it can be a few a million."

"Hey! Are you done?" Somebody knocked on the glass of the back wall of the court. Charlie and Keith were standing in the middle of the court talking. Their time had run out.

Charlie and Keith left the court and continued the discussion on their way to the locker room. The game was forgotten and the new topic occupied their thoughts.

A few days later Charlie and Keith studied the results of the calculations after they made some changes to the logic in the program.

"You see, I told you." Keith said and pointed at the bottom page. "If you have a million accounts, and you perform the calculations with the truncation daily, the balance in the contra account is increased from a few hundred to a few thousand."

"One million accounts, and the balance increase with five thousand per month. Sounds impossible."

"It's not. It's simple. Remember, when you shift the decimal one position, the average truncated per account becomes half of a penny. What is half a penny added a million times? Shift the decimal and see. Five thousand. Like you said, fifth grade arithmetic."

"Wow. Do it for ten years every month, and you have a few hundred thousand. Add interest and you can earn even more."

"Exactly!" Keith leaned back with satisfaction that he was able to figure this one out.

"But I still don't understand." Charlie said with a puzzled look on his face.

"You don't understand what?" Keith looked even more puzzled. "This is basic math."

"The branch where I worked at only had a few thousand clients. Let's say there were seven or eight thousand clients. And, I'm stretching it now. That would give thirty-five bucks per month. How did he get the account to over twenty thousand? They had a wild party the year before I joined the bank, and that must have cost a pretty penny. Where did he get the rest of the money?"

"Who?" Keith asked.

"Mr. Kramer. The bank manager I told you about."

"Oh, him. Maybe he had another scheme going on. This can be huge. If somebody finds a way to implement this, they can make a lot of money from it. The only thing is, there is no way they will get away with it."

"Well, at least we can dream about it."

Project Alpha was in process. The rest of the semester they refined the logic and results before finally submitting their paper. They developed different function modules that could be used to round up, round down, truncate, calculate interest on a loan over a period of time, calculate interest earned over time, and one that compared the different methods of rounding. Some of the function modules developed during Project Alpha they later embedded in applications in their future careers. Most of it though got forgotten, until it became time to start with Project Bravo.

Charlie took the advice from Keith and took Hanna on a second date. They had a heart to heart talk about where their relationship was going. The icebreaker was when they discovered how they were both too afraid to make the first move. They laughed about it and talked about all the good times they missed out on. One evening after a dinner and a movie, Charlie dropped Hanna off at her dormitory. There were only a few minutes left before the final call would be made and the doors locked at her curfew time. When they said good night, Charlie leaned forward and kissed Hanna for the first time. He would never forget the night of the 7th of July 1977.

* * *

CHAPTER 15

Sharky

C harlie's career as a software programmer started at Anglo Bank. It was the late seventies, and financial institutions led the way in acquiring customers with promises of the latest and greatest in modern technology. Enabling the technologies required skills and people. The investment Anglo Bank made into Charlie's education, paid off. To ensure Charlie would not be lured away by competitors, and to tighten the golden handcuffs even more, they offered to pay for his relocation and the first month's rent. Charlie gladly accepted the offer and moved into a nicely furnished two-bedroom apartment located in the midtown district of Pretoria. The apartment was conveniently located and close to a new shopping center. The city bus route was a block away from his apartment and he took it to work. The bus stopped only a few feet from the front door of his new employer. Bus fares were cheap and subsidized for employees of Anglo Bank. He used the time stuck in gridlock traffic to read and daydream about his future with Hanna.

Their relationship had grown into more than a casual friendship. They were planning a long life together. Charlie secretly plotted to surprise her with a small diamond ring and ask her to get married. Unfortunately for Charlie it got thrown off track only a few weeks after Hanna started her new job. They were out for dinner when Hanna broke the news.

"Charlie," she said with uncertainty. "There is something we need to talk about." Charlie's heart skipped a beat or two. He looked at her and immediately realized something was wrong.

"Who died?" was the only thing that he could think of that would cause her to be so upset.

"Nobody," she said with a smile. "But, I have to go away for a while."

Charlie closed his eyes and dropped his chin on his chest. He didn't want her to see how close he was to tears. The day he feared had arrived.

"You made your decision?" he whispered.

"Yes." When he looked at her, tears were streaming down her cheeks. He reached over and touched her hand.

"It will be OK. It's only two years." He tried to comfort her, but inside he was fighting to keep his tears back.

In her final year of studies, a representative of the South African government approached Hanna. The government was in the process of expanding the nuclear power grid and offered her a lucrative scholarship and the promise of a full time position at the Nuclear Power Research Center upon completion of her studies. The only problem was, it would require her to move to London. The scholarship to complete her Ph.D. in nuclear physics was at a prestigious university in the UK. It was a very difficult decision for Hanna. Charlie's initial selfish thoughts about the impact on his life soon changed and he became the supportive friend who helped her work through the choice and make the correct decision for her career.

The NPRC facility was located on the east side of the city. When they went apartment hunting for Charlie together, they found one between his workplace and Hanna's future employer. They promised each other to stay faithful while she was abroad.

Hanna was the one who brought up marriage first. She told Charlie they could consider the next step after her first year of study. If their long distance relationship survived the first year, she told Charlie, it could survive a lifetime.

His attempts to join her and complete his master's degree in computer science failed at the first call he made. Anglo Bank was not interested in his proposition and would not let him out of his contract or put it on hold. There was no way out for Charlie. He wouldn't be able to repay the full amount he owed the bank for the salary he received during his military service. If he could not repay it, his Dad would be on the hook for it. The lucrative scholarship he had received to complete his degree was in the tens of thousand and he had no money to pay for it. He had no choice but to accept the offer from Anglo Bank as a programmer in their centralized IT department in Pretoria. At least he didn't have to go back to the life in the rural areas and small mining communities where his parents lived.

Hanna's departure for the UK was full of tears and more promises were made. Her family was also there to say goodbye. She clung to Charlie's side and regretted her decision many times. Charlie was the one who reminded her of how the time would pass quickly since they would both be very busy building the foundation for their future together. He promised to save a lot, live frugally and visit her in London. Her scholarship included two round trips a year to see family and they looked forward to her first visits.

Loneliness was soon replaced with the hectic life of a programmer exposed to new technology. Charlie spent his first day at the bank mostly with the HR department. There was a stack of paperwork to complete, and he signed multiple contracts that enslaved him for a lifetime with his employer. To completely scare the daylights out of him, the final contract was to confirm the total outstanding balance he owed the bank. The golden handcuffs were slammed on him for at least four years of his life. His new manager, Sebastian Prince, gave Charlie the grand tour of the IT department. He introduced him to the Application Development team, and showed him the pride of the IT department. Like so many other visitors,

Charlie was impressed.

"Let me introduce you to 'Softy'," SP said as they stood in front of the window of the new server room. "This is the best of the best - state of the art future technology. I came up with the cute name," he said and joined Charlie in captivity of the blinking lights of the routers, switches and modems.

"Impressive!" was all Charlie could say.

The entrance to the server room was strictly controlled with a secure keypad. The big windows were to monitor users inside the room, and for visitors to stare at the blinking lights. For some reason the blinking lights fascinated people, and only a few managed to walk by without looking twice at the server room. Charlie was more interested in what was under the hood. Access control was enforced to maintain the optimal room temperature for the servers. The building was old and didn't have a central heating and air system. Executive offices had the luxury of a wall mounted air conditioning unit, while the regular office for employees lower in the pecking order, only had a small noisy window unit. That was, if a room did have a window. In the summer months, programmers would use any excuse to work in the server room. Access was very quickly restricted to only allow users with a valid reason to be in the room.

Charlie was assigned to a project team halfway into the development of a new interface for the electronic fund transfers between banks. The team occupied the eighth floor, and offices were shared between two, and depending on the size of the room, sometimes four programmers. The number of computers cramped into the small offices only enhanced the continued air conditioning problem.

Charlie soon discovered the best time to work was after hours when nobody else was working. With fewer machines running in the room and with an open window, the heat could be tolerated longer. He also discovered the response time was much better when everybody else left to enjoy the city life. With Hanna far away, Charlie had no desire to hang out with co-workers after hours. Being single and new to the department, he soon discovered the perks of working late. It became a habit and he enjoyed the quiet atmosphere with the cooler air at night. Charlie focused on his new job and like a sponge absorbed everything he could learn. He drowned his thoughts about Hanna with knowledge, and became good at what he did.

Charlie and Keith's friendship continued after graduation. When they said goodbye to Hanna at the airport, Marlene promised Hanna to take care of Charlie. Keith and Marlene got married after graduation, and Marlene stayed in school for another year to complete her master's degree in education. Keith on the other hand was lucky to get a junior programmer position at one of the big petro-chemical companies. They interviewed many graduates from the University and Keith was one of ten to join the company. Their IT department was located in the city and Keith and Marlene settled in one of the suburbs close enough for Charlie to spend many weekends with the newlyweds.

Work was frequently discussed and Charlie helped his friend overcome his first disappointment. The team Keith was assigned to was challenged with a huge project to develop a newly planned maintenance system. The ultimate goal was to reduce the total amount of time for the annual shutdown and to monitor expenses during the busiest time of the year. With the production on hold, no cost was spared to perform preventative maintenance in the shortest possible time and get the production process up and running again. Management knew from experience that short cuts were rampant and costs were excessive. A lot of resources and money were thrown at the new IT project that would save the day. The system engineers completed the blueprint phase based on the scope defined by the business. The estimated cost and time to complete the project far exceeded expectations, and the business was sent back to the drawing board to redefine the scope. With no clearly defined system to develop, a bunch of programmers were suddenly looking for a new job. Keith was one of them. Some joined

Anglo Bank and worked with Charlie. Keith was without a job for a couple of weeks before he landed a job with one of the other leading banks in the country. Keith joined the Bank of South Africa, a competitor of Anglo Bank where Charlie worked. BOSA also had in their cross hairs, the long-term benefits an interface for interbank fund transfers would bring. The interface became a frequent topic of discussion when Charlie visited with Keith and Marlene.

Keith used his housing benefit at BOSA to purchase a small three-bedroom home located in one of the affluent eastern suburbs of Pretoria. Charlie helped them move into their new home and observed the excitement on Marlene's face. It was painful at times when he thought about Hanna and how she would have enjoyed helping with the unpacking. Marlene was the one who brought up the subject of being neighbors, and together they dreamed of the day when Hanna would return and they could live next door, or at least in the same neighborhood.

Discussions over weekend visits normally started with current events around rugby and the standing of the local team in the league. At some point, it progressed to work and projects they were involved in. The continuous competition between the two friends was always looming in the background. A big technology race between the financial institutions was underway and Charlie and Keith were on opposing sides. The goal was become the host of the Interbank Clearing Bureau. The ICB, as the programmers referred to the service, was the pot of gold at the end of the rainbow for the winner. Project managers were made aware of the long-term benefits, and frequently reminded their teams about it. Their futures depended on the outcome of the service. The bank in control of the ICB would also control of the pot of gold. The only goal was to be the first bank to implement the service. In the process key controls were overlooked. Overworked and tired programmers got sloppy and careless. Checks and balances were put in place, but were seldom verified to be one hundred percent accurate. Small

149

issues were sidelined and put on a list of topics to be addressed after the first implementation. Progress towards the goal was the only focus point.

The ICB would fill their pot of gold with transaction fees, a small fee charged for handling the millions of transactions between banks. The ICB would be responsible for the daily reconciliation of the interbank clearing accounts. They would control the settlement process between banks and saw it as just another reason to slap a fee onto the competition.

The process was supposed to be simple. Individual transactions would be accumulated by the ICB, and sent in batches to different banks. Cash settlements between banks would be based on the total net value of the clearing account. The account balance was based on the net daily transactions performed between participating parties. It all sounded logical when discussed in the boardrooms of financial institutions. The system architects at each bank thought their ideas were brilliant. The programmers in dungeons and basements had to do the legwork. They spent long hours trying to make sense of the complex design and figure out the complexities required to make the ideas actually work.

Anglo Bank won the race with their concept of the Bank Interchange Transaction System - BITS. The system was put into place and the pilot implementation lasted one month. As expected there were some initial problems, and programmers had to spend more hours to fix the list of items sidelined during the initial build phase.

Charlie was not spared the long hours. He spent many weekends at the office. Eventually he had bragging rights and as promised, Keith had to bear the cost to celebrate the success of Charlie's team.

"Well," Keith said and lifted his glass of wine. "To the winner!" They clicked glasses and Charlie said "Cheers."

"What's your next project?" Charlie asked.

"I'm not sure. Now that the race is over, there are talks about downsizing and we are all nervous. The slackers during the project will be the first to go.

I think I will be ok. My manager already asked if I would be willing to help with an interface to re-balance the ins-and-outs from the ICB. He has a plan to save the bank some costs. We will start writing specs for the new design in a few weeks."

"That sounds great. I'm glad you didn't get cut again," Charlie said as he sipped on his wine.

"Yes, and hopefully my position will be safe this time." Charlie looked at Keith and noticed that he was not very excited and it seemed like he had something else on his mind.

"What's wrong?" Charlie asked.

"I'm not sure. I discovered something that doesn't make sense to me."

"What? Explain. Maybe I can help. After all we did win."

"I'm not supposed to share this with the owners of the ICB you know."

"Hey, we are friends and this is between us. You can trust me."

"Promise?"

"Wow, this is serious." Charlie was not used to Keith being secretive about anything. Keith was the happy one, the risk taker, the biker and the one who always spoke his mind. You always knew where you stood with him. This was unusual.

"Ok, you promised. You remember Project Alpha? The calculations and the bank manager you talked about?"

"Yes, Mr. Kramer." Charlie was caught of guard when Keith brought up his manger at the bank he worked at many years ago. "The truncating during interest calculations and the managers discretionary expense account."

"Yes. I think it is still going on, but at a different level."

"What do you mean, 'at a different level'?"

"Well, I may be wrong," Keith said and hesitated for a moment, "but then again, I may be right. I think I know how the account balance became so high."

Charlie stared at Keith. He could feel his breathing change, and his stomach turn, but tried to brush the feeling aside.

"What? How?" Charlie asked perplexed.

"When we did Alpha, where did we truncate the calculations?"

"After the second decimal."

"Ok, and what would happen if we shifted the truncation to the first decimal?"

"You cannot do that! That's cheating."

"Oh, and half a penny is not?" Keith said sarcastically and laughed at Charlie.

"You cannot show me half a penny, but I can show you five pennies," Charlie responded with the same answer he used before. "If you shift the decimal, the average becomes five pennies and not half a penny."

"Exactly my point. Let me show you." Keith got up, grabbed a pen and paper and started writing some numbers on it. "If you have 100,000 x 0.005 = 500. Correct?"

"Yes."

"Now shift the decimal one position. It becomes 100,000 x 0.05 = 5,000. Five thousand. It increases ten fold."

"Yes, but that would be way too obvious. How can interest calculations always end on zero? Let me show you." Charlie took the pen and paper from Keith and scribbled his own calculations.

"You see," he said. "Somebody would soon notice and then you or me or some programmer would have to debug and fix it. You know the auditors; they don't miss a thing."

"Yes, that is true, and that is why I'm not so sure. I debugged a program the other day and found this out of place rounding function. I think we played enough with rounding during project Alpha for me to know what I'm looking at. Most of the time, the rounding worked fine but then at random, the last digit became zero. That's when I went back to our roots and used a trace table to check my results. I knew something was wrong, but couldn't figure it out. Whoever did it had a shift problem and the decimal was put in the wrong place. A simple mistake you would think, but here comes the funny part. There are two versions of the same program embedded in the source code. The version of the code in the test system and the version running in production, are not the same. Somebody is planning something."

"Ok, and how does this translate to Mr. Kramer?" Charlie was still trying to find out how Mr. Kramer managed to accumulate so much money in the manager's account.

"Don't you see?" Keith sounded excited that for once he could explain something to Charlie. "They already shifted the decimal way back before computers were used. If you do the shift randomly, nobody will notice. When you did the calculations for Mr. Kramer and when we did it on Project Alpha, we never thought about shifting the decimal on the interest. Our focus was on the number of clients. That's why the total stayed small and we could never get to the number Mr. Kramer had in his account. It's simple - shift didn't happen." Keith smiled at Charlie and said: "Remember that? What did you always say?"

"If shift doesn't happen, something else will happen."

"Exactly! We didn't shift the decimal and nothing happened." He tapped on the piece of paper and said, "This guy is randomly moving the decimal to truncate and in the process increasing the pennies tenfold. It all depends on how often the shift happens. If you use a small random factor, the shift happens more frequently. With a larger random factor, the shift happens less frequently. If you do it all the time, it becomes too risky and somebody will soon notice the anomaly."

"So, what are you going to do about it? Fix it?"

"No." Keith said and hesitated. "I want to find out more. I'm going to monitor this and see if I can follow the pennies. I want to find out how they balance the totals. That is what project Alpha was about. If somebody is skimming the pennies, I want to find the account where it is deposited and then I want to find out who is in charge of the account. Maybe I'm wrong, but I would like to know."

"It certainly sounds fishy, but it's not that easy. You know how long we battled to get Alpha done. This is at a different level and real life. I don't think it will be that easy." Charlie did not share Keith's excitement.

"If you are smart enough, it can be done. We were so busy during the race for control of the ICB, not all of the checks-and-balances were put in place. Ask me. I know. I also missed some controls. After BOSA had to relinquish control of ICB to Anglo Bank, we spent some long nights getting the new system in place. We were tired and just wanted to get it done."

"Punishment for the loser." Charlie rubbed in his victory. "Maybe there is a logical explanation for it. Let me know what you find." Charlie sat back and thought about what he heard. If this were true, he really wanted to know more. It just sounded too simple and Mr. Kramer would not have cheated.

"Oh, one more thing," Keith continued. "A different topic. Why are you guys charging such a high transaction fee for debit orders?"

"Fees are regulated and were agreed on by all parties. It's a fixed fee per transaction. We have to make some money, you know? We worked hard and we won the race. Everybody knew ICB was where the money would go. That's why they call it a good return on investment - basic ROI principles. We like our cake with icing, lots of icing on top." Charlie laughed and looked at Keith. While the ICB race was going on, they had each taken it personally. They knew the winner would have lifelong bragging rights.

"Yes, but I need to pay my bills, you know. I noticed on my bank statement this month the fee for my debit orders increased one buck again. All of my insurance is paid by debit order and the bank charges me a fee for each one."

"The good old debit order," Charlie said. "I still remember the days when they came in every month. They were sorted and divided between the data typists. They had a race every time to see who was the fastest. Those ladies were unbelievably quick on the keys. I tell you, it was intense while they were doing the debit orders. Computers have replaced them now, and programmers sit back and drink wine while the machines do the job. I wonder what happened to all of them?"

"Yes, and I have to pay for your wine," Keith continued. "With all of the debit orders, it adds up to a pretty penny out of my pocket every month."

"How much is your fee? I cannot remember if mine increased."

"It was seven bucks last month, and this month it is eight Rand per transaction. I have quite a few debit orders, so I noticed the change this month. We should call the ICB 'Sharky', a bunch of sharks ripping off the other banks. They've got some really sharp teeth and my bank just passes the increase right on to the client. What are you guys doing with all that money?"

"I haven't received my statement yet. I will check it and let you know what I pay. I work for the sharks you know, so maybe I get a discount."

Marlene walked in with some dessert and coffee on a tray. Keith got up, took the tray from her and waited for her to be seated before he held the tray out for her to take her coffee and dessert. He walked over to Charlie and held the tray to him.

"Have you hear anything from Hanna?" Marlene asked.

"Yes, I got a letter from her a last week and I replied the same day. I should have one back soon."

"How is she doing?"

"Seems the professor she is working with is really good. She is working hard, but didn't expand on what she really does. Just said it's a lot of new stuff she has to learn. She wants to know when I plan to visit her. She wants to show me London."

"And? Are you planning to go?"

"Well, the tickets are a bit expensive." Charlie said with disappointment on his face. "I need to save more. Maybe I will go in the winter and experience the summer there. Hanna said the winter in London is cold and miserable. Why don't you two join me? Make it a second honeymoon for you," he said with a smile.

"That would be great," Marlene sounded excited about the idea. "What do you think, Keith? Would you like to see London?"

"Like he said, tickets are expensive," Keith objected. "We also need to save more before we can go. If the sharks would just stop increasing the fees, maybe we could afford it." The stab at Charlie's employer was lighthearted and they laughed about it. Charlie realized how the small increase in the fees affected Keith and Marlene.

The conversation continued and they talked about Hanna, the future, daily life and the upcoming cricket test series against England. Life was good and they were enjoying it, not knowing that it would soon change dramatically.

It was almost midnight when Charlie left Keith and Marlene's home. They had enjoyed another glass of wine together. Keith knew better than to try and get Charlie to have more than two glasses and understood the reason for his decision.

This day was no exception. He stayed until the extra cup of coffee and dessert cleared the effects of the wine. When he arrived home and opened the door to his apartment, he felt bad about the condition it was in. He thought about the clean house he had just left, and realized the difference the touch of a lady made. He saw the picture of Hanna on his nightstand and was sad. He longed to be with her and talk to her. He fell asleep thinking about her and the life they planned together.

Charlie woke up mid-morning and saw the time on the alarm clock. He realized it was too late for church and made some breakfast. While sipping on his coffee, he looked at the stack of dirty dishes in the sink. He looked around and saw the overflowing trashcan and realized he had not cleaned the place in a while.

"This place is a mess. I wonder what Hanna would say if she saw it?" Charlie said to himself as he got up and started to clean. He was normally well or-

ganized and kept his place neat and in order. The long hours he worked the last few months to complete the implementation of REAL-TIME, had taken its toll. He got into the habit of leaving dirty dishes in the sink until he ran out of clean stuff to use. Then he would just clean it all at once. Every time it happened he resolved to not let it happen again. When Keith and Marlene paid him a surprise visit one day, he had to quickly think of an excuse for the pile of dishes in the sink.

"There is a drought somewhere," he said trying to hide the embarrassment with a joke. "I cannot waste water and wash dishes every day. I only do it once a week and do my share to save water."

"I wonder what Hanna would say?" Marlene had commented, making Charlie feel even guiltier.

"If you tell her, we are not friends anymore," Charlie replied. "She doesn't know about my dark side."

"Seems like somebody's habits got to you," she said and looked accusingly at Keith. Keith was the disorganized one, and when he and Charlie shared rooms at university, you could clearly see which side was Charlie's and which side was Keith's. Charlie had a touch of OCD while Keith just wanted to have a good time.

"As long as everybody is happy, everything is fine," Keith said and kissed Marlene on the cheek. They were still very much in love and Charlie missed Hanna more every time he saw how happy they were. He was grateful for their friendship and how they took care of him while Hanna was away.

After cleaning the house, he looked around with a feeling of satisfaction. It was past lunchtime and he decided to have an early supper somewhere else. He didn't want to make a mess again and also needed to stop at the grocery store.

On his way back home, he went by the post office to collect his mail. He ran up the stairs and retrieved it from his mailbox. He normally stopped by once a week to pick up his mail, but when he expected a letter from Hanna, he stopped by more often. He scanned through the pile of envelopes. The normal bills, junk mail, bank statement, some more junk mail, a letter from his insurance company, a finance magazine he subscribed to, the monthly newsletter from church and finally a letter with a familiar handwriting. He smiled at it, smelled it and then kissed the letter. He could not wait to read it. He wanted to sit back comfortably when doing so. He knew he would read it a few times and then he would start with his reply.

He walked to the shelf against the wall at the window and sorted his mail. Things were frequently sorted incorrectly and there was a slot in the wall with an overhead sign that read, "Incorrectly Sorted Mail ONLY". He had no incorrectly sorted mail and moved on discarding the junk mail. He glanced over it and then dropped it in the trash. He opened his bank statement and looked at the balance. He was saving for his trip to visit Hanna, and the balance was going in the right direction. He scanned the transactions and noticed the ICB transaction fee. He remembered the conversation with Keith and smiled. *"Six bucks. Well, at least my fee stayed the same."* He gathered his mail and left, eager to get home.

Charlie sat down in his living room and read the letter from Hanna. She wrote briefly about her classes, other students, and the professor she studied under. She was excited about the places she had visited and listed all the places she wanted to show him. She explained the underground train system and how easy it was to get from one place to another. Closer to the end, she had a long list of questions he would answer in his response to her. She asked about his work and about Keith and Marlene. After reading the letter a couple of times, he went and sat down at the kitchen table to respond to her. He thought about just typing a letter and printing it, but he remembered how disappointed she was when he did it previously. She said writing by hand made it a lot more personal. He took his time thinking about his response and started his letter to Hanna.

Charlie's work routine returned to a normal. The long list of items sidelined during the rush to implement the ICB system still had to be addressed. One of the priority issues on his list was a problem with the ICB interface. After a few hours he came across a piece of code that handled the transaction fees. He thought about the conversation with Keith, and decided to analyze the source code to determine how fees were calculated. He noted the database tables referenced where the rates were stored. He looked at the current rate being charged as a transaction fee. He still thought it was a nice benefit to have a reduced fee. He wrote a simple statement and queried the table. He looked at the numbers and was puzzled by what he saw. *"That's odd,"* he thought. *"The rates are the same for all banks. It's six bucks for all debit orders. I'm not getting any discount. But, why is Keith being charged eight bucks? We are not charging his bank eight bucks. That's unfair!"*

"We are not the sharks!" He said out loud.

"Did you say something Charlie?" a voice asked from across the room asked.

"No. Just talking to myself. Sorry." Charlie apologized to the person sharing the office with him.

The difference bothered Charlie, and the hunt began to find the reason for the additional charges. The real problem he was supposed to work on, completely forgotten. He wanted more details and analyzed the transmission logs and transaction history. He wrote a few queries and traced the transaction fee history. The increased transaction fee came into effect at the same time the ICB was established. Before the ICB, fees stayed the same for long periods of time and seldom changed. Increases only happened a few times and customers would always complain.

"They used the ICB as an excuse to raise the fees," Charlie thought to himself. The new fee started when they switched over from a manual process to the new system. The fee in the system was the same as the charge on his

statement.

"His bank must be loading the fee." He printed a copy of the page and stuck it in his bag. He would show it to Keith when they saw each other again.

A few days later, Keith had a meeting close to Anglo Bank. He called Charlie and they made arrangement to have lunch together. Charlie asked for an extended lunch and SP had no objections. He knew the long hours Charlie had worked during the ICB implementation.

Charlie and Keith met at a small sandwich and coffee shop not far from Anglo Bank. They placed their orders and while they waited for the food, the conversation went from family, to sports and life, and eventually to work. They talked about the different projects they were involved in and speculated about the future trends in the technology industry. Although they were working for competing banks, as friends they trusted each other. Confidential information may have been shared and discussed accidentally, but they never crossed the line on purpose. The discussion came back to the transaction fees for the debit orders.

"I looked at the transaction fees," Charlie said between bites of the steak, egg and mushroom burger he ordered. "The fees are still the same they were when the ICB was launched. My fee didn't increase. The sad thing is, I'm not getting any discount from Anglo Bank. I pay six bucks for each debit order. I don't know why your bank is charging you eight bucks."

"Well, I did some digging of my own," Keith said as he looked around to see if there were any familiar faces nearby. He leaned forward and looked at Charlie. Charlie saw the excitement in his eye, but there was concern in his voice when he spoke. "Something weird is going on. It seems my account was one of a random selection last month."

"What do you mean random selection?" Charlie asked confused.

"I queried all accounts that had the same charge as me. Guess what? Exactly one hundred accounts had a two-buck increase for the debit order fee last month. I queried the month before, and guess what?"

"The same thing?"

"Yes, but it was a hundred different accounts. I went back more, and it seems this has been happening for some time. It didn't start with the ICB, it's been happening for as long as I could go back in history."

"What? Where does the money go?"

"That is where it gets interesting. The amount is split. One buck goes to an internal bank expense account called 'annual office maintenance' and the other buck goes to a personal savings account."

"Did you get the name?"

"Yes."

"And?" Charlie wanted more information and gestured at Keith to give him some more. Keith smiled at Charlie and replied with a straight face.

"It's confidential information. I cannot share account details from my bank with you? You are working for the sharks."

"What!" Charlie sat back and stared in disbelief at Keith who burst out laughing.

"Oh man, I got you. That look on your face."

Charlie faked a smile when he realized Keith was teasing him.

"Oh, come on. So none of it is true?"

"Everything I said is true." Keith continued and he lowered his voice again. "It is confidential, but I know I can trust you. The name and address are both fake."

"What do you mean fake? How do you know? Nobody can set up a fake account?"

"It's very easy if you know what the checks and balances are. This has to be an inside job. I looked at the transaction history. Both accounts are cleared every year around the time we get our annual bonuses. Whoever is involved in this scheme seems to disguise the extra income by taking it when the bonuses are paid. There is very little left in the account at year end, so no red flags are raised."

"Did you get a name and address?"

"That's where it gets even more interesting. The person is a certain 'Sir Archibald Victor Mansion' who resides at 1001 Church Street, Glenmore. Guess what? There is no Church Street in Glenmore. It is a nice suburb, but when you go east on Church Street in Pretoria, it ends where the new highway was built. The suburb of Glenmore starts on the other side of the highway and then the street name becomes Union Way. The house numbers for Union Way restart at one 1-0-0 and Church Street ends around 9-8-7. There is no 1-0-0-1"

"You already checked it out?"

"Yes. I just took a different route home one evening and followed Church Street. It seems most of the houses towards the end of Church street are foreign government embassies. The fake name sounds like a person from a different country."

"What are you going to do about it?"

"I'm not sure." Keith sat back and looked at Charlie. "I thought about it. I, or we since you also know about it, can do one of two things."

"Go on." Charlie said. He waited for the new scheme he expected Keith had already planned out.

"We can blow the whistle and get a few bucks as a reward, or..."

"Or, what? Are you scheming again?"

"Yes!" The excitement was back in Keith's eyes. An uneasy feeling grew inside of Charlie. Something told him he was not going to like this.

"What's your plan this time?"

"We can launch Project Bravo."

"What? Project Bravo?" Charlie had no idea what he was talking about.

"Yes. We copy the scheme Sir Archibald, whoever he is, started. We randomly hijack his logic and include our own little routine in the process. We set up another fake account for his wife. I already thought about a name.

Madam Catherine Victoria Mansion. We then redirect part of the money to her account."

"Ha-ha-ha" Charlie said sarcastically. "As if that would ever work."

"It will" Keith insisted.

"I don't know, man. That's serious stuff you are talking about. It's real money and not some project we can use to pass an exam. If we get caught, we will be in major trouble," Charlie objected.

"They owe me. They stole my money. I will just steal it back. Stealing from thieves is not a crime. Think about it." Keith laid out his plan to Charlie. "We use the same concept Sir Archibald uses. We increase the number of randomly selected clients, add two bucks to their account and transfer the money to Madam Catherine's account."

"Well, I still don't like it." Charlie said reluctantly.

"I know. It's just an idea. But, remember. Somebody is already skimming from the fees and they stole from me. I want my money back. So, do we blow the whistle on them and ask the bank to repay me?"

"No. Not yet," Charlie said deep in thought. This time Keith was the one with the puzzled look on his face.

"No? What do you have in mind?"

"Why don't we set a trap for them. We already know where the money is going. Then we create our own program, and we can call it Bravo since you already started with it. We add the logic from our old Alpha program to the process. We randomly select a hundred clients, and transfer the pennies from the rounding to the account of Sir Archibald. This will be the perfect disguise to test the code from Alpha. If it goes wrong, Sir Archibald is on the hook, and Alpha is just another one of his little schemes. We just need to make sure it cannot be traced back to us."

"Sound interesting. But what's it in it for us? I'm the one who got ripped off by him, you know." Keith was adamant that he wanted his money back.

"Madam Catherine will eventually pay you back. That is where Project

Bravo comes in. We test the waters and see how it goes. We need to find out how to get ahold of the money. How does Sir Archibald get the money out of his account? Does he just walk up to the counter and say 'Hi, I'm Sir Archibald Mansion, and I want to withdraw some money from my account?'"

"No. I already checked. He withdraws the money from an ATM. He must have a debit card for it."

"How did he get it? His address is fake?"

"That part I don't know... yet" Keith said.

* * *

CHAPTER 16

From Bravo to Delta

C harlie and Keith spent every available hour in front of their computers working on Project Bravo. The first step was to embed the logic from project Alpha into a routine used to calculate the interest. The second step was to implement a toggle switch to activate the program on demand. They didn't want the program to run daily, and needed a process to control when it would be executed. Charlie explained to Keith the process he used many years ago to trigger the ransom for Samuel Griffin. The plan was to read a secret phrase from a file placed on an ftp site. The ftp site was a shared repository for files sent between banks participating in the ICB agreement. As programmers for participating banks, Charlie and Keith both had access to the site. The login details and passwords were not difficult to figure out since they were shared between departments. Keith told Charlie about the note he saw on the bulletin board in the break room at work. All the login details for ftp sites were posted there. Controls over the content of the site were non-existent with the justification that information should be removed from the site as soon as it was used. The ftp site was located on a server controlled by the ICB and had limited space allocated. Some smart programmer developed a process to remove all files with a date and time stamp older than three days. No information was retained on files dropped or removed from the ftp site. Everybody preferred it that way. It was exactly what Charlie and Keith needed for Project Bravo. They performed a test by dropping a random file with gibberish in it on the server and waited.

After three days the file disappeared. Nobody mentioned anything and no questions were asked. They dropped a second file that contained a trigger phrase on the ftp site. Their program read the phrase from the initial file, decoded it and replaced it with a new version. In the process, the date and time stamp were modified, and the user ID associated with the file was changed to 'sys-admin'. It was a system-executed process with no specific user linked to the new file. Nobody would know who had placed the file on the server. Three days later the file was automatically removed.

Charlie and Keith celebrated their success briefly and then immediately started working on the third and final phase of Project Bravo. The final step was to remove the pennies from the interest and transfer the money to the account of Sir Archibald.

Keith uploaded the program logic for Project Bravo into the system at BOSA. They left the code in place for a week and waited. Nothing was mentioned in the grapevine about unauthorized changes, and they uploaded a file containing a false phrase for the first test run. Nervously, Charlie checked the file on the ftp site the next day. It was unchanged. Nothing had happened. After three days the file was deleted from the site. They uploaded a new file with the correct phrase and checked the file every day.

"Did you look at the file?" Keith asked Charlie as they met during one of their lunch breaks.

"Yes, still there. No change. Did we do something wrong? Why is it not working?" Charlie was very nervous and concerned. They were both anxious to see some results, and get confirmation that their plan worked.

"When does your bank normally run the debit orders?" Charlie asked.

"Based on my bank statement, early in the month. I checked the files we

receive from the insurance companies. They normally drop between the fif-
teenth and the twenty-second of the month. That gives the 'bean-counters'
enough time to cross check the hash totals. Then it's released for processing
on the first business day of the month." There was a love-hate relationship
between the programmers and the accounting department. The account-
ants double-checked every change made to the system while programmers
thought their work was flawless. It was a constant battle between the two
departments.

"Let's drop the file on the first day of the month and see what happens."

"Ok. I will check how Sir Archibald triggers his process and when the
fees are deposited into his account."

They completed their lunches in silence, each busy with his own
thoughts about what they were doing.

"Is there a way to undo all the changes if it doesn't work?" Charlie asked
after a while. "We shouldn't leave the code in place if it isn't working. Are
you sure some smart programmer will not be able to trace it back to us?"
Charlie was incredibly concerned and Keith had a hard time to keeping him
relaxed and assured that everything was taken care of.

"Removing the code will be simple, or we can just leave it. Without the
file from the ftp site, there will be no trigger for the logic. Nothing will
happen if the function remains in the program forever unless somebody
specifically searches for it or accidently stumbles over it. Nobody will even
notice it. It looks like a piece of test code in the standard rounding function
that didn't get removed. If you don't know what you are looking for, you will
not find it." Keith sounded overconfident.

"Let's see what happens. Give it another week. I will drop the file on
the ftp site as soon as the current one is removed. Call me if something
changes," Charlie said as they left the cafe to returned to work.

A few days later Charlie arrived in his office at his normal time. The
phone immediately rang as he walked in and he picked it up. He clamped

it between his shoulder and ear, and said: "Hello, this is Charlie," as he switched on his computer.

"It worked!" Keith said without the regular greeting.

"What?"

"The file got updated last night. Bravo updated the file. I downloaded the new file to my computer and ran it through the decipher logic. It had the correct account number and the amount in it. The astronomical amount of thirty-four cents was added to Sir Archibald's account. I would love to see his face when he finds the transaction on his statement. He won't have a clue where it came from."

"I'll see you tonight. Let's talk then, not over the phone." Charlie said.

Charlie and Keith sat in the living room discussing the discovery of the day. In the background a cricket match was on the TV. The commentator was doing his best to make a one-sided match sound interesting. The bowlers of the home team were being slammed and the visitors were piling up the runs between the wickets. Marlene sat at the dining room table grading student's test papers. She was not very interested in the work discussions between Charlie and Keith. Her normal reaction to a conversation about work was that it sounded like they were talking in a foreign language. She didn't care about all the technical jargon and acronyms they used. When Charlie visited and the two best friends got lost in their own world, she would use the time to grade papers or prepare lessons for the next day. As a schoolteacher, there was always something to do and she didn't mind the frequent visits from Charlie to keep her husband occupied.

"What do we do now?" Charlie asked Keith.

"We wait and see what happens to the money. I managed to copy Sir Archibald's account and created a new one for Madam Catherine. There is no money in there yet, but we can add her account number in the file and upload it. It worked for Sir Archibald, so the pennies should move into hers when we trigger it."

They were silent for a few minutes. Charlie thought about the impact this could have on their lives. At what point would they have crossed the line?

It was Keith who broke the silence. "Let's do it," he said enthusiastically.

Charlie looked at him for a moment and said: "If the ship sinks, we go down together. No mistakes. Remember what my math teacher told me. A simple mistake can prove one equals two."

"I know. I will make sure our names cannot be linked to anything."

Project Bravo was set into action. Madam Catherine Mansion started receiving small amounts into her account from the interest calculations. Keith continued monitoring the accounts, and although the money kept flowing in, nothing was taken out of the account for months. The end of the year was approaching fast and early in December, as expected, when Keith did his daily check of the accounts, the money from Sir Archibald's account was gone. The account had a zero balance. Sir Archibald had withdrawn the money. Keith scanned the logs to find the location of the ATM where the transaction happened. It was an ATM in the East-End Mall, a big shopping complex in Sandton, an elite suburb on the north side of Johannesburg. With the Christmas shopping season in full swing, it was the perfect spot for Sir Archibald to complete his transaction.

"We need a debit card," Keith said to Charlie when they met for lunch to discuss the new developments.

"There's not a lot of money in the account," Charlie said.

"I know, but I want to test it and see if we can at least buy a drink to celebrate. We know Sir Archibald withdrew his money. Why can't we withdraw some money also? They still owe me for all the fees I have paid." Keith frequently reminded Charlie about the purpose of project Bravo. "Maybe I should change the logic for Bravo. Instead of only taking the pennies from the rounding, we can redirect the fees from Sir Archibald's account to Madam Catherine's account. We'll just upload a file to the ftp server, and when it triggers, the account number will be swapped and the fees will go to Madam Catherine. The next time Sir Archibald's program runs, there will be no file and the money will go back to his account. We do this a few times and soon we will have enough money. Maybe I can buy a new bike. Maybe we will have enough to go with you to visit Hanna."

"That's it," Charlie had suddenly come alive and sounded excited.

"That's what? Another brilliant idea?" Keith asked.

"A foreign bank account." Charlie continued to explain. "We set up a foreign bank account with our own money. That is one hundred percent legal. If you set up an account in Switzerland, the bank promises to never share your information with any person or any government. We go in person and open an account with our own money. They will give us debit cards and we can use it anywhere in the world."

"You are something else," Keith said with a smile and shook his head. "What world are you living in? You sure about this?"

"I can read, you know. With Hanna so far away and work just normal these days, I actually get some time to read. I subscribed to a *Finance Weekly* and there are always a bunch of other financial magazines lying around at the office. I take some home to read when I can. It gives me a mental break from staring at a screen the whole day." Charlie continued to explain to Keith the article and what he already knew about the international banking systems.

"I read about the privacy guarantees in Europe. Apparently banks in Switzerland have the strictest privacy laws of all. They use it to market their services and lure international clients. This might just be what we need."

"And, how do we get the money into the account in Switzerland?"

"We go there and open an account. Easy."

"That's not what I mean. How do we get the money from here to the account in Switzerland?"

"You can transfer money from anywhere in the world and you can withdraw money from any ATM. Of course they will charge a fee for that. But at least we can get our hands on some of the money."

"You sure about this? It sounds too good to be true, and you know the saying: 'if it's too good to be true, then it probably is'."

"I think it will work. Oh, you want to know something else I discovered?" Charlie was on a roll with his ideas and wanted to share it with somebody.

"Go on. Seems your brain has been working overtime. Maybe you have too much free time."

"I think I found a way to hit the big one with Project Alpha."

"Will it be enough for me to buy my new bike?" Keith sounded interested.

"The ICB." This caught Keith's attention immediately since there were still some sour grapes about losing the race after he had worked so hard to win it. He looked at Charlie with anticipation of a weird but brilliant idea.

"The clearing accounts. Do you know what the end of day balances are for some banks? Each bank has a clearing account with the ICB. The balance fluctuates daily from millions in the positive, to millions in the negative. The inter bank settlement happens on the last day of each month. The rest of the month, the money is just parked in a clearing account. No interests are earned, and no interest are paid while parked in the clearing account."

"So how do you use Alpha if there is no interest to calculate?"

"Let's say we combine project Alpha and project Bravo into a single function. We make some minor changes to the logic, and we redirect a portion of the money parked in the clearing account to Madam Catherine's account where the money will earn interest. We leave it only for a day and then move it back to the clearing account. Kind of a revolving door where the money just moves in and out of the whole time. There are millions of transactions automatically cleared daily between these accounts. A reference number and the amount are used to balance the clearing account. The logic matches the same debit and credit amounts based on the reference number. If it finds a match, it clears the transaction. Items not matched are listed as an exception and are resolved manually. We transfer the funds from a few banks and the continuous revolving balance in Madam Catherine's account will remain in the millions. We clear her account every month by transferring the interest to her overseas account. The revolving in-and-out is stopped for a few days before the end of the month. That will allow the clearing process to balance. And, bingo! We've struck gold!" Charlie leaned back in his chair with a smile of victory on his face.

Keith just sat there and stared at Charlie. He was still processing the idea and trying to figure out exactly what Charlie had just explained to him in a few seconds.

"What? Are you crazy? It will never work! How long have you been dreaming about this?" Keith just could not follow the logic.

Charlie used a napkin and explained the methodology he had in mind again and again. Slowly Keith started to understand the details of the plan, but he still wasn't sure about the outcome. He wanted to know how they could manage to hide the transactions and had many unanswered questions. Charlie had a lot of explaining to do. They talked till late that night and for the next few weeks about Project Delta. They would skip Charlie as a project name since they didn't want anything personal tied to their secret projects.

Progress with Project Delta started off slowly. Charlie and Keith spent endless long nights and weekends working on their master plan. When Marlene questioned them about what they were working on, the answer was always the same: "Project Delta." She was married to Keith long enough to know that when he and Charlie were together it was useless to ask questions. The answers were always short and brief. If she did ask for more details, he gave her an explanation that included technical jargon and acronyms she didn't understand. Eventually she gave up asking. It gave her the opportunity to continue with her own tasks. Charlie became like a brother to her and the guest bedroom became his room over weekends. Marlene morally supported them and when they seemed to be stuck, she would force them away from the computers to help with some household chores. She made sure coffee was always ready and available.

They wrote the code in ASSEMBLER and simulated it on PCs they built from parts bought at a local computer shop. They ran the initial tests at home, and when they were satisfied with the results, it was time to move to the real world. Charlie embedded the trigger mechanism for the code inside the ICB system. Keith embedded the calculations and transfers at his bank. They used the accounts of Sir Archibald and Madam Catherine to test the process. They made sure their user IDs could not be associated with any of the code and used shared administrative logins to cover their tracks.

The day for their first test eventually arrived. Charlie was nervous and hesitated for a few moments before he hit the enter key to uploaded the trigger file to the ftp site. A *"small"* portion of the money in the clearing account would be transferred into Sir Archibald's account. From Sir Archibald's account the same amount would be transferred to Madam Catherine's account. In Sir Archibald's account, the net effect should be zero. The money would stay in Madam Catherine's account for a day before it would be moved back to the original clearing account. The program Charlie uploaded at the ICB would then update the reference in the system back to the original reference for the transaction. The auto-clearing process would then clear the amount. Charlie and Keith met for lunch to discuss the outcome.

"Did it work?" Keith asked keeping his voice down.

"Yes," Charlie responded purposely not elaborating. He took a bite of his sandwich and looked at Keith who stared back in anticipation.

"And?" he asked. Charlie took his time to answer.

"The interest for one day was one hundred and sixty-four bucks and thirty-eight cents. That's what she made in one day from interest at 6%. She had a cool million bucks in her account."

"That's great!" Keith was excited. "Multiply that by ten and she will be an extremely wealthy lady very soon. It will fit her title. How long do we leave it in her account? When can we start using some of it?"

"We have to leave it for a month or two to see if anything happens. We cannot use anything until we have the accounts setup in Switzerland."

"Any progress with your plans to visit Hanna?"

"I'm working on it. I just need to get my vacation approved. I called her over the weekend and we discussed the dates. She is very excited about it. Do you know how expensive an international call is? It is almost cheaper to fly there and visit her."

"Nope. I never call international. With inflation so high, all the prices are going up."

"I told Hanna I want to see Europe. She was very excited and said we could take a train ride to visit Paris. I told her I wanted to visit Zurich."

"Did you tell her about the account?"

"No. I will get the bright idea when we are on our way to Zurich. I will use the excuse of using it as an investment account and a safeguard against inflation. We can save money in the account for our honeymoon. I'm sure she will go for it."

"Honeymoon?" Keith said with surprise. "You didn't tell us? When did you ask her? Have you set a date?" Keith was both surprised and excited to hear Charlie mention a honeymoon. Marriage between Charlie and Hanna was a frequent topic when Marlene was present. Charlie on the other hand never wanted to discuss it.

"Wait, slow down!" Charlie said and laughed at Keith's response. "No, not yet, and no. I want to ask her in person. On her last visit we were looking at rings and I have a good idea of what style she likes."

"Can I tell Marlene?

"No! She will tell Hanna. You know they write letters to each other. I want to surprise Hanna and Marlene may just let the cat out of the bag.

Please keep it quiet."

"When are you buying the ring?"

"Already placed the order."

"What? A custom made one? Wow that must be expensive?"

"Remember Bert Skipper from school? He lives in the Coligny area. He once told me there are lots of small diamond claims still being worked in the area. I called him and he got me a good deal on a half carat diamond and a custom made ring. We met a while ago and clinched the deal."

"Are you sure it's not a fake diamond?"

"No. He will get it certified as a true diamond and he showed me a simple test to see if it's real or fake. A real diamond will leave a scratch on a piece of glass. A fake one will not. He also had a small diamond tester we used. I think I can trust him. He convinced me, so I already have the ring ordered."

"You are slick, man; everything planned and ready." They completed their lunch and on their way out, Charlie looked at Keith.

"On second thought, why don't you and Marlene go with me? It will be a nice surprise for Hanna. We can all visit Zurich and open an account for you, too?"

"I don't know. It's expensive and you know Marlene. She will not spend any money on a vacation like that." Keith sounded disappointed, but Charlie was so excited about the idea.

"Let me talk to her. She and Hanna are good friends. Maybe if she hears about the ring, it will change her mind. I will ask her not to tell Hanna about my plans. "

When Marlene heard about the ring and his plan to ask Hanna to marry him, there was no convincing needed. Marlene became the planner and the organizer. Together they decided to keep the ring and extra visitors a surprise for Hanna. Planning the vacation consumed all their time for the next few weeks. The trip was planned during the mid-year school break in the winter. It would make a big dent in their savings, but Charlie and Keith saw it as an investment in their futures. They continued with the refinement of Project Delta and were convinced it would work. The bank accounts in Zurich were the final step in their plan.

Two months later, Charlie, Keith and Marlene were at the airport on their way to London. Hanna was totally surprised to see them. Her excitement reached the ultimate high point when Charlie proposed that evening after dinner. They celebrated with dessert and champagne. They stayed a couple of days in London and Hanna showed them where she lived and the university campus. They took a train to Paris, spent a couple of nights at a Bed and Breakfast and visited familiar tourist sites. After that, they spent two days in Zurich where they rented rooms from a couple that transformed their home into a small inn.

Before their visit, Charlie and Keith continued their research about the international banking systems. They made a few expensive phone calls to a bank in Zurich and discussed the prospect of opening an account with them. They asked about the process to transfer money between bank accounts in South Africa and Zurich. The bank forwarded them the application forms, which they completed before the visit. They were ready for the final step in their plan of becoming wealthy.

There was one item they didn't completely resolve. It bothered Charlie, but Keith always had an answer ready when the discussion turned to the legal and moral side of their project.

"Stealing from a thief is not a crime. The banks have been stealing from their clients for many years. Sir Archibald stole from me. We are just taking back what they owe us."

The answer didn't satisfy Charlie completely, but he left it there and project Delta went live.

* * *

CHAPTER 17

The Accident

C harlie changed his work schedule to fit his new life around Hanna. She successfully completed her master's degree and started her new career as a nuclear scientist. Charlie, Keith and Marlene helped her move into her new apartment. After work, Charlie would normally pick her up and the now engaged couple spent many evenings at the married couple's home. It was not long before wedding plans became the main topic of discussion. Marlene was not only a bridesmaid, but became the de-facto wedding planner. While Hanna and Marlene planned the wedding, Charlie and Keith discovered a new interest in the cricket series between South African and England - anything to stay out of the wedding planning process. They soon learned their part in the process was to follow instructions and not voice an opinion.

One Friday evening while the friends were having dinner at a restaurant, Keith and Marlene announced their pregnancy. Although everyone was extremely excited about the new baby, stress levels increased as plans for the wedding and the new baby progressed. Keith talked non-stop about his new role as daddy and Charlie's nervousness increased as they approached the wedding day. Every item that was added to the wedding budget intensified his concern about his savings that were going in the wrong direction.

Hanna assured him that there was no reason to panic and that she had already talked to her dad. Charlie was off the hook. Hanna's dad had given her a generous budget for the wedding. They set a date for the dream wedding during the summer of 1981. The newlyweds would have enough time after the wedding for a short honeymoon, and to settle into Charlie's apartment before the new year and the new baby came. Life was good the four friends.

It was spring in Pretoria, and the purple Jacaranda trees were in full bloom. It was also the first weekend of the month, which meant Charlie had to be at work on Saturday. The project he worked on for the last three months was in its final stage. The changes to the interface were complete and he had a few minor upgrades to install. As a software programmer for Anglo Bank, Charlie sometime had to work at hours when normal people would be off or asleep. The first weekend of the month was frequently used to implement new changes. If something went wrong, the IT staff had enough time before the end of the month to correct problems.

Charlie planned to leave early. The British Lions rugby team was on tour in South Africa. He and Keith planned to watch the rugby game against the Springboks while Hanna and Marlene continued the never-ending wedding planning. Keith installed a TV in the thatched roof lapa in the backyard. His excuse to get it past Marlene was that with a TV outside the house, he would not wakeup the sleeping baby when he watched rugby. The TV was also conveniently located next to the grill and they cooked outside almost every weekend. Charlie and Keith spent more hours in the lapa than inside the house.

The phone rang on Charlie's desk. He automatically reached for it and clenched it between his shoulder and ear as he continued typing on the keyboard.

"Hello, this is Charlie."

"Hello Charlie. This is Stephen."

"Stephen?" Charlie said and stopped typing. Charlie's brother, Stephen, was a Reverend in the Dutch Reformed Church, and although they got along very well, they didn't visit together frequently. The ministerial duties were understandably his priority, and Charlie accepted it that way.

"Wow, this is a surprise. You never call me at work. How are you doing?" Charlie said.

"Charlie," Stephen said ignoring the customary small talk and cutting straight to the reason for his call. "There was an accident."

"Who?" Charlie asked as he immediately thought about Stephen's family. "I'm sorry to hear. What happened?"

"Charlie," Stephen paused be fore he continued. "It's Hanna. I'm afraid..."

Time froze and Charlie went numb to the bone. He felt the blood leave his face and he became nauseous. He heard Stephen's voice, but nothing made sense and the words faded away as he tried to grasp what Stephen was saying. "... an accident. Keith and Hanna both ... the police ... on a motorbike ... ". He only heard parts of what Stephen was saying. Each word over the phone struck deep inside of Charlie, stabbing him in the heart.

"No! No! No!" he groaned and started to sob. He suddenly felt trapped in the small office. He wanted to throw the phone away but he could not move. He held the phone tight to his ear as Stephen tried to get a response.

"Charlie! Are you listening"? Stephen's sharp voice brought him slowly back to reality. "Is there anybody else at the office? Do you want me to come and get you?"

"There's nobody here." Charlie whispered into the phone. He leaned on the desk and put his head on his forearm. Tears dropped on the desk and ran under the keyboard. He cried and wept while his body became limp.

"Charlie. Stay there! I'm on my way," Stephen said and hung up the phone.

Half an hour later Stephen and the security guard found Charlie in his office still sitting with the phone in his hand. He had not moved since Stephen called. His tears had dried up. Stephen reached down and touched his shoulder. Charlie looked up at him with a blank stare in his eyes. He slowly stood up and they hugged each other. It took Charlie back to many years before. He clearly remembered how he felt when he saw Stephen lying in the hospital bed after he had almost died in a wreck. Charlie started to sob again and Stephen comforted him as best he could. Dazed and moving slowly, Charlie packed a few items in his briefcase and walked toward the door. Stephen led him out of the building to his car, and drove him to the hospital.

In the same day, Charlie lost his future wife and his best friend. He had a hard time remembering anything that happened that day and the order in which it occurred. He vaguely recalled walking with Stephen down a hall in the hospital. The nurses allowed him into the room where Hanna's body laid covered with a white sheet. They didn't want him to look at her, but he insisted. When he saw at her lifeless face, the tears started rolling again and the image was instantly burned into his memory forever. Her parents were still on their way.

From the room next door, he could hear Marlene crying. He walked to the room and when Marlene saw him, she ran toward him and hugged him. They cried about their losses. Charlie's attempts to console her were not very successful. Stephen stood with Marlene's dad outside the door watching the scene unfold in the room. Charlie had to say goodbye to his best friend. Keith's body was in the same position as Hanna's. When a nurse lifted the sheet for Charlie to look at Keith's face, he didn't even recognize him. His face was still wrapped with white bandages to cover the wounds caused by the fall during the accident.

Charlie and Marlene comforted each other, their lives forever changed on that beautiful spring day. A special bond was established between them, but they would never be the same. Marlene and Charlie didn't want to leave their loved ones and stayed together. The trauma intensified when the parents and other family arrived. Eventually a nurse asked them to leave so the bodies could be moved. They stood together as the bodies were rolled down the hall and disappeared around a corner.

Marlene's mother was very concerned about her pregnant daughter. She took charge and asked a doctor to give Marlene something to calm her down. Their lives would also be severely impacted by the accident. They instantly inherited the responsibility to take care of a widow and a new baby that would be raised without a father.

Charlie observed the injection a nurse gave Marlene, and when she turned towards him, he declined the offer. He had enough needles pushed into his arm while in the military by medics in training, and forever had a fear of needles. Stephen took Charlie home with him. On their way, Charlie tried to convince Stephen that he would be fine on his own, but Stephen knew better. Charlie spent a few nights with Stephen and his wife Ester. They had a big house, and the guest room was always ready. Charlie talked to his mother that evening, and she cancelled all her plans to be with him for a few days.

Stephen's experience as a Minster of faith, and his offer to help the families with funeral arrangements, was graciously accepted. As a Reverend he knew exactly who to call and what to do. Charlie and Marlene discussed the funeral with the parents of Hanna and Keith. Together they decided one combined memorial service would be best given the circumstances. Charlie and Marlene agreed that they could not stomach two funerals back to back.

Most of the people attending the funerals were from out of town. Some co-workers and friends showed up and the procession from the church to the gravesite was a long line of cars. The gathering afterwards at the church hall was taken care of by Ester with the help of many willing hands from the church community. The women's ministry provided light snacks and sandwiches with the tea and coffee. A small area was dedicated for immediate family and Charlie and Marlene each sat on a couch. Charlie sat with his mom at his side, and Marlene with hers. Sympathizers came, talked for a few minutes, and then allowed the next person to repeat words of comfort.

The days after the funeral were a complete blur for Charlie. He did as he was told and felt like a zombie. Between Stephen, Ester and his mom, he was never left alone. He did not talk much and most of the conversations he did have, didn't even register. He was grateful for the barrier his family formed between him and the constant flow of visitors.

Charlie sat in an armchair in the corner of the living room at Stephen and Ester's. He vaguely remembered a police officer and a detective in plain clothes asking him questions. He was not very responsive and could not give them much information. He was at work when the accident happened and then Stephen came and picked him up. They asked about his car and where it was. Charlie explained and his mom gave them a piece of her mind for insinuating he had anything to do with the accident. She told them Charlie was still in shock and maybe they should leave and come back later. They switched to ask Charlie about Hanna and her work. During the question and answer session, Charlie realized how little he knew about what she really did. She never talked about her work and her studies in England. The detective's line of questioning gave Charlie the impression they knew more about what she did than he did.

It was a hit-and-run accident with very little information about what really happened. The driver left the scene of the accident and the police were investigating it as a homicide. Their efforts to locate the car and driver involved were fruitless. In a follow-up interview, the detective wanted to know if Charlie knew of anybody that would want to harm Hanna or Keith. Charlie just shook his head. He could not think of anyone that would want to harm the most beautiful and caring person in the world. She was the best thing that had ever happened to him. She would not even hurt a fly. She always wanted to help others and was always ready with a word of encouragement. They had been engaged for just over a year and it was the happiest time of his life. Everybody adored her and he thought he was the luckiest person alive. Charlie loved Hanna and he missed her so much he didn't want to live without her.

A few days after the funeral, Charlie visited Marlene. When she saw him at the door, she immediately started crying and they hugged and sobbed together. They both lost the loves of their life and their best friends. They shared a bond that nobody else understood and they found comfort talking to each other. They felt like brother and sister and talked about the future. When Charlie asked about the baby, Marlene broke out in tears again. She didn't know how she was going to raise a baby without a father.

"Should I give the baby up for adoption?" she asked Charlie. They sat on the same couch Charlie and Keith sat on to watch their last rugby game together. It was only a few days ago.

"And never see the child again?" Charlie responded. "What do you think Keith would want you to do?"

"I'm not sure." Marlene hesitated for a moment. With tears welling in her eyes, she looked at Charlie and continued. "He was so excited to become a father. We were both very excited."

"What about your parents? Will they be able to help?"

"I thought about it and my mom already hinted in that direction. When I mentioned adoption to her, she didn't want to hear about it. But I'm concerned about my dad. He doesn't like the idea of raising another man's child." A twitch of a smile formed at the corner of her mouth as she continued. "My mom really gave him a scolding when he dared to say it."

"If they help to raise the baby, at least you will still be there too. I think Keith would not have wanted it any differently."

For a moment there was silence, both of them busy with their own thoughts. Charlie thought about Hanna and how excited she was when Keith and Marlene broke the news to them. Hanna wanted to start a family as soon as they were married.

"Charlie," Marlene broke the silence and looked at him. "There is something else we have to talk about."

"What is it?"

"Where did Keith get the money to buy the motorcycle?" A bucket of ice-cold water thrown on him could not have shocked him more. The direct question about money caught him completely off guard and he struggled to control his thoughts.

"I'm not sure," he stuttered. "Did he say where he got it?" Charlie knew he had to be very careful with the conversation. He was not sure exactly how much Marlene knew about what he and Keith did.

"I didn't want him to buy a bike. We already had a mortgage and a car loan to pay. With the baby on its way, we just couldn't afford a bike payment too. He said he did some extra work on the side and he got paid good money for it. What was he working on? You were always together and I'm sure he would have told you."

"He mentioned a special project at work, that required a lot of overtime. I thought he used his overtime to buy the bike. Did he not get a good bonus at the end of last year." Charlie tried all the excuses he could think of. He didn't want to lie to Marlene, but he also knew he could not tell her the truth.

"One more thing." Marlene continued to question Charlie. "The cops mentioned that the accident was a hit-and-run. What does that mean?"

Charlie looked at her and saw the pain in her eyes. He vaguely recalled the conversation he had with the police, but in his mind he heard different voices. He could still hear the voice of Mr. Burns, his math teacher. *"With a simple mistake you can prove one-equals-two, and it changes everything,"* The voice of his military training officer echoed in his mind. *"If you don't use the shift, people can die."*

"A hit-and-run? I... I thought it was just an accident. I thought he lost control. I just couldn't understand it because he knew how to handle a bike."

"Did the police not discuss it with you?"

"I'm not sure. Maybe." He looked down and swallowed hard on the lump in his throat. "The last few weeks are still a blur for me. I know I talked to a cop or a detective at some point. But I'm not sure how I responded or what I told them. I think I was too much in shock. They also asked some weird questions about Hanna and her work."

"A couple of detectives came by last week and also asked me a lot of questions." Marlene looked down and fidgeted with a tissue in her hands.

"What type of questions did they ask?"

"They wanted to know what kind of work he did. When they asked if Keith used any drugs, I really got upset. My dad told them to leave. They asked me to give them a call if I remember anything."

"Drugs?" Charlie was without words and just shook his head. "What gave them that idea?"

"I don't know. Did you know they found a witness to the accident?"

"No." Charlie had a surprised look on his face.

"The person said the car deliberately caused the wreck. The driver swerved on purpose, hit the bike on the side and sped away." Her words sent a shiver down Charlie's spine, and he looked around to see if there was somebody else in the room.

"Did the witness see the car? Did they get the license plate number?"

"She could only describe the model of the car and the color. She said it was a black Mercedes, a newer model, and the windows were dark. She could not see the driver or how many people were in the car. She was too far away."

Charlie didn't react and just stared at Marlene. He couldn't move. He didn't know what to say, and after a moment tried to answer her question.

"They call an accident a hit-and-run if one of the parties involved, leaves the scene. If the driver in the car who caused the accident didn't stop, then it is a hit-and-run. You know how ignorant drivers are about motorcycles and you warned Keith every time he went for a ride to be careful. I have seen Keith handle a bike. He knew what he was doing. He learned how to ride in the military and he was very good it. He was a safe driver."

"I know. I told him to be careful when they left."

"Why was Hanna on the bike?" Charlie asked the question that had been puzzling him for a while. He also wanted to change the subject, and not discuss where the money for the bike came from.

"Keith convinced her to take a ride with him. He just wanted to show off with his new bike. Hanna didn't want to go, but he nagged her until she agreed. You know Keith, he wouldn't stop until he got it his way."

"Yes, don't I know it."

"I was standing outside when they left and watched them until they turned the corner. I was in the kitchen when police called and told me about the accident. I didn't know what to do, so I called my dad. I wanted to call you, but I just couldn't. I'm so sorry Charlie," she said as she touched his arm and tears started to stream down her face. "My dad called Stephen and asked him to call you."

"That's ok, Marlene." Charlie reached over and hugged her to comfort her. "Stephen called me, and picked me up from work. He took me to the hospital."

They talked a while longer. When Marlene's parents returned from their shopping trip, they invited him to stay for lunch. He declined with the excuse that Ester and his Mom were cooking for him.

Charlie said goodbye. He knew Marlene was in good hands and her parents would take good care of her. He needed to be alone to think about his life and what he should do next. He got in the car, and before he turned the key, he broke down and cried. When the sobbing stopped, he started the car and looked back at the house. He saw Marlene standing in the window. She waved at him and he waved back. Life would go on, but it would never be the same for Charlie and Marlene.

* * *

SECTION III

Putting It Together

CHAPTER 18

Dinner with Ben - Visas

T he project at First Midwest in Springfield, Missouri, was in its final days. The migration from the test environment into the production environment went smoothly, and minor issues discovered initially were quickly resolved. The overworked and tired project team transitioned ownership of the system to their business counterparts. Charlie, like most of the team, had worked long hours and welcomed the calmness after the storm. The critical care period would last one month and then he would be free.

Fall had started early and Charlie sat at his desk staring out the window. He watched the leaves falling and followed one picked up by the light breeze that blew it to the far end of the parking lot. In the past few days his focus shifted from work to vacation. His attempts to get his hands on the money in his account at The Bank of Zurich were unsuccessful. The account had been dormant for too long and the only way to gain access again required a personal visit to the bank. His request for a new debit card over the phone were declined since he had changed addresses a few times since opening the account and had immigrated to a different country. The bank needed proof of his claim to be a US citizen. There were too many things that prevented the bank from sending a debit card to an address not verified by an in person visit. Exactly according to the instructions on file. It was his brilliant idea when he and Keith opened their individual accounts to stipulate the specific instruction that a new card can only be issued in person.

It was not only the work and the problem with the bank that kept Charlie awake at night. He spent many hours lying in bed considering his options for the future. He flip-flopped between taking Tessa's offer and sticking with PITS. Heinz kept his promise and corrected his compensation rate per hour. His last paycheck brought a smile to his face, but the feeling of vindication lasted only a moment before it turned back to anger when he thought about how long they had cheated him.

His hand reached for his coffee cup, and when he tasted the cold coffee, he got up to make a fresh pot. He walked by the cubicles where the programmers sat and noticed the somber look on their faces. They tried to look busy, but he knew some were more worried about their future, than fixing the minor issues still to be resolved. Charlie felt sorry for them. While waiting for the coffee to brew, he thought about all the rookies he had to train in the past year. It still bothered him that they only stayed for short periods of time. With a fresh cup of coffee in his hand, he walked back to his desk and stopped along the way to talk to one of the programmers working for PITS.

Benjamin Rivers joined the project late in the build phase when the need for programmers reached its peak. Charlie felt sorry for him and understood what he went through. He didn't have a lot of experience when he initially joined the project, but Charlie noticed his enthusiasm and the thoroughness with which he completed all tasks assigned to him. *"You can do a lot with a good attitude,"* his dad used to say, and Charlie thought the same way about Ben. It was Ben's first time outside of his home country and everything was new. He struggled to adjust and Charlie put in some extra effort to get him acquainted in the new country. He gave Ben pointers about the project and helpful tips for the life as a traveling consultant. As one of the lead consultants on the project, Charlie frequently had to deal with new team members. He spent time with Ben explaining the status of the project and the list of tasks to be completed. As a full time PITS employee, it was expected that Charlie would to take care of the company's reputation and provide special guidance to new consultants.

Charlie had no idea where Heinz found all the characters he recruited. Most consultants were from his home country South Africa and the rest from Asia and Europe. Some would stay till the end of a project and then return home. Those who made a good impression would be given the opportunity to return as a consultant for another project. The exceptional ones would be offered a full time position with PITS and the opportunity to live the American dream.

Ben didn't notice Charlie until he stood right next to him.

"Hi, Benjamin." Charlie used is full name on purpose even though he knew he preferred to be called Ben. "Do you have any plans for this evening? Want to grab a bite to eat after work with me?"

"Hi, Charlie." Ben said as he looked up and shifted around uncomfortably. "Not really. I'll just get some fast food and eat at the hotel. Trying to save on expenses, you know."

"I fully understand. You've done a great job on this project and deserve something extra. Everybody can do with a good steak once in a while. How about I treat you for dinner tonight - on the house?"

"Thanks, Charlie. That will be awesome!" Ben was all smiles, and Charlie knew the only thing Ben would think about for the rest of the afternoon was a big juicy steak.

"Ok. Let's meet in the hotel lobby after work. There's a good steakhouse just down the road from the hotel. We can ask the shuttle driver to drop us off."

At the restaurant the conversation started slow and was mostly about project related items. Charlie asked questions and Ben responded with short answers. Charlie probed deeper into Ben's background and work experiences but didn't get much out of him. When the appetizer was served, Charlie was still on his first glass of wine while Ben was already done with his second beer. Charlie emptied his glass and signaled the waiter for another round of drinks. The restaurant was full and orders were slow to be served. It suited Charlie very well and gave him time to wait for the alcohol to take effect on Ben.

"Tell me, Benjamin," Charlie started with his next round of questions, but he was quickly interrupted.

"Charlie, please just call me Ben. Benjamin is what my mom calls me when she really means business. That is what's on my birth certificate and on my passport, but all my friends call me Ben."

"Ok, Ben!" Charlie continued with a smile. "Will your parents come and visit you here in the US?"

"No, it's way too expensive. With the drop in the exchange rate, there's no way they can afford tickets to come visit me."

"Why don't you pay for them? You must be making good money on the project." Charlie used the opening to try and get Ben to talk about money, the real reason why Charlie invited him for dinner.

"Good money? You must be kidding. You may make a pretty penny since you are a full-time employee, but as a contractor, I only get a basic rate for eight hours a day," Ben said with bitterness dripping from every word.

"You work more than eight hours a day and you get paid by the hour. Should be good pay."

"Only if I work more than forty hours a week. I get an extra bonus rate for billable hours over forty."

"What do you mean bonus rate?" Charlie pressed for more info.

"It's simple. I get a basic rate of forty dollars an hour. If I work more than forty, I get an additional five for the hours over forty."

Charlie had to fight the flare of anger when he realized how PITS was screwing Ben and the other programmers. He remembered the rate he saw in the contract he slammed on Heinz's desk. PITS charged Midwest $100 an hour plus expenses for junior level consultants.

"Wow! Really? Five bucks an hour? Whose idea was that?"

"Heinz. He said it's standard practice for the first project. If I do a good job and return for a second project, they will increase my rate." Ben explained the details of his rates between gulps of beer.

"I sure hope you get a new assignment. How long do you plan to stay?"

"Till the project ends. I have to go back in a few weeks," Ben said as he finished the appetizer and washed it down with another mouthful of beer.

"What do you mean you have to go back?" Charlie asked.

"My visa doesn't allow me to stay longer than six months. If I stay longer, I may not be able to come back again."

"That's odd." Charlie tried to hide his surprise, but wanted to know more. The details of the immigration process were nothing new to Charlie. He suspected a scheme was going on at PITS, but had never found any proof. When Michael DeWet and his wife Karen returned to South Africa, Michael had mentioned to Charlie how he got Heinz to pay for their first class airline tickets. Michael said he knew there was something going on with the visas. At the time Charlie had no reason to suspect anything and did not want to know more. He was busy with his own immigration process to become a US citizen. He didn't ask questions and was sure his paperwork was in order.

"It's the same for most of us," Ben continued as the beer took effect and loosened his tongue. "It's a lonely life here and I miss my family. When the project ends, I plan to go back and have a nice vacation, and visit my family. With the strong US dollar, I will have enough savings to enjoy a nice long trip. Heinz said they are always looking for good programmers. I learned a lot on this project, and I hope he will ask me to come back. Maybe you can put in a good word for me."

"I will do what I can. I'm sure there will be something for you. So what type of visa do you have?"

"Well, I'm not supposed to talk about it. Heinz said we can get in big trouble if immigration finds out."

"I know. Been there, done that." Charlie played along and wanted to keep Ben talking. "We all go through that phase in life. I think I was one of the lucky ones. I had back-to-back projects and did not have to go back."

"How did you do that?" Ben asked surprised. "I thought everybody had to go back before six months was over?"

"Six months? Why six months?"

"That is the time on the visa. According to my I-94 document, I can only be in the country for six months. The emigration agent had a lot of questions when I entered the first time. Heinz also made sure I understood it very clearly."

"Oh, yes. Those agents are really something else. I still remember the first time when I arrived. I thought they were going to throw me in jail. They asked all these weird questions and then the guy just smiled and said. *'Just kidding with you, man. Relax. Everything is in order. Welcome to the United States of America. Enjoy your stay'.*"

"I was scared stiff when I went through immigration," Ben continued. "The lines were so long. Then they took a whole family right in front of me to a room and closed the door. There was some serious questioning going on."

"So, what type of visa did you say you had? H-1B or L-1B?"

"No, just a B2." Charlie could not believe what he was hearing. The B2 visitor's visa did not allow a person from another country to work legally in the US. It only allowed a person to visit for up to six months. Upon arrival, the border agent would ask the purpose of his visit, and how long the person planned to visit. The answer was irrelevant and used as a smoke screen to make visitors nervous. Charlie thought it was a game they played. If the answer did not match with what was entered on the visa application, it could mean further questions. If the answer were consistent with the details on the visa application, the agent would enter a date on the I-94 that allowed a person to stay up to six months. Adhere to the time restrictions during the first visit and the next application for a visitor's visa would allow a multiple entry permit. The new piece of information Ben had volunteered explained what Michael indicated when he mentioned the illegal use of visas. Charlie planned his questions for Ben carefully. He wanted to see how much information he could get from him.

Before he could respond, the waiter arrived with their food. The waiter put the plates with grilled steaks in front of them. Charlie looked at his plate and smelled the aroma of the hot grilled sirloin. He had not realized how hungry he was, and looked forward to the meal. He looked across the table and saw Ben already cutting into his well-done sixteen-ounce rib eye steak. He silently wondered how long it had been since the kid had a decent meal, something not bought from a fast food place or heated in a microwave oven. Charlie slowly cut into his medium done steak, and took his first bite. Judging from the rate the food was disappearing from his plate, Ben seemed to inhale his food.

They ate in silence for a few minutes and Charlie had time to digest what Ben had just told him.

"Good steak," Charlie commented on the food to get Ben talking again.

"Oh, this is great. I cannot remember the last time I had a decent steak. We used to grill out every weekend back home. Lamb chops are still my favorite. My uncle raised sheep on his farm, and my parents always got meat at a reasonable price from him."

"That I can agree with. My favorite is the rack of lamb." Charlie kept the conversation going, and Ben eventually started to talk more than he usually did.

"Did Heinz mention if you would be able to come back?" Charlie continued to ask more questions.

"He said Vince had a few projects in the pipeline, and they might need some application developers for a project that starts early next year."

"Yes, I also heard the rumor. Did he mention the client involved in the project?"

"No, just that it is some financial system that needs to be converted to newer technology. They are looking for SQL and C++ skills. He promised me a referral fee if I could find somebody with experience. They are always looking for developers who would be interested in coming to work in the US for a short while."

"Very interesting. Did he perhaps mention the company involved?"

"I'm not sure, but he did mention that BOSA, Bank of South Africa, was looking to expand into the international market. Do you know them?"

Charlie took another sip of his wine. He had to consider his response carefully. He had promised himself many years ago to never lie to anybody and to always tell the truth. The truth for him also meant not volunteering information. Keith was the one who gave him the advice and it helped him many times. *"If asked a question that puts you in a tough spot? Remember, less information is always more."* This was one of those times where he needed to use the advice. He could say yes, and it could lead to more questions, or he could say no and lie. He considered the correct response.

"Yes. Everybody from South Africa does. They are one of the big ones. Did you work for them?"

"No. I started in the insurance business after graduation. When the company downsized, I got word of an opportunity for web developers to work internationally. I applied, got an interview and here I am. I hope to come back again and maybe stay longer."

"What type of visas do the other developers have?" Charlie asked nonchalantly. He needed more specific details and it seemed Ben was a good source of information.

"Heinz told me not to discuss my own or any other employee's visa status." He suddenly leaned forward and with glassy eyes looked at Charlie. "You are not going to rat me out, are you?"

"No, don't worry about it." Charlie said with a smile but sounded disappointed. "If you cannot talk it's fine. I don't want to put you in a difficult spot. I had to go through the same process, and I'm just glad mine is over now." As they finished their meals and the waiter took their empty plates, Ben picked up the dessert menu placed in front of him.

"Can we order dessert?"

"Sure, why not. Another beer for you?"

"Why not!" Ben echoed Charlie's words and scanned the dessert options.

Charlie hoped Ben would want another beer. It seemed the more beer he consumed, the more careless he was about the information he shared. They placed the order for dessert, and Ben continued providing the information Charlie wanted.

"Tell me Ben," Charlie ventured deeper into the topic. "Why did Gracey have to leave the project so suddenly? I was disappointed when she left. She was one of the better developers."

"Yes, I miss her too. We became good friends." Ben said with a sad look on his face. "She wanted to stay and complete the project, but Heinz said she couldn't."

"Oh! Why not?" Charlie expected the reason, but needed confirmation.

"Her I-94 was almost expired. She had no choice."

"How is her replacement doing?"

"Jackson? He's ok. Heinz agreed Gracey could work remotely until Jackson was up to speed with the processes she worked on."

"Seems he knows his stuff. Does he also have a B2 visas?"

"Yes. He came from a different project and he mentioned he could only stay for another three more months before he has to return. The project should be over by then." Ben paused for a moment and Charlie saw he had something else on his mind. "What are you going to do after this project Charlie? Do you have anything lined up yet?"

"Well, I have been here since the start of the project and need some time off. I plan to travel a bit and visit my mom. There may be something in the works for next year, but I am not sure."

The waiter placed the desserts in front of them and Charlie enjoyed his apple pie and vanilla ice cream. Ben had a brownie with hot chocolate sauce and enjoyed every bite with a comment about how good it was. Charlie asked the waiter to call the hotel shuttle for them and settled the check for dinner.

"Thank you, Charlie. I really enjoyed the food. It was very generous of you to pay for my drinks also. I owe you one."

"Don't worry about it. You already helped me a lot," Charlie said as they got into the shuttle and left for the hotel.

In bed at the hotel Charlie mulled over the information he gathered from Ben. If he could only get some proof that his suspicions were true. It was obvious that PITS had more than one fraudulent scheme going on. Heinz lied to him about his rate, but it seemed they had another scheme going on with the rates for other consultants. It was also clear that some consultants did not have the correct visa type to work in the US. Charlie thought about ways to get a copy of Ben's visa. It would be the ultimate proof that something strange was going on.

"How are they getting away with this?" he thought to himself. He remembered the comment from Michael when they had to leave the country and he decided to e-mail the next day. *"Maybe I should visit them while I am on vacation."*

His thoughts turned to the offer from Tessa and the new opportunity for him. He remembered her comment about how they did their homework and wondered if she would be able to help him with information. The more he thought about it, the more worried he became.

"What if they start investigating me and discover the account in Zurich? How do I explain it? What do I do with the money? Can I really spend it? Maybe I should not make the trip to Switzerland?"

It was past midnight when Charlie eventually fell asleep. He had many ideas of how to proceed, but none was without risk. After all the years of living a quiet life, focusing on his work and nothing more, his world had turned upside down in the past few weeks. The only positive thing was the offer from Tessa and the possibility of getting away from PITS.

* * *

CHAPTER 19

Project End

"Thank you again for all your hard work. Take some time off and travel safe. Until we meet again. Good-bye! Meeting adjourned!" The team clapped as Tessa closed the final project meeting.

Team members started saying good-bye. Promises to stay in touch were exchanged and slowly the room emptied. Employees of First Midwest were the first to leave. They now had sole ownership of the new system and took over responsibility for future maintenance and support. The consultants completed the typical lame duck knowledge transfer sessions and for employees it felt like pulling teeth. When the project started a couple of years ago, they relied on the input and knowledge of the external consultants. They knew the day of reckoning would eventually come yet for some it still came as a surprise. Their crutches were taken away and the continued success of the project depended on how much of the knowledge was retained by those staying behind. Some were confident and excited about the prospect, but most were very nervous.

The critical care period lasted for thirty days after go live. The transition went smoothly and the first month-end showed it was a success. A few consultants were retained for an additional fourteen days' remote support but Charlie graciously declined the request. He did not particularly like the after care period. He used his vacation plans and the confirmed tickets as an excuse to get out of the job.

Charlie walked with Tessa from the meeting room to her office. She still had some final admin things to take care of as the project manager and would remain until the very end before she would be able to move on to her next adventure.

"Thank you, Charlie," she said as they walked down the hall towards her office. "You became a true friend, almost like the brother I never had."

"It was my pleasure," Charlie said with a smile. "I enjoyed working with you. It took me a while to realize you were not only an excellent project manager, but also a caring human being,"

"It was a long and challenging project. Lots of things happened, but I think we can feel proud of ourselves. I had a great team, a few stubborn ones, but I think we wrapped it up pretty well."

"Yes, that's a wrap. You did a great job, Tessa. I hope the next project will be just as successful for you."

"Speaking of the next project. Have you made your final decision yet? Will you be available for us if we get the final nod?"

"I need some time off to get my thoughts straightened out. My dad always warned me against making a decision when upset or when things are going wrong. He said you have to make important decisions when things are going well and when your emotions are stable."

"A wise man," Tessa commented and Charlie continued.

"I told you about my plans to visit Europe. It's been a while since I visited my mom and my family. I also plan to visit an old friend while I am there. It's spring in South Africa and the weather is just getting better. October is the perfect time of the year to visit."

"Well, you know where to get ahold of me." Tessa said as they stopped at the elevator. "If you need a friend to chat with, give me a call. I have your contact details and will stay in touch. Let me know if your plans change."

"I will. Good luck with the final few weeks."

"Thanks, Charlie. Stay in touch." She moved forward and surprised Charlie with a hug. He quickly wrapped his arms around her to return the hug. She was really like a sister to him, and when they let go and stepped back, he saw a tear in her eye. His eyes were also watery and he had to swallow the lump in his throat.

"Bye, Tessa, and thank you again. For everything!" Charlie said. He gave her hand, which he was still holding, a final squeeze before he turned around and walked away.

"Enjoy Europe! Bye!" Tessa said over her shoulder and waved at him as she made her way back to her office.

The elevator door closed behind Charlie as he left the place he had spent the last two years.

* * *

CHAPTER 20

Zurich

His flight from Springfield to Nashville was without incident or delay. Charlie had a couple of days to make his final arrangements before his extended vacation. Heinz kept his promise and a nice bonus was included in Charlie's paycheck. They had not talked since their last meeting, keeping all communications done via e-mail. Heinz did not offer any explanation for how he had pulled it off and Charlie did not bother to ask. Heinz confirmed that he had made the arrangements with his bank for a wire transfer when needed. In an e-mail Heinz assumed the transfer would be to a bank in South Africa and Charlie responded with a brief comment to inform Heinz that it would be a bank in Europe. With every e-mail exchange, Charlie felt the urge to ask about the name of Heinz's cat and where it came from, but every time deleted the question before he hit the send button. He just could not get over the uneasy feeling about Heinz.

Charlie enjoyed the luxurious flight from Nashville to Amsterdam. When he saw the difference the bonus made to his bank account, he decided to splurge and upgraded his ticket to first class. He had not been on an international trip for a while and the food and service were excellent. He enjoyed a glass of champagne offered by the flight attendant when he sat down in his seat, and felt like a king. The plane touched down in Amsterdam early Sunday morning and then Charlie boarded a train to Zurich. He had made a reservation at a hotel close to the bank. He was not sure how long he would be there and reserved a room for three nights. At the front desk during check-in, he confirmed that it would not be a problem to extend his stay if needed. His flight from Amsterdam to Johannesburg was booked for Friday, leaving him enough time to complete his business with the bank and return to Amsterdam.

Charlie walked into the Bank of Zurich on Monday morning and approached the customer service desk. *"Seems like nothing has changed since my last visit,"* Charlie thought as he looked around at the impressive architecture and high ceiling. At the desk he asked to see the bank manager. From his experience when he opened the account he knew it would be a very formal encounter with the staff. He had called the previous week to make sure he would be able to see the manager on Monday morning.

"May I ask the purpose of the meeting, Sir?" the clerk standing behind the counter asked courteously. He was an older gentleman with neatly combed hair, a clean-shaven face and subtlety smelling of after-shave lotion. With the dark three-piece gray suit, white shirt and thin red striped blue silk tie, Charlie thought he would make a perfect butler to a king. He showed no emotion, and although his eyes were friendly and reassuring, Charlie also knew that he was facing a professional in his own right. His posture demanded respect, and he treated people with courtesy.

"I need information about an account I opened many years ago. I am not sure if the information on file is current and would like to verify it please."

"Maybe I can help you," the clerk said. "Do you have a passport for identification and the account number please?"

"Yes, I do. There may be two account numbers linked to my name, Mr. Lindtmeyer," Charlie said as he reached for his passport in his bag. He used the last name from the nameplate on the desk and assumed it was Mr.

Lindtmeyer he was talking to. He assumed correctly as the gentleman acknowledged the use of his name and the correct pronunciation of it with a gentle nod of the head, and only the slightest indication of a smile. He took Charlie's passport and the piece of paper with the account numbers. He typed on the keyboard, waited a few seconds and then a question mark appeared on his face. He looked up at Charlie for a brief moment and turned his attention back to the screen in front of him.

"Mr. O'Neal," he said. "Can you confirm the account numbers for me please?"

Charlie quoted the account numbers and waited. He expected more questions, but was not sure what they would be. When he opened the account, he was informed about the strict confidentiality and security. He knew an identification code would be requested to discuss all matters related to the account. The identification code was separate from the PIN number to use when withdrawing money.

"Do you have the identification code?"

"a-l-p-h-a-#-1-9-7-3"

"Thank you, Mr. O'Neal. I do have some more questions if you would not mind." Mr. Lindtmeyer looked at Charlie, and he realized the he was being vetted as the true Mr. O'Neal. "As an account holder, you are aware of our strict confidentiality and security. We want to make sure we only provide information to the account holder or a duly authorized representative."

"I am aware of that, and I do appreciate the thoroughness of the verification."

"The passport number does not agree with the passport number on the account." Mr. Lindtmeyer looked at Charlie through eyes that would take note of every twitch or flinch.

"Oh, yes, of course," Charlie said and opened his bag. "I opened the account many years ago while living in South Africa. I immigrated to the US, and am now a citizen. I do have my old passport if that would help." Charlie handed him his old passport. The look on Mr. Lindtmeyer 's face did not change.

"Thank you, Sir," he said and compared the numbers. He looked at Charlie; looked at both passports, and back at Charlie again. "Do you have your bank card, Mr. O'Neal?"

"Well, that is why I needed to see the manager. I do not have one. I destroyed it many years ago and have not used the account for a very long time. What is the balance on the account?" Charlie asked.

"I cannot discuss the details of the account, Sir. Do you have any other form of identification?" Mr. Lindtmeyer was good at his job.

"I do have my US driver's license with me. Will that help?"

"Indeed it would, Sir." He took the license, studied it and then started typing on the keyboard, reading the responses. Charlie could not see what he was typing, but he knew from experience with bank security systems, that he was accessing security databases and analyzing all his details. He may even have access to Interpol to verify his identity. After a few minutes the typing stopped and Mr. Lindtmeyer continued to read the screen in front of him. Charlie watched his eyes as they moved from side to side while reading the screen. After a few more keystrokes the printer on the desk next to the computer started printing. Mr. Lindtmeyer picked up the phone and dialed a number. Somebody answered on the other end.

"Mrs. Rothschild, this is Mr. Lindtmeyer. I have a Mr. Charles O'Neal from the United States with me. He would like to meet with Mr. Meyer. Is he perhaps available for an meeting?" The person on the other side responded, but Charlie could not hear. "That will be fine. I will inform Mr. O'Neal. Thank you, Mrs. Rothschild." He put the phone down and looked at Charlie.

"Mr. Meyer can see you in fifteen minutes. Would it be in order for us to make a copy of your new identification documents, Mr. O'Neal?"

"No problem, Mr. Lindtmeyer. Go ahead," Charlie said and looked around for a place to sit and wait.

Christo Louis Nel

"We have a private waiting room for Mr. Meyer. Could I offer you a cup of coffee while you wait?" Mr. Lindtmeyer asked very politely.

"That would be very kind of you. Thank you, Mr. Lindtmeyer" Charlie responded. Growing up in South Africa he was also influenced by the British traditions, and recognized the aristocratic manners and cordial way of treating guests and clients.

"Please follow me, Mr. O'Neal." Mr. Lindtmeyer opened a door and lead Charlie to a small waiting room with six comfortable high back antique chairs and a coffee table. In the corner stood a small table with a variety of local newspapers and financial magazines.

"Please wait here, Sir. I will return with you documents shortly. Mrs. Rothschild will serve coffee in a moment."

"Thank you, Sir," Charlie responded and sat down in one of the chairs. A few minutes later Mrs. Rothschild brought in a tray with all the ingredients necessary for Charlie to make his own cup of coffee. He put one teaspoon of coffee in a cup and poured hot water from a silver carafe. He added some milk, not creamer, and stirred it with a silver spoon. He sat down to enjoy the coffee and the rich aroma reminded him of his childhood. He drank his coffee alone and in silence with only memories as company. He remembered when he and Keith sat in the same office many years ago.

A few minutes later Mrs. Rothschild returned with his documents and handed them to Charlie.

"Mr. Meyer will be available shortly, Sir. He is concluding his meeting, and I will come and get you when he is available."

"Thank you, Mrs. Rothschild," Charlie said with a slight nod of the head as he saw Mr. Lindtmeyer did when he acknowledge Charlie's responses.

Charlie put his documents in his bag and browsed through one of the magazines. A few minutes later Mrs. Rothschild came back and escorted him to Mr. Meyer's office. Charlie recognized the office and the furniture, but it was a new face smiling at him. Mr. Meyer stood up from behind his desk and stretched out his hand. Charlie reached over and felt the firm grip of big hands. "*A confident man*", Charlie thought as he returned the firm handshake. The manager had calluses on his hand that reminded Charlie of his uncle. He knew he was facing an outdoor craftsman. It was not as soft and smooth as Charlie's hand that was more used to typing on a keyboard for ten to twelve hours a day.

"Welcome, Mr. O'Neal. Please sit down and let us see how I can be of service to you today."

"Thank for your time, Mr. Meyer, and for seeing me on such short notice without an appointment."

"We always make time for our international clients, Mr. O'Neal." Mr. Meyer said as he opened the folder Mrs. Rothschild had put on his desk. He flipped through the pages, made some notes on a pad, and then turned back to the first page. He typed something on his keyboard. Charlie waited patiently as Mr. Meyer studied the screen, and then typed some more. The same question mark appeared on his face that had appeared on the face of Mr. Lindtmeyer.

"What is it we can do for you today, Mr. O'Neal?" Mr. Meyer said as he locked his fingers and looked at Charlie with piercing eyes. It was clear there was some explanation required.

"Sir, I don't have a debit card for the account and don't have access to the funds. I destroyed the card a long time ago when something personal happened. Over time I completely forgot about the account."

"Forgot? How can someone forget about so much money?" It was the first time somebody confirmed to Charlie that the balance he saw online might just be true.

"It's a long story, Sir. I believe I don't have to explain it all. I chose this bank for its privacy and confidentiality." Charlie did not want to talk about what had happened. It was painful for him just to think about it.

"That is true, Mr. O'Neal, and we are proud of our reputation. We are a bank with the tradition of privacy, security and confidentiality. You can trust me that information discussed in this office stays in the office. If we don't do it that way, we risk losing many clients in the blink of an eye."

"Thank you, Sir," Charlie said before continuing. "I am not sure about the balance I saw online." He was still very careful to not disclose too much of what he already knew.

"There has not been any activity on the account for quite some time. We flag all accounts dormant for more than three years. Any activity will immediately trigger a notification for us to verify the identity of the person accessing the account. If I look at the activity log, I see the password was recently reset. The next thing somebody walks in and enquires about the account. It is obvious, Mr. O'Neal, that we will have questions and we will need to verify your identity. Your identity documents seem to be in order. Before I share and discuss the account details further, I would like to ask some questions that only the original applicant will know. Is that in order?"

"Yes, and I do appreciate the verification."

"Ok, then. Let's see." Mr. Meyer looked at his monitor and pressed a key. "When did you open the account and what was the amount of the initial deposit?"

"It was on June 13, 1979 and it was a thousand Swiss Franc."

"The account is linked to a second account. Can you provide me with any details of the other account?"

"The account is in the name of Keith Thomas James. He was from Pretoria in South Africa and opened the account at the same time I opened my account. We countersigned power of attorney for each other, and it authorizes an in-person discussion of each other's account with a bank official. That is, if the identification of the person can be verified. I believe that is exactly what is happening."

Charlie provided the number for Keith's account to Mr. Meyer. They had opened the accounts when they visited Zurich when Project Delta promised some results.

"And where does Mr. James live now?" The question did not come as a surprise for Charlie. It still caught him off guard to talk about the most tragic day in his life, a day he had tried so many times to forget, but to no avail.

"He is deceased. He passed away during an accident in 1981. My fiancé passed away in the same accident." It was with a heavy heart that Charlie managed to mention the accident.

"I am so sorry to hear that. I did not know," Mr. Meyer said and sounded very sincere. There were a few seconds of silence before Mr. Meyer continued.

"This must sound strange, but do you perhaps have a copy of his death certificate? We can verify it, but that will take some time. If you have copy of the death certificate, it will be easier."

"I do have a copy. His wife has the original one." Charlie opened a folder he had brought with him and searched for the document. He handed it to Mr. Meyer who took it, studied it for a few seconds and pressed a button on the phone. A few moments later the door opened and Mr. Lindtmeyer appeared.

"Mr. Lindtmeyer, I need you to verify something for me. Please make this a priority and also make a copy for our records. Mr. O'Neal here has power of attorney over the account of Mr. James." Mr. Lindtmeyer took the document and disappeared. Mr. Meyer picked up the phone and ordered coffee for them.

"This is going to take a while," Charlie thought.

"Mr. O'Neal. We have a lot to talk about. How long will you be in town?"

"I expected it and made reservations for three days. Will that be enough?"

"More than enough to verify some information and prepare documentation for you to sign."

"Will I have access to the money?" Charlie asked the question he was hoping to get answered to soon.

"Of course. It is your money. It has been in the account for so long and earned some great interest for you. You may use it immediately."

"So, the online information is true?"

"Yes. One hundred percent accurate! Do you need to withdraw some funds today?"

"I would like to. Will it be possible to provide me with a new debit card for the account?"

"We can do that. The fees to withdraw cash internationally are very expensive. We only have our own teller machines in Switzerland and in some major international cities. We do have other ways to make it easier for you to access the money if needed."

"What would that be?" Charlie asked with interest.

"We can provide you with a credit card and link it to your savings account. Charges to the credit card are settled daily, and fees for the use of the credit card are a fraction of the fees to withdraw cash at a foreign ATM. In your case, you will then have more than one way to utilize the funds in your account."

"I do not want any paperwork sent anywhere about the account. No marketing schemes please."

"Mr. O'Neal!" Mr. Meyer sounded upset. "I take offense at that. Do you know with whom you are dealing? We are proud of our reputation and you are insinuating we share information with others."

"Oh. I am so sorry. I forgot," Charlie felt embarrassed for the obvious blunder. "I am so used to being bombarded with marketing from credit card companies that I prefer not to use any."

"It is not a traditional credit card. It is a special arrangement we have and transactions are settled daily in full. No interest and no fees are charged until you deplete your savings account. Then the card becomes invalid and will be of no further use to you."

"Can I use the account online to transfer money between accounts at other banks?"

"Yes. The account status is set back to operational since we have verified your credentials. You now have full control again. We do have to discuss Mr. James's account though."

"I do not have access to his account. Can you tell me anything about it?"

"The balance is not close to the balance in your account. Based on the date of his passing, he did not have significant funds in the account at the time. The transactions that occurred after his death seem to match those of your account for some time, but then stopped completely. The deposits to your account picked up for a while again, and then also completely stopped just before the year two thousand. From then on only interest was added to the accounts."

"Will I have access to his account?"

"Not immediately. The agreement you both signed was only to get access upon death. As soon as we get the death certificate verified and the appropriate paperwork signed, we will give you full access. We can even transfer the money to your account and close the other account."

"Is there any documentation or reference about his wife?"

"None. The same as with your account - there are no beneficiaries on your account. Something you should take care of as soon as possible."

Charlie thought about this for a moment and then looked at Mr. Meyer.

"Can we do something about it immediately? As in right now? I would like to assign beneficiaries before I walk out."

"Do you have the name and address for the beneficiary?"

"I do. There are two people I want to nominate please," Charlie said and handed over a sheet of paper with the name and address details for his mother and his brother, Stephen.

"I will have Mr. Lindtmeyer handle this before you leave."

"I do have one more request, if I may, Mr. Meyer?" Charlie asked. Mr. Meyer looked up from the document he was reviewing.

"And that is?"

"May I request some of the money be wired to Mr. James's widow, please? I believe it can be done incognito?"

"Once we have completed the verification of the death certificate, it can be arranged."

"Thank you, Sir. That will be very kind of you. I also need a single use account number for a wire transfer to my account as soon as possible."

"That is a second request, Mr. O'Neal," Mr. Meyer smiled and winked at Charlie. "But, yes, we can arrange for that too. Anything else?"

"Not today. I will come prepared with questions and requests tomorrow."

"That will be in order. We are here to serve you. Can we meet tomorrow afternoon? We need to prepare the documentation for you and verify the death certificate. Before you leave, Mr. Lindtmeyer will provide you with a new debit card and will arrange for the beneficiary nomination document to be signed. Thank you for visiting us, Mr. O'Neal," Mr. Meyer said as he stood up and stretched his hand out to Charlie, indicating the meeting was over. They shook hands and Mr. Meyer opened the door for Charlie. He saw the next client in the waiting room, and Mr. Meyer gave some instructions to Mrs. Rothschild. She escorted Charlie back to the customer service desk where Mr. Lindtmeyer stood ready to execute the orders from Mr. Meyer as relayed to him by Mrs. Rothschild.

With all the paperwork done for the day, Charlie walked out of the bank with a bundle of cash and a stack of travelers' checks in an envelope. In his wallet were brand new debit and credit cards. He walked a few steps away from the bank, stopped and turned around to admire the building he had just exited. He felt relief slowly returning as the stress from the morning and the last few weeks faded away. He still could not believe what had just happened. After all the years of planning and scheming, after all the long hours he and Keith had spent working on the execution of their plan. For the first time, he could actually feel the money in his hands. The *half-a-penny* calculations from Project Alpha became tangible after so many years.

"Is this for real?" he asked himself as he turned around and walked down the street along the shores of the Zurich-See. The air was brisk, and when he got to a bench along the way, he sat down and cried. He remembered how he and Keith had sat on the same bench many years ago when they first opened the accounts. Hanna and Marlene did not want to visit the football museum with them and were wandering the streets of Zurich taking pictures of the old buildings. Their plan worked and they did not have to explain the reasons for the visit to the bank.

"My life will never be the same again," he thought to himself as he wiped away the remnants of the tears in his eyes. He thought about Hanna and the life they had dreamed about - a dream that came to a sudden end and left him alone. For many years he had managed to suppress memories about her, but just being in a place where he knew she had also been, brought all the pain and sadness back. He walked to the street café where they had all dined together and ordered a sandwich. When the waitress brought his food and placed it in front of him, she noticed the tears and the sadness on his face. She smiled at Charlie, did not say much and left him alone with his thoughts.

Charlie sat at the table for a while and thought about everything that had happened in the last few months. In a way he felt guilty about suddenly having access to so much money.

"Am I a thief? Was it wrong to blackmail Heinz to get what was owed to me? I worked very hard for it." He thought back to the first time he held a system hostage and demanded ransom to be paid. Every time he thought about Sam and Linda Griffin, it made him smile. He made peace with the money Heinz owed him, but still had a battle raging in his head about the 'half-a-penny' that became millions.

"Can I really spend that money? Is it really mine? What am I going to do with

it?" He had more questions than answers so when he left the street café, he went for a long walk along the river. He stopped at places he remembered from their previous visit, and was engulfed and saddened once again by all the memories. Remembering was painful and decided he'd rather go back to the hotel.

The next day Charlie returned to the bank and completed the purpose for his visit. The bank proved their efficiency and upheld their reputation as one of the best banks in the world. They had confirmed the authenticity of Keith's death certificate, and according to the original documents he and Keith had signed, the money from Keith's account was transferred into Charlie's account. He then authorized the transfer to Marlene's account, knowing he'd have some explaining to do when saw her again. It would be difficult, but he looked forward to seeing her and Keith Junior, or KT as she called him, again.

Mr. Lindtmeyer provided Charlie with the details of the single use account number and Charlie confirmed the expected amount to be wired over. He requested the full amount be transferred into his savings account and that all the information linking the two accounts together be removed. Mr. Lindtmeyer provided Charlie with a business card and his phone number. If the funds from the wire-transfer didn't appear online in Charlie's account, he could call Mr. Lindtmeyer directly.

Back in his hotel room, Charlie sent a short e-mail to Heinz with the account number and instructions on how the money should be transferred. He reminded Heinz of the agreed upon twenty-four hours to wire the money and requested a confirmation via e-mail when the transaction had occurred. Charlie didn't expect an immediate response due to the time difference between Zurich and Atlanta. He used the rest of the day to visit the FIFA World Football Museum. Football wasn't his favorite sport since he had been a rugby player in high school, but it was something he had to do for Keith.

When he returned to the hotel in the afternoon, he checked his e-mail and saw the confirmation from Heinz that the money would be transferred as agreed. Brief and to the point, only the essentials mentioned in the e-mail. No personal discussions or references.

On Wednesday morning Charlie stopped at an ATM to check the balance of his account. He printed a statement of the last five transactions and saw the money Heinz had wired. A feeling of satisfaction came over Charlie, and for a brief moment he felt sorry for Heinz. He looked back at the balance on the statement. It stood at 12,233,477 Euros and he quickly converted it to dollars. *'With the exchange rate at 1.114, it gives me 13,946,291 dollars. Wow! I am rich!'* he said to himself. It made him feel better to know that some of the money was his own, but the lines were still blurred between what was legal and what was not.

Suddenly Charlie just wanted to get away. He longed to see his family again, realizing just how many years it had been since he'd seen them. He called Stephen, who was very surprised to hear from him, and was even more surprised to learn the he was on his way to visit. They made arrangements for Stephen to pick Charlie up from the airport and decided to keep it a surprise for their mother. Stephen would ensure she would be available for Charlie to visit her.

The next call was the more difficult one to make. He dialed Marlene's number and waited for her to pick up on the other end.

"Hello, this is Marlene James," a soft and friendly voice said on the other end.

"Marlene, this is Charlie," he said and swallowed hard on the lump in his throat.

"Charlie?" she said, as she did not immediately recognize his voice. "Charlie! Charlie O'Neal! Oh my word! How are you? Where are you?" She sounded excited to hear from him, but Charlie did not trust his own voice. He waited a few seconds before he responded. As always, her excitement was contagious and he struggled to control his emotions.

"Yes. It's me. Marlene, I'm on my way to South Africa. Can I come and see you?"

"You'd better come and see me! I haven't seen you in years. Where are you? Are you ok? You sound strange." She rambled on with questions and Charlie knew better than to try and interrupt her. It made him smile and also gave him time to relax and take a deep breath.

"I am ok." Charlie said with more confidence and excitement in his voice. "The project I worked on for the last two years came to an end and I'm taking a few weeks off. I plan to visit my mom, family and some friends. I would like to see you."

"When will you be here? I can arrange for a day's vacation. You know the life of a teacher this time of year. The matric final exams are not far away and the students need a lot of help."

"If I can get my ticket changed, I will arrive tomorrow. Stephen and Ester will pick me up at the airport. We are going to surprise my mom and I will stay with her for a couple of days. If you have some time next week, I am flexible and can fit in with your schedule."

"Wow. That's great! I still cannot believe it. You really surprised me. Why did you not let me know sooner?"

"It's a long story. I will explain when I get there."

"Ok. Let me call the principal and see if I can get a day off next week. He's not going to be happy, but he owes me more than just one day. Where can I reach you?"

"You can just call Stephen. His number is still the same. I will be with them for a few days and am still working on the details for the rest of the time."

"Ok. I will call when I have made arrangements at school."

"Marlene," Charlie said and hesitated. "There is one more thing."

"Yes?" she asked cautiously.

"Have you checked your bank statement today?"

"No. Why?"

"It's not a mistake. It's yours." There was silence on the phone for a while and Charlie held his breath. He did not know what to expect.

"Charlie, what have you done?"

"I will explain when I see you."

When they said good-bye, Charlie felt good about what he had done. He looked forward to seeing her again.

* * *

CHAPTER 21

Battle of the Mind

O n the train ride from Zurich back to Amsterdam, Charlie thought about his future plans. He found himself opening his wallet a few times just to make sure he still had the cards and it was all real. He enjoyed the first class flight from Amsterdam to Johannesburg, but sleep during the flight didn't come easy. Charlie only managed to get in a few hours of sleep on the 10-hour flight. He tried to follow a movie on the screen in the back of the seat in front of him, but his thoughts kept straying. He envied the passenger next to him who had managed to fall asleep not long after takeoff.

He had enjoyed some upgrades to first class on domestic flights before but it did not come close to the luxury he experienced during the international flights. It had been more than ten years since he had last visited his home country of South Africa, and he looked forward to seeing his family again. He couldn't wait to admire the beauty of nature only found in Southern Africa.

Outwardly he had the appearance of enjoyment and pleasure, but in his mind the battle continued to rage between right and wrong over the ownership of the money and the guilt trips about the death of Keith and Hanna. So many times he went down the rabbit hole of *'what-ifs'*. What if they have never started with project Bravo? What if he and Keith never interfered with the doings of Sir Archibald? He had a renewed fear after the incident at Heinz's house when he was introduced to his cat.

"Who is Heinz really? How does he fit in with Sir Archibald?" Charlie caught himself many times thinking about the incident, and it just did not make sense to him. They lived in separate cities, and personal contact was very little. They had a strict professional working relationship where Charlie kept to himself and Heinz had enough trouble at home to not want to discuss his private life with anyone else.

"Why did he name his cat Sir Archibald? What a name for a cat!" Charlie thought while staring out of the small airplane window at the North African desert below. The sun touched the horizon as they flew south. *"If you can name a dog Beethoven, you can for sure give a cat the aristocratic name of Sir Archibald."* If it were not for his history and past experience with the name, it would have been a cute name for a pet.

When the plane finally touched down on South African soil, his exhaustion was replaced with excitement to see his family again. Charlie cleared immigration and collected his luggage from the baggage claim area. The years on the road made him a light traveler. He only had one checked bag, one carry-on and his laptop bag with him. He walked into the receiving lounge and looked for Stephen and Ester. They spotted him first and waved. When he saw them, he acknowledged the wave, and made his way through the waiting crowd toward them.

The greeting was emotional and tears filled the eyes of the two brothers who bravely tried not to show any weakness when they embraced. *"Men don't cry,"* their father used to say when they were little kids and got hurt in some way.

Stephen was almost two years older than Charlie and as kids they were best friends. Charlie was one grade behind Stephen in school, but they took care of each other, they shared secrets, fought each other like brothers did, and remained confidants for life. They got separated when Stephen graduated high school and the required military service took him away for long periods of time. They had very little contact during that time and Charlie only received updates about Stephen's military experience from his mother. Like many other mothers with sons in the military, she diligently wrote a letter to Stephen every week. Eventually Stephen joined the permanent force of the military and became an instructor at the academy. As a non-commanding officer, or NCO, he experienced the worst side of the war. Charlie noticed the effects on Stephen during one of the seven-day passes when he visited his parents. Conversations would go well until someone would mention the border war, whereupon Stephen would go quiet. He didn't want to talk about the excursions into neighboring countries. Charlie remembered one conversation where Stephen mentioned an ambush deep inside of Angola. He led a reconnaissance patrol across the border where they were caught in an ambush. In the ensuing battle, they lost five men and Charlie realized that Stephen would never be the same. They never talked about the incident again.

Their lives changed drastically the day Stephen fell asleep behind the wheel of his car. He was on his way home for a visit, and had driven fourteen hours straight when the car veered off the road, and he lost control. He did not have his seatbelt on and when the car flipped a few times, he ended up in the passenger seat when the car landed against a tree. A branch of the tree pierced the roof and penetrated the driver's seat. He realized how narrowly he had escaped death and was convinced God wanted to tell him something. A few months later Stephen informed his parents about his decision to become a Reverend of faith in the Dutch Reformed Church. Dad was very excited since it had been one of his dreams to become a Reverend or some kind of preacher himself, but he never had the opportunity or the money to complete the required education.

Stephen worked hard, and after seven years graduated with his Ph.D.

from the Dutch Reformed Church seminary in Stellenbosch. The only thing more impressive than his achievement was the amount of debt he accumulated during the time. Their dad had co-signed for the student loan, and was on the hook when Stephen could not make payments. His first position as a Youth Reverend was at a church in Pretoria, not far from where they grew up as kids. The church owned a house and provided it for free to married clergy and took care of all expenses around housing, utilities and maintenance. For unmarried clergy, the church would pay the rent. Stephen moved into a small apartment in a church member's backyard, and like most young Reverends, barely survived on what was left after his student loan payments. He soon learned about the generosity and hospitality of the congregation where he served.

The church loved Stephen. His commitment to the ministry soon took effect and the attendance registers showed the monthly youth service far outnumbered any of the other services. He started a young adult ministry and met his future wife, Ester, at one of the events. Dating for a Youth Reverend was a complex and closely watched affair, and the courtship did not last long before they got engaged and then married.

Ester Bradford was a music teacher at the local high school. Being a married couple increased Stephen's status as a Reverend and he soon got a raise. They moved into a house owned by the church. It was a big house and had more space than they needed. A few months before Charlie made his decision to emigrate, their Dad passed away at a very young age due to a heart attack. Stephen took care of Mom and helped her through the difficult time. She stayed with Stephen and Ester for a short while, and then decided to move back to her own place where she had more friends and a job. "*There can only be one chef in a kitchen,*" she would jokingly say, but insinuated that being the mother-in-law in the clergy house was not how she wanted to spend the rest of her life. When Mom retired, she sold her house and moved into a retirement village where most of her friends lived. There was adequate security and organized activities to keep her busy. She was happy with her own place to call home.

Charlie stayed in the guest suite and Stephen insisted Charlie use one of their cars if needed. Charlie, with the knowledge of his current bank balance, insisted to at least pay for the insurance portion while using the car. After a lot of friendly squabbling, Stephen relented and agreed. Charlie had other intentions and asked for Stephen's bank account details to transfer the money for the insurance. When he offered to pay rent and help pay for the groceries, it was Ester who chimed in and said it would be an insult if they would take money from a guest living with them. The discussion was very lighthearted and they enjoyed seeing each other again. They talked for a long time and caught up with each other's lives, family, old friends, rugby, politics and happenings in the church. When the discussion turned to Charlie and what his plans for the future were, he was very vague and dodged questions by claiming to be relaxing and enjoying his vacation.

Ester brought out some afternoon snacks and tea, excused herself and left the brothers alone. As the Reverend's wife, she had her own responsibilities in the congregation, and was in charge of an outreach program at the church. The group was meeting to prepare for an event the following day. The church provided soup and sandwiches every weekend to settlers in squatter camps on the outskirts of the city. Volunteers gathered on Thursdays to plan and do the shopping, and on Friday mornings another group prepared the food. After she left, Charlie looked for the right opportunity to have a discussion with Stephen.

"I want to ask your opinion about something," Charlie started the conversation.

"Anytime. I knew there was something bothering you. Although we haven't seen each other in a long time, I counsel enough strangers to know when a person has something on his mind." Stephen said. Charlie realized it had been a very long time since he had talked to Stephen about anything personal. He didn't know exactly how to start or what to say.

"Well, it's kind of personal and confidential. Since we are family and also since you are a Reverend, this will only be between the two of us. Nobody else needs to know, but I also don't want to put you in a difficult spot."

"Wow, this is serious. But I can guarantee you it will stay private. I see and hear a lot of things, and sometimes it is a burden on me to know things about people who sit in the front row of the church, or who may be a deacon or and elder. Believe me, I learned my lesson very early in my career. Let's go to my office and close the door," Stephen said. He picked up the tray with tea and snacks and led the way.

Stephen's office was like a library. Bookshelves rose from the floor to the ceiling, and from wall-to-wall. There were all kinds of books covering the full spectrum of his ministry in the church and the community. There were books on the floor next to his desk and his desk was filled with open books he was in the process of reading.

"A nice collection of books. Have you read all of them?" Charlie asked as he stood in front of one of the shelves looking at the titles.

"If it's on a shelf, yes. If it's on my desk, I am working on it. If it's on the floor, they will end up in a box and go to storage. I don't have enough space for all my books, so I have to store some in boxes in the garage."

"Tell me something," Charlie said and turned to Stephen as they sat down. Stephen sat in his chair behind the desk, with his cup of tea in hand, and Charlie settled in to one of the chairs on the other side of the desk. The furniture was of good quality, but was faded and showed signs of being used frequently. "I am a bit nosy sometimes, but do you own this house now, or does it still belong to the church?"

"It still belongs to the church. The church's finances are very tight at the moment and I offered to buy it so that they don't have to keep up with the maintenance. We are working on the finer details of the agreement and hope to stay in this house and make it our forever home. It has everything we need. It was built in a time when the church had enough money to afford top quality materials and is within walking distance from the church. That makes it very convenient for me."

"I know Reverends and pastors are not always paid that well. Sometimes I think you are working in the mission field and not at a church. Will you be able to afford a mortgage payment?" Charlie knew this was something Stephen did not like to discuss. Stephen took a moment to answer and stalled by refilling their cups with tea.

"Ester and I knew from the start when we moved into this house that there would come a time when we would have to buy our own place. The church provided us with a clergy house and every month we put some money away so we will one day be in the position to buy a place of our own. If we buy this house from the church, it will be a win on both sides. I will get it below the current market value, while the church will get a much-needed financial windfall and also save on future maintenance. There are a lot of needs around us, and you know the church operates on tithes and offerings. I am sure you are aware of the state of the economy in the country."

"Yes, not going that great. Well, I hope it will work out for you and Ester. It is a nice house, and you have lived here for a very long time. It would sure be nice to have a place of your own."

"Well, that's not why we are here," Stephen steered the conversation back on track. He got up and closed the door. "Let's talk about the real reason for the visit."

Charlie took a deep breath. He had not discussed his personal life with anybody and this might just be the time to clear his mind.

"It's a long story. I'm not sure where to start."

"Well, the beginning is always a good place."

"Maybe not in this case. Maybe I should walk it backwards." He hesitated for a moment and then started. "I want to quit my job. I'm not sure I can go back to the company I worked for." Charlie said and Stephen looked at him with surprise.

"What happened? Another job?"

"I may have another option, but that is not the real reason I want to quit. I'm not sure I can trust them anymore. I recently discovered how they have cheated me for many years."

Charlie explained to Stephen what had happened in the past few months. He opened up about his anger and the bitterness was clearly visible as they talked. Stephen, the experienced counselor, had to pull the information out of Charlie in bits and pieces. They discussed the situation for a while and when they heard Ester return from her meeting, they did not stop talking.

"I think I should just not go back to PITS," Charlie said. "With the bonus they paid me and the increase in my rate, I can survive for a while." Charlie had told Stephen about the money Heinz had transferred, but he didn't mention the amount. He only indicated that it was substantial.

"If I were in your shoes, I would have done the same. From an ethical perspective, I think you have enough reason to walk away."

"I agree, but that's not all. I also know they are breaking the law with the way they are using the visa program to recruit new consultants. Some have a valid visa, but I know of many who are working on visitor's visas. That is fraud and they are asking others to break the law in the process."

"Can you not talk to immigration services about it?"

"I don't have proof. I know about it and I know how the process works. I had to go through it myself and it took me years to complete the process. That's why I feel so bad to leave them. It feels like I owe them something since they helped me get my citizenship."

For a while they talked about the different options Charlie had. In the back of his mind, he was still looking for a moment to talk about his other problem.

"One more thing," Charlie started to change the subject.

"There's more? Wow! You sure don't have a boring life," Stephen said lightheartedly.

"More than you will ever know," Charlie replied before he continued. "Let me put it this way. If you suddenly received a large amount of money, what would you do with it?"

"Did you win the lottery? I heard about the big jackpots there in the US."

"No, I did not win the lottery, but let's say you won the lottery. What would you do with it?"

"Well, I would be fired if I win the lottery. The church does not condone gambling and as a Reverend, I don't take part in any form of gambling. So, I will never have that problem."

"So the church would not take a donation if the winnings came from gambling?"

"Absolutely not. If we know it, we will not take it. If we find out about it later, we will pay it back. But why all these questions?" Stephen asked. Charlie wanted to know what Stephen would do if he were in Charlie's position, but he didn't want to put all his cards on the table.

"I just wanted to know what you would do. Let's say the money PITS owed me was much more and I had to sue them for it. What should I do with the money when they finally settle?"

"That's a different story. I know of a lot of things I would do."

"Like what?"

"Well, if it were my money, I would use most, not all of it, for me and my family. Also, being a Christian, I would give one tenth to the church, but that is just me." Stephen continued to talk about what he would do with a large amount of money. Charlie realized that he had not been to church in a while. The ideas Stephen brought up were all about helping others. None of his ideas were about doing something for himself.

"What would you do for yourself?" Charlie tried to change his line of thought.

"Well," Stephen said and leaned back in his chair with his hands behind his neck. "I would buy this house and then make some changes to my office so I can have space for all my books."

"Your books. Of course you would want more space for your books. And maybe more books I'm sure. A real bookworm." Charlie looked at all the books again. "Where would you build more shelves? The shelves already go to the ceiling."

"Well, I would break out that wall and add the space from the bedroom behind it to my office. I would add a couch, a couple of chairs and make my office more comfortable for counseling sessions. I have to counsel from behind my desk or use the living room where there is not a lot of privacy."

"What else?" Charlie asked.

"Let me see. Do you know what ARK is?"

"The ark that Moses built in the Bible?" Charlie was perplexed and had no clue what Stephen was referring to. Stephen burst out laughing.

"No, not that ark! A-R-K - Acts of Random Kindness. We had an outreach program in the community a few years ago. We gave each member of the congregation ten bucks. I asked them to use the money to perform a random act of kindness to a stranger they didn't know. We organized group sessions and each person could share his or her experience with the rest of the group. It was a huge success and it changed people's lives. Although it was only a small amount of money, a lot of people grabbed onto the idea and added some of their own money to it. They would randomly select a person and buy him or her something they did not expect. Some paid for a stranger's meal at a restaurant. One person overheard a couple in the grocery store discussing how many potatoes they could afford. The wife argued for the bigger bag so they didn't have to come back every day and waste gas in the process, but the husband argued that they did not have enough money to buy the bag of potatoes and all the other items in the cart. The person walked to the couple, gave them enough money to pay for all the groceries they had in their cart, and walked away."

"She just walked up to complete strangers and gave them some money?" Charlie said in disbelief.

"Well, she also said, 'God bless!' but she did not ask any questions. Just gave it and walked away. You see Charlie," Stephen continued and Charlie realized why his brother made a success in the ministry. He lived in the moment. Stephen continued with his explanation. "The intent with the experiment was to let people experience the feeling and satisfaction of giving and not of receiving. The person who gave something away spiritually got more in return than the person who received the physical gift. The focus was on the spiritual experience and not on the physical act that involved money."

"I thought it was just a matter of being generous. I always tip waiters and people that serve me well so next time they will serve me even better."

"But that is exactly the problem," Stephen said and waved his finger at Charlie. "Yes, you are generous by doing that, but what is the motive? You give bigger tips to receive better service in the future. The waiters will serve you better next time since they are expecting a big tip and not because it is the right thing to do. Should the waiter not do a good job of serving regardless of the tip size? Should the owner not pay the waiters and kitchen staff better so they will not depend on tips to survive?"

"I never thought of it that way."

"The ARK principal stuck with people and some still use it. For the church, it opened the door to start the soup kitchen. Every week volunteers from our church serve random strangers that they will never get anything from in return. The group goes to the same spot every week, and serves soup and sandwiches until they run out of food. And we run out every week."

Charlie listened to Stephen explaining more about the ways his church was helping the community and it stirred something in him. Slowly it dawned on him what he should do with the money that was not really his own.

"Would you accept a donation from me for the soup kitchen?" Charlie asked Stephen when he had a chance.

"We can use every penny we get. We declined some offers from big businesses since they wanted to use it as an excuse to market their products. We also don't take donations from a politician who wants to buy votes. It all depends on the amount of the donation, and the motive of the person giving it. We do not want to take the opportunity away from our congregation to continue to live the ARK principle. My usual question I ask prospective donors is how much they want to give and why?"

"How much will you need to not run out of food at least one time?" Charlie was not sure how much would be appropriate. He also did not want to let Stephen know that he could actually give a large amount of money.

"We will always run out. There are just too many mouths to feed in the squatter camps. We have set a goal for this year to try to increase the number of meals every week by twenty. We have not received enough donations the last few months to reach our goal, but we still managed to increase every week. With a large donation, we could do a special meal at Christmas."

"Can I make a donation to help with the Christmas meals?" Charlie asked. "I will also make a regular monthly contribution to the soup kitchen so the church can feed a few more people every week. My motive? Well, let's just say I also want to experience what ARK really is all about. Can it be anonymous? I know you will spend it wisely."

"Thank you, Charlie. That will be very generous of you. How much?" Stephen still did not have the full answer.

"Let's say it will be a generous donation. You know I am single. I now have a decent income and some savings. I have everything I need and more. Contrary to you, I have not given my tithe in a very long time and this may be a good time to do something about it."

"Thank you, Charlie," Stephen said humbly. "Every donation will make a difference. Let me discuss it with Ester and with the church leadership first."

Charlie felt relieved. He knew any amount he donated would only be a small drop in the bucket. He also could not let Stephen know where the money came from and was afraid he wouldn't accept anything if he knew the truth. It had to be just enough not to raise any suspicion with Stephen.

Eventually jetlag and excitement caught up with Charlie and when Stephen had to go check on the preparations at church, Charlie decided to stay at home and take a nap. The nap stretched till late the next morning. When Stephen and Ester returned from the church the night before, they found him in a deep sleep in his clothes on top of the bed. Stephen threw a light blanket over him and closed the door.

Charlie woke up the next morning totally confused, not sure where he was nor what day it was. He looked at the alarm clock and saw it was nine o'clock. The house was very quiet and in the kitchen there was a note from Ester informing him that they were at the church and would be back around noon for lunch. There were some freshly baked scones on the table so Charlie made himself a cup of coffee and enjoyed breakfast on his own. He found the phone in the living room and called Marlene to confirm their visit the following week. She had arranged for two vacation days and Charlie would see her on Thursday. He wanted to go see his mom first and planned to leave after church on Sunday. Charlie's surprise visit did not give Stephen enough time to make arrangements for a stand-in preacher so he had to preach before they could leave.

On Saturday, Charlie went with Ester to the soup kitchen while Stephen used the time to prepare for his sermon. The experience shocked Charlie. It was difficult to believe what he saw. The poverty and need was overwhelming and he couldn't understand how the volunteers had kept it up for as long as they did. When they returned home, they had lunch together and talked until it was time for the rugby game to start. Stephen was a devoted

Blue Bulls fan and Charlie enjoyed watching the game with them. They were playing against the Sharks in the Super XV series. The winner of the game would end in the top position for the division championship and secure a spot in the playoffs.

On Sunday Charlie sat next to Ester while Stephen preached. After the service they had the traditional cup of tea with the congregation and the main topic of discussion was the rugby game from the previous day. The Bulls won the game and were headed to the playoffs. Those who did not like the rough game of rugby were by far in the minority and were used to being left out of conversations. They formed their own little group and discussed other matters of the day. Charlie floated around, not knowing anybody and struck up a few friendly conversations with random people. He was glad when it was all over and they could leave.

They traveled in two cars with Stephen leading the way and Charlie and Ester following in her car. It had been a few years since Charlie drove a stick shift or on the left side of the road. Initially it felt awkward, but following Stephen made it easier to get back into the habit. Ester was in the passenger seat next to Charlie to make sure he didn't get lost and also to ensure he stayed on the left side of the road. Charlie found it easy to talk to her and she updated him with news about their kids. Daniel, the older of the two, and Ruth were away at school in Stellenbosch at Stephen's alma mater. They were doing fine, made good grades and life was great. Charlie listened and enjoyed the conversation. He made plans to at least go and greet them when he visited with Michael and Karen, who lived in the south, about an hour's drive from Stellenbosch.

Charlie nonchalantly asked about scholarships and how they were paying for their studies. It was a sensitive subject for Ester to discuss since Stephen handled all the finances. Typically, as per Afrikaner traditions, finances, politics, religion and sex were taboo subjects in conversations. Since they were family, Charlie managed to get some information from her about their financial situation. Daniel had a scholarship because he was a good rugby player and played for the Varsity team. Ruth was studying music and wanted to become a teacher, but there were no scholarships available for her. Stephen and Ester had to bite the bullet for many years to pay off Stephen's student loans. They did not want their kids to suffer the same fate and were living on a very tight budget to pay for the children's education. They were not in debt, and their frugal lifestyle over the years, as well as their discipline to save for a house, gave them enough savings to cash flow the kids' education. She was concerned that they would have to go into debt again if the church board approved the transaction for the house. The finance committee met monthly and they expected a final decision soon. She was very nervous about it as she wanted the house, but she also knew a mortgage payment would make their budget even tighter. Although Stephen was the Senior Reverend and controlled all the church committees, he was excused from all meetings involving himself or his family. The chairman of the finance committee took over when the Reverend's remuneration and clergy house were discussed. They had very little insight into what the outcome would be.

Charlie realized Ester was using him as a confidant and their heart-to-heart discussion was like a relief valve for the pressure built up over so many years. She was the Reverend's wife and had to keep up the facade that everything was fine in the clergy house. She always had to put on a friendly face and lead the women's ministry. Charlie listened and was glad to be a sounding board for her. When he glanced over at her, he saw the tears in her eyes as she continued to talk and discuss her personal feelings with him. She made him promise over and over to never let Stephen know she had discussed their personal lives with him and thanked him for being a good listener.

"Is there any way that I could maybe help you, Ester? I am single and you know why. I don't have any other family, you are my family."

"You know Stephen," Ester continued. "He would never accept help. He is just too proud to take anything from anybody."

"Just like Dad," Charlie said and shook his head. "He was the most generous person and there was always something available to help other people. Seems like Stephen is just the same."

"Exactly!"

"After all these years. You know, I realized that I have built a wall around me. I have neglected my family and avoided contact on purpose. I have worked very hard and I managed to put away some savings. There has to be a way for me to help," Charlie said.

"Thank you for trying Charlie. I know you want to help, but Stephen would rather give everything he has away, and sometime he does, but accepting a gift is very difficult for him."

Charlie knew she loved his brother, but he also knew Stephen's history, and what made him the way he was. It seemed Stephen reacted the opposite way than Charlie did. Stephen wanted to continue their dad's legacy while Charlie hoarded his savings. It was difficult for him to give something away unless he got something in return. With all the money he suddenly had, he didn't know what to do with it. Although part of it was his, he still was not sure what to do about the rest of it.

"What about an anonymous donation? Is that allowed?" Charlie knew his brother's pride and the rules of the church could get in the way very quickly.

"The finance committee has to approve every penny. If we were made beneficiaries of a donation, Stephen would always take it to the finance committee for their approval. The first ten percent would go to the church; half of what was left, he would give to some ministry; he would save part of it to buy the house, and if we were lucky and there was anything left, we would celebrate a birthday or our anniversary at a nice restaurant. Woo-ho!" she said sarcastically.

Charlie listened to Ester and a plan formed in his mind. There was always a way around rules. He had worked long enough with information systems to be able to think differently and consider different options when faced with a problem that needed a solution. There were different ways to resolve it.

"What would happen if I gave you cash?" Charlie asked and looked at Ester. He saw embarrassment written all over her face and she looked like a kid caught with her hand in the cookie jar.

"Please don't tell Stephen." She looked at him with eyes begging him to keep her secret. Charlie nodded and she continued. "If it is cash, I hide it in a small box between all my sewing stuff. I then use it when we need something for the house or when the children need extra money at school. I must be a horrible wife to have secrets from my husband, but it's only small amounts. If it's a check or a large amount, I would always take it to Stephen and he would handle it the way he does all donations."

"Ester," Charlie started and he knew he could trust her to put his plan into motion," can I trust you with something I want to do? Will you promise to never tell Stephen about it?"

It was silent for a few minutes and her answer shocked Charlie, but he also expected it.

"I cannot do that," she answered with determination in her voice. Charlie wanted her to cross a line that she was not willing to cross. "We made a promise on our wedding day to never keep secrets from each other. I know I told you about my secret cash money, but that is the only thing I have ever kept from him and I will not keep any other secret. It's just not worth it."

Charlie knew it was a dead end and he would not be able to get her help. He had to think of something else. They drove in silence for a while and then Charlie asked the next question.

"Can you tell me something about the chairman of the finance committee? Can he be trusted? What type of person is he?"

Ester glanced at Charlie and looked puzzled for a moment, as if she could not understand why Charlie would ask a question like that. After a few moments, a smile appeared on her face, as she realized what Charlie's plan was. She would not have to break her promise.

"I would trust him with my life and with everything we have. Stephen and Derik have been friends since they started coming to our church. His wife, Debbie, and I are very close friends and we work together in the women's ministry. I think you can trust him. He is honest and believes every-thing should be done according to the book. He is an accountant and does our tax returns. He knows everything about us. Although he is the chairman of the finance committee, he never makes financial decisions by himself. The church has an ethics committee that looks at every decision and rule in the church. They can be a pain at times, but if it were not for them, I think there would be a lot more gossip and mud slinging in the church."

"Can you give me Derik's number please? What is his surname?"

"Siebert. I will write it down for you," Ester said with a smile, and scribbled the details on page from the notebook she kept in her purse. She reached over and tucked it in Charlie's shirt pocket.

They continued the drive and talking more about the ministry, and Char-lie realized that Ester's mood had changed. She was her normal self again and her positive spirit was back. It was contagious and they enjoyed the rest of the trip. Charlie felt good about the idea that there may be a way he could help Stephen and Ester. It all depended on the help he could get from the chairman of the finance committee, Derik Siebert.

* * *

CHAPTER 22

Mom and Marlene

The visit with Charlie's mom started with an emotional greeting and a long hug between mother and son. She talked with a soft breaking voice while tears freely ran down her cheeks. She held Charlie's hand with one hand while the other hand constantly rubbed the top of his hand. Charlie looked at her hands and saw the now soft and wrinkled skin with knuckles misshapen from the arthritis. He remembered the strong, sure hands that had spanked him as a little boy, comforted him throughout the years, and hands filled with vegetables from her own garden. Charlie spent many hours with her in the garden where he received life lessons. He could still hear her voice as they talked, and when it went quiet, she would sing the old gospel song "In the Garden". When he missed her, he would hum the same melody over and over.

Charlie spent three days with his mom. He stayed in a hotel close to the retirement village, ate breakfast with her in her small one bedroom townhouse and then hit the road to visit extended family. They drove by places he wanted to see again and along the way reminisced about the past. They visited the graves of his dad and her dad. She cried many times when she told him stories from his childhood. Charlie had to swallow hard to keep the tears back. They drove to the farm where Charlie grew up and they visited the mine where they had lived when Charlie graduated from high school.

They stopped at the bank where Charlie had his first job. Charlie exchanged a traveler's check for cash at the teller. He looked around at the office spaces and cubicles, but it was not the same as he remembered. The place looked old and run down. At the customer service desk, he asked the lady if she knew a Mr. Kramer that was the bank manager a long time ago. She told Charlie that he had passed away a few years ago. He was a loyal customer until the day he died. She showed him his picture on the wall in the manager's office where it hung amongst those of his predecessors and his successors. Charlie thanked her as he and Mom left the bank to continue their trip down memory lane.

In the car Charlie gave Mom an envelope of cash.

"No, Charlie," she immediately objected. "I cannot take this. You worked hard for your money and I don't need it. You have already given me so much with the monthly deposits you make. I cannot take more of your money."

"But Mom, what do you do with it?" Charlie asked.

"I save it," she said.

"For what?"

"For when I am old. Then I will need it." Charlie burst out laughing. "What are you laughing at?" She had an angry look on her face, and Charlie just shook his head.

"Some things never change. You have always been the saver and Dad was the spender." It took Charlie a while to convince her to reluctantly accept the gift. Then she elaborated on how she planned to spend it. As Charlie expected, only a small portion would go towards her own needs, some towards saving and the rest would go towards helping other more needy residents in the village. He wondered if it was his father's or his mother's genes that were passed on to them as children. He was not a sacrificial giver, and would never get close to the level of Stephen or his parents.

"Maybe it's time for me to change," he thought while staring in front of

him at the road as they made their way back to his mom's place. He glanced over to her and saw her head slumped forward as the excitement of the day turned into exhaustion and she rested her eyes for a while. As he drove in silence, he suddenly got an idea that may help him with the dilemma he was in. *"I need to ask her about her will!"* Charlie thought by himself.

The days Charlie spent with his mother passed in the blink of an eye. On the last day they had breakfast together and when the time came to leave, she greeted Charlie with tears in her eyes. She made him promise to come see her again before he returned home. He left her standing alone in front of her little home in the village. As he drove away she waved at him and Charlie put his arm outside the window and waved back. When she disappeared from sight, he stopped waiving. In his heart he believed he would see her again. She was in her early seventies, full of energy, healthy and surrounded by caring friends.

Charlie skipped the highways and the toll roads and took the scenic route through the mountains. He arrived at Marlene's house and sat in his car for a few minutes to gather enough courage to face her. How much of the truth should he tell her? How much does she know? He got out and walked up to the front door. He hesitated for a few seconds before he rang the doorbell. *"Why am I so nervous?"* he thought. When she opened the door, they stared at each other for a few moments, not knowing what to say or what to do.

"Hello, Marlene."

" Charlie," Marlene said and lifted her arms. Charlie stepped forward and gave her a big hug. She was still as beautiful as he remembered and it looked like she hadn't aged at all. There was no sadness in her eyes and she seemed to be happy. The awkward moment Charlie had expected was not there and she led the way to the sitting room. He looked around at the smartly decorated room and the thought that came to his mind shocked him; there was no evidence of anybody living with her. In one corner he saw a small cabinet with a glass door. He stepped closer and looked inside. He saw Keith's helmet, his collections of small motorbikes, a wedding picture, a picture of his coffin at the grave and the sheet of paper with the eulogy Charlie did the day of the funeral. The rattling sound of cups made him turn around and he looked at Marlene with a tray in her hands. She had tears in her eyes. She smiled at him when he took the tray from her and put it down on the coffee table. They sat down and she started pouring tea into the two cups. They had spoken the minimum and they both had no problem with that. They knew the conversation would come soon. Charlie took the cup and looked at her.

"Thank you," Charlie said. "How are you doing, Marlene? It is a beautiful memorial of Keith."

"I am doing great. And yes, I look at it every day. He lives in my heart forever. When I am alone and need some advice, I come and sit here and talk to him. You know, he is a very good listener," she said with her eyes fixed on the memorial. Charlie looked at her, and she seemed to be glowing. Charlie slowly started to crumble on the inside as she continued. "I use this room as my prayer room. I pray with him and sometimes he seems to be right here with me." She turned to Charlie and looked at him.

"And how are you? How was the visit with your mom? Is she still healthy?" She spoke with a relaxed voice and Charlie could not believe how easy it was to listen to her and be in her presence. In his mind he had dreaded every moment thinking it would be awkward and strange and that it would be difficult to have a normal conversation with her. He expected tears of sadness, but he saw the opposite and it confused him.

"How do you do that?" Charlie skipped the answer as he voiced his thoughts out loud.

"Do what?" she asked.

"After all these years, you look great, you talk about Keith as if he is still alive; the memorial you look at every day?" His eyes filled with tears as he talked to her. He had never talked about Hanna, and suppressed any thought about her. "I cannot even think about Hanna without crying. It's like I blocked that time out of my mind, like it never happened. And here you are, so relaxed, so at peace with it all. How do you do that?"

"Oh Charlie!" She said with empathy in her voice and tears in her eyes. "Believe me, I cried my eyes out and ignored what happened to Keith for a very long time. If it were not for KT, I'm not sure I would have survived. I had a lot to explain over the years, and when depression got hold of me, I went to see a therapist. She is a member at our church and does her counseling with her Bible always within reach. I blamed God and everybody else for what happened to Keith and Hanna. The depression was so bad I didn't want to live anymore and I may have done something stupid if it was not for KT. The therapist helped me to process the thoughts and memories and I think I cried more than I talked. One day she suggested I talk to Keith. When I started, it felt strange. I blamed him, I cussed at him, and oh, I was mad at him for a very long time. He did not only take my husband and leave me with a baby, but he also took my best friend. Eventually, I got over it and I believe it can only be God that brought peace back into my heart. When I got peace in my heart, it spilled over to KT, and he became my whole world. He was the sweetest little kid and grew up to become a young gentleman just like his father. And guess what his major is at university? Computer Science, just like his dad." The anger she started with and the calmness she ended with hung in the air. Charlie was amazed by what he saw and what he heard. He just sat there listening to her and shook his head. He could not speak, and he didn't trust his voice or thoughts to make any sense. This was not what he expected.

"How have you dealt with Hanna's death over the years, Charlie?" she asked.

"I don't think I have. I block out all thoughts about her and ignore it. I threw myself into my work and became good at what I do. I lived to work, and worked to live. Did nothing else. I still cannot talk about her without crying."

"You never saw a therapist or talked to somebody?"

"No." Charlie said as he broke down and let his head hang. Tears dripped from his eyes and the soft sobs became louder and louder. Years and years of emotions spilled over and Marlene moved closer and wrapped her arm around his shoulders. He cried and cried like he had never cried before. Marlene said nothing; just held him and in a soft voice prayed for him. It took a while before Charlie stopped crying. He took a deep breath and sat back. Marlene stood up and got some tissues for him to wipe the tears from his eyes and blow his nose.

"I'm going to make some fresh tea," she said and gave Charlie a few minutes to recover. He felt embarrassed about the crying, and when she returned, Charlie stood up and took the tray from her.

"At least you didn't forget your manners at home," she said jokingly and tried to change the mood in the room. Charlie attempted to smile and it made him feel better.

"I miss the formality of drinking tea the traditional way. In the US it's more like everybody helps himself or herself. Equal rights for all you know and you do your own thing."

They talked about his life in America. She wanted to know everything: where he lived, what he did, who his friends were, does he go to church? They talked for a long time. Charlie explained about his work and how it took him all over the country. He talked about all the places he had been, the big cities he visited, the Grand Canyon, and the colors of the leaves during the fall in the Smokey Mountains. They talked about the weather; tornadoes, hurricanes, fires, snow and blizzards. He told her about the incident where a tornado hit the office building he was in and everybody narrowly escaped. Finally, it was Marlene who broke the ice and asked for the real reason Charlie had come to visit her.

"Charlie, you have some explaining to do. Where did the money come from?" She looked directly at him. A shadow appeared over his face and he showed no emotion.

"Marlene," he said and looked at her. "I know I owe you an explanation, but let's just say the money was due to you a long time ago."

"No, Charlie. It will not do. You know me better than that. The Bible says the truth, and only the truth, will set you free. I want to know the truth," she said with determination in her voice.

"Marlene," he started and paused for a moment. He looked up at her and asked her directly. "Did you ever find out who caused the accident that killed Keith and Hanna?" The question was so direct and strong it threw Marlene off track for a moment. Charlie saw that he upset her. He felt sorry, but he was not ready to answer her question.

"Charlie," she said and he could see there were still questions in her mind. "We both went through a lot of questioning and interrogation for days and weeks after the accident. At some point I felt as if I was the driver of the car who caused the accident. None of the witnesses could give a detailed description of the car or the driver, and the best they could do was a black Mercedes. How many black Mercedes' are there? Some saw a similar looking car drive through the neighborhood a day or two before the accident, but nobody could recall the license plate number or the driver. There were rumors of a drug deal in the area that went wrong or that it may have been a gang that targeted the wrong person."

"Drugs? Keith was never involved with drugs?" Charlie said with shock.

"Exactly what I told them! They asked about Keith's work and what he did. Did he hang out with other people from work? What were his hobbies? So many things they wanted to know. The detective followed up on some other leads about an employee at the bank who was involved with drugs, and he thought there might be some link between the drug dealer and Keith. It was also a dead end and nothing came from it. They asked me a lot of questions about my job at school. They asked if somebody had threatened me at school. They even suggested maybe the person mistook Hanna for me. I never received any threats and I don't know of any threats Keith received. For me, the mystery of what happened that day is the one thing that continues to upset me. Whenever I think about it, I get so mad at the driver of the car. If I just knew why. Why? Why did it happen?" Charlie saw the pain in her eyes and heard the frustration and anger in her voice. He felt the same way, but they both dealt with it differently. She voiced it and moved on. He tried to hide everything and blocked it all out.

"I have the same question. Why did it happen? Maybe that's why I shut out all memories about that day. The detective asked me a lot of questions about Hanna and her work. They thought she might have been the target because of the government work she was involved in. She never talked about what she really did at work - she mentioned something about nuclear energy and how it could be the long-term solution for the country. When I wanted to know more about her work, she always said it was complicated and classified. *'Government stuff'* was her normal excuse."

"So, we still have no answer. We just have to live with it," Marlene said with a touch of bitterness, but also surrender, in her voice.

"Yes. What else can we do? We have no option," Charlie echoed Marlene's feelings

"Are you going to answer my question?" Marlene asked again.

Charlie hesitated and then started to explain.

"Do you remember the trip we took to Zurich in 1979? When Hanna and I got engaged and we decided to explore Europe for a few days?"

"Yes. Hanna was still at Cambridge and could only get off for a few days. Was it not in her final year? She was busy with the last stage of some research project and felt bad about not being able to have a longer vacation. But what does this have to do with the money?"

"The day you and Hanna went shopping in Zurich, Keith and I were supposed to visit the football museum. Well, we never actually went. Instead, we went to the bank and each one of us opened a bank account. We had all sorts of ideas of how to make lots of money and searched for a bank outside of South Africa where the money would be safe. The Bank of Zurich was one of the top international banks. We were looking for privacy and we knew the bank would not share customer details with any government. We wanted to make sure the accounts could not be traced to us."

"Why did you need accounts that couldn't be traced? Did Hanna know about this?"

"She did not. Keith and I planned to save as much as we could and transfer our savings every month to the accounts. We thought the compounded interest over many years would make us millionaires and then we could retire early. Remember the house at the beach you always wanted? Hanna and I dreamed about living next door to you and Keith." Charlie attempted to dodge the question and steer the conversation in a different direction, but was not very successful.

"I know about the beach house. Keith and I talked about it many times. He never mentioned how we were going to do it. But you still have not answered my question. Where did the money come from that you put into the accounts? I looked through all of Keith's papers when I had to file the claims for his life insurances. I cannot remember any reference to a bank in Zurich."

Charlie's brain was working overtime. Deep in his heart he wanted to tell Marlene the whole story. He had carried the burden of the secret alone for so many years and it weighed heavily on him. He felt the urge to share it with her. He wanted to tell her about Project Delta, Sir Archibald, Madam Catherine, about the cat and the unsolved mystery about Heinz. He wanted to tell her about his fears - the fear that somebody may still be looking for him after all these years, the fear that he would end up the same way as Keith and Hanna - just another unsolved murder. When he talked to Stephen, he wanted to tell him, but did not want to burden him with it. Now, he had the same urge in his heart to share it with Marlene.

But his brain told him something else. His brain said no. He did not want to shatter all her memories of Keith and the good person she loved and married. He could not break her heart after all the pain she had gone through. Keith and Marlene loved each other and when she announced they were pregnant, Keith was in seventh heaven. If he told her the truth of what had happened, the whole memory of Keith would be ruined and she would hate Charlie for that. He had no idea of how she would react and he had no idea how to handle a woman with a broken heart. He stared at Keith's memorial in the corner of the room and remembered her face when she looked at it. He wished he had kept more pictures of Hanna, something to keep her alive in his memories. Oh, how he missed her. He was so heartbroken and devastated after the accident. When Hanna's mother asked if she could take care of Hanna's stuff when Charlie planned to emigrate, he had no objections. He had to get away from it all, the memories, the guilt and the fear. He felt bad about not telling Marlene the full story.

"Do you remember all the long hours Keith and I worked when Hanna was still in England? Project Delta was a side job we worked on. We hoped to someday make big money from it by selling the copyright to the system. We dreamed big back then. Well it seems our efforts did pay off. I just didn't know about it. Over the years we received small amounts every month and the money was transferred directly into the accounts in Zurich. Initially it was only small amounts, and at some point we thought it was a dead end and we gave up on it. With everything that happened, I erased it from my mind in the same way I blocked out memories about Keith and Hanna. I completely forgot about the accounts and I never went back to Zurich. Until I needed to use an offshore account again."

"But," Marlene started and sounded confused. "Why did you need an offshore account? Where did you get the details again?"

Charlie looked at Marlene and started to explain what happened with PITS and how they cheated him with his rates. He told her about the bonus he received and the money Heinz wired to his account. He told her just enough to make her believe the money was really left over in Keith's account. After he withdrew money to buy the motorbike, there was not much left. After the payments, as he called it, started again, he also earned interest on his money.

"What should I do with the money?" Marlene asked after Charlie completed his story and his version of what happened.

"Why don't you retire?" he asked.

"Retire?" She laughed at him and the sound of her laughter broke the tension between them. Charlie relaxed. "And do what? I love my job and I love helping my students. I still have a few years before I will even think about retirement. I am not planning to quit soon."

"What about the dream to live at the beach? Buy a beach house and spend your summer vacations at the beach. Property is always a good investment."

Marlene looked at Charlie and smiled at him. It made him uncomfortable. She was silent for a few moments before she asked the next question.

"Did you never fall in love again, Charlie? Do you have a girlfriend?" The question was like ice in Charlie's face. His thoughts about the beach vanished as her question cut right through to his heart.

"Why do you ask? Why didn't you ever marry again?" he countered to avoid answering the question.

"I had KT. That was more than enough for me. Being a single parent was not easy and if it were not for my parents, I don't know what I would have done. They basically raised him." She hesitated before she continued. "You're a smart and handsome guy Charlie. You could easily have found somebody to love again," Marlene had a slight blush around her neck when she talked to Charlie and they both looked away from each other. Charlie thought about his response and after a few moments replied.

"I was just not interest in any relationships. I don't really know why, but

I never really made time for it. I just had no interest in going through the pain of losing somebody again. When my dad passed away, it was very painful, but it was not even close to what I experienced when Hanna died. I can never love somebody as I loved her. I don't want to go through that pain again." Charlie had tears in his eyes as he looked at Marlene. It felt like she was looking right into his heart and mind, as if she could see deep into his soul.

"I can understand that. I felt the same way. At some point there was a teacher on staff who was interested in me. We are still good friends. He asked me on a date, and I said yes. But it was like I was cheating on Keith and I couldn't go through with it. We had to cut the date short and I never went on one again."

They sat in silence for a few moments, each busy with their own thoughts.

"Let's go get something to eat," Marlene said and got up. "Since we have all this money, we can celebrate and have a good dinner. There's a nice restaurant I've always wanted to go to, but I never allowed myself the luxury. I also didn't want to go alone." She took her keys and purse and walked to the door. "I'll drive," she said as Charlie followed her to her car.

At dinner Charlie and Marlene talked a lot about the past and life after the accident. They shared stories and discussed how they learned to cope with life. Charlie was the one who struggled, but the relaxed way Marlene talked about her life after Keith made Charlie rethink his way of dealing with the loss of Hanna. They talked about the emotional times and how they handled it. They talked about the future and what their individual plans were. Marlene wanted to complete the dream she and Keith had and buy a beach house. She did not want to live in the big city forever, and really wanted to live in a small place with a long white beach. They talked about the different areas in the country where the beautiful beaches were. Charlie told her about the beaches on the east coast of the US. They talked like old friends who saw each other every day.

After dinner they went back home to get Charlie's car and he followed Marlene to her parent's house. Marlene had arranged for Charlie to stay in their guest room and she decided to also spend the night there. She stayed in the bedroom KT used when he stayed with her parents. They talked till late that night. The next morning after breakfast, Charlie packed his bags and got ready for the trip to Cape Town. Saying good-bye was suddenly not easy. He said good-bye to Marlene's parents first and then Marlene walked with him to his car. When he opened the door, he turned to her.

"Thank you, Marlene. Yesterday was the best day I've had since the accident. Thank you for listening and for understanding."

"No, Charlie. I am the one to say thank you. You changed my life and my future, and I have hope again. I still think you didn't tell me everything, but that's ok. I know you have good intentions and at some point we will talk about it again." She looked at him and pointed her finger at him. "Please don't disappear and go quiet on me again. Come and visit before you go back to the US even if you just come and say good-bye. Just don't ignore me like you have been doing for so long. We have a bond that nobody can take away and we have so much in common. I'm sure we can help each other." Tears filled her eyes and her voice faded as she moved forward and gave Charlie a hug.

"I will definitely do that. I still have a couple of weeks before I go back. I'll stay with Stephen and Ester for the last few days before I leave. Maybe we can have dinner with them. That is, if it's ok with you."

"I would love that. I have not seen them in a very long time."

They hugged again and Charlie got into his car. He opened the window to say his last good-bye, and they looked at each other. Charlie saw something in her eyes that made him realize how much he missed the friendship and camaraderie they once shared. The gaze lasted longer than a normal good-bye and he didn't want to leave. He realized that she didn't want him to go.

He started the car and said good-bye one more time.

"Bye, Charlie. Drive safe and don't be a stranger. Promise me!"

"I promise," he said and backed out of the driveway.

He waved at her as he drove down the road. In the rearview mirror he saw her standing in the road, waving until he turned at the corner. He had a long road ahead of him and now he had one more thing to think about.

"What just happened?" he thought to himself. He felt good and drove with a smile on his face and lightness in his heart. He could still picture her face and he thought what a gorgeous color her eyes were. *"Blue like the sea or blue like the sky?"* He remembered her smile, and thought about her long dark hair. The picture was burned into his memory and deep inside of him he knew he would see her again. He wanted to see her again. He thought about Hanna and for the first time, he didn't cry. He remembered her smile and he started to talk to her. Tears formed in his eyes, but they were no longer tears of sadness, but tears that soothed his soul.

* * *

CHAPTER 23

Michael and Karen

C harlie stopped for gas in Beaufort West, about a 6-hour drive from Cape Town. He got out of the car, stretched his arms and legs, and twisted his body to get rid of the stiffness from the long hours behind the wheel. The previous day he visited The Big Hole museum in Kimberly. The last time he was there he was a child with his parents and brother. There was not much to see the rest of the way, but he enjoyed the changing landscape. He considered booking a flight, but he wanted to travel the road he had been on so many times as child, just one more time. The cities had changed; the roads had deteriorated and at times he had to swerve hard to miss a pothole in the middle of the road; but the countryside, the beauty of nature and the friendliness of the local people had stayed the same. He enjoyed interacting with the locals and hearing the different accents as he drove from the northern parts of the country to the south. He skipped hotels and looked for bed and breakfast signs along the road. He purposely drove during the day to see the country in the daylight. He stopped early at the guesthouses so he could have dinner with the hosts and talk about life in the rural areas. He remembered the ARK principal Stephen had told him about and although he had always been generous with gratuities, it suddenly had a different meaning for him.

The road trip from Marlene to Michael and Karen took three days. Michael was surprised when Charlie contacted him a few weeks ago, and typical Michael, he invited Charlie to stay over before Charlie could even ask. Michael arranged some vacation time for the week Charlie planned to visit the Cape Town area. They greeted each other like long lost friends and battled to keep the tears of joy away. Karen had their guest room ready and they helped Charlie carry the little baggage he had to his room. They showed him the rest of their house and Karen and Charlie stopped at floating shelves in the living room full of pictures of their three grandchildren. Karen glowed as she showed Charlie pictures of each one, and explained their personalities in a typical grandma fashion. Charlie let her enjoy the moment and noticed how different she was from the last time he had seen her. The depressed and lonely housewife had become a beautiful lady in the prime time of her life.

In the garage, Michael showed Charlie his new Harley Davidson, but Charlie struggled to match the excitement of Michael. He declined the offer from Michael to take it out for a test ride.

Dinner was the traditional South African style "braai" or cookout, and Charlie had more meat on his plate than he normally consumed in a week. He had a couple of glasses of wine with Michael, who had double or triple the amount while Karen only sipped on hers. They talked till late that night and reminisced about life in the US and how returning home had impacted their lives. The brain drain from South Africa to the rest of the world had opened new opportunities for Michael. He initially became a freelance developer in the telecommunication and cell phone area, and with the help of a silent business partner, built an application enabling cell phone users without a bank account to buy airtime at retail outlets. One of the major retailers bought into the idea and Michael earned a small percentage of the sales. He had a lucrative contract for the installation and maintenance of the system and he managed a small team who travelled all over the country to support new customers. They had a steady income from the royalties and fees, and if they wanted to retire, his partner was ready to buy his share in the company. They still had a few years to go and already lived in their dream house close to the beach. They had no plans to move and when they did retire, they planned to just stay where they were.

The conversation eventually turned to PITS and the reason for Charlie's visit. Karen gave her thoughts about Heinz, and Charlie heard the bitterness in her voice as he realized she still had some very deep resentment. Michael was more content and at peace about their experience in a different country. Although it had set them back a few years, in the end, it all turned out for the better. The kids were happy and they were close to their family. Michael asked about The Three Musketeers, and Charlie updated him with how the company was doing. Karen did not want to hear about them so she decided to cleanup before going to bed. They helped her take all the dishes to the kitchen, and their offer to help was fiercely declined. She ordered them to go sit outside and talk about "those three mosquitoes" as she referred to Heinz, Dan and Vince. Charlie and Michael laughed and made their way back to the porch. Michael selected a bottle of liqueur and two small glasses from his drinks cabinet. They sat down to enjoy a nightcap and Charlie took his first sip of the sweet, smooth, silky taste of the Amarula cream liqueur. He complimented the great selection and then resumed the conversation about PITS.

"Michael. What happened between you and Heinz before you left? I know something went down, but I'm not sure what it was."

"Why are you asking?" Michael asked with skepticism in his voice.

"I had my run-in with him recently. I may just call it quits when I get back. I think it's time to venture out and become an independent consultant."

"You should've done that a long time ago. What happened?"

"Something to do with my rate. I discovered how they cheated me on the last project. I just happened to see the agreement between the client and the staffing companies. They were not allowed to take more than twenty percent of the rate they paid their consultants. There was a full disclosure agreement in place and the project manager accidentally showed me a document where my rate was listed. They charged the client double what my rate was."

"So, they are still doing it then." Michael said with a smirk.

"What do you mean still doing it?"

"I had the same run in with Dan before Heinz joined them. They used some kind of formula to calculate a consultant's rate. It was supposed to be based on what they charged the client. They not only cheated me, but I know of a few others who had the same problem. That's why they lost so many senior consultants. I am amazed that you stayed so long." Michael paused and looked at Charlie. "So nobody told you about what was going on?"

"No. I was just working to get in as many hours as possible. And also to forget about what happened here. You know, with Hanna and my friend, Keith."

"Yes, I remember. You told me about it. Karen and I were glad to help you in the beginning. Man, you were an introvert when you started. Never joined us on outings, worked like crazy and never talked to anybody about your personal life. Until I got to know you, I thought you were a snob. It was only after I learned of what you had been through that we got to know each other better. Sorry I did not spill the secret to you then, but I was so caught up in finding a job for myself, I wasn't thinking about anybody else. I should have warned everybody."

"There is something else I need to know." Charlie wanted to get as much as possible out of Michael about his experience in the early days of PITS.

"Let's hear it. I know those guys very well. I was one of their first recruits and they really did screw me in every way they could."

"What visa did you work on when you were there?"

Michael laughed out loud, emptied his glass and filled it again. He leaned over and topped off Charlie's glass too. "Don't tell me it's also still going on. When are those guys going to learn?"

Charlie was dumbstruck with Michael's response. He realized that in his effort to hide his own hurt from the world, he became oblivious to what was going on around him.

"What do you mean still going on?"

"Come on, Charlie, be honest with me. After all these years, you don't know they are three lying and cheating bastards? How do you think Vince and Dan can afford the cars they drive? And the mansions they live in? They cheat with every contract they sign, and with every person they hire outside of the US to work for them. They tried it with me too. I discovered very early what they were up to, and threatened to blow the whistle on them if they did not correct my visa. There were many consultants who were not interested in settling in the US. They had no problem working on a visitor's visa and getting paid under the table. When you convert dollars to the Rand, you can earn more in six months in the US than you can earn in a whole year in South Africa. Who wouldn't want to work for six months, have vacation for five weeks in South Africa, and then go back for another six months? That's what they have been doing the whole time. I'm just not sure how they get away with it."

"I only recently heard about it. One of the rookies I worked with on my last project let it slip after he had one beer too many at dinner. He was apparently on a visitor's visa and could not stay past the date on his I-94. He plans to go back next year again."

"Exactly. That is what they did back then too. When I was still working for PITS, they had a few consultants working on visitor's visas. They used one person's visa and made copies of it. They only changed the name on it when a client asked for proof of work authorization. The clients did not really care and only needed a body to fulfill a need. The immigration services were not as strict when I worked there, but after 9/11 it seems to have changed a lot. At some point they are going to get caught and I hope they rot in prison for a long time. I just feel sorry for all the consultants who will lose their jobs and get deported. Pure greed! Man, I tell you, those three guys are bad news. They don't care about the people. I am just so glad I am out of there."

"Tell me something. How did you get Heinz to pay for your relocation back here?"

"I told him straight up I was going to USCIS. He begged me to keep quiet and offered us first class tickets back home. I got him to pay for the move of our furniture also."

"So, where do Vince and Dan fit in? Seems like Heinz is the one really doing all the illegal stuff."

"No, no! Don't be mistaken. He is only the pawn. Vince and Dan are the brains behind the schemes."

"But, I thought Vince made his fortune from a business he sold and money he had inherited?"

"The business was a failure. I don't think he made much out of it. He got more from his inheritance than from the business. The way I know the story is that he gave his business partner an ultimatum to take over his share, or he would sell it. The business was on the downhill and Vince knew it. His partner thought he could turn the business around if Vince was not involved anymore. They agreed on initial lump sum, and then a monthly payment for the balance. The business did not survive long and when they lost the government contract, it was all over. He tried to sue Vince, but Vince had already left the country."

"Why did he leave?"

"He emigrated soon after his parents passed away. He was the only child and got a boatload full of money from their insurance policies. He sold the properties he inherited and some of the investments his dad had. He used it to emigrate."

"His parents died at the same time?" Charlie asked.

"Yes, it was a terrible accident and a real tragedy. It was all over the news when it happened."

"Wow! That must have been a shock for him. How did he handle it?" Charlie sounded sincere, and for a brief moment the pain returned. He realized something had changed. He could think about his loss without the urge to get up and do something to escape from the pain. He thought about his conversations with Marlene, and how she had helped him gain control of his emotions when thinking about Hanna. Michael's response brought him back to reality again.

"I did not know Vince at that time, but the local newspapers and radio stations covered it in depth. His dad was a big shot at BOSA, and there was a lot of gossip about the accident. His dad grew up in the bank, was a bank manager at different branches all over the country, and moved around often to advance his career. He eventually made it up the corporate ladder and became the Chief Data Processing Manager. They lived in Sandton at the time and Vince got a scholarship from the bank to study computer science. He graduated from WITS and joined his dad at the bank."

A cold shiver made its way up Charlie's spine, raising the hair on the back of his neck. He knew Vince had worked at a bank, but he did not know his dad had also worked at BOSA. The same bank Keith worked at.

"They lived in Sandton?"

"Yes. They had a beach house near Hout Bay.

"But, how did they die?"

"Apparently he lost control over the car while driving through Chapman's Peak mountain pass. The car flipped a few times before it dropped over the cliff, landed on the rocks below and then fell into the sea. The autopsy said they drowned, but they would have died from their injuries if they had not drowned."

"That's terrible. Poor Vince. What was the gossip about?"

"Money. What else? Rumor had it back then that Vince's dad was involved in some embezzlement scheme at the bank. He was not the only one - a few bank managers were involved. Apparently it was a long-standing practice of bank managers. One of them got too greedy and got caught with his hand in the cookie jar. Apparently Vince's dad knew about the scheme and was also involved in it when he was a bank manager. Some said he took the easy way out, and instead of facing the music and prosecution, decided to commit suicide. Others said he was silenced. They claimed a person who commits suicide, would normally not kill somebody else also. They never found a suicide note and to this day it's a mystery."

Charlie just stared at Michael in disbelief. Deep inside he felt sorry for Vince, and could not believe what he was hearing.

"Vince's dad was a bank manager!" Charlie said and shook his head. He knew exactly what the *'long-standing practice of bank managers'* implied. He remembered his first manager, Mr. Kramer, and the black journal in his bottom drawer. Deep inside he felt a twitch in his stomach.

"You ok? It looks as if you have seen a ghost," Michael said. Charlie sat with eyes wide open staring at him.

"You wouldn't believe me if I told you; just a flashback from the past. You know, I also worked at a bank before I left and joined PITS."

"Yes, you told me at some point."

They sat silent for a moment, and looked into the flames slowing dwindling. Charlie looked up at Michael and asked.

"This may sound strange, but what car was he driving when the accident happened?"

"His car? I'm not sure. It was a while ago, but if I am not mistaken, it was a Mercedes. They had a picture in the newspaper when the car was recovered from the shallow waters. I think it was a dark color. Not sure if it was black or dark blue. Why do you want to know?"

Charlie stood up and walked a few paces away from the fire and stared into the darkness. He gasped for air and took a deep breath as he felt a panic attack growing stronger. *"Control yourself Charles O'Neal,"* he said to himself. He took another deep breath and held it for a few seconds before slowly releasing the air from his lungs. He blinked a few times to clear the tears that formed and look up into the sky and the Southern Cross. *"Can there be any link with Keith and Hanna? It's not possible! It is just a coincidence."* He turned around and slowly walked back to where Michael sat at the fire pit stirring the fire with a stick. Charlie sat down and stared into the flames.

"Are you ok? Sorry, I did not mean to stir some memories for you." Michael apologized with concern in his voice. Charlie waited a few moments before he answered. He knew he could trust Michael, and they had been good friends many years ago. A lot had changed since then and he did not know if he should ask his next question, but he needed to make sure. He looked at Michael and decided to go ahead before he made his final evaluation whether he could trust him or not.

"Have you ever heard of a Sir Archibald Mansion?" Charlie asked and looked straight at Michael to make sure he did not miss anything in his reaction.

"No, doesn't ring a bell. Who is he?"

"Never mind," Charlie felt relieved. "It's just an e-mail I got the other day from a Sir Archibald from Sandton. Must be one of those money scams again." Charlie didn't want to change the subject yet.

"Were there any other rumors about the accident?" Charlie asked.

"What is it with you and the accident?" Michael asked puzzled. "It was many years ago. I worked at an insurance company in Bellville when it happened, and there was a lot of talk, but no evidence. He was heavily insured, and it seemed like every person had his or her own opinion of what happened and why. They wanted to make something out of nothing. The conspiracy theorists had a field day and it became the talk of the day in the office. Why are you interested in the rumors?"

Charlie waited for a few moments and with a voice thick with emotion, answered the question.

"I don't think I ever told you this, Michael," Charlie paused to control his feelings. "Hanna and I were engaged when she died. Keith was my best friend. They were killed in an accident on a motorbike and a witness saw a black Mercedes leave the scene of the accident. She claimed the car deliberately caused the accident."

"What? You never told me. I am so sorry Charlie," Michael said softly and Charlie continued.

"And you know what, Keith also worked at BOSA. The cops had a lot of questions about his job, and what type of work he did. To this day their accident is also a mystery. I will never know what really happened. When you said the car was a dark colored Mercedes, I could not believe the similarities. Is it just a coincidence, or are the accidents related? Was Hanna just collateral damage in the same way as Vince's mom was? Two bank employees killed in different places, and in both cases an innocent person was killed too. Can you see where my brain is going? Is this just another conspiracy theory?"

"That is something else. I knew Hanna died in an accident, but you never gave me any details. You never wanted to talk about it and didn't bring up her name. Are you ok to talk about it now?"

"I am. I had a good talk with Keith's wife, Marlene, and she gave me some tips on how to cope with it." Charlie attempted a smile, but it barely made it to his face as he slowly nodded his head and said again, "I am ok."

"Well," Michael continued. "There were theories that Vince's dad was made the scapegoat for a bigger problem at the bank. Some even said he was murdered to hide fraud and money laundering. The accident started a big shakeup in the leadership of the bank. Not long after the incident, BOSA announced a merged with a big bank from the UK, and the new BOSA became the leading bank in the country. That of course started more rumors. Some newspapers claimed he was murdered because he blocked the merger. Somebody claimed the brake line was tampered with, causing the accident."

"What do you think?" Charlie asked. Michael thought for a few moments before answering.

"For me, the idea of a mechanical failure, or a tampered brake line, makes more sense. If you want to commit suicide, you don't take your wife for a scenic drive on a Sunday afternoon and just drive over a cliff."

"When did all of this happen?"

"Oh, this was in the mid eighties. Karen was pregnant then. We lived in Milnerton just outside of Cape Town and we liked to drive the Chapman's Peak pass, and stop in Hout Bay for ice cream. After the accident, Karen was not as keen on driving there anymore. It took a while before we made the trip again."

Charlie realized the accident of Vince's parents and the one involving of Keith and Hanna, were not far apart. He wondered if Vince would be able to tell him more about the rumors.

"What was Vince doing at that time? Do you know?"

"He lived somewhere in Pretoria. He worked at the bank until his student loan was repaid and then he quit. That's when he started his new business. You know, the one that installed access systems in government buildings. Vince was the software expert and his partner was some electronics engineer that took care of the hardware design and installations."

Karen joined them again, and they sat around and talked until the fire turned to embers and ash. They decided to call it a night. Charlie asked Michael if he could use his network connection to check e-mails, and Michael showed Charlie his office. He took a spare cable from a drawer and plugged it into the router.

"Much faster than the old dial-up modems we used before," he commented to Charlie. "I don't have Wi-Fi yet, but maybe next time you come visit I will."

Charlie hooked up to the Internet, logged into his account and scanned his e-mails. He noticed the ones from Tessa and Heinz. He read Tessa's e-mail first. They both had similar questions - asked about his wellbeing, when he would return, and if he was available for a call. Tessa provided a bit more information and said she wanted to finalize the deal regarding the next project. The merger was moving forward and could be made public knowledge soon. He wanted to respond immediately, but thought about it for a moment and decided to wait until the next day. He scrolled through the rest of the e-mails, and one from Dan caught his eye. He opened the e-mail and read it.

The e-mail didn't have much social content. He said he was happy they could correct the error and hoped they could count on him for the next project. The rest surprised him and the further he read, the better he felt about his future.

Dan mentioned that PITS was in the final run for a big project about a bank merger. They depended on his skills to be available for the venture and they, meaning The Three Musketeers, were willing to review his rate. He promised to personally make sure Charlie would not be disappointed by the offer. Dan also mentioned that they were busy with a new recruiting effort and had plans to form a partnership with another staffing company who had access to the Asian technology market. They would be able to provide a strong bench for a pool of developers. Charlie shook his head in disbelief as he read the rest of the e-mail. *"Just more cheap labor to profit from,"* he thought. Dan mentioned how close they were to finalizing the deal. The project would run for at least eighteen months, and it would be a great opportunity for everyone involved.

"This could become interesting - a bidding war for my time. Maybe I can make a killing with this one and retire. Never have to work again," he thought to himself. The next sentence drained the blood from his face for the second time

that night.

    'One of the key components of the project will be an interface to a global network of ATMs. They are looking into a new process for the reconciliation and redistribution of usage fees between banks. With your interface skills, and Vince and my experience with banking fees, we can clinch the deal. I'm not sure if you know this, but both Vince and I worked together at BOSA after graduation and we implemented an ATM fee management system for the bank.

    Let me know when I can give you a call.'

Charlie had to read the e-mail a few times before he realized that it might be the missing link he was looking for. He closed his computer and walked out of the office to the guest room. He knew sleep was out of the question. In the hallway he heard voices from the master suite and realized Michael and Karen were still up talking. Charlie knew sleep would not be possible for him. He settled in the living room and picked up the local newspaper. He had to get his mind and his thoughts away from everything he had discovered that day. He needed time to think. He browsed through the paper, and read some of the local news for a few minutes. On the back page he studied the weather forecast and realized the next day would be a perfect day to be outside. He planned to drive around Chapman's Peak and take a long walk on the beach to think about his response to the e-mails. After a while he put the paper down and went to bed.

* * *

CHAPTER 24

Daniel and Ruth

The drive through the mountainous southern tip of Africa and the scenic curves along Chapman's Peak restored calm and peace in Charlie's mind. In Hout Bay, he stopped and followed Karen's advice, eating ice cream during a long walk on the beach. He sat down on a rock, looked out over the vastness of the ocean and followed the waves as they came rolling towards the beach. He thought about the last few months and everything that happened. He knew his life would never be the same again, but he was still unsure about what his next step should be.

He thought about Vince and the tragic accident of his parents. He compared it with his own feelings after Hanna's death in the motorcycle accident, and in his heart he felt sorry for Vince. He wanted to know how he had managed to get through the terrible time of sadness and grief. Did he also run away from the memories and work to forget? He thought about Vince and how he always seemed to be in charge and controlled the atmosphere when he joined in a conversation or entered into a room. Was it admiration or fear that made people pay attention to him?

He thought about the e-mail from Dan he had read the night before. Who was Dan really? He never knew that Dan and Vince had known each other before they started PITS. The new knowledge that they had worked at the same bank as Keith sent shivers down his spine. Was there any connection between the accidents that had claimed the lives of two employees of the same bank?

He thought about the e-mails from Heinz and Tessa. His uncertainty and uneasiness were replaced with a feeling of vindication. He looked forward to the opportunity to negotiate and knew he could win this round. He thought about how to start a bidding war between Heinz and Tessa to get an even better deal than he knew he already had. For many years he work at a rate far below that of an independent consultant and he only filled the pockets of The Three Musketeers. Finally, he had a chance to break away from the hold they had on him. There would not be any go-between company to take a cut from his rate and this time he would dictate the terms of the deal. He wanted proof of the rates on both ends and he wanted all expenses paid. In his mind Charlie made a list of all his demands, and smiled at some of the ridiculous things coming to mind. He also considered what would happen if he overplayed his hand, and in the process lose the opportunity. But he was ok with it. He still had the money in Zurich and thought he could live off of it for a while. For a moment he felt bad about the money, and it brought him back to reality.

He thought about his brother and sister-in-law. In his mind he listed all the ways he could help them, but he also knew the difficult position Stephen was in. Charlie did not want to complicate life for Stephen and he knew Stephen would flat-out reject any donations from him if he knew the true origin of the money. Charlie thought again about his conversation with Ester. *"Maybe it's not a bad idea,"* he said to himself as he thought of the chairman of the finance committee.

He left the beach and returned to Michael and Karen's home. He had dinner with them and they visited like old friends. He told them about his plans and the next day, after breakfast, Charlie left to visit with his niece and nephew. Stephen had arranged for them to meet at a restaurant in the shopping mall close to the University of Stellenbosch.

The visit with Daniel and Ruth started awkwardly and they talked like strangers. The last time Charlie saw them, they were still little kids, and now he sat in front of two beautiful, intelligent young adults. They talked about life on campus, their degrees, the future, rugby and food. Charlie told them a few things about himself and their dad, and how they grew up together. Slowly they warmed up to Charlie, and started to remember bits and pieces of the time before he emigrated. They remembered the accident and knew they had an uncle who lived in America, but they never saw him. When the food arrived, they commented on how long it had been since they could afford to eat in a restaurant. Charlie used it as a lead-in to gather more information about their student loans and how they paid for tuition. They confirmed the story Ester had told him, and gave him even more information. The longer they talked about life on campus and how they had to turn every penny over, the more Charlie felt the urge to help them. Charlie paid for the food and left a generous tip, making sure Daniel and Ruth noticed it. He smiled to himself when he saw the look on their faces and the way they glanced at each other as they walked away. They strolled through the mall and did some window-shopping. They refused the offer from Charlie to buy something they needed. Pride, and the strict rules from Dad, prevented them from accepting gifts from anybody. He spent a couple of hours with them and walked to their car to say good-bye. When Charlie saw the car they were driving, he could not believe his eyes. It was his mom's old VW Jetta! After all these years, the car was still running. He walked around the car, asked if he could start it and looked inside. The car was kept clean, well taken care of and on the odometer he noticed it had more than three hundred thousand kilometers. He looked at Daniel and Ruth who stood outside smiling at the fuss Charlie was making about the car.

"How often do you go home?" he asked with his hand on the steering wheel.

"Only during school breaks. It's a long drive, but the car runs ok. It's a diesel and we get good mileage, so gas is not too expensive. Dad says we can easily get half a million kilos with the car. We keep it in good shape. I have a friend who is a good mechanic and he services it for us every time before we go home." Daniel showed no shame or resentment for driving an old car, and seemed to be content with it.

"How do you both get to class if you only have one car?"

"We live on campus and like most other students we walk. Ruth uses the car the most during the week since the music conservatorium is on the other end of campus. We are used to coordinating things, and everybody on campus shares rides. Welcome to our world!" Daniel said with a smile.

"When are you going home again?"

"Our finals starts in a few weeks, then we will pack up and go home. We can leave most of our stuff in a storage space at the dormitories. Thank goodness we don't have to take everything. Ruth has so many clothes, there's no space left in the car for mine." Daniel ducked just in time as Ruth tried to slap him at the back of his head. Charlie laughed at the teasing between the two, and could tell they took care of each other.

"He's a big liar. It is he who has all the stuff. All his rugby gear would fill a truck, never mind the trunk of this little car," Ruth responded to Daniel's comments. He grabbed her and gave her a brotherly hug. She just stayed stiff armed and did not respond.

Charlie looked at them and looked at the car, and got lost in thought. Ester's car was only a couple of years old, about the same size as this one and in excellent condition. It was still a long drive back to Pretoria and he did not look forward to it. Maybe there was a way out for him and a way to help his nephew and niece in the process. He just needed to talk to Stephen, or maybe Ester would be a better one to talk to in this case.

"What are you doing on Saturday? I need a ride to the airport," Charlie said.

"I can do it in the morning. I need to practice for the piano exams, but can do that in the afternoon." Ruth offered before Daniel could, but he didn't want to stay behind.

"May I come too? Maybe we can have breakfast together." Daniel said.

"Ok. Let me talk to your dad first. Who can I call to make arrangements with?"

"Talk to Ruth. She is better at making plans. I will just fall in with what she tells me to do. Rugby is over for the year, so I sleep in on Saturdays."

The awkwardness they had started with had disappeared and they hugged good-bye like family. Charlie watched them leave and in his heart he felt good that he had made the effort to visit with them for a short while.

Later that afternoon, Charlie called Ester and talked to her about his plans. Initially she was very upset and didn't want to hear about it. He tried to convince her to accept his offer and put her on a guilt trip about the safety of her own children on the long dangerous road from Stellenbosch to Pretoria with an old car. As expected, she said he had to talk to Stephen. She handed the phone to Stephen and it was shockingly a lot easier to convince him. Charlie mentioned the ARK principal and Stephen fell silent for a moment. In his mind, Charlie pictured him sitting behind his desk with his head bowed down, praying. He finally agreed with Charlie's plan to leave Ester's car with Daniel and Ruth and they would pick him up at the airport Saturday evening.

While Michael ran some errands, Charlie used the time to book his flight and respond to the e-mails. Tessa was the easy one. He confirmed to her that PITS was also in the run for the merger. He mentioned they had made him all kinds of promises to keep him on their team and asked her if she could do better on her offer. He kept it short and simple. *"Less is more,"* he said to himself as he hit the send button.

The e-mail to Dan and Heinz took some more thinking. He combined his response in a single e-mail, and added Vince to the e-mail. He went through multiple iterations and had to start completely over a few times. He just couldn't find the right words to keep it from sounding like a threat or blackmail. After a while, he abandoned the effort and saved a draft to review later.

Michael returned from his trip and Charlie joined him in the backyard where he had already started a fire for another traditional braai that evening. He boasted about the good deal he got with some lamb chops at the butchery and offered Charlie a cold beer. Charlie did not like the bitter taste of beer, but decided to have one with Michael as they settled down and watched the sun set over the Atlantic Ocean. Another beautiful evening on the southern tip of Africa.

They talked about food, weather, rugby and cricket, and then Michael asked Charlie about his plans for the future. He explained his situation with the next project, and asked Michael what he would do. Michael thought for a few moments and then looked directly at Charlie before he responded. Charlie knew he was serious when he started.

"Charlie. Be very careful with what you decide. I don't trust those three for one minute. The sooner you get away from them, the better for you."

"Why do you say that? I thought about Vince and his loss and felt sorry for him. It must not be easy to lose both of your parents on the same day. I wanted to go and talk to him about it."

"What." Michael said with a bewildered looked on his face. "You want to talk to Vince about the accident?"

"Yes. Why not? I know what it feels like to lose two people you loved very dearly at the same time. I can just imagine how he must have felt when he lost both of his parents." Michael shook his head in disbelief and looked out over the ocean. Charlie could see he was upset, but did not understand why.

"He didn't love them. He loved their money. He was a spoiled brat who always wanted more. If you really want to have trouble, talk to him about it. I overheard him one day as he went off on Dan. I don't know the exact reason, but Vince went ballistic on him. I was in the office next door, and Vince slammed the door so hard you could feel the walls vibrate a mile away. I heard them through the wall, and really felt sorry for Dan that day. I had no idea what was going on back then, but I think I know now."

"What do you know?" Charlie asked and studied Michael's face as he turned to Charlie and smiled.

"My neighbor next door is an editor at one of the local tabloids. One day we discussed life in America and I told him my story and about The Three Musketeers. We talked about Vince and the accident of his parents. A few days later he brought me a file with some very interesting articles. I still have it. I will make you a copy and you can read it when you have time. Maybe on the plane back home."

Charlie realized there was still more going on than he knew and was at a loss for words. As the evening progressed, Michael continued his attempts to convince Charlie just to quit and not go back to PITS.

"Just tell them you have another offer for a new project. Don't give them any specifics or any details. Take the offer from...what is her name?"

"Tessa." Charlie filled in.

"Yes, Tessa. Take her offer and don't look back. Just stay away from Vince."

* * *

CHAPTER 25

Saying Good-bye

S tephen and Ester picked Charlie up at the airport. He exchanged a brotherly handshake with Stephen and he kissed his sister-in-law on the cheek. Ester was not her normal self. She tried very hard to be cheerful and was a lot chattier than before. Stephen on the other hand was silent and seemed to be very focused on the road in front of him. Charlie sat in the back seat, smiling to himself as he observed the two in the front seats. He knew he would eventually get an earful from Stephen, but for now they chitchatted about his trip and how the kids were doing.

Charlie used the opportunity and jokingly blamed Stephen for putting his kids at risk with such an old car. Stephen countered and said Charlie had no reason to interfere with how he raised his children and what they had or did not have. They were very much content with the car and mentioned that it was still in excellent condition despite its age. Eventually the real reason for Stephen being upset at Charlie surfaced.

"How am I going to explain this to the congregation? The finance committee will grill me and have a million questions. They always have lots of questions when I buy a new car or anything that one of them could not have. And where do you think I am going to get the money to make payments on a car?"

"Oh, so the Reverend's image is more important than the safety of his children," Charlie said from the back. The look Stephen gave him in the rear-view mirror made Charlie burst out laughing. Ester turned around with a smile on her face as she winked at Charlie.

"You look just like Dad! He always looked at us in the mirror like that. The apple didn't fall far from the tree," he said and smiled back at Ester.

"That's not true. What are you laughing at?" Stephen asked Ester as he looked at her trying very hard to stop her giggles.

"How old are you two? Maybe I should do the driving because it sounds like I am with two teenagers in the car."

"I thought you were on my side?" Stephen looked at Ester with a surprised look on his face. Charlie enjoyed the scene in front of him and knew it was more a facade rooted in pride than a real objection.

"Stephen," Charlie said when it became silent for a minute. "I explained it to you before. I have enough savings and would love to help you for once in my life. I was cheated for a very long time and the bonus was more than enough to be able to do something about the ARK principal that somebody in this car explained to me." He knew he had Stephen when he mentioned ARK and that the objections would go away.

"But I'm not a stranger to you. It doesn't work with family," Stephen tried again, but Ester quickly looked at him and responded with sarcasm in her voice.

"Oh? And who made that rule? Another one of the Reverend Stephen's 'humble thyself' rules." Charlie enjoyed the moment and tapped Ester on the shoulder.

"So, Ester, what car do you want?" Charlie asked and looked at Stephen to see his reaction.

"Why does she get the car?" Stephen jokingly objected and looked at Charlie in the rearview mirror.

"It was my car you let Charlie drive and leave with the kids." Ester quickly responded. "So, it's just fair that I get the new one - at least this time. I always get the old one since the *'Reverend'* has to have the new one."

Charlie listened to his brother and sister-in-law squabble over the car, and for a brief moment he wondered what his family would have been like if he and Hanna had gotten married and had children. If they were just given the opportunity to have a family, he was sure Hanna would be a great mother. Where would they be in life if she had not been killed in the accident? *'Why did it happen? Who did it?'* he thought and the conversation with Marlene flashed through his brain. It was a lot easier now for him to think about Keith, and Hanna and the accident. He clenched his jaw as he silently resolved to find the identity of the killer. He had a good idea where to start, even though he was not yet sure how he would execute his plan.

The following day at church, Ester introduced Charlie to Derik Siebert and his wife, Debbie. They talked for a few moments and Ester skillfully took Debbie away with a request to help her with something. Charlie used the opportunity to ask Derik for a private meeting. Derik wanted to know the subject and so Charlie explained the car situation to him. He just wanted to clear it with Derik as the chairman of the finance committee. He specifically also mentioned that he did not want Stephen or Ester at the meeting and wanted to meet in private. They arranged a time on Monday just before Stephen walked up and joined in their conversation.

Monday was a normal workday for Stephen. He spent some time in his office at home, made a few calls and then left for a meeting at church. It was the first time Charlie and Ester were alone.

"I talked to Derik yesterday," Charlie said as they sat down with a cup of tea. "He said I could stop by this morning and we can talk. Can you please drop me off?"

"Of course. I need to do some grocery shopping, so that will give you time to talk in private. Charlie," Ester stopped and wiped a tear from her eye, "thank you for what you are doing. You don't know how much I worry every time Daniel and Ruth have to travel so far in that old car."

"Oh, it's nothing. They are family and I'm very glad I can help."

"You know, I have prayed and asked God to do a miracle for them. Now God had sent an angel." Charlie felt embarrassed and guilty.

Ester left Stephen a note on the kitchen table. She said they had gone grocery shopping and would be back later. She dropped Charlie off at Derik's office and went shopping.

Charlie and Derik settled in and talked about their respective backgrounds and careers. Charlie asked questions about the role of the finance committee. He wanted to make sure he could trust Derik. The discussion went well and Charlie saw no red flags. He got the impression that Derik was an honest and trustworthy accountant. He understood why Stephen and Derik were such good friends. Derik was a man of principle and wanted to do the right thing, regardless of the consequences.

"Derik," Charlie said and got down to the real reason for his visit. "I have told you about the car, but there is something else we need to discuss."

"Well, now is always the right time. What is it?"

"Stephen told me about their plans to buy the clergy house from the church."

"That is correct," Derik said. "The committee really want's to just give it to them, but we cannot. The church building needs some renovations and we need the money from the property to finance the project."

"What if I make an anonymous donation? I will give you fair market price for the property. Knowing Stephen, I know he will not approve and so I want to stay anonymous. I know his pride will get in the way, so the church can still sell it to them for a nominal price they can afford."

When Charlie mentioned the clergy house and laid out his plan, it was he who suddenly found himself questioned and scrutinized. Derik wanted details of where the money came from and how he was going to pay for it.

It was the accountant that asked the questions and Charlie had to explain to Derik how PITS had cheated him and then gave him a "substantial" bonus if he did not report them to the IRS. The moment he said it, Charlie knew it was a mistake.

"Did you blackmail them to get the money?" Derik asked with suspicion.

"I see it more as restitution. I had the proof of what they owed me and only asked for what I could prove. I did not claim a penny more than what was owed. You are an accountant and I'm sure you understand the power of compounded interest. If you do the calculation you will realize that they owed me much more than what I actually received."

"I see," Derik said and made some notes on the pad in front of him.

"Besides," Charlie continued, "I don't have a family of my own. Stephen has sacrificed a lot to help others while in ministry. I will not only help Stephen, but also his wife and their children. They are my family. What would you do if you were in my shoes?" Charlie was on the brink of tears and his voice was wrought with emotion.

The discussion lasted for a while. Charlie made sure Derik understood that Stephen and Ester should not be informed about their discussion about the clergy house.

"Charlie," Derik said and looked at him, "this is not the first time that somebody wanted to make an anonymous donation to Stephen. The problem is not with the finance committee, but with him. He is the one that normally declines to accept any donation for him or his family. I think you may have found just the way to make right with him. As his friend, I want to thank you for this offer. I will discuss it with the committee. I am sure there will no be objection from them. I have an idea of how much they have in savings and I will make sure there is something left over."

Derik took it on himself to use his influence and friendship to help Stephen, for once in his life, to accept the gift in good faith. The church would ask a nominal purchase price for the clergy house and once the deed to the property was transferred, the money would be returned to the Reverend as an appreciation bonus. Derik explained to Charlie a rule in the church's guidelines he could invoke. The rule allowed for a special bonus to be given to the Reverend of the church when a substantial gift was made to the church and he was specifically nominated as the recipient.

Ester returned from her shopping and Derik's secretary opened the door, asking if they wanted tea and informing them that Ester had arrived. They accepted the offer and Derik asked her to invite Ester to join them.

Ester walked in and nervously sat down next to Charlie. Derik asked Ester some questions about the donation for the car and how she felt about it. She hesitated for a moment and first looked at Charlie and then at Derik. She did not like to discuss the situation without Stephen being present. Derik reassured her that he would discuss it with her and Stephen again, but he just wanted to get her opinion. She had enough experience as a Reverend's wife to select her words very carefully and gave only a vague and neutral opinion. She had no objections and said Stephen was the one who deserved it. Derik pointed out to her that she had sacrificed just as much, if not more than Stephen, for their ministry.

The discussion continued and after they had their tea, Charlie and Ester prepared to leave.

"Ester," Derik said as he greeted her at the door, "I will talk to Stephen. There will not be a problem with the car."

"Thank you, Derik. Just remember to tell him it is my car," she said and smiled at him.

"I will make sure he gets the message," Derik said and turned to Charlie.

"It was nice seeing you again, Charlie," he said as he took Charlie's hand. He held it for a moment and looked at Charlie. "I don't think you will ever know how much this will mean to our church. Your generosity will save us from a financial disaster and will open new doors for us." Derik had tears in his eyes and Charlie realized he was shaking the hand of a man of deep integrity. Stephen had a good friend that was closer than a brother. He left with a warm and satisfying feeling inside of him.

Charlie stayed with Stephen and Ester for the last few days of his vacation. Marlene came over for dinner with Stephen and Ester the evening before Charlie would return home. It was an enjoyable night, and when it was time to say good-bye, Charlie and Marlene both had tears in their eyes and promised to talk more often. He looked into her beautiful blue eyes and smiling face. Something stirred deep inside and he knew he wanted to see her again. When Marlene's car disappeared from view, Ester came and stood next to Charlie and locked her arm into his.

"I think you will see her again, Charlie," she said softly. Charlie looked at Ester and she gave him a meaningful smile.

"I think so, too. I never realized how much we have in common. We became good friends."

"Maybe more than friends, if you ask me," Ester pulled on his arm and they walked inside. Returning to his roots had been a healing experience for Charlie. He wanted to stay longer.

The drive to the airport in Ester's new car was somber and quiet. At the airport, they said their good-byes and Stephen thanked Charlie again for what he had done for them. They hugged each other and Charlie was surprised to hear the depth of emotion in Stephen's voice. Ester could not hide her feelings the same way as the two brothers. Charlie smiled when he looked at her and saw her cheeks streaked with makeup mixed with tears. He hugged her and kissed her briefly on her cheek. He picked up his bags and started his long journey back to the US, and reality.

Charlie checked in and went through the security checkpoint. He turned around and waved at Stephen and Ester one last time. He had no idea when he would see them again and hoped they would visit him someday in the US. When he originally emigrated from South Africa, he had good intentions to return more often, but life didn't go the way he had planned.

Work became his life and in the struggle to suppress his memories of Hanna, he also forgot about his own family. *"This time, it will be different,"* he thought to himself as he walked to the departure gate.

He sat down at the gate and opened his backpack. The expression on his face became stern when he saw the folder in his bag. He clenched his teeth as he thought about The Three Musketeers. He reflected on the conversations he had with Michael. If everything he had heard and read was true, he knew revenge would be sweet. He wanted to bring down the house of cards and let it fall to pieces. He felt sorry for the innocent who would be affected, but he also realized that in the long run it would be better for them. The injustice could not continue. The abuse of the innocent had to be stopped.

"If shift doesn't happen, something else will. The wheel may turn slowly, but it is turning. God does not sleep!" he thought to himself as he stood up to board the plane.

* * *

SECTION IV

Project Romeo

CHAPTER 26

Call to Tessa

The long sixteen-hour flight from Johannesburg to Atlanta gave Charlie enough time to read and reread the news articles in the folder Michael had given him. Among all the gossip and conspiracy theories, there was one article that caught his attention. A good piece of investigative journalism, it included details from the police inquiry into the condition of the car. Although it had been completely destroyed in the accident, the writer asked a simple question that caught Charlie's attention. *'How did a paperclip get lodged into the brake line of the rear wheel while rolling down the cliff?'* Charlie read the articles over and over, and nowhere else were it mentioned. The theory of another car involved was noted a few times, but there were no witnesses. One theory implied the driver was drunk, but the blood alcohol level was so low it couldn't have impaired the driver. The weirdest theory was that the driver and the passenger got into a fight, which caused the driver to lose control.

Again, Charlie couldn't sleep, and when the passenger in the aisle seat next to him stood up to go to the bathroom, Charlie did the same. He stretched his legs and got his laptop from the overhead bin. He started working on project "Romeo". He skipped the other letters of the alphabet and decided on the letter "R" because it was time for "Revenge". He thought back on his high school days and smiled as he remembered how he had enjoyed making mistakes on purpose when the bullies forced him to do their homework. Project "Romeo" is going to be sweet revenge.

It took Charlie a couple of days to get over the jetlag and adjust to the new time zone. He called Tessa and they had a friendly conversation about his visit and his family before the discussion turned to the next project. Charlie was ready for the negotiation phase. He had rehearsed the conversation in his mind before he called and anticipated her possible responses. He even prepared himself to just say no and walk away from the deal. He hoped she would be ready with a counter offer and then planned to ask for more time to think about.

The discussion stayed professional, and Charlie realized it was not the first time Tessa had to negotiate rates.

"Charlie, you know I'm depending on your expertise for the project, but you cannot use that as leverage to get a even better rate. It's already above the market rate," Tessa object against Charlie's request.

"I am sorry, Tessa," Charlie said with a smile. "I can use the same argument. You know my relationship with PITS is coming to an end and you cannot use that as leverage to not give me the best deal available."

"In your e-mail you mentioned an Asian company who wants to partner with PITS. Do you know the name of the company?"

"No. I have not talked to Heinz yet. He is next on my list. I wanted to call you first and see how serious you are about our agreement."

"It's not going to be an easy sell to my boss, but I think I can do it. Remember our agreement and the confidentiality. Don't mention it to PITS, please. What is your final number?"

Charlie thought a moment.

"If you give me a 20% allowance for expenses on top of the hourly rate, we have a deal."

"Charlie! You are killing me! I thought we were friends?"

"This is business, Tessa." Charlie waited and for a moment he thought he overplayed his hand.

"On one condition," Tessa said.

"And that is?"

"You stay for the full duration of the project." It was Charlie's turn to be silent. He thought about the money in his Zurich account and his discussion with Stephen. *"I could just quit and live off the money in the bank, but he also knew that was not really his money."*

"Deal."

"Thank goodness! What happened to you in Africa? You were always an easy customer." Tessa said with sarcasm. She shared more project information with Charlie and reiterated that she trusted him.

Although the rate negotiations went a lot easier than Charlie thought, he was exhausted from the intense discussion. He smiled as he realized he got a better deal than he had hoped for. Tessa increased her offer and with an additional twenty percent allowance for actual expenses he was satisfied with the result. *"Not bad,"* Charlie thought as he calculated what he could potentially earn if the project lasted the full 18 months.

"Don't be too excited. I have not yet handed in my resignation. You know they are not going to take it well," Charlie told Tessa.

"Oh, they will just have to get over it. Now that we have secured you on our team, they will not get the project and we'll have it in the bag."

"So, you are convinced you have it. How do you know?

"Charlie. I told you before. We do our homework very well. We know who we are up against. We submitted the resumés of our key resources for the project and your name stood out like a sore thumb. You were the only person submitted by two of the three companies in the final run. The project manager called me and asked for an explanation. He wanted to know how sure we were about your commitment. I told him that you worked for me on a previous project and I had information they did not have."

"It was confidential. You were not supposed to discussed it with anybody."

"Charlie. I made a mistake once when I assumed something. I don't make the same mistake twice. I only told them we increased our offer. Not about what happened in the past."

"Oh, sorry. I am little bit stressed."

"Seems like it. Anyway, I told him to verify the individual rates and compare it with the cut taken by the staffing company. I assured the project manager that I had you on my team."

"How did you know we would reach a deal?"

"Were you not the one who reminded me of the old saying of, *'Fool me once shame on you, fool me twice shame on me'*?"

"You win. I will be more careful making comments to you in future," Charlie said teasingly. He relaxed when he realized he had made the right decision. If he didn't break his ties with PITS now, he would regret it for the rest of his life. The house of cards would soon come down.

"I have another request," Charlie said, "as a friend, and not as my future boss."

"Anytime. What can I do for you?"

"This may sound strange, but I need a contact person for a safe deposit box at my bank. There are some important documents and my last will and testament that I need to keep safe. I don't have any relatives in the US, and I need somebody I can trust to take care of it if something happens to me."

"Charlie, this sounds creepy. What is going on? Why do you need a safe deposit box at the bank? Just leave it in a safe at home."

"Tessa, I cannot explain the details now, but will update you when I see you at the kickoff meeting for the project. There will be instructions in the safe deposit box about what to do with the contents. You'll just need to follow them."

"Are you sure you are ok?"

"Yes, I'm just stressed. I told you they would not take my resignation easy. I also have something else I need to take care of and I'm not sure about the outcome. If anything goes wrong, I will not be available for the project."

"Are you in trouble? I can make some calls if you need a lawyer. You can talk to our legal counsel anytime. Just let me know."

"Thanks for the offer, Tessa. Don't be surprised if I take you up on that one. I cannot say more right now. I don't want to get you involved unnecessarily."

"Charlie. You are one of our key resources, and without you, I'm not sure if we will get the project assigned to us. Please don't do anything stupid. Talk to me if you need some advice."

"Tessa, don't worry. I will not do anything stupid. I have to go." Charlie did not want to continue with the discussion. He was afraid he might say too much. From experience, he knew how easily Tessa could get to the bottom of an issue with a few good questions.

"Ok. We will talk to again. Bye, Charlie."

"Bye Tessa," Charlie felt relieved and hung up the phone.

* * *

CHAPTER 27

Prince Justus

C harlie was not yet ready to talk to Heinz. When he got home, he listened to the voice messages Heinz and Dan left on his answering machine. He decided to stick with e-mail communications. When his phone rang, he let it go to voice-mail. He finalized the e-mail he had prepared, and made sure all three executives of PITS were included as recipients. He read it one more time.

Subject: The next project.

To: Heinz and other members of the executive team.

I do not have to remind you of my history with PITS. I want to sincerely thank you for the opportunity you gave me to settle in the US and ultimately become a citizen. I am very grateful and thankful for what you have done for me in this regard.

What I am NOT grateful and thankful for is the way you have knowingly and purposefully deceived me over the years. I have worked diligently and sacrificially on every project I was involved with as a PITS employee. I trained many new consultants over the years just to realize that you were not only cheating me financially, but you were doing the same, and more, to the young and inexperienced people.

I think you can understand very well why I will be looking for some new opportunities in the future. If you are still interested in my services as an independent consultant, it will be on my terms, and at a totally different rate than what was previously agreed to in the contract you so frequently reminded me of.

If the above is not acceptable to you, then consider the attached letter as my resignation from PITS.

Sincerely,

Charlie O'Neal

He had typed and retyped the e-mail a few times over. He wanted to say so much more but decided once again that less is more. He tried to be as vague and non-specific as possible. He wanted them to think he would still be available for the project they were bidding on.

He did not send the e-mail yet. Project Romeo was not ready to be launched and he first needed a dry run of his plan.

He sent a copy of the e-mail and the attachment from a fake e-mail address to himself at his PITS e-mail address. He logged into the PITS network using the VPN connection the company provided to consultants. He opened his e-mail and clicked on the attachment. He waited for a few minutes without leaving the screen he was in and then closed the document. He logged off from the network, and scanned his computer. He knew exactly what to look for, and used the command line editor to find the hidden file. He manually executed the file and studied the screen closely to make sure there was no indication of a program being launched in the background. He analyzed the memory details. For a novice, everything would seem to be working just fine. He performed a few simple tasks on his laptop, typed a short memo and then closed all open programs. He waited for a few minutes and then logged into the ftp site he had setup. He searched for the file that should have been created in the last few minutes. He found the file and opened it with a text editor. It looked like garbage and contained only hexadecimal characters. He ran the string of characters through his Romeo decipher program and converted the memo back to normal ASCII characters. He studied the results. He was able to read the message he had just typed, and the file contained all his keystrokes. This was exactly what he wanted. Project Romeo was ready to be launched. He just needed to create one more e-mail.

He scanned his junk mail, and found an e-mail he planned to use. It looked like the typical scam from a prince in some foreign country who offered him a share of his inheritance in return for some personal information. What made his different would be the name of the prince and the content of the letter. Only somebody familiar with Sir Archibald Mansion and his wife Madam Catherine would pay attention to the e-mail. The message contained the same fake street address Sir Archibald used many years ago when he opened his bank account. Charlie added specific details of the accident on Chapman's Peak and described how the Mansion couple had died in the accident. The e-mail concluded with a request for help to resolve the murder of his parents and offered a substantial reward for information about the cause of the accident.

Charlie was ready to launch project Romeo.

He sent his first e-mail to the executive team from his personal computer and expected them to click on the attachment and read his resignation letter. Embedded in the attachment was the program that could log their keystrokes. The next step of his plan depended on the second e-mail from the prince, and the curiosity of the reader to open the document attached to the e-mail.

Charlie switched to an old laptop and used a virtual instance of an old version of the operating system. He logged into the fake e-mail account of Prince Justus Archibald Mansion and completed the final preparations. He hacked the IP address used and changed the machine serial number so that it could not be traced. He scheduled the e-mail to be sent with a date and time stamp that matched the east African time zone of the IP address. He sent three individual e-mails - one to Heinz, one to Dan and one to Vince. He gambled that one of them knew something about Sir Archibald and would click on the link to display the attached document from Prince Justus. Unlike the specific detail in the e-mail, the document contained only a few words:

"I know who you are and what you did. I know about the money in the off shore account. I will be in touch.

Prince Justus."

Charlie was interested in what the next action of the real Sir Archibald would be. He hoped the person would log into a bank account to verify the balance of the account. The keystrokes recorded would provide him with all the details he needed.

The next few days were nerve wrecking for Charlie and he anxiously checked the ftp site every few hours to see if a file had been generated. He hadn't received a response from any of the executives and got concerned. He didn't know what to think about their silence. Were they all involved in the scheme? Were they trying to figure out what to do next? Was he in danger? Could they trace the e-mail back to him? The questions spiraled around in his brain and caused a few sleepless nights.

And then there was a file on the ftp site.

He downloaded the file onto the virtual machine. He immediately disconnected from the Internet before running the file through the Romeo decipher routine. The file was from Dan's computer didn't contain other information. The keystrokes captured indicated he must have shut down his computer immediately after opening the attachment from Prince Justus. It didn't make sense to Charlie. How was Dan involved? He never seriously considered Dan as somebody who would be involved in a scheme like that. For the visa fraud? Yes, but Sir Archibald? Never.

"He's not smart enough for it," Charlie thought to himself.

Before Charlie went to bed that night he checked the site again and found a few more files. There was nothing generated from Heinz's computer and so Charlie assumed he did not click on the link to activate the program to log keystrokes. Charlie was very interested in two specific files - one from Vince's computer and another from Dan's. The time stamp showed they had both accessed the file within minutes of each other. The file from Vince had a lot more information and Charlie scanned the details in the log file. It contained exactly what Charlie expected. Vince first accessed the website of a bank in South Africa and a few minutes later accessed the website of a bank in Mauritius, a popular vacation spot for the wealthy from South Africa. The third website Vince visited was for an online e-mail service and Charlie expected an e-mail in the account of Prince Justus. He logged into the account, and when he saw the e-mail from Vince, his excitement abruptly turned from winning and accomplishment, into fear and flight. He felt the anxiety growing inside, and had to read the e-mail again and again to be sure of what he was reading.

"Prince Justus

We have an idea of who you are. You can run, but you cannot hide! You'd better not be on your brand new motorbike or drive too fast on Chapman's Peak. Amazing what can be done with a paperclip. Expect the unexpected. We are coming for you.

Archibald and Alexander"

Charlie's thoughts went round and round. Sleep was out of the question.

"Who is Alexander? Where does he fit in? Did I find more than I bargained for?" He had no idea what he was going to do next and sat in front of the screen staring at the message until it was burned in his mind. When he closed his eyes, he could still see it.

"But his cat's name is Sir Archibald. How does Heinz fit into this? Is he Alexander?" The more he thought about it, the more confused he was. *"I have to get out!"* he said to himself and grabbed his car keys. He drove aimlessly and after a while stopped in a parking lot. Thinking about a destination took his mind away from the e-mail. He decided to find a place where he wouldn't be alone and when he looked up, he saw a billboard advertising the Gaylord Opryland Resort and decided to go there. It had a beautiful indoor garden where he could walk around thinking about the e-mail and what it implied. He passed a restaurant, saw there was no line and asked for a table in a quiet corner. The atmosphere inside was relaxing and a pianist sat in the corner playing soft, calming music. Charlie ordered a steak with a fried egg on top and crisped vegetables. The waiter was baffled for a moment but was sure the chef would not object. He ordered a glass of wine to keep him company and calm his nerves. He sipped his wine slowly and processed the new information in the e-mail. He thought about what he read in the folder Michael gave him. Suddenly he was filled with dread. He realized the implication of the e-mail.

"No! I have to warn Michael. For some reason they think he is behind this e-mail." There was no doubt in his mind that the story from the journalist in the article he had read was true. He had just found the evidence in the e-mail from Vince. Michael was right - he had to be very careful of Vince.

His food arrived and the aroma from the sizzling steak made him realize just how hungry he was. He broke the egg yoke and took his first bite.

"Perfect! Nothing like a good steak."

After a while he started to think clearly again and planned his next response. His first priority was to call Michael. He looked at his watch and realized it was still too early to call and made a mental note to do it.

He then thought about Heinz and the next project. He needed an excuse to call and the project was a perfect reason. He promised himself to be calm and professional, but not too friendly. He did not want to give Heinz any indication of what he was up to. The only thing he was sure about was that his time with PITS was limited.

Next on his list were Vince and Dan. According to Michael, they worked together at BOSA, but according to their company bios, they only met once they were in the US. Conveniently, nobody knew them well enough to dispute the information. *"Why do they want to hide the fact that they knew each before and worked together? What else are they hiding?"*

Charlie continued to reason with himself for a while. He knew he still didn't have enough evidence to prove what they may or may not have done. *"I need to get some hard facts to prove to the USCIS and the IRS what scheme they have going on. They got away with murder. I am not going to let these bullies get away with abuse and fraud also!"* he said to himself. Charlie shivered every time he realized he might just have been working with the one who could actually be responsible for the accident that had killed Hanna and Keith. He felt sick just thinking about it. He thought about what Michael had told him about the accident on Chapman's Peak. Charlie knew deep inside of him that, without a doubt, Vince was involved. The rumor about tampering with the brake-line of the car was true.

"Why did he mention a paperclip? He knew exactly how it was done." Charlie had once owned an old car that required a lot of maintenance. He'd also spent many hours with his Dad under a car when he was a little boy, so he was easily able to picture the brake-line and where a paperclip could be placed to make only a small hole that would cause the brake fluid to drain each time the brakes were applied. Eventually the system would run out of hydraulic fluid, and when brakes were suddenly needed at a critical moment, there would be no way to stop the car. Through the scenic drive and winding mountain pass of Chapman's Peak, it could be fatal. Many accidents did occur there, some fatal and some not. The outcome of the brake failure depended on where it happened. In this case it happened at the wrong place for Vince's parents, but at the right place for Vince.

Just thinking about it made Charlie feel sick and he pushed his plate away. He couldn't finish his meal. *"What type of a monster is he to plan the death of his own parents?"*

"Excuse me, Sir?" The waiter brought Charlie back to reality and he looked up to see a concerned look on his face "I noticed you have not eaten much. Is there anything wrong with the food? Can I heat it up for you?"

"No, no. Nothing wrong," Charlie said. "I just lost my appetite. Can you bring my check, please?" Charlie needed to get out and after settling the bill he walked around in the inner garden of the hotel. He sat down on a bench and stared at the water running down a small waterfall in front of him. Memories flashed by and he mulled over the many ideas of what to do. His plan slowly started to take shape. The key point was his assumption how they would react. The only thing he really wanted was justice for Hanna and Keith. *"How long has it been? More than twenty years?"*

He thought about the e-mail again and the names at the bottom. *"Archibald and Alexander? Vince and Dan, or Vince and Heinz?"* The only thing he was sure about was that Vince was involved. Charlie thought about all the possibilities. The only conclusion that made sense was that Vince and Dan were Archibald and Alexander. They had known each other before they started PITS. Heinz must have overheard them talking about Archibald and took the name for his cat.

"What is happening? Do they really know who Prince Justus is, or do they think they know? I have to finish this!"

Charlie walked out of the garden at the Gaylord Opryland Resort with determination and resolve. He knew what he was going to do.

* * *

CHAPTER 28

Call to Heinz

Early Saturday morning, Charlie called Heinz. He thought about waiting for a more civilized time, but he also wanted to make sure he caught Heinz unprepared. He expected Heinz to answer his phone, because he knew he took many calls on Saturdays from employees who needed to change schedules.

Heinz was totally surprised when he answered the call. Charlie could hear the relief in his voice when Heinz greeted him like a long lost friend. They talked about his trip and Charlie responded kindly as they briefly talked about his visit with family. Heinz mentioned the e-mail he had received about the next project and Charlie was relieved to know at least one of them had read it.

"Charlie, we really need you for this project. It will be a nice long project and I hope we can put things that happened in the past behind us. I promise you, I will take care of you. No more hidden agendas. You will have full access to the contracts and the rates. All cards will be on the table."

"Do Vince and Dan agree with you?"

"We briefly discussed it, and they gave me full authorization to negotiate with you. They seemed to be very upset about something yesterday. I'm not sure what's going on, but the two of them were behind closed doors the whole day. They were also on the phone the entire time. They must be in the final negotiation stages for the project."

Charlie was caught off guard with Heinz's change in attitude towards him. The explanation about what Vince and Dan were doing was totally unlike Heinz. He never talked about their inner workings. And for Dan to allow Heinz to make a financial decision, that was even more obscure. Dan was the CFO, kept rates and contracts under his reign and was an absolute control freak. *"Are they setting a trap for me? Is Heinz being used as the bait to lure me in for the kill? Be vey careful, O'Neal!"* Charlie thought to himself.

"So, the project is not secured yet?"

"Not fully."

"Is it still moving forward?" Charlie asked to stay on point with the reason for his call.

"Oh, yes. We are making good progress. Just to show you how open I will be with you, I will let you in on a little secret. Just please don't mention to Vince or Dan that I told you. We are in negotiations with a consulting company from Asia. Their rates are extremely competitive, and I mean extremely! They have enough resources available to staff the full project requirement for programmers. We met with some of the partners and the plan is to set up a strategic alliance between PITS and ACG. Vince and one of their senior partners will be the project managers. Sound exciting?"

"Who is ACG?"

"Oh, ACG - Asia Consulting Group."

"They must be close to signing the deal if they are already talking project management positions," Charlie replied. He was stunned by the fact that Vince would be part of the Project Management Office. Vince managed some of the projects in the early days of PITS when there were only a few consultants and the durations were short. In the last few years, he had stayed away from projects and only showed up for special occasions to entertain sponsors for dinner, of course it was on their dime.

"Yes. I think it's close," Heinz continued to explain what was happening. "They want to expand more internationally, but their programmers lack experience with financial systems and mergers and acquisitions. We, on the other hand, have the experience, but have limited resources. If we join forces, their rates will give us the competitive advantage on the short list. I am working through some resumés and I will need your help to separate the fluff from the facts."

"Depends on your offer. Do you plan to use some of the team who worked on the project in Springfield?"

"Yes. We already have a few working on the final proposal. We received the final statement of work a couple of weeks ago. You will be happy to hear that Ben is one of them. Seems you have trained him well. He had lots of good things to say about you."

"That's great news. He's a smart guy."

"Will you join us for our year-end celebration next Friday? We had another record year and owe the staff a big thank you."

Charlie had heard enough and ended the call with a promise to join the celebration. In his heart he didn't want to go, but if he wanted to go through with his plan, then he had to be there. The good news was that Ben was back in the country. He just needed to convince him to help.

* * *

CHAPTER 29

The Response

C harlie checked the ftp site constantly. He studied the logs and downloaded ones he wanted to analyze in more detail. He flip-flopped between his laptop and the virtual PC on his old computer. He used a flash drive to move files between systems and, although it was old school technology and a very time consuming, it was perfect for the job at hand. The virtual instance could be wiped out instantly or be restored just as quickly from a ghost image if needed. The logs soon bored Charlie and did not render any new useful information. After a week of analyzing them, he suddenly noticed something. Dan accessed the same folder on the internal network drive a few times daily. Charlie recognized the folder as the one where employee files were stored. He helped setup the structure and it was still in place.

Charlie logged into the PITS network just as he did daily when working remotely. As one of the employees who initially help set it up Charlie still had administrative privileges to the servers. His admin rights had never been questioned or revised since he had installed them. He was taken aback when he got a system message telling him he was not authorized to see the folder.

"That's odd. I had access to the files before. Why did they take it away?" he

thought to himself. He went back to the logs and studied them again. He found the last time Dan had accessed the folder and saw the same pattern of keystrokes being used after accessing the folder.

"They changed the username and password. Why didn't they let anybody know?" He used the username and password from the logs and opened the folder. When he looked at the details, he saw multiple folders all starting with three letters followed by a five-digit number. He scrolled through the list, found the one with his initials and employee number and opened the folder. He saw the same list of documents he had seen before - project agreements and HR documents. He looked at the file dates and opened the most recently modified file. It was a draft of the new agreement between him and PITS.

"Typical!" he said to himself and shook his head as he read through the document. It was a copy of his previous contract with a new date and a change in the rate. He printed a copy of the document and scrutinized the familiar content word for word. While he read the document, he downloaded a copy of all the staff folders to his flash drive. *"Never know when I may need it and what I will find. They may just change the password again. If I quit, they will take away my access."*

Charlie looked at the rate in the document and was impressed. They almost matched the rate he had from Tessa, but the expenses were capped at the usual twelve percent of the consulting rate. He smiled as he thought about his negotiation with Tessa to get a twenty percent expense rate. He had a far better deal with Tessa.

He scrolled through the folders and documents and randomly selected a few to open. The more he studied it, the more excited he got. On the one hand it made him angry, but on the other it gave him exactly what he was looking for. He had all the proof he needed.

Each employee had a folder that contained all the images of their personal documents. He saw copies of passports, visas, social security cards, bank details, resumés, etc. *"You must be kidding,"* he though as he realized exactly how they were committing the fraud. He just could not believe they had gotten away with it for so long.

He opened his old computer with the virtual instance and logged into the fake e-mail account of Prince Justus. It was time to respond to the e-mail Prince Justus received. He kept it short and simple, smiling while he typed. He made some obvious typos to maintain the image of Prince Justice.

> *"Dear Sir Archibald and Mr. Alexander*
>
> *Just to informs you that I boughted myself the motorbike as you suggested. What do I do with the paperclip? I will sent copy to you to do the needful.*
>
> *Yourses truly,*
>
> *Prince Justus of the state of Northern Nigeria"*

Charlie paused a few moments as he once more considered the consequences of his plan. Eventually he took a deep breath and hit the send button. He shutdown his computer and went to bed.

* * *

CHAPTER 30

The Whistleblower

C harlie called Ben a few days before the planned year-end party. They exchanged pleasantries and Charlie asked Ben when he had returned. Ben confirmed what Heinz already told him.

"Will you be back next year?" Charlie asked.

"It all depends. If PITS gets the contract I will be back," Ben said and something in his voice gave Charlie an indication that everything was not as great as it sounded.

"If? So the contract is not in place yet."

"As far as I know, nothing is confirmed yet."

"Who else is working with you? Anybody I know?"

"There are seven of us working on the proposal and the detail plan. We all go back in a couple of weeks."

"Why? Why not stay until the project starts?" Charlie knew he was running out of time if they were going back so soon. If he wanted to do something, now was the time to put his plan into action.

"Dan called us in and explained the situation with the contract. The final decision will only be made at the end of the month. The project start date is early next year. We have to be out of the country for five weeks before we can return again. If we go back now we'll maximize our time when we return in January. We will be working from the offices in South Africa until the big kickoff meeting. He wants us back for that."

"That's sounds interesting." Charlie realized he knew more than Ben. "Listen, Ben, I am driving down for the function this weekend. Want to have dinner again? How about I take you to a good restaurant, like we did in Springfield?"

"Really. That would be awesome!" Ben suddenly sounded more excited than he had just a few moments before. "Anytime. Just let me know where and when."

They arrange a time and a place, and right before Charlie ended the call, he had one final request for Ben.

"Ben. Can we keep this confidential? Just the two of us, ok? Nobody needs to know I will be in town early or that we will have dinner together."

"Not a problem. Will keep it quiet."

"One more thing," Charlie said. "Can you also bring your passport and visa? Remember what we talked about in Springfield? I just want to check on something for you. I want to make sure you will not get into trouble when you come back again."

"Thanks. I appreciate that. I'm nervous every time I have to go through customs. Last time they asked a lot more questions than before. I don't like lying to them. It will help to talk to somebody who knows the process."

"We can talk. Just trust me and keep it quiet."

Charlie and Ben met at the Capital Grill in Buckhead, just north of the downtown area of Atlanta. It was far enough away from the PITS office located on the northwest side of Atlanta. Charlie was sure none of the staff would be in the area on a Thursday night. Ben appeared out of place in the upscale restaurant and Charlie asked for table in the back of the restaurant. Ben struggled with the menu and all the choices. Charlie helped him to select a rib eye steak and fries. For himself, he selected the sliced beef brisket with cheese grits and stir-fried smoked Brussels sprouts with bacon. From experience he knew the big chunk of meat would not be a problem for Ben. He ordered a couple of beers and they started talking. Charlie got the normal office and life outside the office discussions out of the way. The waiter brought out their food, and the look on Ben's face when he saw the steak confirmed to Charlie that Ben's focus would be on the meal and nothing else. Ben asked for another beer and Charlie knew the question and answer session would be easy.

"Did you bring the copy of your visa?" Charlie asked between bites.

"Uh-huh," Ben said with a nod and a mouth full of food. He reached into the pocket of his jacket hanging over the back of the chair and presented an envelope to Charlie. Charlie opened it and smiled at the picture of Ben stapled to the visa. *"Still a kid"* he thought and studied the document. It was a type R with a B1/B2 class printed in the top right corner. The I-94 document had an expiration date the following year. Charlie returned the document to the envelope and, as he cut another bite of his meat, he closely observed Ben's reaction to his next question.

"Tell me something, Ben. How are you paid if you don't have a social security number?"

"Oh, I'm not paid over here. Our salaries are paid through the company in South Africa." Ben gulped some more beer and worked on the next bite of steak. He didn't even think twice about what he implied. PITS was involved in visa fraud by paying workers on a visitor's visa. The beer did its work and Ben was a lot more relaxed. He answered all the questions without hesitation.

"And your expenses?"

"We get a weekly allowance. Each person gets a debit card to use. If the money runs out, we have to pay with our own credit cards and claim it back from PITS. They reimburse us through the company in South Africa."

"You mentioned on the call there are seven consultants. Do they also have debit cards?"

"Yes."

Charlie could not believe how gullible Ben and the other consultants were. Did they even know they were involved in an illegal process?

"Ben. Do you know it is illegal to work in the US under a visitor's visa?"

"It's not illegal." Ben said with confidence. "Heinz and Dan explained it to us. We are working for PITS South Africa, not for PITS America. We are only here for a few meeting, and the rest of the time is paid vacation. Nothing illegal about that."

Charlie knew it would take some time to convince Ben that it was illegal. He tried to explain the different visa types and told Ben to do some research. He took a napkin and wrote down the web address for immigration services and gave it to Ben.

"Go and read about the jail time you can get for working on a B1 visa. If you get caught, you will spend some time in jail and then get deported. You will not have the opportunity to visit the US ever again." Charlie was upset with the ignorance of Ben and the other consultants. What upset him even more, was the way in which PITS abused them. Since childhood Charlie hated bullies and couldn't stand people who took advantage of the innocent. "Once you find out about the punishment, let me know. I have a way for you to come clean, and start over again. It will take some guts to do it, but you will reap the rewards later." Ben stared at Charlie as the seriousness of the situation started to get through to him.

"Jail? What do mean? I'll ask Heinz about it."

"No! He should be the last one you talk to! I asked you before not to tell anybody about our conversations. If you talk to him or one of the executives, you will go home immediately, and..." Charlie looked at Ben and saw the fear growing inside of him. "You will be out of a job, too."

Ben just stared motionless at Charlie. His forearms rested on the table with the steak knife in one hand, the fork in the other hand as he leaned forward over his plate. His face was a mix of fear, anger, disbelief and innocence.

"It's that serious," Ben said with wide eyes. Charlie looked at him and suddenly felt sorry for him. He was still a young man with a lot of potential who had gotten sucked into something he did not ask for or understand. *"Greed knows no boundaries, and will stop at nothing. Not even murder,"* Charlie thought. He realized Ben had gotten caught in the same trap he had managed to get away from. He wanted to take Ben by the shoulders and shake him so that he could wake up. He didn't realize how serious it was - the danger they lived in.

"You don't believe me?" Charlie asked and waited for Ben to respond. Ben was still staring at him, his mind in places Charlie did not know, and did want to know.

"No, I believe you. It's just..." Ben's voice broke down, and he swallowed hard. Charlie let him be for a moment as he realized he might have triggered something Ben already knew. After another long drink from his glass, he continued.

"After our previous talk, I did some research of my own. I also talked to some of the other consultants and we were all very nervous. The questions at the embassy in Johannesburg and at customs at the airport are more intense every time. The agents want to know more about the purpose of our visits and I don't like to lie to people. But how else am I going to get to work here? You know the situation in South Africa. There are no more jobs for us."

"Lying to a customs agent is serious business. They are federal agents and you can get in a lot of trouble. If I were you, I would plan to not come back unless you have the right kind of visa. Next time PITS asks if you want to come here for a work assignment, make sure you have an L-1 visa. With your qualifications and experience from the project we worked on together, it should not be difficult to get one. Do your homework before you return again."

"Ok. I will. What do I do now? I don't have a job in South Africa. My parents cannot take care of me forever."

"I think there is a different way for you to earn a permanent visa. But," Charlie stopped and tried to stay as calm as possible, "it's not for the faint of heart. You will have to man up for the task. It will be risky, but the rewards may be worth the effort." Charlie was ready to launch his battle against The Three Musketeers. He just needed to get Ben on his side.

"I have nothing to lose," Ben said with a sad look on his face. "If I cannot come back to America again, I will have to stay with my parents even longer. I am saving every penny I can so I can survive until I return. What else can I do?"

"Do you know what a whistleblower is?"

"No, some kind of referee? Like in rugby?" Charlie had to smile at the answer. *"Really still an innocent child,"* he thought.

"No, Ben. It's not a referee. It's somebody who informs the authorities of fraud or crime at a workplace."

"Like a *'rat'*, who tells on somebody?" When he said it, Ben suddenly sat up straight as he realized what he had just said. Charlie tried to keep a straight face, but inside he smiled when he saw the shock on Ben's face. *"He knows exactly where I am going."* Ben looked around nervously to see who could hear him. "You want me to be a, what did you call it, a "whistleblower'? How? What do I have to tell somebody?"

Charlie explained the details of his plan to Ben and added some information on all the fraud PITS and The Three Musketeers were involved in. He wanted Ben to know exactly how serious the situation was and that they didn't have much time. Ben's resistance and doubt slowly changed to anger and determination to get involved. Charlie's instinct that Ben was a man of good character seemed to be correct. Ben wanted to set things right even more than Charlie.

Charlie laid out his plan. Ben would make copies of all his visa documents and print out all communications he could get ahold of about his visa application process. Charlie instructed him to write a detailed log of when the process started and how it had progressed.

"Write it down in your own handwriting, exactly as it happened with dates, times, places and the names of people involved." Charlie kept on giving Ben instructions. He asked him to discreetly talk to the other consultants he could trust. If they worked under the same visa class, then they obviously also lied to the customs agents each time they entered the country. Ben would make copies of their visas and I-94 documents, if possible. He had to make detailed notes of how they were paid and make copies of any pay stubs and expenses he had filed. He should save any electronic documents to a flash drive and always keep it in a safe place. Charlie made him understand the danger of the situation if a manager or one of the admin staff discovered what he was doing.

"What do I do with all the information then?" Ben asked.

"Put it on this flash drive and hold on to it." Charlie handed Ben two flash drives he had prepared. "Keep it in a safe place with all your documents. Save all your documents on the blue one. The red one is password protected with some more information. I will give the password to you when you need it. Just don't loose the drives."

"How long is this going to take?" Ben asked.

"I will let you know. Maybe next week, but it will be soon. If you decide to chicken out and not do it, I will completely understand. Just remember the consequences." Charlie had some more work of his own to do. He also had to make sure that he wanted to go through with his plan. It could become very dangerous for both of them. He had done his own homework and had all his files ready, not only for the USCIS agents, but also for the IRS. He just needed to make a few more calls.

"So," Ben said after a few moments of silence, "and then I am without a job. Where do I find work again?"

"Let's first make sure you want to do this. Go think about it and let me know tomorrow evening at the party if you still want to go through with the plan. Once you have all the information together, we'll talk about the next step. If and you want to move forward, we will arrange for another dinner."

The waiter brought the check and Charlie settled it in cash, leaving a tip that made Ben look twice at him. Charlie wanted to give Ben some extra money, but at the last minute put it back in his wallet. He did not want to give Ben the idea that he would be paid for what he would do. There would be other ways to reward him if they could pull this off. Outside the restaurant they said good-bye, and Charlie had one last word of encouragement for Ben.

"Ben. You can do this! Just remember, the reward is not always in the form of money, but in your mind, in your conscience and in your heart. Become a person of integrity and do the right thing. Always." When Charlie said it, he knew he was also talking to himself. He still had the money in the bank in Zurich and silently resolved not to use it for himself, but to help other people. The ARK principal was still fresh in his mind every time he took out his wallet.

* * *

CHAPTER 31

Vince

The hall at the Marietta Country Club was packed with attendees for the PITS year-end celebration. The air was filled with excitement about the successes of the year gone by and with the prospect of a better year ahead. Vince, as the top showman, performed his CEO duties with flamboyance and flair. He silenced the crowd with a delicate tapping of a spoon against his glass, and welcomed everybody to the event. He invited the audience to mingle, meet some new friends and have a free drink until the dinner announcement. He joined many of the small clusters of employees in the foyer, cracked a joke here and there and moved from group to group. Charlie stood silently with his group and observed the performance from a distance while occasionally answering a question directed at him.

Charlie's heart skipped a beat when Vince suddenly appeared next to him.

"Hello, Charlie. Have minute?"

"Hello, Vince. Yes, sure." They walked to the window overlooking the 18th green. Charlie thought about all the things he wanted to say to him. His fear of the outcome was greater than his desire to let him have a piece of his mind. He played the role of the submissive employee.

"How was your trip?" Vince asked. Charlie focused on news and updates about his family. He intentionally did not mention his visit with Marlene or with Michael and Karen. The conversation turned to work and Vince totally surprised Charlie.

"Charlie. There is something I have to say. Thank you for your loyalty all these years. You always put in more than what is required, especially during the last project. Thank you, again. I hope the bonus was proof of our appreciation for what you do. It was well-deserved."

"Thank you, Vince. Yes, it was very generous of you. Did you get my e-mail?" Charlie asked and looked at Vince to see his reaction. Vince stared at the lighted putting green in front of them. He slowly lifted his glass and took a drink from it.

"Yes. I was kind of surprised by it. I gave Dan and Heinz a piece of my mind about the error they made. It will not happen again." He turned to Charlie and looked at him. "Maybe we can forget what happened in the past and look to the future again."

Charlie was at a loss for words. Vince explained the situation as if he had no idea what happened. Charlie had to bite his tongue when Vince started talking about the ethics of the company and how they always play according to the rules. The next question made Charlie realize that he had to be very careful.

"You mentioned in your e-mail something about the treatment of new employees. Is there something I should know? Did anyone complain?" Charlie looked at Vince and weighed his words carefully. Although he had expected a question about the e-mail, he had not expected Vince to claim innocence.

"You know how it is with 'fresh-off-the-boat' consultants. They join the team with great enthusiasm and eagerness. Then after six months they go back home. Some come back, and some don't. Why can't we just keep them longer? It's a waste of time and resources to constantly train new blood. Do you know how many times I had to explain the same thing over and over? I am sure it costs the company a pretty penny to find replacements all the time. Why can't they stay?" Charlie made sure Vince understood his frustration was about the new employees.

"You know the process, Charlie. We put in a lot of effort to vet them carefully. Not all of them are consultant material and some just don't fit in. We have to weed out the bad ones and focus on the good ones. Look at you! You are still one of our best. Wish we could have ten consultants like you. The executive team discussed your future and your role in the new project. We don't want to lose you, Charlie. We discussed your contract and Heinz will send you an offer soon. I am positive it will meet your expectations. If it doesn't, please talk to me personally."

"Thank you, Vince. I can't wait to see it. I will ask Heinz about it." Charlie attempted his best smile and tried to hide the sarcasm in his voice.

"Oh, and watch the news in the next week. There will be some interesting movement in the financial sector. We hope to be part of it next year. I can't say much more, but just listen." The conversation stayed professional, and Charlie let Vince do the talking.

"Thanks again, Charlie. I will see you around," Vince said and turned around to leave. He hesitated for a moment and then turned back. "Just one more thing. Did you get time to visit Cape Town on your trip home?" Charlie was caught off guard. His heart nearly leapt out of his chest. He took a sip of wine and nodded slowly.

"Yes. I visited my niece and nephew in Stellenbosch. They are at University there. I drove from Pretoria; stopped at a few places, drove along the garden route from George and stopped in Hermanus to do some whale watching. Why do you ask?" Charlie noticed the look on Vince's face become more relaxed and the muscles in his neck release the tension from a few moments ago.

"Just wondering. I loved to drive through the mountains along the coastline. My parents lived in Clifton and they loved to drive around Chapman's Peak. They died in a terrible accident there. Not sure if you knew about that."

"Alice mentions it to me during the party at your house. She didn't give much detail. I'm so sorry to hear that," Charlie said. He wanted to ask a question, but Vince was ready to move on.

"It was a long time ago and life goes on." Vince turned around and walked away. Charlie watched him as he joined the next group to continue with the show. Charlie knew the question was not without purpose. He just didn't know if he had convinced Vince with his response.

Charlie replayed the conversation Vince over and over in his mind, analyzing every word. The only conclusion he could come to, was that Vince had tested him for some unknown reason. He realized he didn't have much time. He searched the crowd and saw Ben with a bunch of new consultants. *"It must be the group he is working with on the proposal,"* he thought. He watched the group interactions for a few minutes. They laughed and talked like any other group and seemed to be having a good time. Ben, on the other hand, had a somber look on his face. He managed a fake smile for some joke everybody else enjoyed. It was obvious that he was not having fun. Charlie made sure no one was watching him and made his way to the group Ben was with. He said hello to everyone, asked their names and inquired about their backgrounds. They all responded positively and he encouraged them about the project they were busy with. He got ready to move on, and turned to Ben who stood next to him. With a nod he indicated for Ben to walk with him. They stepped a few paces away from the group, and Charlie made sure they could not be overheard. The group continued their conversation and Charlie looked at Ben.

"You still on board?" He asked in a low voice.

"Yes. I have it all ready."

"Did you talk to anybody?"

"No."

"Ok. I will call you soon." Charlie touched his shoulder, and looked at him.

"Ben. Please be careful. Don't let them notice anything. Just be yourself and act normal."

"I will do my best."

Charlie turned and walked away to another group.

Charlie managed to avoid Dan the whole evening, but he had no way out when Heinz approached him. He said as little as possible and let Heinz, who had one drink too many, do all the talking. Heinz apologized profusely about the past and promised multiple times that he would take good care of Charlie in the future. He again mentioned the excellent offer he had prepared for him.

"I have to run it by Dan once more, but that will be easy. It will be a win for us all," Heinz said and tapped Charlie on the arm before taking another sip from his glass. Charlie just stared at him and listened to him talk about the offer. Charlie decided to make use of Heinz's condition and thanked him for making sure the offer would be great.

"Still have your cat?" Charlie asked and steered Heinz's attention to something else. Charlie hoped to get an answer to one of his bigger lingering questions.

"Yes. He wandered off for a couple of days, but he is back again. I always wonder where he goes."

"What was his name again? I know it was something strange, but I cannot remember. Where did you get such an unusual name?"

"Oh! Sir Archibald. Just some name I picked up shortly after I got him. I overheard Vince and Dan talk about someone named Sir Archibald. I think he was some rich client at a bank, and I decided it would be a nice sophisticated name for a cat. The name fits his personality, but I mostly call him Archie."

"Interesting story; a beautiful cat. You take great care of him, Heinz" Charlie said. He got the information he wanted, and was relieved when dinner started. They made their way to the dining room and he was glad to be seated amongst some of the more experienced PITS consultants who he could let to do most of the talking.

Early on Saturday morning, Charlie left the outskirts of Atlanta and returned home. He would work from home until the next project started. It suited him perfectly. He had enough time to prepare for the calls he had to make.

* * *

CHAPTER 32

Phone Calls

B en answered his phone almost immediately when Charlie called.

"This is Ben."

"This is Charlie. Are you ready to move forward with our plan?

"Yes," Ben said nervously.

"I made a reservation for you at a hotel in Chattanooga. Pack light and be ready move around in the next few weeks."

"When should I leave?"

"Leave as early as you can tomorrow. Check in at the hotel and stay there until I call you again."

"What about food? I don't have a lot of money, you know."

"Yes. I know Ben. I made arrangements at the hotel. You can order room service and I will take care of it. Just go slow on the drinks, please."

"Wow. I can get room service? Sounds great, Charlie. Thank you."

"One more thing before you go. I will send you the reservation details and a link to an ftp site. Download all the files on the site to the blue flash drive. The login info will be in the e-mail, but not the password. Can you write it down?

"Just a sec," Ben said and Charlie heard some noise on the other side coming through the phone. "Ok. Give it," Ben said again.

"The password is 'Romeo#2004' with a the first character a capital letter. Remember; protect the drives with your life. The information on the flash drives will be your bargaining chip to cut a deal with any prosecutor. It contains names and visa details of all the consultants involved in the visa scam. The password for the zip file on the red flash drive is 'Zulu#73'. Do not give the passwords to anybody until you have a signed letter from the prosecutor. Remember what we talked about. In exchange for the information and your testimony as a witness for the state, you will not be prosecuted. They may still deport you, but at least you will not spend time locked up. If the wrong people get the information, I'm not sure what will happen, but it may get us both killed."

"I am scared, Charlie. Are you sure this is going to work?" Ben sounded very nervous on the phone.

"It's good to be scared Ben. That will make you careful. I can't guarantee anything. If you don't want to continue, you have to tell me now."

"No. It's ok. I'm just nervous, that's all," Charlie could hear the fear and emotion Ben was trying to hide.

"Ben, the next few days, and maybe weeks, will be a roller coaster ride for us. Just remember, we are in the same boat. I am also scared, but I cannot sit still and let them get away with this scam any longer. Just think of all the other consultants they have taken advantage of. We worked our butts off for them to become rich, and what did we get in return? Peanuts!"

"Ok. Who do I give the drive to?"

"It will be some federal agent or a cop. I will give them your details and you can trust them. If possible, I will give you a call at the hotel to let you know when they are on their way. Stay close to a phone."

When he hung up, Charlie thought for a long time whether they should go ahead with their plans or just let it go. He did not want to put Ben, or anybody else, in danger, but he also knew that the futures of many innocent people would be wrecked if The Three Musketeers were not stopped. They had gotten away with their scam for far too long. He didn't even want to think of what would happen if they managed to join with ACG. With another partner involved in the process, the scam may just grow bigger. His only regret was that he didn't have any hard evidence to pin the accidents and murders on them.

He looked at the three envelopes on the kitchen table and it gave him hope. At least the real Sir Archibald will know that somebody is aware of his involvement in the crashes that killed Hanna and Keith and Vince's parents.

He got in his car and drove to the post office. He dropped three similar looking envelopes in the mailbox. Inside was a single sheet of paper with a web address and login details printed on it. Taped in the middle of the page was the biggest paperclip he could find. The information on the website contained everything Charlie knew and a warning that somebody would come knocking on their door very soon.

"This is it! If shift doesn't happen, something else will!" he said to himself as he turned away from the mailbox and walked back to his car.

At home, he called the whistleblower hotline and gathered all the information about the process, confidentiality and protection. The person on the call wanted more details, but Charlie said he did not want to discuss it over the phone. He asked if there was somebody local he could talk to in person. The operator put him on hold, and a few moments later the voice came back and gave Charlie the name and number of a federal agent in Nashville. Charlie hung up and walked around like a trapped bull. He took a few deep breaths and tried to control the anxiety building up inside of him. He picked up the phone and put it right back down again and again. He just could not make the call. Not yet.

He went to the kitchen and made some tea. He opened the fridge to get something to eat, but just stared at the contents and closed it again. He had no appetite. He sat down in the living room, and drank his tea. He thought about the call he had to make. After a few minutes, Charlie got up, walked to the phone, and dialed the number he had written down.

Agent Wesley Payne took the call and listened to Charlie's story. He asked some questions and agreed to meet Charlie in person. Charlie drove to the USCIS office building near the Nashville airport. The security guard verified his ID, confirmed his appointment and directed Charlie to the elevator. Agent Payne met Charlie at the elevator on the 5th floor. He took him to a small conference room and they talked for a few minutes. Agent Payne excused himself and returned with a bottle of water for Charlie, a tape recorder, a legal pad, a pen and another agent. He introduced Agent Mark Hastings to Charlie and started the question and answer session.

Charlie did his best to explain his reasons for his suspicion and why he thought his employer was using the visitor's visa program to employ staff from outside of the US. Agent Payne warned Charlie about the implication of making false accusations and asked if he had any proof. Charlie told Agent Payne that he could do even better - he could give him a witness working for the company. The witness, Charlie explained, wanted a plea deal and a pass from prosecution in exchange for his testimony. He told them the witness also had electronic documents to verify not only the visa fraud, but also the scheme the company used for tax evasion and possible money laundering. The company withheld taxes from employees working on the visa program, but did not pay the equal amount to the IRS. The agents became more interested, asked more questions and wanted to know the identity of the witness.

Charlie avoided providing Ben's identity until he could get it in writing that Ben would also receive the reward for providing the IRS with the necessary information. Charlie felt sorry for Ben, and was trying his best to help him stay out of trouble. The agents could not guarantee anything and promised to at least put in a good word for the witness. In exchange for the information he provided, Charlie wanted to remain anonymous and be a confidential informant. He did not want PITS to know he was the one who had provided the agents with the information.

They left Charlie alone and Agent Hastings returned every fifteen minutes to check on him. After an hour, Agent Payne returned with Special Agent Patrick Banes from the Treasury Department. They switched the recorder on and questioned Charlie at length about the accusations he made against his employer. It got to the point where Charlie thought he was the one going to jail and he regretted even contacting Agent Payne. Charlie managed to stay calm and kept to the facts. He refused to give them Ben's details until he could get assurance that there would be some kind of protection for Ben. He told the agents he was afraid of retaliation and was concerned about Ben's safety as an immigrant. The agents assured Charlie that nothing would be done until the claims could be verified and they promised to take Ben to a safe place.

The questions continued for hours and when the agents were satisfied that it was credible, they requested Charlie write down his statement. Charlie asked for his bag, and Agent Payne left the room to get the bag from his office where he put it when Charlie was taken into the interview room. He placed the bag on the table in front of Charlie and carefully watched as he took out some documents. He placed two documents in front of the agents - one contained the details of the visa program, and the other one had details about the tax evasion. They studied the documents, looked at each other and special agent Banes gestured with his head to Agent Payne to talk outside. They got up, instructed Charlie to wait and closed the door behind them.

Charlie again waited for a long time. An agent brought him another bottle of water and removed the empty one. He asked if Charlie was hungry and he said no. Charlie waited alone with his thoughts and memories. From time to time an agent would open the door to check on him and asked if he needed anything. Charlie said he was okay and his repeated question about how long he would have to stay didn't get any answer. He paced. He counted the tiles on the floor just to keep his mind occupied. At some point he rested his head on his arms and tried to take a nap, but sleep did not come. After three hours that felt more like 3 days to Charlie, Agent Payne returned to the room.

"Sorry it took so long, Charlie. We just had to verify some facts. What we could verify checked out. Hang in there. We are getting the paper work to make you a CI."

"What's a CI?" Charlie asked.

"Confidential Informant. That will give you some protection, if needed."

"Oh. And the other person, will he also become one?"

"Yes. You just need to give us his details. Do you have them?"

Charlie hesitated for a moment and looked at Agent Payne. He decided to trust him, and took a copy of Ben's passport and visa from his bag and handed them to Agent Payne. He studied the pages.

"This seems to be in order. I'll be back," Agent Payne said and left the room. After a few minutes, he returned with the documents and asked Charlie to read and sign when he was ready. He showed him the same document with Ben's details. He asked if Charlie needed any protection. They discussed the reasons and the risks involved, but Charlie was more concerned about Ben's safety than his own. As long as they kept Ben in a safe place and kept Charlie's identity a secret, he would be ok. He told Agent Payne about his plan to resign from PITS and that he would start soon with a different company. They talked for a few minutes about Charlie's travel plans for the future, and Agent Payne asked him to keep him updated with his movements for the time being.

When Agent Payne asked where Ben was, Charlie gave him the name and address of the hotel in Chattanooga. He explained to Agent Payne about his agreement with Ben, and asked if he could call him and give him the name of the agent he could release the information to. Agent Payne left the room and returned with a phone he plugged it into the wall socket. He handed Charlie a piece of paper with the name and badge number of an agent who would pick Ben up in Chattanooga.

"Hello, this is Ben."

"Ben, this is Charlie. You still OK?"

"Yes. Food is great here. Where are you?"

"I am in Nashville at the USCIS."

"Oh. What did they say?"

"Ben, I have a name and badge number of the agent that will come pick you up. You can trust him. Make sure you verify his badge before you give him the flash drives. Remember what we said about the passwords. Do not give it to anybody until you have signed the document to become a Confidential Informant. I have just signed mine."

"Wow. Charlie. Are we really doing this?"

"Yes. We are."

Charlie handed the phone to Agent Payne and he talked to Ben for a few minutes. He explained the procedure to Ben and what would happen next. Agent Payne assured Ben that he would be taken care of. They would first bring him to Nashville for questioning and then put him up in a safe house or hotel with protection.

After they got off the phone Charlie and Agent Payne talked for a few minutes and he answered the rest of Charlie's questions. Agent Payne escorted him to the elevator and they said good-bye. He reminded Charlie once again to stay close to a phone and to let him know of any changes in his travel plans. He promised to be in touch with Charlie soon.

Charlie left the federal building of the USCIS and when he got outside, he saw the sun was setting in the west. On his way home, he stopped for some fast food, and ate dinner at home. He thought about the day and all the questioning. He felt emotionally drained and had the urge to talk to somebody who would not twist and turn every answer, but who would just believe him.

His first thought was to call his brother Stephen, but then he thought about Marlene. She did ask him to stay in touch, so he decided to give her a call. He looked at the clock against the wall and realized it would still be the middle of the night in South Africa. He decided to wait a few hours and call her in the morning. Although he was tired, there was no way he would be able to sleep. At 1:00 AM in Nashville, he called Marlene. It was early morning in Pretoria when she answered the phone. She was somewhat surprised, but still excited, to get a call from Charlie. They talked in general for a few minutes, and then there was a pause in the conversation.

"Charlie?" Marlene asked. "Are you ok? You sound different. Is something wrong?"

"Marlene, you have to promise me to not to talk to anybody about what I am about to tell you. I..." She interrupted him before he could complete his sentence.

"Charlie! What did you do?" Marlene sounded upset and he heard the fear in her voice.

Charlie briefly explained to Marlene the events since his return from South Africa. He told her about his visit with Agent Payne and the questioning. He told her about the information he had provided to Ben and about the visa scam and tax fraud. Marlene was a good listener and asked a few questions, but Charlie did most of the talking. They talked for a long time and when Charlie eventually said good-bye, he felt different. He felt refreshed and the stress and anxiety had disappeared. It was so good to hear her voice. For a few minutes he sat in his chair and stared at nothing while he thought about Marlene. *"It's so easy to talk to her,"* he said to himself. He could not remember the last time that he had felt this way after talking to somebody.

He thought about Hanna, and began to cry. He thought about the good memories and not about the accident. He got up and went into the attic. He searched for the box where he kept some pictures from the time in his life he had been ignoring. He found the shoebox tied with a piece of string and he carried it down to the kitchen table. He unpacked the contents and looked through the pictures. With a smile on his face and tears running down his cheeks, he enjoyed the memories from when he was young and in love. He found a picture of himself with Hanna, Marlene and Keith. He stared at it for a long time and remembered the week they had spent in London. The picture was at a train station in the London underground when Hanna showed them her daily commute to work. They asked a stranger to take the picture. They were young, happy and had so many plans for the future - a future that never happened.

He placed the pictures back in the box, except for the one of the two couples in the train station.

* * *

CHAPTER 33

The Raid

Ten days after Charlie met Agent Payne for the first time, he was back in the same room facing him again. Beside him sat Agent Hastings and the atmosphere in the small room was a lot more relaxed than during their previous meeting. The stern face of Agent Payne was replaced with that of a regular person confident in the task at hand. He had called Charlie the day before and invited him to his office for a discussion about events and findings since their previous meeting.

As the conversation continued, Agent Payne from time to time slid a page from the folder in front of him over to Charlie. The pages contained the evidence they found at the office of PITS and he explained to Charlie how the investigation unfolded.

The raids took place early on Saturday morning at the break of dawn. Federal agents targeted the homes of The Three Musketeers and were swift and precise. They seized computers, and anything that looked like a document. They asked for their passports and travel documents and the three executives were each asked to accompany the agents "downtown" for questioning. Vince and Dan's wives had no idea what was happening so an agent stayed behind to explain the charges to each of them. They were advised to call a lawyer. Tears were in abundance, including terrified children. Lives were changed in an instant.

The PITS offices were raided at the same time. The floor where offices were located was *'locked down'*, and they use yellow tape to block the entrance. A uniformed police officer was stationed outside the elevator to protect the scene. The federal agents removed computers and files from the offices and loaded the evidence into a white van parked at the front entrance. The two locked filing cabinets found under the desks of Vince and Dan were also taken away. They did not force them open, but just took the whole cabinet on a dolly and loaded them into the van. They looked similar to the ones found at their home offices. The cabinets contained the final proof of the visa scam and the tax evasions.

When employees arrived at work on Monday morning, nobody had any idea of what had happened over the weekend. The front desk person of the service company arrived first and was surprised to see the police car and those of federal agents at the front entrance. An agent explained to her what had happened and she immediately started to make some phone calls to her manager and other employees.

PITS employees were directed to a conference room and were not allowed into their offices. They sat down and talked in small groups, speculating about what had happened. The front desk informed them about the raid by the USCIS and IRS. She didn't know where Vince, Dan and Heinz were and suggested somebody call their homes and ask. Nobody answered the phones at home. The rumors in the conference room were rampant and everyone had a different idea of what they should do. Somebody mentioned that they had not seen Ben for a few days. Gracey, one of the consultants, who worked with him on the proposal for the new project, informed the group that Heinz had told her that Ben had to take some unplanned vacation days due to some sort of family emergency. Heinz didn't say how long he would be away. Speculation continued and somebody suggested contacting the office in South Africa. It was useless as they were just as surprised as the group in Atlanta. Nobody had any idea of what was going on. One of the senior consultants took charge and asked for volunteers to drive to the homes of the executives to see if they were there.

They were all still planning their next steps when the front desk person entered the conference room with a few federal agents. They could see a few more standing in the hallway. An agent explained what was going on and somebody started crying. The agent opened a folder and started to call out names. One by one, the consultants on a visitor visa were called and escorted out of the room by USCIS agents. The employees that remained either had valid visas, green cards or were US citizens. The agent suggested they go home and wait to hear from the executives who would appear before a judge later in the day. The agent had no idea how long they would remain in custody. He suggested they contact the wives who may know more after the hearing.

The agents left the building and a short while later the few remaining employees also left. They had no idea of what was going on or what to do. Slowly the daily routine for the other businesses in the office building where PITS was located returned back to normal. Only a few people were aware of the drama that had taken place on the fifth floor.

Charlie browsed through the list of names of the employees who were arrested. He recognized a few he had worked with in Springfield, but most of them he did not know.

"What will happen to them?" he asked.

"Those on the list were all deported back to the country they came from. They will not be allowed back into the US again."

"I don't see the name of Benjamin Rivers on the list. What happened to him?"

"He is one of the lucky ones. The information he provided was spot on and will help the prosecutor to build his case. He is still in protective custody, and if everything works out as planned, he will be placed in the witness protection program. With his skills, it won't be difficult to place him in some government office under a new name."

Charlie felt relieved and was grateful that Ben would be ok.

"There is one more thing we need to discuss Charlie." The tone in Agent Payne's voice changed and Charlie looked up in surprise. Agent Payne looked uncomfortable and had a sad look in his eyes. He briefly looked at Charlie and hesitated for a few moments. He slid one of the two pages in his hand over the table to Charlie.

The first page was a copy of an article in a paper from many years ago. Charlie knew the contents as he also had copy in the folder Michael gave him. The article was about the accident on Chapman's Peak.

"Where did you get this?" Charlie asked with uncertainty.

"It was in one of the filing cabinets we removed from the offices. Do you know about the accident?" Agent Payne watched Charlie very closely. Charlie knew this was not the moment to lie.

"Yes. A friend showed me the article not long ago. What about it?"

"We got a confession from Dan Oliver. He told us the whole story."

"Dan?" Charlie stared at Agent Payne and could not belief what he heard. "It was Vince's parents who died. Did Dan do it?"

"They were in it together, but in the end turned against each other."

Agent Payne explained to Charlie how the two longtime business partners had planned the accident together. Vince's Dad was accused of running a scheme that allowed branch managers to use creative methods to redirect service fees charged to customers for personal expenses. The bank blamed him for another scheme where fees were randomly transferred to a fake account and the funds were withdrawn as cash at an ATM. Apparently it was not his dad, but Vince and Dan who were involved in the second scheme. When Vince's dad confronted him, he and Dan planned the accident. Vince made sure he had an alibi and Dan executed the plot.

Charlie listened to Agent Payne and slowly shook his head. He could not belief what he heard. *"So it's all true. Michael was right about it,"* he thought to himself.

Agent Payne looked at Charlie and slowly pushed the second page over the table. The two men stared at each other for a moment and Charlie slowly looked down at the picture in front of him. It was a crumpled motorcycle smashed against the railing on a highway. There were skid marks on the road and parts of the motorcycle were strewn everywhere. He didn't have to look long at the picture since deep inside he had filed it away in his memory. Slowly it returned to him.

"Charlie. I'm guessing you have seen this picture before?" Agent Payne said with a compassionate voice.

"Yes," Charlie said softly. Silence hung in the air for a few moments.

"They confessed, Charlie." The words were like ice water thrown into his face except he couldn't move. He stared at Agent Payne.

"They did it?" he whispered.

"Yes. They said Keith was interfering with their scheme and they wanted to scare him. They didn't plan to kill him."

"And Hanna? They killed her too?"

"They thought it was Keith's wife. They didn't know who it was and only found out later. I am so sorry Charlie," Agent Payne said and looked down. Charlie knew it was not easy for him to break news like this to those who are left behind.

"So they knew all these years. They knew who I was and what they did to me. I hope they get what they deserve," Charlie said with bitterness in his voice.

"There is one more thing, Charlie."

Charlie looked at Agent Payne with a blank stare in his eyes. All the will to fight had left him. He just wanted to get away.

"There is more?"

"We talked to the South African police. I'm afraid it is not good news."

"What do you mean?" Charlie asked with a puzzled look on his face.

"We provided them with the information we got from Vince and Dan. Apparently the South African government has no interest in opening an investigation into cold cases from the previous regime."

"What? So they will get away with murder? Can they not be prosecuted here?"

"It is out of our jurisdiction. We could use it to build our case, but a good lawyer would get it thrown out as not relevant to the fraud charges."

"Where are they now?"

"That is why I wanted to talk to you, Charlie. They posted bail and were released. They have a very good lawyer."

Charlie felt a twitch deep inside. He was uneasy about the fact that they were out on bail.

"Do they know I talked to you?"

"No, but they know Ben talked to us. We have him protected and they will not be able to find him. I am worried about you. Do you need protection?"

"I don't know? Why would I? Do I need it? " Charlie sounded confused and unsure.

"The local police are aware of the situation. You will see a patrol car more frequently in your neighborhood. If you see or hear anything suspicious, call me immediately. The executives are not allowed to talk to any employees. They were made fully aware that any contact will be regarded as witness intimidation and they will be locked up. If any one of them contacts you, call me."

Charlie left the federal office building and returned home. He caught himself a few times on the way home glancing in the rearview mirror to see if he was being followed. At home he packed a bag with the essential items he normally took with him when he traveled. He put the bag in the trunk of his car just in case he needed to leave in a rush. He paced the living room and looked at the phone a few times. He wanted to call Marlene, but wasn't sure if he should.

After a few minutes of agonizing and reasoning with himself, he sat down and made the call.

* * *

CHAPTER 34

Christmas Day

It was Christmas Day 2003, a few weeks after Charlie's conversation with Agent Payne. He had not heard anything from his previous employer and none of his old colleagues had called him. All the employees of PITS were officially unemployed and Charlie looked forward to starting a new chapter in his own book of life.

The call Charlie made to Marlene after his visit to the USCIS offices started a series of phone calls between them. The calls became a routine, but he could never tell her everything he knew. He wanted to tell her, but he didn't know how to explain it over the phone. He felt he should do it in person. He asked her to visit him during Christmas break, but she did not want to come alone. Together they planned a surprise for his brother and sister-in-law and invite them also. Marlene conspired with Ester to surprise Stephen, but they were not very successful in their efforts.

Ester tried to convince Stephen to take a longer break than the usual few days between Christmas and New Year and do something different. Stephen was set in his ways and did not want to budge. He didn't want to be away from his congregation for the traditional Christmas Day and New Year's Eve services. Eventually Ester surrendered to his stubbornness and had to break the surprise to him. Stephen was overwhelmed by the invitation and became more excited than a kid in a candy store. He called Charlie to thank him and the first question he had was if they would see snow. Charlie laughed and said they could plan a road trip to a place where there was snow. They would spend Christmas and New Year's with Charlie in Nashville.

Charlie sat in front of the TV with his brother Stephen. He tried to explain the rules of American football, but Stephen could not understand why they had to wear all the protective gear and helmets. Charlie and Stephen both played rugby in high school and never had to wear any protective clothing. Stephen was convinced the helmets actually made the sport more dangerous and that the only purpose of them was to inflict injury on an opponent.

Charlie was relieved when Ester and Marlene joined them, thanking them for the rescue. He quickly changed the subject to food before Stephen could continue with his stubborn arguments about the dangers of football helmets.

They woke up on Christmas morning and exchanged small gifts. The Reverend in the house called them to order and reminded them what the day was really about and the true meaning of giving of gifts.

"This day is not only to celebrate the birth of Jesus Christ, but we also rejoice in the gifts of salvation and eternal life. We give gifts to each other because we are grateful for the gift we have received. Today, we are also grateful to be here with you, Charlie. Thank you for not only inviting us to come and spend Christmas with you, but also for the tickets you included. It was very generous of you."

"This will be the first Christmas since I immigrated that I will be with family. "Charlie had to clear his throat a couple of times to get all the words out, but he was happy. "Thank you for bringing Marlene with you." Charlie looked at Marlene and smiled at her. "Thank you for coming. It means a lot to me."

They all had to help in the kitchen to prepare the traditional Christmas meal. The day before, Ester and Marlene had taken charge of planning the meal and the shopping experience turned out to be an event of its own. Charlie battled to translate and explain all the names of ingredients. The conversion of metric to Imperial made for a very long shopping experience. The end results turned out great. They enjoyed the traditional turkey cooked the American way while the side dishes had a South African twist.

They talked and took turns complimenting each other on the food. It was cold outside and the light rain made the warmth inside so much better. Charlie looked at his guests around the table, and for the first time in a very long time, he had peace in his heart. He was glad he could share this special day with them.

The phone rang in the living room, and he decided to ignore it. Stephen looked at him strangely.

"Aren't you going to answer it? It may be somebody who needs your help," the Reverend commented. Reluctantly, Charlie got up and answered the call.

"This is Charlie! Good morning and Merry Christmas to you." He said before he even knew who was on the phone.

"Charlie, this is Heinz."

"Heinz?" Charlie said and sank into the chair next to the phone. The blood drained from his face and it became very quiet around the table in the kitchen. Marlene stood up and walked over to sit on the couch across from Charlie. Her hands covered her mouth as she tried to keep the fear inside.

"Where are you?" Charlie asked.

"At home," Heinz said with a soft voice on the other side.

"Are you ok?" Charlie asked concerned.

Stephen and Ester also got up from the table and stood in the doorway listening.

"Charlie, Vince is dead," Heinz said. Charlie could hear him sobbing over the phone.

"Vince, dead? What happened?" He looked at Marlene, and their eyes locked while he listened to Heinz. The blood drained from Marlene's face. She covered her eyes with her hands and bent forward with her face on her knees. Ester sat down next to her and put her arm around Marlene.

"They told me everything, Charlie. I am so sorry."

"What did they tell you? Who told you what?" Charlie asked with uncertainty in his voice.

"I didn't know about his parents. I had no idea what they had done."

"Whose parents?" Charlie asked. Marlene suddenly sat up and stared at Charlie with disbelief.

"Vince's parents - the accident on Chapman's Peak. He and Dan planned it to get the money."

"What! What money?" Charlie asked with anger in his voice. He had a very good idea where the conversation was going.

"The money his dad had stolen from the bank." Heinz sobbed on the other side and he was breathing heavily. "Charlie, they talked about Hanna and Keith, too." The words came with stutters and between sobs. Heinz sobbed more and Charlie heard a cry from deep inside over the phone. He sat with the phone in his hand. Too shocked to move and with anxiety slowly building inside of him, he took a deep breath and closed his eyes. He could feel Marlene staring at him. He opened his eyes and looked at her before he continued.

"Hanna and Keith? What about them?" He saw the shock on her eyes when he asked the question. The shock turned into pain and she began to cry. Ester wrapped her arms around Marlene and held her tight. For a few moments the only sounds were the sobs in the room and over the phone. Then Heinz continued.

"They caused the accident on the motorcycle. Why did they do this to me, Charlie? After all these years! They lied to me. They used me and now,

now I will be the one going to jail." Charlie heard the disappointment and confusion in Heinz's voice. He realized it was not only Heinz's emotions that were making it difficult to talk, but that he also had too much to drink and was slurring his words.

"Heinz. Are you okay? What's going on? What happened to Vince?" The anxiety grew in Charlie. He had more questions for Heinz but he was also concerned about him.

"He jumped bail and made a run for Mexico. He didn't want to go to jail." Charlie heard gulping as Heinz drank something.

"Did he make it to Mexico?"

"No, he didn't. He crashed into the back of an eighteen-wheeler on the highway. He was speeding and didn't have his safety belt on."

"When did this happen?" Charlie asked.

"Yesterday. I don't want to go to jail, Charlie!" Heinz cried over the phone and gulped some more.

"Heinz? What are you drinking?"

"Charlie, will you take care of Archie?" Heinz asked. The alcohol was in full effect and Charlie knew Heinz had far too much to drink.

"Heinz? Heinz! What about Archie?"

"Will you? Promise me you will take care of him."

"Yes, yes. I will take care of Archie. Where are you going?"

"To hell!" Heinz shouted and Charlie heard the phone drop to the floor. The shot echoed through the phone. Charlie heard glass break as Heinz's body dropped to the floor next to the phone. He sat stunned as he listened to the last sounds of a dying man over the phone.

"Heinz! Heinz!" he shouted a few times into the phone, but there was not a sound on the other end. He looked at the phone, and then he looked at Stephen. Tears formed in his eyes, and he let go of the phone when Stephen took it from his hand and put it down.

"No! No! No!" was all he could say as he dropped back into the chair and started to cry. Marlene came over and wrapped her arms around him to console him. He cried and sobbed. It was a while before he managed to control himself. Marlene let him go and sat on her knees in front of him. He looked at her and remembered the day he and Keith became friends. With an expressionless face and blank eyes, he just stared at her and couldn't utter a word.

"Are you okay, Charlie?" Marlene asked with a soft voice as she touched his knee.

"It's been thirty years," he said without blinking an eye. "Thirty years!" he repeated.

Marlene had no idea what he was talking about.

"Thirty years? What about thirty years?" she asked and looked at Stephen who had confusion written all over his face. He also had no idea what Charlie was talking about.

"Christmas Day, thirty years ago. That's when Keith and I met for the first time. Shift did not happen, and they died."

"What?" Marlene asked shocked. She got up from the floor and took a few steps back. "What are you talking about? Who died? What does Keith have to do with this?" she asked with an angry voice.

Charlie looked at Stephen and Ester. His eyes slowly returned to normal and he took a deep breath. Then he started to explain.

"It was Christmas Day, 1973. Keith and I met in the army in the Caprivi on the Angola border. Somebody made a mistake and some troops were killed. They were not supposed to be on the road. Keith and his biker squad had swept the road and cleared it. Lt. Lambert did not use the shift factor when he coded the message for the daily report to clear the roads. He made a mistake and one of the patrols from Alpha Company went down a road that was not cleared. Their vehicle struck a landmine and four soldiers died. That was the day Keith and I became friends for life. Thirty years ago, on Christmas Day, four soldiers died. Why did Heinz have to do it today?" he said as he looked at the phone and started sobbing again.

Marlene stared at Charlie, eyes brimming with tears.

"Charlie. Keith told me the story once before we got married. He never discussed the details and we never again talked about it. I never heard the two of you talk about it either. I am so sorry, Charlie." They stared at each other for a long time.

Stephen and Ester were silent spectators of a life-changing scene in front of them. They knew from experience there was a time to just sit back and let things take their course. Stephen took Ester by the hand and they walked to the kitchen.

"I think they have a lot to talk about," he said as they said down at the table. After a few minutes, Charlie and Marlene joined them.

"Should we call somebody?" Stephen asked as Charlie sat down. He thought for a minute and then got back up.

"I'll call agent Payne. He will know what to do," Charlie said and walked back to the living room and called agent Payne. Charlie briefly explained to him what had happened. He returned to the kitchen and sat down again.

They ate in silence for a while - each busy with their own thoughts. Stephen and Ester used their pastoral experience and skillfully changed the atmosphere around the table. Slowly the conversation returned to planning for the week and where they could find snow.

* * *

CHAPTER 35

The Confession

Charlie knew he still owed Marlene an explanation about Vince and Dan and their involvement in the accident that had killed Hanna and Keith. He looked at Stephen who sat across from him at the other end of the table. He had so much he wanted to say, but he just didn't know where to start. The last thing he wanted to do was to compromise the renewed relationships with his brother and Marlene. How much could he explain without mentioning the bank account in Zurich?

Marlene came to his rescue when she suddenly stopped eating her dessert and put her fork down loudly. She folded her hands in her lap and stared at her plate without moving. Charlie looked at her with concern.

"What's wrong?" he asked.

She looked at Charlie for a few moments and then asked the question he feared to answer.

"What did Heinz say about Hanna and Keith?"

Stephen and Ester looked at each other and then at Charlie as he slowly put down the knife and fork in his hands. After all the years of living with guilt and in fear, he was ready to finally come clean.

"Maybe it's time to talk about it," he said and looked at Marlene. He turned to Stephen and asked: "You're a Reverend. What do you do if somebody tells you something confidential?"

Stephen looked surprised to be put on the spot and paused briefly before answering the question he had been asked so many times in his life.

"Well. It's normally right before somebody unloads a life secret or hidden sin that I get that same question. I have heard many confessions over the years, and we..." He paused and touched Ester's arm lovingly. "We have our share of confidential things we harbor and do not discuss with others. If we cannot be trusted, then we should not be in the ministry. If you want it to be confidential, it will stay that way. We have heard some really terrible things in our lives." Ester smiled at Stephen and it gave Charlie the reassurance he was looking for.

"So, what you hear from me will remain confidential? Even though we are family?"

"Since you are family, it will be difficult. A Reverend would normally refrain from counseling a family member. But, there is always an exception. I would say this would qualify as an exception."

Charlie started with the day he and Keith met and became friends. Stephen, Ester and Marlene listened to him in silence as he explained.

He told them about Project Alpha. How they worked on it in remembrance of the soldiers from Alpha Company who had died when shift did not happen. He explained how they used the interest calculation and shifted the decimal point around to round the results. He explained about Sir Archibald. How they uncovered the scheme and how they channeled the money to the bank in Switzerland. He explained why he thought Vince murdered Hanna and Keith. He explained about the paperclip discovered in the brake line of the black Mercedes that went over the cliff on Chapman's Peak. He told them about the e-mail from Prince Justus, and how Vince indirectly confessed to murdering not only Hanna and Keith, but also his own parents. He explained about the letter he had sent and the website that contained everything Charlie knew about Vince.

Marlene, Stephen and Ester stared in total disbelief at Charlie who continued with his story. He explained why he never could talk about the accident and why he had kept everything to himself. Once he started talking, it was like a floodgate had opened and he unloaded anything he could never tell anybody.

He told them about the documents and pictures Agent Payne showed him. The filing cabinet in Vince's office contained more than they expected. They found the letter with the paperclip, and when Agent Payne confronted Dan and Vince, Dan was the one who put all the blame on Vince. They were partners in crime and had worked together on multiple schemes. Vince's dad was a bank manager, and Vince uncovered the scheme bank managers used over many years to redirect fees to a discretionary expense account. Vince's dad got him the job at the bank and the bank paid for his tuition. Dan and Vince worked together at the same bank as Keith. They were Sir Archibald and Mr. Alexander. They discovered Keith's code in the system and saw how half of the money was transferred to a different bank. They couldn't trace where the money had gone, but did discover he was the one making the code changes. They didn't know about Charlie's involvement in the scheme. They wanted to scare Keith, but it turned ugly when Hanna and Keith were killed in the accident. They cleared the accounts, split the money and resigned from the bank. Vince used his share and became a partner in a company who developed and installed security systems. Dan used his share to finance his way to the US and took an offer to work as a programmer at a consulting company. Dan was the one who started the visa scam and contacted Vince to join him in the US. Dan was the financial officer and he planned the scheme to withhold taxes for those who worked illegally on the visitor's visa. They needed money to get their scheme off the ground and Vince told Dan about his dad's secret fund in Mauritius. His dad discovered that Vince took money from his account, and when he confronted him it turned violent. He threatened to expose Vince to the police about the death of Hanna and Keith. Together Vince and Dan planned the accident that killed his parents.

Heinz was used as a pawn in the visa scheme. They bribed him to participate when he needed money to finance his divorce and when he was blackmailed.

He explained how he forced Dan to transfer money to an offshore account in Zurich and how it led to his discovery of the money in the account in Zurich. It was pure coincidence that he found it at the same time he learned how PITS had cheated him with his rate.

When Charlie was done, he looked at Marlene for a long time. When she stopped crying she looked at him. There was no hate or accusation in her eyes. Charlie could only see the pain.

"I am so sorry, Marlene. I wanted to tell you so many times, but I couldn't. I felt guilty and blamed myself for the deaths of Hanna and Keith."

"Charlie, I knew about it. Keith had told me everything." She looked down with shame on her face, and then continued. "He made me promise to never talk to you about it. He wanted to end it after he bought the motorbike. We had a big fight about the money because I didn't believe his story about the overtime pay. He confessed and begged me over and over not to tell you. He wanted to talk to you personally and stop the project you were working on. He never got the opportunity. I wanted to tell you for so long that I knew, but never had the courage to start a conversation about it. I never blamed you, Charlie. Never! We both lost so much on that day. If we had just talked to each other, then maybe it would have been completely different."

Charlie looked at Marlene and for a long moment there was complete silence in the room. Marlene stood up and stretched out her arms to Charlie who slowly got up and put his arms around her. He looked over Marlene's shoulder and saw Stephen looking at Ester with a grin on his face. He winked at her and she smiled lovingly at him. Deep inside Charlie knew everything was going to be ok.

* * *

CHAPTER 36

Epilogue

S tephen explained to Charlie and Marlene the different stages of grieving. It became a lot easier for Charlie to talk about himself and what had happened to Hanna. They took a few short road trips and Stephen, Ester and Marlene saw snow for the first time. At the end of the visit, Charlie and Marlene seemed to be more than just friends who had lost loved ones. They had more in common than they realized, and Ester pointed it out to Stephen. They agreed that something was happening between Charlie and Marlene and they were happy for them.

Charlie still had to deal with the money in the Zurich bank. He did not want to use it for himself and when Marlene shared her plans with him, he liked her idea. She planned to set up an education trust fund for KT who planned to complete his Ph.D. in computer science at the Michigan Institute of Technology. The fund would pay for his tuition and would still leave enough for her to visit him a few times a year. She also planned to make an anonymous donation to the soup kitchen at the church Stephen pastored. She planned to use some of the interest earned from the money to buy the beach house she dreamed about near Cape Town.

Charlie thought it was a brilliant idea. *"Whose money was it after all? It was only interest that was earned, and the capital did not really belong to any-*

body. Nobody will miss it," he reasoned.

Charlie and Marlene discussed their plans with Stephen and convinced them to become trustees of the fund. They already had a food ministry at church and this would allow them to expand the program even more. It took some convincing, but eventually they agreed. On their return home, Stephen and Ester started the charity in honor of Hanna and Keith. The foundation bought a building closer to the townships they served and volunteers from many churches joined in the local community outreach program. On Fridays volunteers prepared sandwiches and soup and on Saturdays they distributed the meals in the townships. During Christmas they prepared a small gift bag with candy and a toy for each child. They always ran out of food on Saturdays and gifts on Christmas Day as the numbers of those in need continued to grow.

Charlie asked Stephen to also set up an educational trust fund for Daniel and Ruth. Stephen and Ester were speechless and gladly accepted the donation on behalf of their children.

KT, Daniel and Ruth continued their studies in the US. During a college recruiting event, global companies offered them jobs and then sponsored their legal visa processes, putting them on the path to become citizens of the United States of America.

Charlie's efforts to locate Archie to fulfill his promise to Heinz were in vain. He couldn't find the cat and believed he had found a new home on his own.

Charlie worked with renewed vigor and dedication. Tessa's company won the bid for the merger and acquisition project and Charlie started working on it early the following year. Tessa noticed the change in Charlie, and when she asked him about it, he said it was a long story and best to discuss over dinner. At dinner, he confessed to her that there may or may not be a woman responsible for the difference she saw. He explained to her briefly what had happened at PITS, leaving out the part involving Hanna and Keith.

She was shocked to learn about what had really happened. Charlie showed a lot more compassion towards the people around him and became even more successful in what he did. With the rate increase he received, Charlie had enough money to change his lifestyle. He sold his property in Nashville and bought a beach house on the Atlantic Ocean near Jacksonville, Florida. It was conveniently within driving distance of Orlando where the new project offices were located. After the merger and acquisition project, Charlie negotiated for short-term contracts as an independent consultant and worked more from home.

Marlene retired from her job as a teacher and moved to her beach house. With KT living in the US, she visited more frequently, and in the process saw Charlie more. The relationship evolved, and when Charlie asked Marlene to marry him, she said yes. Marlene moved to the US and lived with KT until she and Charlie were married. She enjoyed summer on the beach while Charlie worked.

When Charlie had to travel for work, Marlene went with him and together they explored different areas of the country. During the winter months in the northern hemisphere, Charlie took a break from consulting and enjoyed the summer in the southern hemisphere at Marlene's beach house. Stephen and Ester had free use of it when Charlie and Marlene weren't there. Every year during Christmas, Stephen brought their mom to spend Christmas and New Year's with Charlie.

On his 60th birthday, Charles Guillaume O'Neal sat on the porch with a cup of coffee in hand. He enjoyed the peace and quiet of the early morning and watched the sun rise over the Atlantic Ocean. A cloud moved in front of the rising sun and turned a bright reddish-orange color. It reminded him of what happens when shift doesn't happen. He then decided to write a book about it.

* * *

THE END

About the Author

*I*n his debut fiction novel, author Christo Louis Nel takes his reader deeper into the life of an IT consultant outside of the corporate meeting rooms. Christo has a Bachelor of Science, and combines it with more than two decades of IT experience to make the story about Charlie O'Neal so real, it may just as well be true. Christo and his family immigrated from South Africa in 1999, and lives in Bartlett, TN, a suburb northeast of Memphis. He is married, has three daughters, two sons-in-law, and seven grandchildren. Writing is a hobby for Christo and he is still employed full time as an IT Consultant. In July 2002, he co-authored a technical book about CRM Analytics, "CRM Analytics the E.piphany Way".

From the author:

"Thank you for purchasing this book. I hope you enjoyed reading it as much as I did writing it. Please take a moment and leave a review on Amazon and/or GoodReads. This will encourage me as I continue with my next novel."

Please visit my website at **ChristoLouisNel.com** and add your e-mail to my distribution list.

Christo.